Melonnie

The Dark Side of Truth

Melonnie

The Dark Side of Truth

Written by:
D'Avion

ISBN: 1-58820-857-5

This book is printed on acid free paper.

1stBooks - rev. 12/04/00

Special Credit to:

Kim Yung Im

Mark Donnaruma
Christian Martin
Ryan Cupp
Mathew Bernius
Mark Cardona
George Cloud

Joen Krueger
Kerstine Krueger
Stephanie Krueger

A Word to the Wise

For further details concerning the release of this novel or its history please visit.

www.deavion.com

The content of the following story may not be suitable for children or individuals of deep faith, as it borders in part on beliefs not explored by common Christianity

You have been forewarned

Table of Contents

The Reason to his madness
Writer's Note

First I must say. You cannot conform to society, if you want to be a writer. For years I have seen the unseen, heard the unspoken and even felt feelings that supposedly have never been felt. I define society, as a unit within a populated location that is subjected to common daily rituals. However, for the ones purposely selected to build our tomorrows, we must be able to see more than the day-to-day task. Throughout all the places I've visited there is a sense of togetherness, much like a family. This is a good thing if you have a good family. Let us face it. There are good families that believe in God, there are good families that do not, and there are families that believe in devil worship. Please do not tell me that you are surprised.

My point is truly quite simple. There are just too many variables, too many reasons why, and the poor soul needing to pick one is a lost soul. Most of us are lucky. Our parents were the strong influence, (perhaps border line brain-washed) who instilled in us our primary beliefs during the early stages of life. This influence causes us to naturally assume and understand certain ways of worldly living. This can be a good thing, if you learn completely and with entirety. But just imagine for a minute that they are wrong. Not about something, but about everything. Let's say that what is truly important in life is not what we as humans do, but why we do them.

Knowing that there are always consequences to all that we do, we should have greater understanding behind the meaning of that, which we do. We should also consider the effects those consequences will have on others and the consequences that others will have on us.

You must be twisted to be a writer. What does this mean? Or perhaps the question should be: "Why does he say this?" It's simple. You, the writer, the actor, or the singer are the twisted soul because you must take society apart and delve into its method of reasoning. The final product of that tormented soul is finally the product of music or literature. Getting into the mind of an artist is a deep subject- a maze if you will. And the only tour guide is the composer himself.

I would like to clarify that I don't believe man has the power of creation. You might say that the argument is of a semantic nature and has no direct importance to your life. However, how many arguments could you have personally avoided had you known or understood the true origin or content of the argument? The only true creator is woman. Sometimes I believe that man has forever been jealous of her, that he has manipulated vast opportunities to punish woman.

No! I am merely a composer, secretly watching matters from the corner of my eye. I have truly been there, to those places I often mention. I have touched the soil and spoken to the people. I have lived among the people. I know that there is a dark side of truth. A dark side of truth that is powerful and disturbing. And thus the question arises, "If you really knew who you were, would be afraid of yourselves?" The most innocent of actions can be the most terrifying, if you were to wear the shoes on the other foot.

The stories I compose, are not of what but of why. I refuse to write of what my characters are about, but I merely show why they have done the things they have. So, when you find yourself involved with them and torn by the things they do, it is only because you have touch that dark side of truth. The one we are so often afraid to admit exists.

Life is indeed short, and perhaps I shall die - unknown. But I have seen that dark side of truth and it has awakened me. Each night I pray for morning. Each night I check the closet and under my bed. Each night I ask God to watch over me, because there are things of this world I've yet to understand.

The reason that I write is not to make "THE GREAT."

I would like for the world to understand that we truly do not know the things we believe we know, until you've looked into the eyes of history. We cannot come to understand until we have been part of that which we fear. I ask that as a society, as needed a thing, we should be more understanding of each other, while defending the world we live in and the ones we love. I ask that we press on until death with honor and pride.

Prologue

"I need to catch my breath! I have to press on! Ouch!" Running up the stairs she crashes against the side of the wall. "My shoulder is going to be sore. *I'm* going to be sore! If (straining her voice and moving up the stairs) I don't get my ass up these stairs and onto higher ground, I'm toast. Time! So little of it, or so much. It all depends on the way or method from which we *choose* to exist. (she focuses on the next step) Got to control my breathing. Ouch! (she crashes against the next wall) That is *really* going to bruise. Shit! They're behind me! I can tell by the expensive noises their cheap shoes make. Or can it be the rattling of their clothes? I can't believe that I can actually hear that! They must be two flights behind me, I bet. Still I have to press on!"

"There it is!" Her eyes focus on the door ahead. "*That* should be my way out." Her opposite shoulder crashes against the door, forcing it open.

"Good! That gives the other shoulder a rest." The fresh breeze cools the burning sensation against the surface of her so recently scraped and bruised skin. Quickly she walks to the edge of the roof, directly in front of the doorway. Her dark outline is an obscured silhouette against the city lights and its horizon. The raindrops fall like heavy pellets against her shoulder and pools underneath her feet, soaking them as the water seeps in through the seams of her shoes. She stands motionless, waiting for the enemy to reach her. Turning around, her eyes set focus on the doorway she has just exited. The sounds of footsteps echo more clearly. The falling rain striking against her skin is warmer than she expected. Trailing down her face, the rain sooths the abrasions now etched crimson streaks, shining badges of her battle up the stairs. The rain rolls down her long western raincoat. Taking a deep breath and closing her eyes, she takes a moment to herself, calming herself and reeducating her emotion.

The two men in pursuit push their combined weight against the odd door. Their tired bodies push against the dark metal door, forcing their appearance out into the open. Unable to clearly focus and nearly out of breath, they stagger (one to the left the other to the right) reaching for cover against the doorway. Their backs strike the brick wall breaking their momentum. Panting, they sneak quick glances around the edges of the brick structure. Panting, they gasp for air and try to arrest the silence.

"Edgar Allen Poe," her voice quickly speaks, "said that if you want to hide something effectively, you should lay it in the most obvious place." Between the falling pellets of rain, they try seeking out the origin of the voice with no luck. She takes aim. Fires! One of the men doubles over and falls to the ground. "Death to the man on the right." She says almost in a playful manner. (lightning) The second man's pistol fires a round, hoping to hit near what he thought was her silhouette. The sound of a small rocket echoes into the hollow of her ear, missing her by a close distance. She takes sight. She fires once again. Her bullet strikes the last man. His expression denotes a severe loss of stamina.

"I guess I have the better aim." She says coyly watching the man's hand loose its grip on the pistol. For the moment he is surprised that he is still alive. His eyes travel over to his partner's corpse lying motionless in a puddle. For the moment his expressions read of doubt. "Make no mistake there little man. You live for the moment at my appeal." Bending his knees and sliding his feet outward, he attempts to hold himself against the coarse unforgiving wall. The drops of rain clinging to his face become warmer as they mix with his sweat. The feeling of nausea comes in waves: a burning sensation boiling the pit of his stomach, he fights the shock. He vomits. With saliva stringing unevenly from his mouth, he wrestles with consciousness to slowly form words.

"Who are you?" He asks. His voice is raspy, but she finds charm in his accent.

"Do you really want to know? And with this question answered, will you rest easy where it is that dead humans go?" Walking towards him, her manicured fingers remove her jacket. "Let me shelter you from the rain. I know that I can do at least that. I can see by your face that you are sincere. (she cleans his face) Let me explain. I owe you that much since we are from the same cause." The drops of rain create a spectrum of rainbow colors as they roll off of her skin-tight high-tech suit. Reaching down she takes a fist of the jacket she has used to shelter him. A streak of lightning illuminates her face. Seemingly with little effort, she drags the limp body to the edge of the building. The man remains silent for the moment, as he watches the small stars pulse randomly on her suit.

"I sit upon hills of windows, high above cities. I watch the young humans within their man made vehicles drive the streets. (she looks down onto the street) I can tell they're young by the way they drive. Experienced minds know well how to maneuver. As for myself what can I say? I watch carefully, as I have all of my life. My Profession makes me see things that I perhaps shouldn't. Nonetheless, here I am with you. " The wind plays with her long coat and she takes notice.

It is dark tonight and though darkness fills the air, the moon's radiance caresses the outline of the rain clouds. "This is my curse, or my blessing. When I attended public schools, the teachers would tell me that the world was whatever I made of it. (the man coughs)

"My teachers said the same." He smiles attempting to disguise the pain. "What if the world gave me lemons? Wouldn't you know it?"

"There is a bumper sticker for that. I believed that it read- 'if life gives you lemons, make lemonade.' The same day I saw another bumper sticker. This time it was on the back of a tractor-trailer: 'If you don't like my driving, call 1 800 EAT SHIT! Yes! (she places her hand on the dying man's head) Humanity, in all its rich and powerful ways, is most definitely the *being* with the most incompetence. Have a bad hair day? Didn't get enough fries with that shake? Guy stood you up? Kill'em. Then flee. Then get caught or turn yourself in - which ever. It doesn't matter, because most of you humans don't understand the importance of humanity. Then they say 'I'm sorry' expecting forgiveness, as if their lives has more meaning than the ones they've tortured. Damn the ignorant bastards! Damn them all!

"If I were God, I could see the interest with such retards! They are in constant need of attention. But I don't know. You tell them how to live correctly. You show them that certain things make sense? And they still screw up. Perhaps I'm too young. (she looks around her) I won't kill you. At least not till morning. Take this time to thank God for the splendid and fullness of the life you have received. Ah yes! Morning. Come you, daylight! (she calls out at the world) And touch the flesh of my kind, once more! Perhaps I will not welcome you this time! Perhaps I shall become what is necessary to keep these pests of humans alive!"

She passes the cuff of her sleeve past her mouth, wiping the rainwater from it. She kneels down and places one hand near the edge of the top of the building. She overlooks the view below. "You just don't understand. Do you? And even if I made you understand, you still wouldn't understand. Would you?"

"Try me." Says the dying man. "Let me live till morning." He repeats his plea again trying to bring himself closer to consciousness, fighting the waves of nausea and the chilling tremors of shock from the trauma his body feels. The wound has gone numb, but he is strangely aware of her words, her presence, understanding somewhere deep within himself, almost instinctually, who she is and the importance of her words.

"Sure friend. As I said previously, I shall not let you die just yet." She reassures him. "First! Go easy on yourself. You did as you thought to be your own will. You will know hell soon enough. (she places her hand on his wound) Questions? (she presses down) An eternity of them. But their answers are very scarce. Should I decide to continue my life like a human? Then I would have an abundance of opportunities. I mean I- I- I- could be a kind person that is kind to animals. I could be a psycho killer. No! Better yet! I could be a psycho killer that kills psycho killers. (they both laugh) Or I could be a Vampire! Like my mother. (the dying man reaches up to her for a better view) Then I could have the responsibilities of saving the world from the few sorcerers and creatures left."

"My God! The worlds most feared and respected professional assassin is kin to a Vampire?" He catches his breath beneath his throbbing pain. "You are real? How?"

"Save your breath. (she places her finger gently against his lips) Where did this all begin? Hmm? Shit! (she rubs her forehead then lowers it) I know what Father, Markus has told me. And whatever I can scavenge from fading memories." She pushes herself closer to the edge of the building. "The world is a funny place today. In our search for freedom, *our individual freedom*, life has become more of a slavery. Somehow I knew it would lead to this, but I wasn't prepared to find a darker side of truth. I'm so confused. My head swirls with thoughts and thoughts of thoughts. It fills with questions and questions of questions. (she sighs) The world has changed so much. In our reach for personal freedoms and personal goals, the world somehow lost its sight of what truly holds it together.

"During the last years science has broken through new boundaries- new truths. They found a man that talks to horses, this in 1997; the Titanic was discovered earlier there after; the discovery of Astro-Projections found between dogs and their masters. Amazing it has been to your kind that a dog could know when their masters were returning. Lasers were being used in medicine. And the most popular of all was when scientist created the perfect clone of a sheep. The media pulled the world together; and through its electronic channels there was a massive overload of information. All of it stored on individual silicon chips scattered throughout the planet like weeds for the picking. Animal Research in Telepathic fields became the craze before the millennium.

"Then strange happenings occurred as reality churches took control of humankind's faith.

"Mysteriously, the airways suffered unexplainable plane crashes, both civilian and military.

"All because your kind could not understand that the balance of the universe is within individual lives. Humanity stopped believing in itself and forgot that certain strengths that balance the world are within the souls of individual beings. This side of the truth was left untouched by scientists as they paraded with their infantile discoveries.

"The media has totally misled humanity. The ability to communicate with creatures and the understanding that they also had feelings and emotions that were predictable of their nature was insignificant compared to the other side of truth, the dark side of truth. The truth from which I am now born.

"Many religious leaders have tried to convince the world not to pursue the new scientific route, but their voices have long been diminished and replaced by the Sect of Reality Churches. The church cultivates, and then harvests their ignorance and fear. They have lost their majestic hold of society and are now ignored, politely set aside from the scientific rule.

"Further tragedy struck while also in 1997, the Princess of London, Diana Windsor (once of Spencer) died in a fatal car accident. It seems that photojournalists, for the love of their money gods, created and participated in a high-speed chase that ended in this tragedy. What was she hiding? Mortals and their secrets! (she shakes her head) She was one of the keys holding the locks that would help prevent the spread of evil.

"But tragedy struck the heart of heaven when the never yielding Mother Teresa died, failed of health in her old age. With characters such as these dead and no one to take their places, the locks were being twisted open for Evil to spread." Placing her hands on the edge of the roof, she sits. Dragging the man closer to her, she places his head on her lap. He is speechless. "Evil! (touching his nose) Not creatures mind you, for I am a creature and I'm not evil.

"Forget my face and forget my hair, forget even my faith, my religion, my fangs, and see my heart- for within the heart and soul is where Evil lives. (her calves lean and swing, by the cliff of the building) Silly Mortals! Silly man." She looks at the dying man inspecting his vital signs. "They, with their bumper stickers. How easily they've taken the value of life and exchanged it for paper currency and worthless coins. Now the world hangs in the balances of truth and the dark side of truth.

Little does man understand that the Truth is not what it seems and to live they must know and understand the darker half."

"The Dark Side of Truth." He says as if knowledgeable.

"Silly humans! To think. I could be like them. Truthfully, I'm glad I'm not! Their social realities and religious barriers do not bind me. Nonetheless I will stay here till dawn by your side and think things through. I will someday write this story and draw to paper the pictures in my mind, allowing for survivors to understand. But for now? I shall share this with you in case you meet with my father when I kill you at first morning's light."

"Where did this begin? My mind is weak. These finger-cut knitted gloves can barely keep my fingers alive, while I lay here on this rooftop half sheltered from the rain." He says looking down at his hands soaking in his own blood. She reaches into her vest pocket. Pushing the man under an overhang, she shelters him from the rain.

She leans back, relaxing her shoulder on the roof. Her eyes, wide open, never even bat at the falling raindrops. A grin debuts across her fleshy face. She chuckles as the clouds roll and drop heavier rain.

"Well human, it started in the beginning of time, but for my purposes France, 1987 Strasbourg."

"My name is Patrick."

Leaning towards him, she searches for the wound and places the neon blue stick against it. "It seems, Patrick, that a few naturals, that is what my mother is, had been placed in secret hiding by a fellow French Priest. (the neon light rubs against the wound preventing further hemorrhaging) He was one of the last seekers of the truth. He sought the Dark Side as well as the common side of truth. For decades they were underground waiting to be awakened. For they had knowledge, that could change the fate of the humankind as well as the fate of the world. They waited for someone to remove the soil that was burying them. The priest who held their secret was destroyed." Her voice changes to that of an eerie storyteller.

"Go on I'm listening." He says to her feeling slightly more comfortable.

"This was given to me to know, that among the world of the living, the world of souls and the world of angels, there was yet another society, thought to have disappeared along with the unicorns, fairies, goblins and ghouls. Holy Men never recorded this species. At least not accurately, since they were changed during the war.

"The war I refer to is the one started in Heaven. The angels of God and those of Lucifer challenged each other for power and understanding, for love. Just where did this war become sour? Neither man nor creature can answer. As a result of this war many of the celestial creations were removed. We know that the serpent that spoke to Eve was changed and demoted to slither the world instead of walking upon it.

"Among creatures like these were winged beings and like angels, they would populate the sky. Their wingspan accented the clouds, and all creatures lending them sight would remember God, their creator. And life was simple then.

"Then came man, and man was good. At least for a time. But the war in Heaven raged and earth, with its life, was threatened unknowingly. The angels came down and fought to remove the winged creatures, but it was too late. Eve and Adam had already taken from the tree of knowledge and poisoned the world.

“The winged creatures fought for their right to exist. Unknown to me the results I can only say this... God found mercy and took their wings.

“Because of their upset with mankind, they were banished for a time. Their only hope was for their children to prove to God that their love was as pure in intent as that of man’s.

“But like man, there was corruption and the once Angelica mimes rebelled against man. And thus war was created between them and man. The legend grew of men that would come during dark nights, as mist brought death to those who had souls.

“But this story is not about their rage against humanity or for their terrene, powering for the essence. This is the tale of a creature’s soul and a sole creature discovering the forgotten sense of love..

Chapter 1

Wolf's Eyes

Shadow Show

What was once laughter
Now echoes,
In the graveyard,
Where the carnival tents
Once stood
Against the
Lifeless sunset.

Red,
Yellow,
Orange,
Autumn color overshadows
White and red tents.
Flame eaters
And
Zipper faced clowns.
They are just playgrounds

I remember the children running
Toward the gothic gates
Hidden by carnival signs
Then waiting in line for their turn
On the carousel
They never came back.

Something wicked this way comes
Something wicked

[1st dream]

Images! Too many Images! I can't stop them all! How can I wake up? Am I yet not awake? I feel awake. Pourquoi cette noirceur? (Why does so much darkness around me?) Quel jour sommes-nous? (What day is it?) Will this feeling ever end? I can't see anything. It is too dark. But why? "Shh!" What's that? My God why? Why? Her eyes! They are black and of solid shine. The reflection within them! What is that? Reflections of angels flying in the sky above? Pretty, how they're soaring through the sky. They are beautiful and majestic. But why are they at arms? What of their Holy Essence? What of their peaceful nature? Armed with holy swords? What is happening to my world? Why can't I do anything? If God knows all - then why?

Images! Too many Images! I can't stop them all! (flash to darkness. She touches her eyes. They hurt) My eyes are open! The air here is barely breathable, she thinks to herself. Wood? Against my fingertips? Stretching her fingers, she feels her way about her. Wood splinters into her damply pruned hands, as she realizes she is boxed. She stomps beneath her. More wood! "I'm still in here?" She realizes she is still within the coffin. The small amount of stagnant air smells of must and mold and deathly silence as it carries her nightmarish screams into the world of the unhearing. "Why have you forsaken us?" Pained and confused she bangs the palms of her hands against her incarceration. "Father where are you? Let me out of this coffin!" Leaning her head within the dark, she comes to rest against the unseen wood surface. Lacking of fresh air and filled of tormenting fear, she faints falling to the mercy of her nightmares once again.

[2nd Dream]

The air smells heavy. Moving her hands about her body, she feels out with them investigating her incarceration. Her delicate fingertips glide carefully over the surface of her body. Reaching her shoulder and coming down to her breasts, they round and excite to the gentle rush of her investigation. Expanding and collapsing ribs draw the damp and ill breath into her lungs. The sensation fills her wakening with the sense of erotic images of pleasure. Her mind envisions the play of swords clashing. Her feelings of pleasure quickly diminish. (swords clashing) The once sensitive and delicate fingers stiffen. As her blood turns icy they wrap themselves around her heart trembling with fear she has never known. Her mouth opens; her lips pale.

Focusing her eyes above, two angels clash swords. Locking blade to blade and pressing against each other, their talons stretch out from their fingers, reaching out and ripping at each others', their bodies like savages enraged. Blood, angelic blood, leaves deep and unforgiving wounds, as gouged flesh cools the heat of their combative palms. Though fatal wounds, the blood of Gods is visible to them. The heavens are not at peace this day, for it is a dark day. The sun has lost its luster. The stars may shun their majestic mystery. The land has been filled with grief and chaos. What is to become of God's creatures? What is to become of me? Plumes fall not gently to the ground, for the air is thick with descending debris. Every few moments she witnesses a wounded angel plummet to the Earth's hard surface. And to what reason or unreason has all this become? Who has dared to break the delicate binds that hold truth, as pure to them as life itself?

Look there! How they crash against the hard Earth. The Earth that has never seemed so hard. The Earth that God himself said was good. And what for? Power? Jealousy? And what of man? Where is man in all of this? Perhaps he lays protected in the Garden of Eden. Perhaps he has or will take of the fruit symbol to that will break the order in heaven. Man! The Earth relies heavily upon you. What are you doing? Or the question should perhaps be stated, "What have you done? What is this?" Her deep fear deepens further. My fellow creatures? Two Angels standing before me? What is this unprecedented fear I am feeling? Is it my turn to be destroyed? The Angel closest to her turns to face her. Canting its head to one side, the angel opens his hands with his palms facing heaven. There is sadness in his dark eyes. She notices that his eyes are similar to hers. His wings made of the very same fibers. I was made to remind man of you, she understands. They approach! "Mother!" a sense of sadness fills her eyes. "Why are you doing this? This is not the Way!" Though able to hear her thoughts and see her fear, they approach her with a sentence of death fixed in their eyes. Her fears become unsettled, as fear, itself, becomes her defending armor, her fingers stretch outward. Talons of black elongate into hardened daggers like instruments of death and destruction. The first Angel runs forward at speed near invisibility. She leaps over him, brushing the face of one with her breast. The Angel's face is pushed back. With her lower extremity, she claws at the Angels neck, gouging the flesh. His blood pushes outwards to his body and she descends to the ground. The Angel falls to a knee, with red fluid escaping the wound. With the other Luciferian Angel not advancing, she turns to the wounded and sets herself to the ground beside him. She glances back. Between strands of her beautiful hair, her face radiates sadness and torment. Her marble, black eyes cry for the first time and though she doesn't understand what tears are, she knows now their meaning. The small droplets fall to the earth leaving a ruby imprint on the soil. The broken contour of her lips sends out the fragmented question - "Why?... I love you."

The Angel acknowledges her love. A sound from behind, as the Luciferian Angel pushes forward with his sword. She takes the sword from the fallen one. Without a word or so much as a look, the Luciferian Angel takes to the sky. Finding the threat to her existence diminished, she drops the sword. (a small cloud of dust forms under it) Bending to one knee, she places her hand against His wound and applies pressure. Her other hand caresses his face and whispers in his ear "I love you. God's mercy." The Angel's eyes fall silently, gracefully. And though he has spoken not a word, she knows he has understood. Turning her eyes to the red heavens, the war rages on above her. Angel against Luciferian Angel and Angelica against them both. Her long slender, razor sharp talons clench the hilt of the sword. Her muscles flex. Her wings expand. And for the very first time known to her, there are emotions of revenge, fear, and hatred. Raising her sword, she wages war on them both, as one more Angelica finds herself entrapped in the fine threads woven from the Black Widow spider.

Unseen by the Angelica, but spotted by another, an Angel lands to earth attacking her. He strikes his blade at her throat - she blocks! Her eyes move over top, spying on the second Angel passing over her head. She rushes forward - falling him off balance. Spinning her body (sword in hand), she moves behind the first Angel. Her blade makes contact with the second Angel's blade. The second Angel strikes his fist across her face. (a loud smack) The fist leaves its immense impression against her face. For the first time she feels the sting of physical pain. The force from his strike propels her body uncontrollably into the First Angel. The First Angel turns toward them both. In his drawing motion, he carefully anticipates the destruction of the Angelica. Then a fourth creature appears having descended from the red sky. He seems the same as the other two, but somehow different. All with blades and having tasted the fresh blood of others now fallen, the two Angels, the Angelica and the newly arrived Luciferian Angel stare each other down. The Luciferian Angel rushes forward towards the Angels. She can see the difference now. The Angels have sorrow in their expressions, as the Luciferian Angel has the harsh lines of anger. Running past the Angelica the Luciferian Angel strikes her with his elbow. Her face is forced away, as she falls to the ground. The Angelica is spared, for the moment, as she is not presently the focus of his rage. The Luciferian Angel catches both Angels' swords in a loop. Forcing their swords away from their hands, he leaps into the air and forces his body against them. The impact sends the two Angels plummeting towards the hard Earth. Their palms strike out against the Earth, breaking their falls. Extending talons penetrate the soil under their hands as they push away and come afoot. Both the Angels and the Luciferian Angel charge at one another. She can see their hands and feet transformed into dark tools of destruction. Colliding against one another they fight viciously hand to sight. The Luciferian Angel strikes his sword against the two. Steel to talons, sparks are the witnesses to the tiny explosions created, as sparks are the witnesses to deadly blows. And the sparks will dare not speak for they die as quickly as they are born. The Luciferian Angel kicks at the Angel flanking his right.

Her back aching, her face scratched and bruised, and her mouth bleeding she mutters, "What is this that I feel? What is this that I bleed? What is this color that escapes me?" Another Luciferian Angel falls from the sky, landing near the female Angelica.

"It is pain. (the Luciferian Angel whispers close to her ear) It is blood. It is freedom! You are now knowledgeable." Fear and mistrust moves her body away from the Luciferian Angel. He follows taunting her, mimicking her. With her ears catching the sounds of grunts from the distance and the clashing sword and talons near to her, she circles him face-to-face and blade-to-blade. Her eyes meet with his.

"Why does Angel against Angel fight to the death?"

"First! It is Angel against *Luciferian Angel.* And all this doth have the means. It has begun! (he smiles) *Can't you smell it?*"

"What has begun?" Her question is sincere yet strongly voiced.

"We are now free! God has no more reigns upon us. We are welcoming free will. Lucifer will be our king now! We have *free will.*"

"Lucifer? Who is Lucifer?" Her confusion and frustrations further deepen.

"He was God's right hand, (mockingly) before God gave so freely the soul to man."

"But man is our friend."

"No more. He is now your enemy. Doth that not have the smell that enriches the soul?" He smiles. The grinning lines surrounding his face somehow settle undesirably within her. And though he may paint the truth, the color is not all it seems.

"But we all played together and he has named us after the Angels."

"Now the woman has taken the fruit and man has followed. Look the Angels now come for you."

"No! This is not born from truth! It cannot be! There is a greater reason."

"Then how come you to a road that leads you in two paths? How come is it that your mind makes room for the hour of deceit? Be with us the Luciferian Angels or be alone in the battle."

She fades to darkness...

[BLOOD RAIN]

It seems that the last feather has fallen to the ground. The sounds of unknown metals clashing together, the sounds of flesh and blood torn from beautiful heavenly and once heavenly bodies, and the sounds of screaming voices are now silent. After Seven moments times seven, it seems the new beginning is to take place. The land is peaceful, but sad. The Mountains have lost their color. The air smells thick and with a scent that is heavy. Within the same air, there is a pasty feeling. A new emotion emerges among the Angelica. It is an uncertainty, a sense of not knowing, and a sense that overwhelms the other senses. The sense is purely fear. And what of man? Did man also fear this new disturbance? After seven moments times seven, the sounds are clear. The earth is changed. ' I sit here naked, knowingly so. My knees pulled to my chest, my arms holding them. Why is the blood of Celestial Angels and Luciferian Angels on my body? There were many Angelica, but now there is no telling how many have survived this battle. How could it be that so much, for so long, is suddenly lost? Would it now be forgotten? I never knew what time was. I never knew what emotions were. Were they here all along? Had I only not noticed them? What of this thing called free will? And what of my wounds? Will they leave my body and bring back the flesh that was once there? Worst yet? What is next? What do I say to my fellow Angelica surrounding me? We've barely spoken in days. I'm so tired.'

In the distance is a cloud that seem to expand forever. Around us - a wave of invisibility that moves brushes. "It's going to rain!" she says

“Rain? What is that?” says one.

“Objects falling from the sky!” says another Angelica.

“Does this mean more battle? When will this all end?” – Says yet another

“No this battle is now over! What is coming will show us. But I fear that in the future there will be no peace, but only moments of peace.” Angelica answers.

A sound of someone weeping comes from the corner of the unlit cave. She walks toward the dark, dragging her sword by the hilt.

“Please come no closer.” Says the weeping voice.

“Who are you? I am Gabrielle!” (exhausted)

“I ask again, Please! Who are you?” Asks the Angelica

“I lead this battle.”

“You are responsible for this falling?”

“No! (alarmingly) I have not the blame.”

“But you say that you lead this battle, therefore you are responsible for this falling.” She picks up her sword and points it into the dark corner.

“Yes, but there is more than just this. In battle there are others to blame.”

"Then who is to blame for this flesh torn, (pushing into her stomach) these feelings in the pit of my stomach? (pointing to the collected bodies) How long before my fellow Angelica wake?"

"Forgive me. I shall tell you this now. They cannot wake. They are now returned to the beginning of creation." The Angel drops his view of her.

"Then (regaining her strength and charging a sword toward the Angel) they shall live again!"
"No. Death is final. Only man has the chance of bringing this to order." He says pushing her sword gently to the side.

"But the Luciferian Angel told me that man had taken from the Tree of Knowledge and has now condemned the Earth!"

"The Luciferian Angel who has spoken has told truth, but beware his tongue for he speaks with halves of what the truth truly means. He (sounds of motion) is a fallen angel. He (light reflects onto his face) is a fallen angel. He is the true reason we war."

"What is this smell?" she demands.

"God shall rain the Earth with (he breaths deeply) *with* the blood from His Angels lost to battle. Drink from it. As it may be your only means of survival."

"What is happened? Tell me this oh loved and wounded one! Tell me why has God forsaken us all. His dark eyes, glossed by vague glimpses of light, tear. The tears fall to the Earth. "Please!" His face contours to pain. The angel looks upon her, reaching out to her physical. Touching her face he feels the convulsion of pain.

"I have touched pain. I have touched sorrow. I have touched- love. But never have I've been so moved as to feel that which is felt by my hand just now!" His head lowers. Drink the rain, but only after the sixth day. Let it be the seventh, for God rested against this day and called it holy. Take it upon yourselves to seek Him out and He will always provide for you." He drops his hand from her face.

"Something more terrible has come. Hasn't it?"

"Yes my love. Something more terrible has happened. Let it be known to your kind that times of torment and times of hunger will appear. This is the age of change and change shall be forever constant."

"I shall return to you again and before the sixth day. During these days be true to your heart and don't be mislead. If you make this, on the seventh day rising I shall tell you truths that will save you and your kind. I must leave now; the rain is about to fall. Remember my words, dear Angelica mother of Melonnie. Love and God be by your side. In time of need, let me show you how to *prey*..............."

The wounded one motions toward the entrance of the cave. "You are so brave Gabrielle."

"Angelica, know my strength. And let it be with you." He turns to walk towards the Angelica. Startled and fearful, she moves back and against the rock wall. He lifts his left arm and presses it to the rock layers. "I loved all of God's creation; I love you with equal strength. You must survive, Angelica." Their eyes lock. A breath at a time, his breath and hers meet together and are inhaled by each other. His arm pushes away and with it his body. His voice fades. His warmth retreats. Before she realizes it, the Angel takes flight. Running to the cave's entrance, she looks to him. With her vision steady to the sky she watches as other Angels, some struggling while other less that, unite in the sky, forming one solid cloud of light. The light, unlike she has seen before, it radiates no warmth. It does not blind her. Yet it fills her with hope.

Now the light vanishes slowly. The Earth feels of difference. "I must drink the rain on the sixth day. I must have faith. He shall return to me on that day before the seventh. But what is hunger? What was all that he spoke of? Why am I unknowing of all that? I truly believed I understood." The others look to her and then their dead, but remain silent.

Lightning races across the sky in search of victims like veins to a cloud. In the distance she can see that all Heaven-died in battle are struck. Small clouds of smoke appear at the distance. Angelica looks on with fear and interest. Her blood soaked hands hold her, now, dead brothers.

"Help me!" she reaches down taking hold of her brother's corpse. The other follows her actions. For the first time in days there is sound from her fellow kind. They all take hold of dead flesh, dragging their dead outside into the open grounds. The lightning approaches rapidly. "Pull! Pull!" With one body out they return for another. The small explosions continue in the background and still approaching. "Pull! Brothers!" The lightning is vast and soon upon them. It strikes the first of their dead, very near to them. Fearful, they run away. It strikes the second body. The explosion expands the air surrounding them, and as a result they are pushed away with great force.

For several more minutes the wave of light lashes out like whips, collecting evidence of the dead. Then there is thunder and with the first deafening clap the rains fall. Each drop that falls is formed from blood, much like their own, only deeper of color and richer.

"He must be purifying the land." Says Angelica the first to have spoken.

"Perhaps. But I fear that far worse will come....."

[Melonnie Rises]

The clouded skies fall their souls within the shadowed forest. The falling rain strikes first at the treetops. Like bleeding veins the water follows the contour of the soaked bark and drowns the ground beneath. The thunder makes profound sounds and is menacing, as it chokes every cloud. The air is left with a heavy scent- the scent of fear and death. Lightning races across the skies, branching its many fingers across the vast oceans of space that now seem to collapse into themselves. All sounds of life are quiet now, all sounds are quiet-all sounds of silence are present. On the soil top there is motion breaking the barrier of what sleeps underneath- now awakening. Things like fingers break the soil; hands reach out towards the sky. The dark ground is pushed away by fingers attached to, what seem to be, hands. In the darkness of the clouds hides the truth of tonight's event; For there is knowledge in the night of what soon will come forth and within the knowledge there shall be secrets of past happenings. The fingers, now become hands and the hands expose further assembly of a creature seemingly not human, seemingly unformed. Through the softened soil, carried away by the persistence of the rain, pale paste-like skin appears dimly reflecting the light of the moon.

The thunder wrestles with the crowded sky. And as the lightning strikes at the sky, even the clouds fear their own reflections against the surface of the Earth. Four heads emerge from the rain-darkened soil, combining to form a circle. Black pearls capture images of their surroundings, as their eyes are freed from the darkness once again. Their pale flesh, airs with illness. Blinking their eyelids, they clear the rainwater mixed with soil and debris. Stretching mouths mimic their struggle to awaken. Their shoulders move forward and back and forward again, while their long fingers sink the soil about them. Their bodies struggle, like snake's prey hoping for the escape. Reaching for nearby brush and roots with enough consistency to aid their release, they pull weakly. The elongated hands and snouted faces manage to pull themselves from the deep vacuum-cavities keeping them prisoner. Pulling with every ounce of will, they bend their ears near to the dark tunnels and struggle for fresh breath.

Once free, they lay without motion for the event is exhausting. For a time they lay without motion, panting and taking in their existence, a breath at a time. The rain falling against their bodies is cold and stinging. It shows no mercy. Like plastic pellets, the tiny droplets shoot from the cloud cannons, hitting their dimly reflective bodies. It is a dark night, much like the dark side of truth. The dark truth, which is much like the core of reality before man, takes to polishing it with his selfish manipulation. But these four creatures are truer, than man could ever imagine. These creatures are true to life and beware, for the one who comes against them with impure heart will suffer the consequence.

Clutching air, rain, water, and soil, their tired, naked bodies pull themselves together, gathering themselves exhausted and clenching to one another. They chant quietly and out of breath, reaching out for each other's support. Their flaring nostrils, their expanding veins, their glistening solid black eyes are all signs of their strength reaching growing heights. The one more muscular and obviously stronger presses against the ground with its front limbs. It roots itself and extends its nose into the air. With its snout keen and eyes sharp it searches for a scent. Rain falls onto its face and rushes down- down passed its blue-like flesh and into the soil- the soil where we all come from. The others raise their sights searching for a sign of promise.

Scanning between the clear liquid pellets and occasionally shutting an eye, it attempts to stand upright. The ground gives way and the creature is fallen, exhausted almost unable to move.

Disappointment. A sense of sorrow! Seeing that there has been failure among them, the other three gather and crowd. The stronger one crawls on all quarters to reach the circle. The larger one places its mouth to over top of another. Rain streams from its chin and onto their backs. Grinning it bears its teeth. The others remain motionless. The larger one nips (a cry of pain) at one of the members, blood pours slowly from the wound of his neck. The creature shivers, but otherwise is still and is accepting of its fate. The blood mixing with the rain will not be wasted. The two uninjured lap the escaping blood droplets with long, thick, pale tongues. Aside from the exploding raindrops, the surrounding thunder, the howling wind, and the cry of a comrade, the world is very silent to them. As they huddle together, they are alone. They are very alone. A sad loneliness of existence shrouds them, as it so has been since their last burial. The strongest creature sips from the wound as the others lap the spilling blood. To them blood, is life and life is blood.

A sound! The others see the ears of the strongest twitch at the capture of a sound so faint. Its eyes take to an easterly direction, as its face snouts even further and claws elongate even further. Its body stiffens. Like pine needles, a coat of black fur like emerges from within its skin. Once projected the fur quickly becomes damp by the rainwater. Soon it is wet and finally fallen like that of a black wolf's fur. The three others watch, filling their appetite with hope, as that is all they have strength for and for the moment all is still among them. The small nips of the wounded start healing, but slowly- too slowly. They lay still. They lay quietly. The wounded creature still shivers. Against the loosening soil, the dying one moves his eyes back and forth searching for the hope of survival. Its eyes, losing strength, try maintaining focus on the strongest creature of the pack. A drop of rainwater falls against its eye. It closes, and then opens again. The strongest leaps upward (the ground explodes without percussion).

Debris falls against the onlookers, catching their faces. The dying one closes his eyes to the falling debris. Above, the creature crashes its claws against the tree. The fragments fall scattering towards its final resting-place down to the Earth. Striking its hindquarters, against the tree it continues to climb paw over paw and leaping from tree limb to tree limb. And in doing so the darkness and the mist swallow him, carried by the night. Lightning strikes at the emptiness of space, creating shadows of the creature above. Weakening the one injured shivers. The other two turn to it licking his wound and his face, trying to comfort it. Still, they are all too weak. They can only wait as patiently as one can for death. Standing their guard, they are at their most vulnerable. And with sad expression the figures wait...

[Time passes]

Sitting. Barely sitting, (a rustling from afar) they hear a struggle (more sounds from afar). The ferocity of the sound seems increasingly powerful, as it is coming closer. As quickly as their bodies are weakening, it must be close. It has to if they are to remain alive. Attempting to pay closer attention, they find it is a difficulty in their perishing state. (a stumbling sound) A puff of exasperated air clouds over a powerful beast, suddenly appearing. The beast presents itself as ponderous and commanding. Within its fangs the beast retains another beast before itself. With fangs of power fastened tightly around foreign flesh, the strongest has returned with another beast hunted, still and unmoving. Approaching as conqueror, the beast paws at the ground beneath. Claw after claw, the strongest stumbles over the hunted creature's dead weight. The hunted creature holds life by dragging moments. Its companions, though tainted with the colors of death, look on with great aspiration that they shall survive this rude awakening. Anticipation and relief are the first two emotions to come forth, as they watch the dragging creature brought to them. The beastly food is laid down before the perishing.

Dropping its head in reverence, the strongest gently moves within distance allowing her dying comrades to feast.

They ravage the hunted flesh, and tearing at it search for bleeding veins still carrying the essence; they position their bodies correctly. All but their mouths are still. Tonight there is a new sound in the forest of natural wonders, there are sounds of life from death, and there are sounds of creatures feasting on the "King of the Jungle". Tonight the lion will not be king, but a slave to give birth to a new creature for a new future.

Looking down, the leader's eyes catch and lock with one that does not move. The hunter's claws shape-shift into human hands, fur turns to body hair and body hair to flesh; a human form is born into existence. She extends her delicate hands aside her body. Who would ever beware that this delicate female could ever bring down a Lion? Still shape-shifting, her pain filled eyes turn sight to the dark and evil sky (lightning strikes at the treetops). "Why? Why have you forsaken us?" Opening her hands the shadow of her body casts the symbol of a cross across the feasting. "Why?" The profound sounds of her anguish projecting from within her voice pierces the clouds and enters the heavens. She covers her face with her hands, washing away all evidence of blood. Her knees give way and her heavy burden, naked and natural, collapses against the ground. The rain beats against her naked figure. The cold frosty mist caresses her, blanketing her, as with the greatest patience she waits for her fellow comrades to replenish their natural strengths. Tears falling from dark eyes meet with tears falling from the heaven, and together mix with the soil condemned many, many years ago. She remembers a time where they were once a part of creation and not just- apart. But there is no time for thoughts of despair or thoughts of pity and so she stands guard while the others gain their conscience selves. Her keen eyes survey the land for dangerous possibility, as do they also look down to her beloved. He has given himself of free will so that the others may live and now her life is that much more precious. For it was so precious that he gave his life for hers.

"Pour l'éternité, je serai tienne.(Eternity belongs to us)... My love? I will see you in a better place and perhaps then this war will be over. Perhaps then our lives will be as once they were meant to be. Man may never pay for what he has done, as we have paid for his sins. But I will set our story straight or straight as the sword buried within wounds of my ancestry; I will die at my attempts!" Compassion returns to her senses, as she strokes the dead creature's face and brow. Her nostrils flare, as she lets out a growl. "Jacques? Mon Jacques. Je t'aime. Je t'adore..."

Chapter 2

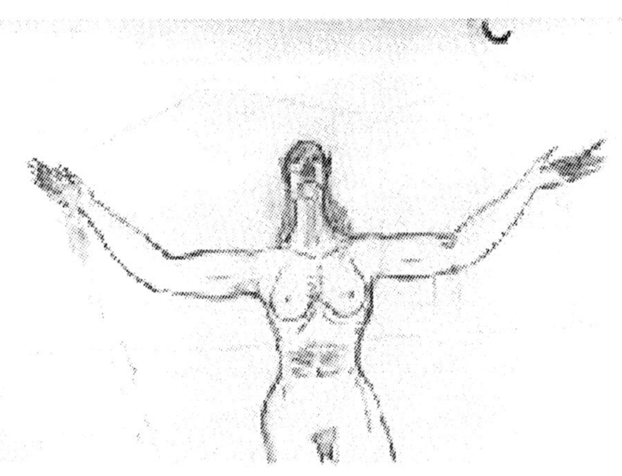

Melonnie Rises

When the wind Whispers

In the distance,
Wind chimes
Take a brief moment
Of silence
Where they hang
On a shredded string.

She kneels again
As she washes away
The red liquid
Encrusted
On black talons of her hands
Mixed with her salty essence…

The Dark in the Light

[Vigore]

While the moon sets on one side of reality, the same is true of another side. A darker side. In a sleepy town, with no mystery and no fear, lives a small sleepy community. If a community it can be called. The sun is falling and the cold night air seeks its refuge. But there is no refuge in this sleepy town. No refuge for mankind. "Oh! And darkness so beautiful in the eye of its maker. So are the comforts of mankind, to have mankind, *that is*." A voice speaks; if a sinister sound can be called a voice. A dark leather glove wraps its fingers around the hilt of an ancient dagger; a relic that has seen blood shed many times over. It is a relic as old as its master. And within the glove there is a powerful menacing hand. The hand, that clutches at the heart of this sleepy town, much like threads that cling to the hem. "Ah! I must admit that soon, very soon, humankind will allow me my rule. I will teach them of pain and persecution, as it has been taught to me throughout the centuries. But only to those who have forever waged war upon me, will I give the bliss of a slow and torturous death! Only to those whose ancestors have not yet changed their paths, will I first hunt and make of them a choir of tormenting tortures." He nears himself to the stony wall. "Look there! Sun. There and here." He points at the rays as if mad. "Here is where I rise against you. And soon it may be darkness forever."

A quick move and he finds himself pressing his body into the wall. His body turns quickly and in place. Reaching out with his right hand, he digs his fingers deeper into the stonewall. Taking a large step backward and pulling at the stone, he forces into plain view the appearance a figure camouflaged within the castle wall. The stone-like, unstable figure of a woman fades and with changing color. Squeezing, what seems to be the throat of a woman, he gains better control. A cape appears, legs become more defined and even its height increases. Forcing the camouflaged woman into plain view, the powerful master, displays his arrogant confidence. The woman struggles to breathe and he enjoys hearing her struggling lungs pull at whatever small amounts they can from the vise that grips. Raising the woman off of her feet, he looks carefully into her eyes.

"One should watch what one says in the company of walls. For walls do have eyes. What say you?" He breaks his character with a sinister smile. Releasing the hold around the woman's throat. She falls to her feet, seemingly unharmed and with a maddening smile, she takes in what freshness of air she can.

"You are too clever my lord Vigore! But never-the-less, (Vigore walks to the edge of the balcony) I will continue my skill, as it only increases my ability to serve you better." With her elbows pressing to the rear of her body and long slender arms wrapped with black leather, she approaches the master. "What will it be tonight, sir? A child? A virgin child? A small boy perhaps? (savoring the thoughts) No wait! You prefer little girls. You like the way they scream and then die lifeless." She moves from side to side catching her weight on each heal.

"Not tonight Zethia." - Vigore

"Have you no appetite? My lord? What disturbs you?" His look changes as so do her concerns.

"Your skills have improved! (she bows her head, bashfully) I fear that someday your skills will be the only things that will keep you alive." He says shrouding a mystery. He paces to the window.

"I don't understand?"

"This village is not all there is child. Beyond the borders of this forest keeping us safe, beyond the wolves, and the werewolves at the edge of our kingdom, are other worlds. Worlds I shall conquer." He leans his arm over to the window's edge. She waits anticipating his next words. Staggering confidently backwards, he falls his body to the trust of a small throne facing the window. The sun has completely extinguished itself and will rest now.

"Go on my lord," unable to hold her curiosity in order.

"There are changes to the Earth today. There will be war."

"What kind of war?" Her eyes widen.

"War like the old days. The days where our kind severed many heads of our once beloved brothers and sisters."

"My lord, vampires and wolves live here in harmony. Are you implying that beyond our boundaries there are still those of my kind posing threat? Haven't they learned *yet?*"

"Yes. Something to that sort. Our old enemy."

"Who is right?" She asks. Her face fills with questions and questions of those questions.

"That all depends on whether you wish to live and correct what mankind has begun and whether you are of weak ability and wish to allow man to continue polluting the world." He pulls his chair closer to the window. She turns to him and sits down on his knee.

"Is this where you go at times? Is this where you go to retrieve these treasures called technology?" -Zethia

"'Tis true. I do search for the treasure that will insure our species to exist. And for this I am called evil, cruel, and discerning." He places his hand to the small of her back, resting it. Her body is muscular and cool to the touch.

"Why have you spoken this only now in recent? Is there a greater relevance?"

"Perhaps I wish to offer you a chance to choose for yourself. Perhaps it has been a point of weakness. Perhaps, my child, I wish you to have the chance at life rather than death as it has always called for me in the hollow of dawn."

"You speak as if death will be upon us, my lord." She says slipping down between his legs and onto the floor. As she becomes comfortable, he strokes her hair gently with his fingers.

"Perhaps not this season child. Perhaps during seasons to come. I have lived for so many hundreds of years. Among the creatures that live are two who I feel fear of."

"Tell me who they are and I will defeat them. If vampire! I swear their ashes will be brought to you in an urn. If Human his head on a platter of gold, or perhaps you would prefer in at the end of your sword, his skin I will retrieve and decorate your wall with, and his blood will be the food of the less worthy." Vigore looks down to her, smiling amusingly.

"My dear little darkened soul? My how aggressive you've become." The words leaving his tongue contain the music of sinister comfort.

"I...(her right eye forms a tear) I...(her left eye) I just don't want anyone to harm you. I could think of a million things you could be, and you are not either of them. You keep the cattle well fed, well clothed, you allow then mating in private. You allow them to work and be meaningful and you seldom have them killed."

"Unfortunately they are the reason we war. This cattle had a name once. And they were free to choose and to live among many creatures." - Vigore

"Yes! But they've polluted the world! They caused war and agony. They've even killed each other without mercy. You have given them rule and understanding! And so I fail to comprehend what is their depth of thought!" She paces back and forth, looking at him and looking at the distant horizon. "I don't understand how anyone would oppose you for that."

"I know how you feel. But war is not avoidable. There will be death. (a sound from behind)". Both, as quick as the whispering sound of wind separating, they break away from each other. Turning, coming to an *on guard*, they face their swords prepared for the intruder.

"My Lord Vigore?" The voice explodes through the doorway and travels to Vigore's ear. The sound is familiar and so he returns his sword into its sheath, docking his sword. However she is less trusting.

"Yes, Servanté?" Vigore's voice is understood to be yielding and willing.

"There has been word that the Naturals have come to surface." Vigore's excitement molds his face of a rare joyous norm.

"Where Servanté? (Vigore focuses onto Servanté) Where?" Servanté's long Black Coat with red lining suits him well. Beside him, quietly, stands the psychic.

"That? We could not know. But an approximate where about is known." His voice changes to that of a more confident nature.

"How useful will that be?" Zethia ejects. Looking down she accepts that there is no further threat and drops her guard, placing her sword into its sheath.

"I'm afraid that the Naturals will have to be sniffed out. Presently they are in Europe. I've dispatched a team of Black Coats and Red Wolves to pursue them. We believe that they are in the Black Forest of Germany, but I can't be sure, as other indications are that they may be at the border of old France. I have our navigators searching the area and mapping out possible locations." Servanté bows his head

"Why there? And for so long?" Vigore's voice sounds threatening.

"There have been secret colonies of Religious freedom there for quite some time." Responds Servanté.

"Where is my advisor?"

"I've taken the liberty to detain him for proper disposal."

"But Sir," interrupts the young woman, "there hasn't been a public execution here for quite some time." She stares at his eyes with deep concern. He turns to her. Her eyes glisten with rays of the moonlight reflections.

"I've taken the liberty to prepare a quiet execution within chambers of torture." Servanté's words seem confident.

"Who will be the executioner?" Ask Vigore

"Yalta."

"How entertaining." Vigore grins. She smiles. Servanté and the psychic follow suit. The pale psychic bows his head. His eyes close, hiding his solid black eyes behind pale blue eyelids.

[Within the Chamber]

Within the chamber of the executioner another psychic receives the message. She is also of blue pale skin. She turns to Yalta and Yalta reads her thoughts. Her body expands and contracts lightly, as the breath of life fills her. She has never seen an execution before and for the death of one so knowledgeable it was a moment truly filling with pleasure.

"Yalta? We have been friends for so many years. (he swallows hard) Please don't do this. I'm not the one to die here. Release me. If not for myself and that of friends past, but for the love of God and the salvation of man." He pleads for his reasoning. Pulling at the bindings, which stretch him out against the wooden table, his head rests on the blood soaked stains of others whom have been victims of Vigore's wrath.

"You are a traitor! And my friend! (his voice mimics comedy) Your mind and knowledge will never leave us. I'll take my guilt, pain and suffer of killing you to the grave with me. Oh! It will be a regret unbearable." He lifts the ax, inhaling a deep breath.

"The psychic powers in me are not the same as your master's. That power which Vigore possesses is power that will be used for the purpose of Satan." His eyes, bulging with fear, shift their view towards Yalta. Yalta's hand falls to his side, relaxing the axe in the crook of his arm. The axe sways back and forth within it, as if contemplating his choices. Allowing it to fall down, it chips the stone floor beneath. Striking the stone, the sound of metal echoes the room for the moment. The traitor is relieved of stress for the time. Looking directly at Yalta, the psychic looks on with question.

"So you're telling me that you too believe in God?" Yalta's voice becomes hushed and secretive. Unable to believe what she is hearing, the psychic's head moves from side to side. Shaking, as if saying no quietly, her mind fills of concern.

"Yes." Yalta exclaims with a bit of desperation and relief.

"The same God who made man and blessed him with a- a- a soul? And whose understanding and passion will redeem us no matter the cost? And all this because we are all part of his creation?" His words are picked carefully.

"Yes, my friend. I do believe in Him."

"Then please! Now! Please undo these bindings and set me free, so that I can make all this right. We need not even kill the Psychic." Sweat from his forehead rolls down to his face. Collecting at the tip of his nose, it falls to the surface beneath. But for the most part he is calmed.

"You are my friend." Yalta speaks out with sincerity. "To think that I thought you the bore. You are very kind to humor me in such ways." He takes a deep breath of air and lifts the rather large ax.

"No wait! Please wait!" His mouth screams out in horror; his eyes observes the edge of the ax.

"Waiting time *is* over." Straining a bit, he pulls up at the ax.

"Please let me speak. Let me pray." He begs for understanding. Yalta swings down.

"Pray?" The axe falls down to the stone floor once again, blanketing the floor with small sparks of fire. The chime echoes against the four walls louder this time. The psychic present watches through the eyes of confusion. Yalta places one hand on his hip.

On the balcony where villains make plans, the psychic smiles and covers his mouth with his index finger and fist lightly held underneath. Vigore takes observes of his amusement.

"Why do you smile?" The psychic shares his thoughts with them, now they too are revealed the illusion of the court jester.

Focusing their thoughts once again, they theatre into Yalta's endeavor.

"You truly believe in *this* prayer?" Asks the executioner, while cautiously navigating to the prisoner.

"Yes! (a gasp for air) It has great powers."

"Will it save you from all this madness and chaos?" Yalta's question enters at the base of his ear.

"Yes. Do you feel the need to understand prayer?"

"Yes! Indeed! Quickly tell me! Will it save your soul?" The sentenced man reaches out hoping to fill his reason.

"Yes! It will bring you to where we once were created." Yalta kneels down near to him. He places his mouth near to his ears.

"Tell me where is your statement of resolution."

"When one says Amen." Yalta smiles.

"Pray my friend." The droplets of sweat pool underneath him. His dark black eyes close and his lips mumble with prayer. Carefully he watches his lips moving, praying.

Vigore looks on with salivating anticipation, lip reading the prayer. Some of the words are known, while others not.

Yalta takes a step away from the man. Twisting his hips and lifting the axe over his shoulder the praying man's words are suddenly silenced to a horrific sound of metal striking through his neck and into the dense wood.

As his head falls to the basket, the sound still chimes in his ear. "So be it!" Yalta says with sarcasm.

Upon the balcony the watchers are pleased.

[Melonnie]

Walking toward an uncertain and undefined scent, the three remaining survivors reach a cleared area. The trees have been moved with some type of uniformity. The ground was suddenly unnaturally hardened and down the center of it are two obviously painted lines. Finding this new and, seemingly, unique creation, the three survivors wait there with little motion and yet much curiosity. One looks to another " Est-ce un chemin?" (Is this a route?)

"Oui! Melonnie, mais pourquoi?" (Yes! Melonnie, but why?) Asks Erasmus.

"Je ne sais pas? Où crois-tu que nous trouvons ceci? (pointing) Où nous trouverons l'Homme, nous trouverons notre nourriture." she replies. (I don't know. Where else do you think we would find this? Where Man is found, food is found!)

"Très Bien!" (Very good!) Says Miguele to Melonnie.

"D'accord!" (I agree!) Says Erasmus to Melonnie with a touch of sarcasm.

By way of movement, Melonnie instructs the others to wait on the opposite side of the road. However, Miguele, requests to stay by her side. Pushed away by her cold hand, he observes the visage of regret and pain that torments her. Her loss is evident, but the grief she bares is hers alone. The impressions of her fingertips on the surface of his naked body slowly erase. Realizing that she is alienating him, she reaches a hold of him with her opposite hand. Pulling him close to her face. "Cher Miguelle, je m'excuse!" (My Miguelle, excuse me!) She reaches her snout to his, communicating her affection. He responds to her with equal understanding.

"Je te comprends, Melonnie." (I understand you, Melonnie.) He blinks his glossy, dark eyes at her and then to her fingertip still clinging to his collar. Taking her fingertips and carelessly placing them to his lips, he gently kisses each one. Her hand floats down gracefully from his lips to her side, as they part.

Agreeing, at Melonnie's command, to wait on each side of the man-hardened ground, they wait for the mysterious to happen. Unknown to them is the way of this world. Unknown to them is the time, the era, the life where they have entered. Still, bravely, but with fear and caution at their sides, they wait for what must be done.

Moments become minutes, minutes to hours, and the hours to tiresome waits. "Bon Jour! (Miguele raises his head) Ça va?" He whispers loudly.

"Ça (smiling) va!" Melonnie giggles, kicking her feet at the near by debris. Reaching out into the gentle crisp air, she stretches her body. The calm steady wind carries a sense of cold within it, streaming from the East. Her skeleton cracks away at her stiffness. Her naked body brushes with the earth. Mist settled on her body, glistens with the reflection of the moon.

"Shh!" Smirks the Erasmus. Miguele shoves at Erasmus' shoulder.

She pushes away at the condensation, collected from the long moments of absolute stillness. And for a brief encounter, her memory permits her to think of Jacques. Her ear twitches, her nostrils flair. Miguele and Erasmus, also pick up the sound and the scent, carried from the Easterly gust of air. Sounds of clunking metal and whinny gears, come across as welcomed sounds. They can hear the wind breaking rapidly, and a rising glow fills the mysterious mist air ahead. "Qu'est ce que c'est?" She says to herself. Could it be a sun? But no sun has ever risen so low and so small. She looks down to her hands pressing her up from the stone ground floor. It aches, reminding her of once when she was not strong enough to withstand the power of the sunrays and so burning her. Indeed this was only one of the many scars attained, from just one lifetime.

The two Burning lights appear from the depth of darkness. Their eyes squint, aching and adjusting to their approach. They look like lanterns, but they are approaching much too fast to be that. Miguele, preparing himself, snouts his face and elongates his claws. The other two follow his lead, raising their hindquarter and digging all four sets of claws deep into the soil. "C'est une machine!" Melonnie calls out, nearly breaking her whisper.

"Oui!" (Yes!) Miguele squeezes out the anticipation.

"*Oh*! C'est du métal!" (It's made of metal!) She says again noticing a rhythmic sound of metal traveling to her ear.

"Oui!" He replies with greater emotion.

"Ecoutez!" (Listen!) She asks.

"Oui! Melonnie! Oui!" He presses down on the ground, as the machine comes closer to them. Digging their hindquarters deeper into the soil beneath them, they prepare their attack.

"Un, Deux. Trois-" They leap!

Their eyes reflect off of the headlamps of the machine that brings a shimmering glisten to the creature's body, as they stretch out their leap. Noticing that the creatures leap from each side, the driver is taken by surprise. Unable to maneuver the vehicle left or right, the driver's heart beats with unprecedented terror. Miguele is the nearest to reach the vehicle. Able to see a passenger, beyond the image of himself reflecting on the widow's surface, he targets his fangs for the passenger's throat. Miguele's snout leans into the glass. It breaks shattering into small fragments, sent flying across to the opposite side of the machine.

Shards of tempered glass fall against the driver, creating minor lacerations. Just as the shards strike scratches at his face, the driver's side window explodes. The two victims find themselves caught between the debris of sharp edges. The woman screams as the man driving holds in what will soon be the inevitable. Miguele's claws piercing the through the door of vehicle, bend and fold the metal skin taking strong hold of the still moving machines. Melonnie too sinks her lower claws clear into the skin of the machine. Her forward claws clear the door, fall into the cab of the machine.

Erasmus' body penetrates the front windshield, uncontrollably tumbling into the vehicle. Melonnie and Miguele instantly, as if rehearsed many times before, penetrate their fangs into the base of their victim's necks.

The first sign of blood squeezes its way out of the man's throat, spurting out from his wound and smearing the front windshield. The smearing of his own blood obstructs his view. In an instinct of panic, the driver drops his foot against the brakes and freezes with his hands locked he holds the steering wheel steady. Tires screech at an attempt to respond against the melting friction between the tires and the road. But at the current speed, the attempt at halting the vehicle seems an unrealistic goal.

The sudden pressing of the brake forces Erasmus to roll forward. He stumbles within the vehicle, still forcefully pushed towards the front, until his body is projected through the front glass. The thick surface cracks, bending outward, and finally gives way in an explosion of glass fragments and splinters to the weight of his bulky and heavy body. Rolling over the hood of the car, his body caves it in. At the edge of the hood and with the car still halting, he falls outside of the machine rolling forward and nearing the front end of the vehicle.

"Oh my God!" Yells an unseen body from the rear seats, followed by screams of horrid nature. Two more humans sink into the furthest reaches of their seats. The car sways left and right, as anti-lock brakes attempt their best to keep the driver in control. The noise from the semi-squeal of the tires, metal puncturing, and growling, allow him the courtesy of not hearing the sounds of his own neck being crushed under Melonnie's powerful jaws.

Desperately searching for a firm place to grab hold, she digs her talons deeper into each side of the machine. Reaching deeper into the machine, her fangs sink deeper into her prey. Outside Erasmus slides off of the hood, dragging his hindquarters on the pavement and underneath the machine. Desperately he attempts to pull himself up and out of danger. With his claws sinking, clinging, into the hood of the vehicle, he manages to hold himself steady for only a brief moment. With the vehicle striking a pothole, forces him to turn about. Looking straight to his front his eyes squint to the point of tears, as he tries to block the burn produced by twin suns. The machine grabs at the ground beneath him, focused on its attack against Erasmus as viciously as he once attacked it. (another pothole) The force of the metal beast in motion swiftly pulls his body under. With his hard body scraping the under carriage, the car lifts. Breaking traction the car is forced in a to skid. Spinning four times and then falling to the side of the road, the powerful machine is defeated.

Miguele, with claws sliding and tearing the leather upholstery, thrusts himself further into the car. Melonnie's lower claws scrape at the yielding metal, creating sparks as her claws slide and slip. The car rocks back and forth with great violent forces, as their creature's forms fight to gain their balance and a hold of the vehicle. The screeching high-pitched sounds of the claws gouging encourage the two screaming rear seat passengers to scream with greater horror. Melonnie's eye rolls to the young man and young girl doused with fear.

Their screams heighten their intensity, catching sight of her deep enamel. The girl instinctively kicks her legs at the seat in front of her, but her attempts to discourage the creature only sinks her mother further into the jaws of peril.

Feeling that death is closing in on his life, the young man reaches out for the door with his cold hands. His tiny shaking fingers pull on the release lever. He pulls at it, with little result. Frantically, he storms at the door with his shoulder. Striking at the stubborn and unyielding door, his shoulder bruises. However, he continues his assault. The door moves to a small open. And so, being only part way open he fills with hope. Miguele, busy with his feeding, swings his large powerful tail crashing it against the side of the door. The door gives to its power bending it; slamming it shut. The violently swift return of the slamming door strikes back at the little boy's shoulder. Pushed onto his sister's lap he grabs at his shoulder, only to be pushed away by her shaking hands. Pinned between her knees and the front seat, he feels the violent frenzy of his father's body being eaten alive. Pushing his hands against the floor, while trying to avoid the powerful kicks of his sister's heels; he forces his way to his seat. His sister strikes his face. He falls down once again pinned between her legs and the front seat. (a distinctive growl from the front seat) Sounds of a creatures feasting. The fear rushing through his veins straighten his arms. He pushes away quickly. His sister kicks him again. A small trail of blood flows from his cut face. But fear allows him the strength to overcome the assault. The young man tries his hand at the door once again. (screams) Sweat pours down the sides of his face, as he pushes his shoulder against the door. But, again, his efforts are of little use. His small muscular frame is no match for the beasts. The door has been jammed.

In her ravish, Melonnie brushes her elbow against the dome light switch, allowing for better witness. Blood paints the inside of the vehicle with great passion. It smells more of death, as the two young people clearly see the fangs of the beasts digging further into their parent's cadavers.

The car continues to brutally rock back and forth, as the two yet unsatisfied creature's tear out more carnage from the cadavers. Miguele pulls his snout from the corpse. His head turns to the young man still trying to break the door free. Pale, the young man immediately presses his body deeper into the seat. His eyes focus on the flesh streaming from between the teeth of the strange creature's mouth. Flesh that once made his mother.

Though fear holds him steady, he shakes violently. His eyes are painted red with blood vessels ready to burst. His nose and ears fill themselves with the very same. His pants are wet with his parents' blood, as so are his face and hands. With his hopes diluted, the young man retrieves his hand from the door, as cautiously as possible. Miguele returns to his business, understanding that the young man will no longer be of any immediate threat. Looking down into the cadaver's punctured wounds, Miguele sniffs at the area surrounding the fatal punctures. Moving flesh and blood aside with his snout, he finds a coarse spot to bite down on. With one great haul and defeating motion, he pulls the cadaver out of the broken window. As if practiced a thousand times, Melonnie follows suit.

The two survivors suddenly feel the car's emptiness and hollow of death departed. Sounds of their own deaths have now departed. All that is left is the dome light, the stench of blood, blood slowly dropping from the rooftop, and a faint sound of bodies dragging from each side of the car. The young girl pulls at her skirt, trying to hide legs soaked with blood. And nothing is left to the imagination, except for the faint sound coming from the rear of the car. They exchange glances at one another in their state of fear. Wide-eyed and pale lips fumble the words of denial. Their confused eyes shake with the hopes of waking from their nightmare.

There is nothing more to hear. There are no crickets; No passing vehicles; No idling engine; No airplanes; No joyous melody coming from the radio; nothing! Nothing but the faint sounds of cat-like claws tapping on the pavement.

Her shaking continues as he begins to move breaking the bonds that bind him. He turns to her. Her lips are so pale. She turns to him (the sound grows louder). His face is paste-like (the sound is upon them). They turn their heads to face the rear window. It explodes! Without so much as a brief introduction or expectation, Erasmus's snout takes hold of the young man sinking his teeth into his collar, snapping the frail body. The young man reaches out taking a hold of his attacker. Their collision forces the girl upward and away.

Her body lifts from the chair, her head comes against the rooftop. (a large white star and all is silent)

Chapter 3

Melonnie Rumani

When the wind Whispers

In the distance,
A faint sound of screaming
Disturbs the whispering wind,
The ghost-like movements
Of the air.

In the distance,
Wind chimes
Take a brief moment
To whisper about
The demented silhouettes
Standing over her
Standing over her own shadow.

"Melonnie?" Asks Miguele, placing his hand on her shoulder.

"Oui?" She inquires quicker than he can finish his breath.

"Are you going to be ok?" His eyes peer at her through the rear-view mirror.

"What do you mean? Mais Oui! (But of course!)"

"We've never blended with the thoughts of a human before. Especially with a child so small. Her ideas and emotions may not be all complete. You know how children are. They have a lot of fantasy."

"Our kind has blended before. It's not common, but it has been done," she answers.

"Wait! What are you guys talking about?" Erasmus interrupts. Without a word Miguele leans his eyes towards Erasmus and then back at Melonnie. He gets the idea.

"Wait! Melonnie that blood-letting and chanting that you did with that little girl- You have never done that before?" -Erasmus

"Non." She says within the time of a short breath.

"What the hell did you do? I don't need another one of my comrades to lose his life."

"Her!" She snaps back at him.

"What?" She requests in confusion.

"Her life! And what did you expect me to do? Learn the ways of the world through a pleasant 5 hour conversation over a handful of this damned rain." She says while rubbing her head. "Listen, it worked. We have a new vehicle and I can drive. I also know a few things more about this time. (her lips curl) It's confusing but it's better than what we had! OK?"

"Melonnie, I am just feeling concern for you. That's all. I'm not questioning your ability or your decision. If you would have told me then I-"

"You what?" She snaps.

"I could have worried a little longer for you." He says his finally defeated words. "I realize. It's something that had to be done." He falls back into the seat, trying to overcome his concern for her. "How do you feel?"

"I feel a little warm. A little flustered. This rain is not helping. Merde! (hitting his fist on the side of the door) Fucking rain! Does it ever end in this time period?" Miguele waves his fist. The expression fastened to his face displays his great discomfort.

"So Miguele? You've learned English well enough to use the worse parts of the language? Did this little girl teach you that?" She takes a small glance at the young girl, still not awake. Miguele glances at Melonnie's mirrored reflection. Erasmus speaks out towards him, mocking Miguele's domineering accent.

"I'm sorry, Erasmus. Words slip my tongue. And as for the accent? What can I say? The world can be grateful I don't speak with a potato in the mouth- like you." He says as politely as he can, taking a small glance at the human girl sitting still in the front seat.

"Potato in the mouth? The world should be grateful?" Erasmus snaps back, feeling at a loss.

"He is right, Erasmus. It's been raining forever. (Melonnie slaps her hand down on the steering wheel) I can barely see through this glass. And all these moving lamps make my eyes hurt." She looks into the rear view mirror. She can see Miguele, but not Erasmus. Moving to the right, a bit, she takes a healthy glance at the little girl sitting beside her, possibly still in shock.

"You like her?" inquires Erasmus, almost making a statement.

"Will you stop reading my thoughts?" She says in a kindly voice.

"Who needs to read them? I make that distinction by the glances you steal from her." Not able to ignore Melonnie's charm and beauty, Erasmus smiles at her. His grin is obvious and cuts clean to the emotion. Though invisible by way of the mirror, she can sense it him smiling ear to ear. Leaning over from the depth of the back seat, Miguele caresses the sleeping beauty.

"Ironic is it? That this reality is born from the seeds of necessity and not otherwise. It makes the pleasure all the more painful." Miguele's words sink into the ears of each traveler bringing a sense of sweet pain. It is a paradox of emotions, as their lives and deaths have always revealed the meaning of the word.

"I need to find the church. And soon! (she gasps for air) I need it soon!" She speaks out loud.

"Melonnie?" Miguele softly asks.

"Yes Miguele?" Her words snap out from her mouth, wiping the moisture from the windshield.

"There should be a city coming up soon. Perhaps when you clear these wooded roads." Miguele holds up a map he has found inside a door pouch in the car.

"Merci- I mean thank you, Miguele. But how do you know this?" She looks up into the rearview mirror.

"Saw it on a print- The last station. What do you call that? Service station. Eh?" His manner brings smiles to them all.

"I'd say there was very good service there." Erasmus picks at his teeth with his little finger, while sucking at it. "I still don't know why we didn't eat her." He points at the little beast still sleeping.

"She is so cute." Melonnie's eyes fill themselves with the girl's image. Unsuspecting she forces the car to weave. The rear passengers weave with the vehicle. Feeling the unease of the road, she brings the vehicle back into control.

"Motherly instincts?" Erasmus' response is first of sarcasm and then breaks into a chuckle. Miguele, trying to hold himself, soon follows suit.

"You guys! Quit teasing me!" Her response is a bashful one.

"You know it's about that time. That natural clock ticking and all." He says turning to Miguele, as if talking only to him.

"Be quiet!" She interrupts.

"After all a woman is not so until she has had the blessing to bear a child." Erasmus continues. Miguele, despite his attempts at hiding his acceptance of Erasmus' humor is trapped in a cycle of giggles and chuckles.

"Be-quiet. You'll wake her." She says in a low careful and nurturing voice.

"That's not what is waking." At his last word, she swerves the vehicle purposely. Hands and arms wave back and forth, attempting to take hold of anything that will hold them steady. "OK! OK! I'll behave." Erasmus screams out in his last word of surrender. The hard turns wake the little girl.

Struggling to find the perfect stretch, the girl moves about slowly. Melonnie fixes the vehicle's mirror, creating a clear and un-obstructive view of the road behind her. The little girl, finding the most comfortable spot, lets out a wide and rested yawn. Reaching out with her senses, the little girl takes short glances of her surrounding. Stains of blood smears on the car's inner surface are ignored, as her mind has not come to terms with what has happened. And perhaps, for the moment, it is better that way. Obviously still suffering from shock, her face has unpredictable expressions. As she becomes more and more awake, she focuses around herself taking longer stares for longer moments in time.

Opening her eyes and bringing the objects above her head into focus, she looks into the rearview mirror. She makes her complete round. Melonnie's eyes meet with hers. Both Erasmus and Miguele bring their lungs to an UnNatural halt, afraid to breathe or make a sound. Both sit completely startled and arrested by the hands of fear. As ironic as it may seem, they understand that they must understand their fear. For it is the understanding of that fear that unites humanity. To Melonnie this was a small human. She is a real human and much the cause of her torment. On the other hand this human was the cause, for which they indirectly claimed to protect.

To the little girl, however, this was not a monster, but a different kind of woman. Surely she is one never before encountered, but there were many things that were new to her. It is ironic then, that the lack of fear has saved her and fear has also brought them together. Melonnie's eyes slowly move to the front of the vehicle, facing the flow of traffic. The car is silent of conversation for the moment. No one makes a sound, except for the little girl.

Canting her head to one side, the small child places her attention onto the driver.

"Hello?" The little girl calls out, touching Melonnie on the lap, seemingly not effected by the blooded walls surrounding her or by Melonnie's semi-monstrous look.

"Hello, little girl." Answers Melonnie, trying to smile and hide her fangs. The others still remain silent, curious of the outcome, as if they had not yet been noticed.

Unexpectedly the young girl places her hand to her mouth, holding back her laughter. Melonnie observes her movements, while taking short glances of her reflection between passing lights. At first it is a bit alarming.

"What is the matter, little girl? Why do you hold back your laughter?" Asks Melonnie.

"You speak funny." She giggles. Unsure, but feeling less threatened, Melonnie allows her smile to widen. The tips of her fangs protrude the curve of her lips. Melonnie pulls herself further up the seat and realizing the innocence of her statement, she too giggles. Erasmus and Miguele also relieved of the situation, let out their laughter. The small girl is slightly startled, but mostly curious. She turns quickly to face them. Her eyes meet with theirs, studying them one at a time. Her mouth drops her smile, stopping her laughter as abruptly as it began. All but the car ceases to move. The silence the crucial witness to their discomfort. "What is your name, mister?"

My name? Ah! Of course. My name is Erasmus." He says, as would a theatrical actor. She is amused.

"And you mister? What's yours?" She asks, squeezing her words through her full feminine lips.

"Miguele." He says out loud with his favorite accent.

Quickly turning around in her seat, she sinks into it. The seat of the car seemingly absorbs her.

"And you? What is your name pretty lady?"

"Lady? Well thank you. (taken by surprise) My name is Melonnie?" She says with amusement. The small girl laughs; this time more loudly. "Why are you laughing now?" Melonnie's voice is one of curiosity.

"Because you speak funny." (hands to her face)

"I don't speak any funnier than Erasmus or Miguele." She says somewhat pushing her complex away.

"Sure you do." The little girl pushes back.

"No I don't." Melonnie calls back.

"SURE YOU DO!" The others say in disharmony.

"Well little wonder, what is your name?" Melonnie looks into the rear view mirror, rolling her eyes at Miguele and the inviso-man.

"My name is Katia." She says with great pride.

"Aha! See! That is a very funny name!" Melonnie forces out her laughter.

"You can't laugh at my name. You have a funnier name!" Katia laughs loudly, as to overcome her competition. They laugh at each other, while both Erasmus and Miguele laugh at them.

"Melody? Why are your eyes so dark." She asks with a sense of innocence. Melonnie reaches out for the rear view mirror. Fixing it, she observes her own reflection. Within the darkness of her eyes, the headlights of oncoming cars produce their signature. There is no sadness to her expression, however she looks at the obvious differences.

"It's Melonnie. And they are different because God doesn't make all things the same."

"But mommy says that all things are created equal."

"Perhaps all things are created with *equal love*, but not ability, or color." Melonnie corrects her.

"Oh!" She says as if thinking of the words just mentioned. But the truth that Melonnie's voice projects, penetrates her mind with a sense of fearless wisdom.

"Is that why there are people of different colors and languages?" The little girl says calmly flexing her knowledge.

"How do you know all this?" She asks searching for further conversation

"I watch the educational shows on TV." Another proud moment.

"Oh TV, sure I watch that all the time."

"What is your favorite channel?" She asks with urgent curiosity.

"Yes Melonnie? Tell me too? What is your favorite channel?" Erasmus asks, satisfying his simple pleasures.

"Stay out of this invisible man." She stabs at him.

"Ouch! Melonnie, that hurts." He says on a different note and backing out of the immediate conversation.

"Yeah Melonnie? Is it channel 13, 7 or 6 or-" Katia calls out remembering some of her favorite TV shows.

"12. My favorite channel is 12." She says with such confidence.

"But there is no 12!"

"There is where I come from. See you don't know everything. Do you?" She pokes between the little girl's ribs, tickling her.

Lifting her eyes over the steering wheel she focuses on the distant city lights. A light mist, much like a cloud spread thinly. The car drives over a hill and begins to descend. In that same distance the symbol of a church appears lit and looming above the ground and through the mist created by the rain. "Ah! The symbol to my death."

"What's that Inviso-man? Something of a phallic symbol, causing you fear?" She grins, looking at the mirror she feels his warmth. "Look! Don't worry. I'm sure that they have an old shack or something they can store you in."

"Melonnie? What about- you know what?" Asks Miguele.

"Look there, Miguele." Says Katia while pointing.

"Where?" he says looking at many places all at once.

"You see? You are not all that smart are you?" The small girl picks at him.

"What on Earth's drowning rains are you talking about?" He says to the little girl with a sense of teasing.

"You fell for a trick."

"And your point? (scooting to the edge of the seat)"

"I know what 'you know what' means. Right Melonnie. Tell him. Tell him! (Melonnie focuses on the sights ahead) Melonnie?"

"Not now ." Her tone is consistent and nearly monotone. Hearing the stress in her voice, Miguele looks forward beyond the pane of glass. Erasmus too cants to one side, catching a glimpse of what is ahead and slightly beyond the reach of the headlamps. The vehicle moves forward, not acknowledging the four figures standing to the sides of the street.

The small misty figures make their way to the center of the street. Two stand in the direct center. The street lines seemingly touch the soles of their black heavy boots. They lift up their arms, holding them briefly to their faces. The remaining two stand clear and away, as if waiting for the go-ahead. Too far away, Melonnie and her team are not sure what their purpose is.

"Stay low! Katia, how do you make this go really fast?"

"Dad always takes the stick, puts it two channels down and steps on the gas, (Melonnie downshifts) but this is not dad's car. And I don't think it works very- (she floors it)" Katia sinks into her seat, pushed by the sudden increase of force. The others too, mimic the small girl. Katia's eyes grow larger. She covers her ears, hearing the car's spinning tires. Breaking friction, the tires spin the car left then to the right before taking firm control of the ground. Melonnie watches the two middlemen lower their hands, while the furthest of them kneels to a crouch. Seeing their comrades drop their hands, the two crouched soldiers lunge forward and commence their running approaches. Moving forward at increasingly phenomenal speed, they accelerate leaving a small trail of water streaming into the air behind them. Using this to her advantage, Melonnie's eyes begin tracking them.

"It's the Red Wolves!" Erasmus calls out. (a small reflection) Melonnie takes notice of the two oncoming bolts fired by their enemy's deadly crossbows.

"They are firing arrows!" Her fingers fasten sternly on the steering wheel. Her eyes search for a quick escape route. Taking a deep breath, she pulls the steering wheel hard to the left. Forcefully the car veers away from the immediate danger. Pressing down firmly, she hits the brakes, causing the vehicle to fishtail and start to spin. The massive vehicle spins around itself, while still moving forward.

Now broadside the leading bolt nicks at the metal brace holding the windshield in place. A large spark illuminates Katia's face. Lifting her hands, she covers herself. Melonnie looks into the skid. "Wow. Very different from the old chariots! Much better (she smiles)." (a sound of glass breaking) The second bolt shatters through the rear side window. The loud sound sends chills through Katia's spine, setting off a series of screams.

Passing deathly close to Miguele's neck, the flared razor sharp edges slice his throat open. Burning with intense pain, he wraps his fingers around the wound. Melonnie, closing her eyes, turns away form the explosion but is unable to avoid the debris.

Through the spaces between his fingers, Miguele's blood oozes. For the moment he is unable to speak and slowly forces small amounts of oxygen into his lungs. Katia, now frightened and confused, lets out one scream after the other, holding her clenched first defensively to the side her head.

Melonnie hands pulls at the steering wheel in an attempt to correct the path of the vehicle. The look on her face is one that is very descriptive of her determination, while along her face a small stream of blood insignificantly descends.

From the outside two Black Coats scrape their feet against the asphalt. Unexpectedly though, Melonnie's maneuvers have made drastic changes to their linear attack.

Originally prepared to enter the front cab of the car, they now find themselves having to avoid the seemingly out of control vehicle. Only but several feet away from it, they leap into the air hoping to clear the large bulky object. The first Black Coat to leap does so with little effort, as the vehicle approaches his direction. The second Black Coat finds no such ease. Located at the opposite end of the car, he leaps attempting to avoid the large bulky object. But less lucky than his accomplice, the vehicle spins around striking at the back of his heels. The force somersaults his body into an uncontrollable spin, smashing his body onto the hood of the car. Immediately the hood caves, absorbing the heavy slab. His eyes bulge feeling the bones snap, as the wave of pain ripples down his spine. One after the other, they fracture like the crack of a whip. There is a quick disorientation of his eyes before blood escapes his mouth, obviously from crushed lungs.

Puncture holes open in his chest, as his ribs pierce through his leather jacket. Blood, first released in small spurts, now slowly drools out. His body falls instantly immobilized and slithers from the hood of the car much like gelatin. He falls onto the asphalt. Ass first he falls against the street's hard and unyielding surface. The broken edges of his bones hit one another, splintering further. The car spins for another pass taking his legs underneath its tires. Capturing one leg under, the broad side of the car strikes the rest of his body forcing tearing him away from his leg. The impact forces his numb body down the grating street. There are only small and minute movements coming from his body, as it begins to decompose and smolder.

Inside the vehicle, Erasmus frantically claws at the roof, hyper-extending his fingers. His nails, hardening, pierce beyond the thin metal. His facial features express his enormous strength, as he begins cutting the surface away with his talons, he breaks through the roof of the car freeing himself from the vehicle. His ears fill the horrifying sound of little Katia screaming.

Suspended like the rain cloud, two more Black Coats observer the vehicle and arm their crossbows, taking aim. One points his weapon toward the driver's area, while the other aims to Katia's seat. Between the raindrop and stretching to the clouds, Erasmus takes notice of them. He leans, undetected by the soldiers, towards their direction. Though he has difficulty seeing through the clouds and rain, the two guards take heed of the vehicles torn roof. But for the most part it is too late. Erasmus' speed and ability has out matched them. With claws extended and increasing speed, Erasmus reaches out to one of them. The Black Coat squeezes the release trigger. The retention of the crossbow begins to minimize, pulling away the safety. With unexpected silence, the Black Coat feels a certain gripping cold that only the grim reaper can deliver. (a shadow in the clouds) The Black Coat's death is sudden. He has not even the pleasures of hearing his own bones breaking. His heart, ripped from his chest, falls to the earth below, leaving a trail of his blood streaming down like a crimson vine and denying him the pleasure of seeing his killer's face.

Erasmus, still in mid air, rolls, mounting his next victim from the back side. He takes the Black Coat by the head and lands, pressing his clawed feet into his back. Erasmus, pulling at the Black Coat, pushes his clawed foot down on his enemy's spine. (small sounds of bone breaking underneath his buried claws) Erasmus absorbs the profound delight of hearing his enemy's neck breaking. Blood flows recklessly from the enemy's neck and down his chest. Erasmus, baring his teeth, pushes the victim away, allowing only the hard surface of the street below to break his fall. "Two down. How many more?" Lightning illuminates a half moon-shaped weapon within the clouds. But the image is too sudden and Erasmus dismisses it for only a shadow in the passing clouds.

His eyes catch the reflection of the rain rolling off of another Black Coat. He draws a dagger from his leather jacket. The Black Coat, near aim, stops in mid flight not aware of the eyes stalking him. Erasmus too, takes aim and with great haste and flicking his wrist, he allows the dagger to slide from his fingers. Carefully sighting his enemy, the Black Coat is interrupted by a sharp pain. He coughs abruptly, rocketing out what seems to be blood drool from his mouth. Finger in trigger, he pulls. The bolt is released.

Below, Melonnie's car crashes into a crowd of parked vehicles. Still holding her hands to her face and screaming, Katia's door crushes in towards her, forcing the armrest towards her and striking her side. Sounds of metal bending fills her mind with illusion of disaster and doom, as the door is instantly jammed shut. Jolted, her head strikes the side of the window. The breaking glass slides across her face, cutting many tiny wounds into her exposed flesh. The car comes to a complete halt. Small sounds of falling glass and settling metal litter the otherwise quiet night. Melonnie pushes her shoulder into the door. It moves little. She pushes harder into it. Metal to metal the door makes reluctant sounds of an uneasy opening. Reaching over to the little girl's lap, she mangles at the buckle. It bends and gives way, un-restraining her. Reaching over with her left hand Melonnie fills her fist with the girls clothing. Pulling her into her lap she cradles her. Melonnie pulls the girl across her lap, and onto the street. The door swings back against her arm. She pushes at it even harder.

Behind her, Miguele opens his door and places his right foot onto the street, moving outwardly. (a sudden sting) His eyes look back onto his leg. Weak from bleeding, he pulls at the bolt buried through his leg and holding him prisoner to the car chassis. Melonnie, hearing the struggle, takes a quick look at Miguele. Her eyes are saddened, watching his struggle to free himself. He motions for her to leave. Extending his bloodied hand and waving his fingers at her, he tells her to leave. Beyond the hand her eyes fill themselves with the anguish of pain painted onto the surface of his face.

"No!" She yells out. The thought of losing another one of her kind, strikes at her heart with as much pain as the wound to his leg. Stepping out of the car and looking carefully around, she notices the approaching cluster of monsters. She slams her fist, pounding and caving down the roof of the vehicle. "No!" She screams again. The sounds of her horrific shrieks ring music to his ears, as he can feel her love.

"And this is how I know that I have lived." His voice trembles. His throat scratches and burns. "To die for love, is the greatest honor." Controlling her panting, Katia screams holding her finger as steady as possible. Melonnie looks towards Katia's scream. In the distance and behind the vehicles, there are images of more Black Coats running towards them. The misty air surrounding them cloaks their numbers. She turns her view desperately searching her surrounding, searching for the cross once seen on the highway. The misty, cloudy sky breaks. She finds it. "It isn't far." She bends down and sets her view to Miguele. Miguele reaches out with a small piece of leather. It sways within the tips of his fingers and is stained with his blood. Melonnie's skin becomes cold and clammy. Her fangs protrude as primal fears take better control of her form and physique. The deep felt sadness expresses itself as she feels her tears rolling down her face. The moment seems to last forever.

Taking Katia's hand, she turns to leave. Knowing that she must climb, she places Katia on her shoulders. The little girl wraps her arms around Melonnie's neck and takes a fistful of garment, holding herself seemingly secure. Grabbing Katia's legs, Melonnie scurries to the nearest building. There, in an alleyway leading to a dark path, she contemplates her method of defense and escape. Breathing heavy and looking up, she focuses her eyes on the top of the building. Powerful legs leap vertically, as she begins her climb. Her great power and strength make it seem as though she is scaling the stonewall effortlessly. Katia looks down and grasps tighter around her neck. Melonnie feels the pull against her throat. Her foot slips, crashing her body against the rough texture of the building. The coarse abrasive stone tears her skin making small wounds into larger ones. Taking a better hold, she begins her climb once again.

"Don't look down sweetheart!" She says to Katia. She can feel the little girl nodding. The falling rain, washes away Melonnie's tears, as ironically she is forced to look to heaven. "You got a lot of explaining to do." She mumbles under her breath and onto heaven.

The tired and blood lost Miguele can now hear the sounds of feet scraping the streets. They sound like wild things of the night, like a pack of hungry savaged wolves. Truly, it is an ancient tactic to bring fear into the heart of their enemies. Enemies to their order like himself. In a way he is satisfied that it will end this way. He is loved by those of his kind. He is honored by his kind. And he understands that, though unwritten and unfair, there are rules of combat. He too has killed the enemy and has done so successfully. The sounds of feet stepping to the street are now consumed with other sounds.

Rocking the vehicle back and forth, as the enemy climbs onto it, the metal of the car screams in its torture as it is ravaged and ripped open in their search to mutilate Miguele. The back window explodes, startling him even further and pushes Miguele's head forward where he can see now those fierce creatures, which have come to destroy him. Small shards of glass penetrate and burn as they lodge in his flesh, tearing the skin and burrowing deeper with every motion. His semi-jammed door makes reluctant sounds as the enemy pulls at it, hoping to obtain a better hold of him. He fights them off as best he can, but every motion he makes only brings him closer to death, as his wounds continue to drain the blood from his body. It soaks his clothing and drips steadily, effortlessly to the pavement below. Gurgling sounds of discomfort come from within his throat as it too begins to fill with blood, choking his every breath, choking the life from him.

Others take to the hole in the roof. Their tough black hands shine against street lamps, as they claw the opening making it larger. Like savages they rock the car back and forth, allowing them more exposure to Miguele. Reaching through the mass of hands, claws and teeth, Miguele takes a hold of one of the Black Coats by his head. Twisting him down to his lap, Miguele claws his face. But for his efforts there will soon be no rewards. Yet, he continues to defend himself; though he knows his attempts are feeble. He will die defending himself, he will not give up; he will die valiantly. From behind he feels the pressure of claws taking a hold of his collar. The bone snaps. He lets out a ghastly yell.

Both Melonnie and Erasmus hear the horrid scream, while Katia blocks out the sound. The chills are sent out, striking fear in the ears of their enemies. The roof of the car, now torn open, allows for more of them to grab at their favorite points of tortures. Erasmus takes to the sky, hunting out existing Black Coats. Trying to ignore his friend's horrible yells he insures that Melonnie has the advantage. And so with pain and rage, he protects Melonnie.

The raindrops falling heavily, matt Katia's clothing to her small form. Hand in hand they run, leaping from building to building. Hoping that there are no more of the Black Coats surrounding them. As if in slow motion, Melonnie's keen eyes catch what looks like a glint of something shining ahead. Their destination is in sight. A momentary flash of lightning reveals the cross atop the church much closer now than from where she first caught sight of it. Sanctuary and rest fuel her to surge ahead, the young human girl still with her. She forces herself to one knee, losing Katia's hand. The little body falls hard against the cold wet roof. Falling onto her small chest she slides down the wet tar-paved rooftop, as pooled rain rushes over her shoulders.

From beneath the steady sound of rain falling comes the sound of metal striking brick. Melonnie draws her dagger. Still on one knee and dagger in hand, she strikes blade down. Rain falls down her face. The knife pierces the Black Coat's foot. (a painful yell) She reaches up and takes a hold of the hilt of his sword. His mouth is open and his screams pour out as loud as the thunder, but she cannot hear his voice. To her all is silent. All is slow moving. Holding the hilt of his sword, she exposes his hand towards the sky. Using the blade of her other hand, she strikes at his wrist. The sword is freed. Stepping as far as she can in front of him, she spins much like a ballerina. Extending her arms, she allows the sword to float across his neck. She grins, thinking revenge has been sweet. She pushes the body aside and moves on to pick up the little girl. Taking a hold of the small human and picking up her speed, she catches sight of the cross. The cross is closer now. (a sense of danger fills her gut) She comes to a sudden stop. Between raindrops falling from a darkened sky, Melonnie's glossy black eyes search for a suitable route. Her mind, though reminding her that Katia is expendable, focuses on saving the human's life. The loss of lives within the last days has been terrible. She is not going to compromise any longer. Besides Katia has an entire life of experiences ahead and to make right so many things that have been wrong in the past. Looking down to her, the wet girl stares into Melonnie's strange dark eyes in search of hope.

Katia looks at the mountain of salvation standing near her and holding her hand. The rain had filled her shoes a while ago, but now her feet feel uncomfortable. Exhausted, frightened and beyond the normal realms of shock brought on by such traumatic experiences, she moves her toes around within her shoes. Melonnie takes notice, not showing additional affection. Melonnie looks down, nodding to her, to her with a look determined to protect. Katia watches the slow motion stinging beads of rain pearls falling from her the corners of her face. She reaches out to touch them. It seems to her a far distance to touch the rainwater. Melonnie looks up and away, desperately searching the heavens for Erasmus. The beaded water falls onto Katia's hand. Melonnie observes her pale skin, soaking in the rainwater. Katia stares carefully, making out the differences between the rainwater and Melonnie's tears. (lightning flashes) Silver tips reflect the light of unnatural substance.

Melonnie reaches down for the little girl. Picking her up, she places her close to her breasts. Tucking Katia's head close to her chest, she crosses her feet and spins her feet vertically, as if taken by a mystical tornado. Once behind the brick roof's building entrance, two bolts, shot down from unknown crossbows, strike the rooftop where she stood merely seconds before. They penetrate firmly. They must not be so far, (pushing her eyebrows together) she thinks to herself. Moving across the brick, she finds a layer of wood. Green? She realizes it is a wooden door, painted green. Side stepping, she scooting the little girl over until she before it. Pulling and twisting at the knob, she finds that the door is closed. Carefully looking down at the door's edge, she finds another metallic surface. She remembers the locks on the car doors. Drawing her hand back and making only half a fist, she punches forward and through. (rolling thunder) The door panel cracks and breaks. On the other side of the hole, just created, she feels for a locking device of any kind. Another sound strikes the rooftop. This time it is heavier, and more solid. Finding and grappling a metallic object, she pulls. Giving way to her strength, her ear is quickly satisfied to hear bending and breaking. As she removes the object, the bolted wood breaks along with it. She opens the door, just enough to slide a small person through. (someone is walking on the roof)

"Meet me in front of the building." She whispers to Katia. She pushes the little girl through the crack. Melonnie reaches for the edge above the door. Trying to maintain silence she slithers up the wall with sword in hand. With less on her mind to distract her, the sounds of wet leather and metal buckles are much more near.

Two Black Coats, appearing from opposite sides of the door, wield their swords striking at emptiness. The metal sound chimes out, striking at the wood and steel, but is subdued by the sound of lightning. Small sparks ignite, as the two blades strike. Sliding their swords one over top of the other, they draw their weapons down to their sides. Moving into view and peering out of the side, they find nothing more than themselves.

From above the door the rainwater sliding from the tips of their blades mesmerize Melonnie's eyes. The small beads glisten, anticipating death. Feeling the advantage, Melonnie somersaults above the two Black Coats. They turn their heads following her movement. Melonnie deftly swings her sword across them. The hilt of her sword carries across to her hip, where it rests for a brief moment. Facing the wall, the Black Coat, immediately before her, stares coldly and seemingly lacking expression. His eyes are fixed to hers. A small rocking motion and his severed head falls forward. The living Black Coat wields his sword under his arm, striking down across her shoulder. Melonnie raises her hands, blocking. (the dead body slithers down the brick wall with his leg kicking pointlessly) Holding the aggressor's sword still, they stare into each other's eyes with great rivalry. Dropping his shoulder, the Black Coat holds his sword ready to engage his opponent.

Pulling his sword into ready position, he tucks the hilt near to his right hip. Pushing off with his hind foot, he plunges his blade forward, attacking with long thrusting stabs at the nimble woman. Melonnie, rotating the hilt of sword, meets the blade. Fanning away the deadly blade, her motion is quick and precise. Melonnie returns, cutting the side of his throat. He chokes for a brief moment, spitting out the blood from the wound.

"Does it hurt?" She asks in a raspy voice. The Black Coat says nothing, but his expression speaks out with enormous hatred. Folding his knee and falling onto it, he circles his saber over top of his head, thus blocking Melonnie's second strike. The force of his defense pushes Melonnie stumbling backwards.

With the same momentum, he continues to swing his sword at Melonnie's muscular legs, trying to disable her, to bring her down to his level of incapacity. Leaping away, Melonnie's foot makes contact with the wall. She compresses her body into it. Springing back towards the Black Coat, she uncoils her body and leads her assault with her left leg with the lethal grace of a ballerina. The movement is accurate enough that she is able to strike across his face with her heel. His face is forced backwards and his mouth fills with his the taste of own blood. Melonnie's blade returns with a forward thrust. His face turns back towards his opponent. With the broad side of the blade facing to the sky, Melonnie makes contact. His jacket presses inward. The blade's tip penetrates and sinks deeper and deeper into his body. Motionless, he watches his heart pumping his own blood onto her sword. Captured by the hand of Death, his fingers lose hold of his own blade. She watches, resting for a moment, the blood running down the length of her sword. His sword falls from his hand. Striking the rooftop with most of the weight pressing on the tip, the sword holds itself upright. His left knee gives way, then his right. Melonnie, panting and without a word, follows him down. (the sword falls) He reaches forward with his left hand. As if trying to speak out to her his last words, but his mouth moves with no sound. Melonnie pushes the blade further, while twisting it and running the sword through until the hilt meets with his chest. His mouth opens, allowing a small cloud of eerie mist to escape.

Now eye-to-eye and breath-to-breath, she insures he feels the gripping hand of fear. (another dark figure looms in the clouds holding a sickle) Reaching out and taking hold of him by the throat, she sinks her claws into her enemy. Her other hand pulls the sword away from his body. Dragging him to where his swords had fallen, she picks up his sword and drops him to the floor, the water puddles splash. "I guess now I have to finish it?" (the rain falls heavier now) Like using a cleaver, she slams his sword down. His head severs. (the image of a young frightened girl enters her thought) Coming a-foot and securing her weapons, she rushes to the end of the building. Looking up and then down, she dives from the edge.

[Entering the Church]

The door to a rather large church stands before Melonnie and Katia. Melonnie pulls back the pitted, dark, iron ring. Repetitively, she strikes the door with it and listens as the sonorous echoes disperse beyond the entrance. The rain still pours down, but for the moment the large concrete awning shelters them from their harassment. The wind is a bit warm, but not enough for Katia as she shivers uncontrollably. Melonnie's ears tune to the sounds behind the large wooden door. "Ouvres la porte! Open the door! My name is Melonnie! I have been sent from the Angelica!" (Metal sounds from the other side of the door) Melonnie is relieved for the moment. The door swings open. In front of her stands an elderly man; beside him a younger man with a most curious look. She reaches out to him, touching his scar. Then placing her hand to her face she touches her own scar. The young priest is surprised, but accepts her sign of curiosity. Seeing the display of affection Katia's tense and strung out emotions relax as she sighs with a sense of relief.

Falling to one knee, but keeping her ears alert, Melonnie speaks out to the elderly man. "Father! Forgive my intrusion as I only have moments to spend with you. I am Melonnie from Angelica." The Priest stands there for a brief moment and no words to offer. He stands there without so much as a motion.

"Angelica? As in- my child (he kneels beside her) I have thought of you as often as I could. I've read about you in the dark books. I am please to have you with me. The mark! Please." Her fingers unlace the front of her blood stained blouse, allowing it to fall over her shoulders and down her back. The young priest shifts his attention to her obvious physique, while the Elder walks around her to observe the legend scrolled on her back.

She lifts her eyes up to the younger Priest. "If you are going to stare at me like that, Please introduce yourself." She says teasingly.

"Brobova. (he swallows hard) The Elder is my mentor."

Seeing the scar tissue on the blades of her shoulder, he stands in awe. His warm hands touch her healed scars, as she kneels there sadly reminded of her persecution. "You're being chased?"

"Oui!" she answers out of breath. He pulls her blouse up around her shoulders, covering her delicately.

"You're French?" He says smiling, while taking her by the shoulders and rushing her inward.

"I've lived there for well over a lifetime." (the door closes behind her) Katia's hands wrap themselves around Melonnie's leg, as she seeks refuge and security, afraid of what could come next.

"You count time in human lives?" The elderly man seems intrigued.

"Oui. It's easier." Except for projections of small light pockets, from torches burning, creating spots of illumination, the inside of the castle is dim. Katia is a bit silent. To her the world had changed too sudden and too drastic. And such was their way. Once an Angelica comes into your life your world changes. Change! Neither for the better nor for the worse. The results of this change would depend completely on individual interpretation. In many cases past, human contact with Angelica would leave one dazed and confused. For some unfortunate soles that could not handle the dark side of truth there would be madness.

The room is relatively quiet. However, the sound from shoes scraping tile floors denotes that there is life within these walls. The young priest looks on not exactly knowing what it is he's looking at. There is the sense of still within the air of these walls they call sanctuary. Each step Melonnie takes is that of sincerity and purity. The Elder's movements mimic hers, while their subtlety displays a friendship deeper than anyone could ever achieve in one lifetime and for that matter they have just met. Even their clothes move in rhythm with their motion. She holds her hands abreast.

"How come you this far?" This question is sincere, yet urgent. He knows that perhaps time will not allow a lengthy chat. And worse yet, he knows that her visit will mean certain death.

"I've a mission!" She answers.

"You bring guilt with you?"

"You are human and among the last of God's kind. I suppose, as in the creatures trying to survive. I have tried to overcome that, that is put in front of me and I too live."

"But you serve such a higher purpose in life. Surely you understand that among lives yours is the most precious?" Says the Priest in a comforting tone of voice.

"My father, all life is precious. One should not place more value on a subject or a matter that is beyond the understanding. For in pricing do we lose the true value. I'm quite pleased to see that spirituality still exists among men. I'm afraid though, that my life may be in peril." She says this with the tone of sadness. Still, it is evident that she is quite content that man has somehow maintained purity no matter how impure he may be. He looks into his eyes facing sadness and listening to his tone against the fires burning. Her sadness is reflected by his eyes and so acknowledged. Katia moves slightly away and walks slowly behind them.

Melonnie questions her own methods. As she thinks to herself, she thinks, not only about herself, but also of what will occur beyond the span of these next few days. And despite her newly attained knowledge, she knows that there's still much to learn. What will happen to her? And the most important question of all -why does it have to happen at all? Still, for the moment, she is aware that time is pressing. Too many decisions to make. Not enough answers for the questions. And so they must push on, leaving questions unanswered and thoughts provoked within the words not spoken.

Exhausted, Melonnie rests on a pew. The priest sits next to her.

"Forgive me. I find you so interesting, so amazing, and most of all so beautiful." She loses herself within his words.

"Equally I can say the same of you. To think that you're kind has fought for so long. I find it fascinating to see that you to have survived." She places her hand onto his. He accepts with a warm smile.

"Your hands are fascinating. They are so warm. They remind me of love." A gentle smile, more like a gentle scar healing. The priest knows there is much pain beyond the site of her words or her deep dark hypnotic eyes.

"Ahh yes! Love. The two powers that power the forces that govern the universe. Tell me Melonnie? Do you love?" His ambiance changes to that of a dreamer.

"Yes of course! But at last he's dead, but not forgotten. (sounds of metal and stone) but I would like to think he is carried deep within me. He gave his life for me. He gave his life for this mission." Her face drops only a bit, but it is enough to bring a small detail of the depth of the pain she has survived. For this aspect alone, he believes that man is truly the blessed soul. For what is 90 years to a man or woman, when the Angelica have lived at war for centuries in a lifetime? She feels his understanding coming through his motion and words. Perhaps this is a tie that such binds the trust.

Katia, still taken by the emotion of the moment, brushes past them and comes to a stop in front of Melonnie. A curious but well-known sound of metal against the ruff of the tile, ears a well into her subconscious. Standing between them and the illuminant of candles burning their light, she looks into each of their shining eyes. Melonnie extends her reach, offering the little girl comfort. Her dress clings to her small frame with the same fear as she clings to Melonnie. His old and experienced eyes glide down the small girl, gently scanning her and noticing evidence of a violent struggle.

Melonnie stares at the floor hoping for forgiveness or at best- understanding. Though courageous and strong willed, Katia looks on dazed, perhaps still in shock. Life was simple before playing this hand monogrammed by the Reaper that so longs for our deaths. For the dead have no worries and the living must carry on performing to their best. The Elder Priest, places the puzzle together, but knowingly chooses to say nothing.

Melonnie reaches down, careful not to startle her. Katia feels the compassion flowing from Melonnie's heart down, down to the tips of her fingers. Taking a deep breath, she holds in the tears of anguish. Melonnie's too holds her tears back finding them so short of regret within the barrier of her eyes. Feeling vulnerable, Melonnie places her head against the chest of the priest. "Father-"

"I know my dear. But this war will end someday. This planet will exist only in memory. It will be displayed as a trophy between heaven and hell. I can only say that because I believe it and somehow- s*omehow* you've believed the same as I do. It is sure that life is more than uncertain. You're no stranger to that. In fact you're one of its finest warriors." He ends his statement with hope, as one would expect from any good priest.

The dragging of metal on the background stops. Within the illumination glimmers the bright steel. Brobova's face too appears as he holds a golden hilt lending meaning to the shimmering blade. "They might hear!" Katia whispers.

"Here is something that may aid you. If I remember correctly and hopefully I do. This is a very old sword. It is one that has survived many battles. If tradition still holds true, this is the way combat is done. I'm not quite sure of the origin, we're in the belief that it may have belonged to your people at one time." He says this with pride and with urgency.

At the other side of the door there is a knock. A knock. But not so loud as to be heard, one can taste its evil from across the room. The delicate white, wet hands take the old silver sword. And instant rage fills her face. It contours to the form of her facial structure, as would war paint to the Indian. Shaking her head from one side to the other, she pushes away the strands of hair that mark her femininity. Katia's fingers run through the strands of her own hair, mimicking her heroine. Finding her elastic buried with her hair, she removes its and hands it to Melonnie. Feeling a smaller hand pushing delicately against her thigh, she shifts her view to the small girl. In the other hand there's a small object, a small elastic object.

Observing Katia rising hand, as if giving her something, Melonnie's mood changes for a brief instant. She lowers the sword. Its point holds steadfast on the rough edges of grout between the tiles. Resting the hilt of the sword between thighs, Melonnie reaches out with both of her hands. Katia's fingers expand, allowing her palm lay open. Melonnie reaches for the elastic, smiling with thanks. She gathers her hair as close to a pony tale as she can and fastens it to her hair. With her hair set to perfection, Melonnie stares down at Katia. Katia is now satisfied to know her friend will be safe; her lucky charm has never failed her before. Reaching down once more with both hands, she fastens her grip around the sword given to her. Her index finger extends, pointing out like a miniature replica of the blade.

Similar in uniform, the outer layer her body transforms to that of light armor. Her hands harden and roughen along the edges bordering the joints, long fingers protrude and like daggers are fierce, her eyes produce a pale yellow-green slit down the center and her fangs erect. "Now I'm ready!" (pounding at the door) Brobova, who had handed her the sword, creeps away stumbling into the nearest line of pews and pushes himself away from the line she has drawn between her and the door. (again the pounding,) Hearing the loud obtrusive disrespect, she walks up to the door as domestically as she can retain and stops. Standing there before the door, she takes a deep breath releasing it with such force as to extinguish a few of the candles nearby. Bringing the polished steel within inches of her face, as to create a meaningful separation between who she is and what she must do, she seizes of her emotions.

Gripping the door latch, her motion comes to a sudden stop. Sounds from the other side. She swings her body to the right, pressing her back into the wall. The large wooden door explodes! Small fragments of wood and metal attempt to gouge at the stone doorframe and floor. Sparks and confused debris blow passed them, as two very large enflamed creatures burst through the center of the debris, entering the church. The stench of burning flesh quickly arrests the relaxing scent of the peaceful church. Katia holds her nose and with panic runs into Brobova's arms. With each step deeper into the church, their bodies disintegrate further. Their flesh pops and wheezes leaving a looming, eerie feeling. The sound becomes louder, as their bodies are engulfed.

Within the church, both Brobova and the Elder Priest move about quickly. For understanding the meaning of this battle, they find that their lives are insignificant compared to the future of their kind. With the door broken, the smell of rain filters through and mixes with the foul air. The priests show their signs of laughter, amused by the feeble attempt to defy what has always been the barrier of good and evil. Melonnie swings her body to face the door. Creating her momentum, she lunges forward, leaps at a time. With her hands, she begins twirling her sword while renewing her inner strength. Reaching deep within herself and bringing out her deepest, most sinister fury, she transforms her mind and body for the coming battle. Clearing her way into the open street, she comes to an abrupt stop. Water seeps into her shoes, standing in a large puddle. "Fucking rain!" Raindrops fall from the roof of her eyes, striking at her cheek, only to roll down and make the puddle larger. Standing in the middle of the cobble stone street, three Vampires surround her, creating a large circle. With their swords drawn, sporting their long dark leather coats, they slowly close in on her. The leader raises his leather glove, extending his finger- pointing at her. Melonnie focuses on the tip of his finger, where the seam of his glove drips saturated from the rain. "Does that jacket keep the rain out?" She inquires lifting her sword slightly taking their attention away from the battle.

"Yea! You want one?"

"Sure! I don't suppose you'll hand it to me?" She watches the UnNatural shakes his head slightly to the left and right. "Naa. Didn't think so." She blows away at a raindrop collecting at the tip of her nose. "Fucking Rain."

She monitors their action carefully and to the detail. A streak of lightning crosses the sky, illuminating the ground they stand on. The UnNatural squints at the sudden light. Just the break she needs. She charges forward. Their eyes blink open. Finding themselves unable to react to her speed, the dark coat nearest her, feels the sudden sharp slither of her blade crossing his throat. His hands drop his saber, as he reaches for where the pain baits his attention. But it is of no recourse; blood flows between them like that of broken damn. The cut, though several inches deep, is not enough for a kill. With blood escaping beyond the grasp of his hands, he falls to his knees, obviously weakened by the loss of blood.

Unable to speak and unable to move he kneels there without motion, hoping that it repairs quickly. Not able to see her, the other two warriors draw their swords tighter into them, while pressing their backs to one another. Scanning the rain filled sky, they search for the female warrior. They can sense her presence between the raindrops crashing against the ground. The rain drops precipitate into puddles and puddles flow into sewers, making it more difficult to hear. But the feeling of sudden inferiority makes them quiver with anticipation and anger. They can hear quiet whispers of her demonic laughter between the falling streams. But the night is too dark. Street lamps can only enlighten a portion of where they stand. Looking into the sky, raindrops fall into their eyes, forcing them to blink frantically. They would wipe their faces pushing off the rain. But why? The rain is falling down too heavily. Besides, that would only mean that they are weak, and so they clench at their swords more tightly. One of the two Black Coats closes his eyes. Feeling out with his senses, he feels her presence nearing him.

With great courage and fear, he allows his blade to travel to where only premonitions can lead. (a feeling of desperation, a pressure) With deadly timing, he swings his blade in the shape of an ellipse traveling up to the sky. The sounds of two blades meeting in the pitch of darkness ring out. The chime of contact startles him. The other Black Coat panics a bit more. Hearing his partner's sword deflect. Melonnie's body falls to the ground. Rolling over onto her left side, she picks up her sword and comes afoot. She swings the long blade between the wet sky and wet ground, as two to one they begin their attack. The first Black Coat swings across, aiming for her throat. She blocks vertically. The other uses his sword to cut downward, aiming low, hoping to cut her at the knees. Jumping in place, she brings her knees to her chest. The sword swings underneath her, missing. Still in mid air, she kicks. Her foot strikes at the side of her enemy's face, solid. The heel of her shoe catches his cheek, cutting into it. The small gash bleed, forcing his face to fall backward, and his body is forced to follow. As his motion forces him to fall onto his back, the other Black Coat returns a second swing. She uses her weight to fall her down to her hands and knees and avoiding his aim. Missing once again and not being able to retrieve his sword, Melonnie kicks at his supporting knee.

Her kick is exact, catching two inches above the joint. The expression of the Black Coat is one of unease. Hearing the cracking of his bones, vibrating through his skeleton, and the horror sounds lodge to the back of his ear. He falls down upon his broken knee. (he screams at the sky) Raindrops fall into his mouth. (the other Black Coat starts to stand) Holding her sword low at the hilt with one hand, and resting the broad side on her lower arm, Melonnie to falls down to her knees. The blade tip pierces through his leather jacket and then through the Black Coat's heart. The Black Coat seems out of breath and quite stationary. Feeling an aggressive strong hold against her shoulder, Melonnie is pulled away from the Black Coat and forced to fall on her back, splashing down into a large puddle of water now hosting her enemy's blood. Her sight focuses on the narrow tip of the saber and for a moment, a brief moment, it seems, as there is a bright shiny star in the middle of the storm clouds. The star becomes bigger; she rolls over her left shoulder. (a chime) The sword misses leaving its permanent impression on a cobble stone street. The sound, the chilling sound, echoes only inches from her ear. From the furthest reaches of the darkness, she notices Black Coats appearing at the end of the street. "Just their style!" She says out loud.

For a normal human being, the cold rain would have been enough to create the feeling associated with surrender. But Melonnie understands that there is no choice in this matter. Kicking her leg over her own body, she brings herself to her fighting stance and she clashes swords with her enemy. Her face is focused on her opponents. It almost seems as though she is not afraid to die. It almost seems as though death is not the issue, for there is no choice in this matter. The human race and perhaps the entire planet are at gamble. Holding his saber with equal force to his, she lets out a small antagonistic grin, confusing her opponent. Quickly and with great agility he pulls out a dagger. Thrusting it forward, he buries a portion of it into her shoulder. Blood fills her wet blouse, painting it with signs of her pain. The sharp pain blushes her face, but reluctant to show weakness, she smiles back into his face. Her opponent is impressed. Taking a step back, she kicks out at his chest. She strikes hard and with full contact. (bones crack) The Black Coat is propelled against the floor behind him and at least for the moment he re-thinks his method of attack.

Turning to the other two on coming Black Coats, she points her saber directly at them. She inhales deeply, allowing her chest to rise and fall. Without warning, she turns her back, supporting her weight on one knee. They stand there in place with the look of caution.

Watching the Black Coat trying to regain his posture, she forces herself to her feet charging him. Her sword makes contact. The dark blood trails down the blade and pools at her hand. "Why can't we all just play nice?" Melonnie looks deeply into his disoriented eyes. Using small movements, as not to be seen by the on-comers, she removes the dagger stabbing at her shoulder. She estimates their distance using her keen sense of hearing. In a single swift stroke, she twists around sending the dagger flying at enemies. One of the two men standing, catches the fast traveling speck of shimmering light. Holding out his hand, the man center to it all, prevents his partner from taking another step. With his other hand he creates a small luminance protecting his partner's face and neck. The dagger nears closer. Jolting to a stop, the Black Coat's face pushes into the illuminant. The almost unseen dagger, stabs at the blue radiance. With the guard of the hilt striking flush against the illuminant, the blade comes to a sudden stop, but not until the point of the dagger cuts the base of his neck. "Ah! A deadly one!" answers the Spell Master.

Melonnie is surprised. She knows now that Vigore's allegiance has increased in power. 'Who is this spell caster?' She questions. Looking at her shoulder, she watches herself bleed. The Spell Master reaches his fingers into the blue illuminate, removing the dagger from mid air. He observes the intricate design of the knife. "Perhaps you would like this returned?" Pointing his two fingers at her, the knife is thrown back. Her eyes open wider. She moves, but it's too late. The blade slides into her other shoulder, burring itself into it. Missing the bone the tip of the blade comes out through the other side. (a feminine grunt) The impact pushes her to another direction. As her head turns forcefully and out of control in the direction of the striking dagger, her hair moves accordingly and for the moment it seems the tables have turned. The victor will now be the victim. On her knees and having fallen onto her wounded arm, She rests trying to absorb the pain. Her hands grip at the air, muscling. Her face in water, she drinks unwillingly from the puddle of rainwater now red with her life. The Spell Master, still holds his arm against the second Black Coat. Inquisitively, he takes a moment to observe the surroundings. The streets comes slowly to life, as the remaining Black Coats come to their feet. The Black Coat comes to a stand, with his face seemingly bleeding as a result of Melonnie's attack. The two, already standing, do not move.

The Spell Master drops his hand and walks forward, but still displays greater care. Placing his attention to the one who is closest to her, he signals for the distant figure to investigate. The distant Black Coat nods his head, moving at his command.

"What is the matter, little one? Forgive my poor sense of hospitality. But you rank among the finest of warriors. I know what you're capable of doing. The reason should be plain as to why I came. Hand it over! Hand it over and perhaps repent (his eyes scale the wall of the church). I'm sure there are good places for you in Vigore's domain. After all, we all make bad judgments; it is the strongest of warriors who learn to correct what bad judgments they've made. You are obviously such a warrior." The Spell Master yells out between drops of rain. At his chin waterfalls like a stream.

Trembling and refusing to surrender, she takes the sword into her hand. With a deep breath and deep will, her chin whips at the air, facing him. Her look is one that is constructed from the solid foundations of her beliefs. Her hand and fingers wrapped around the hilt, she smashes the point of the sword on the ground. Placing her weight on the sword, much like a cane, she helps lift her body from the asphalt. The chime, reaches his ear, the Spell Master gives the death command to the Black Coat nearest her. His body comes to a complete still, acknowledging the request with serious convictions.

With his back turned to the Spell Master; he rushes towards Melonnie, sword in hand. Melonnie, at a stand, pulls out the buried dagger. With the Spell Master maintaining his distance, the Black Coat nearest him (long hair flattened by the rain) waits for the Spell Master's order join the attack. The one nearest Melonnie draws his blade for the attack and swings at forty five-degrees towards her clavicle. Melonnie blocks the sword allowing it to slide off to one side. She kicks out, hoping to catch his knee, but the Black Coat dodges the strike, lifting his knee into the air and releases a crescent kick.

Rain mixed with sweat pours down her face, adding an annoyance to her loss of blood and fatigue. Melonnie rocks backwards, permitting his blow to travel through and beyond the point of contact. Leaning his leg forward, the Black Coat throws a back-fist at her, making impact with the side of her face. (a loud smack) The Spell Master hears the sound of flesh striking flesh and pleased, he smiles. The woman, standing near to the Spell Master, paints a grin on her face and nods with approval.

Moving with the motion, Melonnie sweeps at his foot. The back of Melonnie's heel makes contact with his heel forcing him to loose his balance and fall, as his body spins horizontally to the wet cobblestone underneath in the direction of the Spell Master. Both of Melonnie's elbows point to the wet and dirty heavens, as she pulls her sword from behind her. As it seems she is preparing to strike down her blade, finishing yet another Black Coat. But, there isn't any strike at all. Within his gyration, he extends his own sword, once tightly tucked against his body. Reaching out with his hand, he prepares to break his fall. Melonnie's wet pruned hands release the sword, throwing it forward. The Black Coat, having completed his rotation, mimics her as well. Both swords, hurl at the Spell Master and the Black Coat nearest him. They carry themselves through the dense rain, they sever raindrops they trail to their victims. Almost parallel and almost at the same distance they travel through the air towards their enemies.

Fearful eyes affixed to the message of his doom, the Spell Master brings his hands together in front of him. Slapping his hands together, the collected rain is forced away creating a dry bubble. Squinting his eyes, his lips move quickly chanting out another spell.

Melonnie's sword is the first to make contact, then the other. A large illuminating flash, much like blue lightning scattering in many directions, blinds the Spell Master, feeling the impact of the large heavy blade. With equal and such great force, he is propelled backwards and into the darkness of the street. The female Black Coat is not as lucky, as she feels the steel point separating her sternum. Inch by inch the sword slides deeper into her, severing her flesh and breaking her bones to make way for full penetration. Images allowing her to feel her flesh separating, slicing, like that of wet, cold meat against a dull, but maiming steel invades her mind. The hilt strikes her chest suddenly and without warning. Unable to penetrate deeper, the impact adds to injury crumbling what little structure is left. The sounds vibrate through her body, as the very last conscious sensation is that of her ribs snapping like that of brittle pencils. Her eyes are final witnesses to her death, glimpsing at the strangeness, own blood bursting out from her mouth. Now at the point of death she has not even the benefit of hearing the sound of blood splattering onto the already wet floor. Her body staggers violently backwards into the darkness until her legs can no longer carry her. (the odd sound of a body falling)

Satisfied, with the sound, Melonnie grins. She extends her hand down to the stranger, lain down against the street, soaking what little more his dark coat can of the rain. “Thank you Erasmus!”

“Sorry I had to strike you.” He mentions. She balls up her hand making a fist and strikes down at his face. There is a sudden sound of surprise accompanying the sound her first striking his face against her knuckles.

“C’est rien!” (It’s nothing) Don’t mention it.” She says kindly.

“I won’t next time.” A small trickle of blood falls from within his nose, unnoticed. He pinches the point of his chin.

“Where is Miguele?” she inquires?

“I don’t know.” He exclaims accepting her hand for support.

One step. A smile. Lightning! A flash of energy strikes at them both. Melonnie and Erasmus fall opposite one another, hitting the ground crashing down like a clap of thunder that the lightning bolt had forgotten. They move, but move slowly. The smoke lifting from patches of their own scorched clothing and flesh forces entry into their nostrils, forcing their lungs to cough. Having fallen separately, the eerie mist from the near beyond, comes forth the Spell Master chanting out, what seems to be, a more powerful spell. He walks confidently forward with a frightening glow retained in his hands.

With each second that passes, his hands glow more powerfully. Looking up from the corner of her eye, she catches sight of the Spell Master behind the glowing hands, but she is unable to move about. Her eyes trail down to the wound on his chest. Her eyes let out the subtle air of defeat, as she thinks to herself- if only I were a little faster it would have penetrated and killed this bastard! Both Melonnie and Erasmus search for energies hidden, struggling, staggering. Erasmus comes to his feet. “Ouch! That hurt. “Tell me who you are before I have the pleasure of killing you." He says half-cocked and twisted lost between standing and resting.

"You needn't know my name."

"But you are the infamous Erasmus. Aren't you? Tell this to me, How goes your wondrous quest for peace?" He begins to laugh, projecting his confidence and evil. Erasmus mentions no further words, but it's obvious he is tormented by the question. The glow from his hands dissipates unwarranted and unexplainable to him.

"Greeting Warlock!" A voice sounds off from the direction of the church.

"I have no plight with you!" (he points) The Elder stands away from the church steps and into the streets.

"I do well sir. Thank you." Erasmus responds with relief.

"Ah so speaks the cat when he has no claw nor fang for defense." The Spell Master raises an eye to Erasmus. Erasmus smiles as he's done every time he's cheated death.

"I heard no breath from you, when you believed to have the advantage. Beside I am poking only a little fun. After all it doesn't matter how you play the game. Does it?" Erasmus tone of sarcasm strikes its intended mark.

Erasmus cracks his neck and with instant speed, surrounds the two spiritual combatants in an ellipse, allowing no one to retreat. From within the circle Erasmus creates, allows the small hint of his blade. Standing before the Priest the Warlock chants out at him, so does the Priest. The friction and chanting before them produce streams of energy, swirling the air with many electrical discharges. Their hair, charged with static, on both chanting men stands on end. Their eyes open wide, focusing their complete attention on each other. Their bodies enlightened by the old ways, raise their shoes only inches from the asphalt.

Katia and Brobova walk out the entrance of the church, with quiet caution. The small girl clenches Brobova's arm, while the other hand holds on to Brobova by the waist. Brobova holds his goblet filled with water and moves slowly forward. The warlock's face begins to deform, as bubbles form from within the layers of his skin trying to break him apart. The Elder's flesh, on the other hand, allows evidence, of the struggle, as his veins expand to near rupture. Blood escapes him by way of his nose. Still, hands trembling, he continues his chanting. The Warlock, unable to move because of Erasmus gyrations, turns the focus of his eyes towards the approaching Brobova. The Warlock's head commences to shake violently, as Brobova's energy is also set into defense. Brobova hands Katia his goblet. She takes it into her hand with innocence, expecting the goblet and the water within it to protect her. Glimpsing at Melonnie's still body, she wonders if she will recover. Taking a few steps backwards she trembles with fear, as Brobova moves forward to the circle holding his hands open. Holding a humble goblet filled with Holy Water, she stares with disbelief as the water reaches up and over the beveled rim. Gently making its way through the air as if it were a magic stream, it leaves the cup never emptying itself.

The water makes its way through the circle, produced by Erasmus. It filters through, missing contact with him. However, Erasmus feels the potential danger. A few of those drops and I'm toast, he thinks to himself.

Once inside the circle the Holy water pools over the Warlock's head. He takes a look upwards. Fear stricken, his canting comes to a paralysis. The water drops over him. A brilliant flash of light! Much like an explosion the heat from the blast is felt strongly by the on lookers. However, there is no sound and very little percussion. The Warlock is gone. The brilliant flash, Erasmus loses focus, as so do the others. He miscalculates and throws himself into the brick wall of the church. The pain penetrates through his body shaking his skeleton like an earthquake. Katia stands near to him, still observing the oddly and impractical cup. The water is there, where it always has been.

Bleeding from multiple wounds, Erasmus observes the little girl. "If you drink that the Angels will always protect you." The wide-eyed little girl looks at him, still displaying her fear. Erasmus nods his head. The small girl brings the goblet to her mouth and gulps the liquid down. He nods, "Good girl." Rubbing his nose with his index finger, he smears a small streak of blood collected underneath, across his face.

Compassionately, Brobova aids the elder. He looks a bit tired, but other than that all is going well. Taking the Elder by both arms, Brobova makes himself useful. The Elder, with the most delicate motion, raises his hands a short distance. On queue, Brobova ceases to move. Almost standing motionless and with all eyes upon him, he looks at the young priest.

"Tend to the wounded." Without a word, Brobova walks towards Melonnie. She is still on the wet ground. The rain droplets crash against her body. Melonnie scrambles the last bit of energy left within her. He touches her with a great deal of caution. Her own attire outlines her body in a most flattering manner. He looks at her, while extending one hand offering her support. Taking a deep breath, she throws out her hand and grabs a hold of the Priest. Her rough scaly armor takes him by surprise, yet he motions not. Her black eyes set focus into his. She continues to turn towards him. Facing him front to front, his eyes look at her form. It is truly perfect. Unlike perfection for humanity, she is an original of Gods creatures.

Unlike myths and stories, there she is and carrying information that could save the world. "You have beautiful eyes, Angelica."

"With these eyes I have seen centuries of men, but not one as chivalrous as you are on this day. Please forgive my attire-given the circumstances." She replies honorably.

"Oh it should be *I* who should be asking for forgiveness. Let me offer you some shelter and rest from tiring elements." He brings her to a stand. The loud rain pellets commence to fall harder. Melonnie makes her way to the large church with Brobova at her side. "What about these bodies?"

"Leave them Brobova, they will burn at first light." Answers the Elder.

"As in the legends?" he asks.

"As in the legends." he answers back to him with a softer voice.

Erasmus looks into the sky and then down again. There is still time, he thinks to himself. He glances back at the girl, moving his eyes down her neck and staring at the cross necklace. He smiles at her. She is young, but rapidly gaining knowledge.

"You are afraid of this?" She asks taking a hold of the cross.

"Not exactly afraid, but I do keep my distance." He answers. More priests tend to the door some with tools, while yet others combine their efforts to carry the replacement door. Though confused of what has happened exactly before them, they focus only on the task at hand. Thunder crackles and lightning fluoresces, bringing shadows are brought to light where there are none. Taking the first step onto the stairs Melonnie passes through. She reaches out, first touching Erasmus on the shoulder and then taking a hold of the little girl by the hand.

"Come Katia. You should be in bed. Enough TV for one day."

"Thank you for protecting us Melonnie." She answers.

"You're welcome ." She says with tones of regret. Deep inside of her soulless body she feels a responsibility for what she has done. She knows that she seems ruthless, perhaps even abrasive to mankind's cultural truths. She feels the disharmony within her blood brooding and spilling over like water boiling over a caldron. She has questions of her own that wait patiently to be answered. And within arms of understanding Holy Men, she finds comfort for the moment. They are not so hurried into fear as the common peasant. At least through their touch and their existence, she can feel a respect for humankind.

"Wait here young Erasmus. I will return for you." The Elder calls out. Erasmus nods his head with agreeable manner. Putting his shoulders up against the wall of the church and taking a deep breath, he too has questions. Looking out at the street, he remembers how he too was brought to become what he is and what, till the turn of the century, had become the Red Wolves. Still, looking into the pools of blood collected by the many raindrops' tiny hands, he stares at what he most fears- the Red Wolves. "Sure! (he smirks, looking at the sabers lain with no order), They can be killed. But they are truly something to be reckoned with. They are so agile. Years of combat training, did I say years- centuries! As long as it's not tonight. I am too tired to fight any longer. It's been a hard and tortuous few days. I hope that Melonnie finds what she is looking for."

To think he was once in the ranks of the Red Wolves. "And the thought of that the Spell Master knew my torment grabbed his perishing sense of sanity. He knew my past. Yes! But he is dead now and I am still un-living. This should be of some comfort. Though tortured is my mind and tormented is my soul, there are thoughts of peace within my unrest that no one can take away. Some may call me mad, others may call me Monster. What do I care? They both begin with the same letter of the alphabet and so do the words Me, Melonnie, Miguele and Miracle. How Ironic (he spurts a bit of laughter) I stand before the church of God, who I once loved and perhaps if not for my illness I would still. And, like the fool, I wait for the miracle.

Does he not see me today? I have become a Vampire and in doing so have I become also invisible? I wish mine *enemies* could find me hard to see.

"It would make it all the easier of completing the Mission. Ahh! There! Another word that begins with the letter 'M'! If I could only love you again. (he shakes his head) If I could only feel those feelings I once had for you. Then and *maybe then*, would I be seen through your eyes. I have so many questions to ask you. And now here stranded on this big, blue island I sit, with no rescue. No love in my heart. No direction other than belief. (he sighs deeply). If I could know if there would be a place in heaven for me. If I would be let known that a small compartment of space is reserved for the un-living, I may have a ray of hope. We that must prey on the blood of humans- Aye! There sleeps the paradox. To take human life is sin against the Holyness-ses. And of course in that, is the situation that leads my mind astray. I call out to empty caverns, receiving only my echoed voice to accompany me. (he raises his voice) God do you love me? Answer me! That is the Miracle I wait. In your book you claim that man cannot be saved by merely his deeds, but the purity of his heart and the power of his faith shall judge him. But what am I? I cannot give, but my deeds."

The other Priests, listening on, feel the stress of his heart. Coming to his feet, he walks towards the door. It is opened wide; he looks into the forbidden walls. He can see the serenity that peace and love leaves behind. He reaches out his hand, unknowingly and slowly he inches its way into the door. His eyes are heavy and tearful. A fellow Priest reaches for Erasmus' hand, protecting him from harmful outcome.

"Brother! Please." his voice is gentle, compassionate, and sullen. It fills his ear and captures his conscience. Erasmus, feeling cared for, stills himself.

From within, steps out the Elder. Over his shoulder is the sight of a fellow priest kneeling and commencing to pray. "Erasmus!" Says the Elder with much enthusiasm. In his hands he carries blankets, a set of dry clothes, and two folding chairs. Come friend we have little time before first light. Pushing his way through, the Elder lays the clothes neatly on a dry corner. Unfolding the chairs and setting them down, "Come friend sit with me awhile. (a pause of sympathy) So you spoke out against the church in your early days." He smiles and laughs with a friendly tone. Erasmus returns to him with a smirk on his face.

"Yes those were my days." He admits.

"And today, have we changed?" asks the Elder.

"I wish we had. And do you speak out old man?"

"I have, but now I mostly speak in."

"To your other priests?"

"Yes. To them- to myself. When I was younger, I taunted the Elders and with ridicule of their ways. I can't say that they were correct in their manners of thoughts, but for some other things they were. I carry many regrets within me. I have heard over a thousand human confessions this year alone. I know that no matter who you are there will be regrets."

"This is true! Tell me? How can you live this humble life?"

"Humble. Keeping these men in line is more than a task. Are you kidding me? The worlds computers today couldn't keep these sweating, God-needing, men in line?"

"Surely you jest? How can you speak that way of such men?"

"Aye! Erasmus! (the Elder waves his hand at him) I have heard your story up to the point where it was thought you were dead?" Erasmus laughs. "You know as well as I that the words mean not a thing?" He interrupts himself into silence. Then he explodes, "tsobudabagh!" Erasmus not understanding the words returns with a blank stare. "I just finished calling you a son born from a pig. (his head tilts and he laughs at Erasmus)"

"You are truly someone to be reckoned with?" He says believing his previous disbelief.

"Aye! But don't tell the others. They need a clear path. They still think that by punishing the flesh it brings them closer to God." The Elder shakes his head. "I remember too, when I had thoughts of that same nature. It's not what you do. You know? God is much too smart for such shallow perceptions. It's all in why you do it. He knows, unlike us, our methods and intentions." The Elder shakes his head and finger.

"Aye! You are more knowledgeable than I thought." Erasmus mentions and starts laughing at the complexity of his multi-dimensional character. "'Tis truth you speak. Words brought forth without passion are merely sounds. A shame it is that many more people do not understand."

"It must be tremendous for you- having to put up with all that knowledge back in your day."

"Aye it was. It seems that the only creatures not ruled by their complete emotion or complete intellect were the actual people of the Earth! How can any one man call himself complete truth? (his eyes catch the Elder nodding to his agreement) Even the worlds most profound man, Socrates asked the world that single question-"

"Don't tell me. 'Who is the most intelligent of men?'"

"Yes! Of course! And though unwilling to answer, for fear and dismay, he concludes that he is the most intelligent."

"Aye! But the reason, my friend! That reason- so sound!" The Elder claps his hands together and rejoices in the conversation. The other Priests fixing the door are awakened from their dormant task. Erasmus lowers his voice, noticing them noticing them.

"Not good enough, I believe for those who claimed to be the most intelligent. (his voice changes to a tone of more quiet concentration) He was brilliant! He concludes- that-- he is the most intelligent! Not for knowing all of Gods good reasons and wonders, but because of the lack there of. Is that not brilliant?"

"Of course. Ours is the path of discovery and no matter how hard we try to keep life and its social civilities in control, the paths will change."

"Oh! One last thing I would like to say! If I may, of course?"

"Please! It's enlightening talking to one of more age than myself. (he chuckles) Compared to you, I feel like a young man."

"Not all men are created equal. Race is race, gender may be gender, but equality will never be achieved. Similarities, perhaps. But equality? Never." No two people are the same. After all, think of the 4092 decisions to be made on a daily bases. We are confronted by situational affairs each and every day of our existence. And the knowledge we interpret from these matters is stored in that fleshy substance (he points to his head). This could never be the same for each. Too much has to happen for this to be a 'life' fact." - Erasmus

"You should be careful of such arguments. Humans may take offense. Though I am not partial to any one race or kind, I can see how what you say can be true. Now there is something that you don't know. Scientists have finally broken the barriers of DNA and the inner working of the mind has been mapped." - Elder

"This has been said for so long- I can't believe this anymore. Tell me will they change their discoveries in a future decade?"

"It does seem that the order of man is such, and that he makes statements of absolute for reason only discovered by accident." The Elder's reply is one of obvious observations.

"And let us not forget the opposing force that always is reluctant to change." - Erasmus

"Aye! Let us not forget." The Elder mirrors his statement, while nodding his head. Watching Erasmus retract his finger while making his statement, he continues. "Man has a hard time understanding that most of what he touches is indeed transient."

"The only things I know to be not so are the images of the stars and images found in nature."

"Aye! It seems reality has set into you deeply, Erasmus."

"I've had more than a few human life times to figure this out. Tell me Elder! How many years does a healthy strong man live today."

"Oh, that is a difficult question. No one man has an accurate life span. The world is changing, as you know it always does. How man as a race, in these parts, can live to be a century old I'll never understand. But, most men I would say-80 years." - Elder

"I recall when a man would be ready to die at 35 and women had born children by the age 15."

"15 is too young today. You'll go to jail now."

"Much to learn. Much to see. And is the world any more corrupt or less corrupt today?"

"No. But you can watch much of it on the television. Rather depressing I might add."

"Katia mentioned this thing. This television. What is it?"

"It is a glass and through electronic signals recreates an image of ourselves. But you can't believe everything you see in it. There are things called documentaries- those are factual discoveries. With those types of films you can believe 90 percent of what you see. There are the news programs, which are filled with sensationalism and they try to pack in a lot of information. This type of program you can believe what you see and be careful what you hear. Then there are movies and sitcoms. These are shows, which are not of true situations, but the people, called actors, are a good clue of a few stereotypes. Perhaps you should watch it sometime- it'll confuse you."

"Complicated world you live in Elder." Erasmus says almost in a monotone voice.

"I don't know what you are talking about. I live in this church. It is often very dark and damp here. (he smiles at

Erasmus' overwhelmed look) Welcome to our century sleepy vampire."

"Yea! Right! Old man."

"Where did you pick up that phrase?"

"Katia." -Erasmus

"So tell me about the little one." The Elder's request brings out a feeling of regret.

"We were lost and confused, hungry in the forest. A vehicle passed through these man- made- ah- streets. We attacked. (he bows his head) There was a woman, a man, a boy, and Katia. She witnessed their deaths."

"Was it a horrible attack?" The Elder's question ears of profound concern.

"I believe so. How would I know? It was like a pack of hungry wolves."

"Does she know that you killed them?"

"I believe so." His face is filled with shame. The expression of the Elder leads Erasmus to believe that he has come to certain understanding. After all, it was his own kind.

"Tell me son?" The escaping words play rhythmic to the songs of peace. *Son, what a beautiful sound.*

"Yes Father?" His answer is equally as beautiful, as he has waited centuries to say the words and yet, they come naturally to his persona.

"When was your last confession?"

"A few hundred years ago?" (shrugging his shoulders) His answer is frank, but within the words there is deeper meaning.

"Do you pray?" Asks the Priest.

"Does he listen?" He answers with a sense of despair.

"You've prayed for your conversion?"

"Yes! Each day, each night, and every moment I come to rest, and every moment I take a life. (shaking his head) I can't rest until I kill them all." He looks between the falling raindrops, against the dead.

"Before you count the victims of your revenge, know that there are others out their willing to destroy all of God's good. They too are like you and it's only you that can help us survive. God watches over all his creatures. (placing his hand above Erasmus' head) God watches over *all* of his creatures. *You* included." The Elder can sense the struggle within him. The other Priests, finished with their task, move closer to the Vampire. Careful not to startle him, their curiosity surface as they move closer to him. Tired and perhaps feeling the power of compassion, Erasmus kneels before them. The other Priests circle him and they kneel. Erasmus feels a presence he has not felt for what seems to be an eternity. The presence of God is felt. With a sense of reverence and respect, the Elder's fingers grab his cross, suspended by a red ribbon. Feeling the texture of the ribbon, images of his moment come to mind. His mentor handed this powerful tool down to him as so it was done through the generations. Witnessing the event, the surrounding priests bow their heads and pray within whispering words. Extending his hand, the Elder holds the cross to Erasmus. The cross sways in the wind near to his lips. The cool, pale vampire cannot hide his confusion or fear.

"Say your peace. Erasmus, our kind and our ministry owes you many apologies. Say your peace with God. Say it now." Looking into the Elder's eyes, his mouth quivers with fretful anticipation. He reaches down to the cross very slowly. Many thoughts rush through his head. The cruelty of his life's conscience is obvious. Until this moment he has been forced to hold back the anguish and torment powering the cells of his vengeance. Now such energies of pain and regret pour from his softly whispering words. His forehead beads with sweat. Inches away from the gold; he leans his lips onto it. His eyes close, feeling years of anger and angst diminish into the darkest deepest of seas. Pulling away he feels nothing more that a slight vibrating sensation on his lips. The cross smokes, burning his saliva from the surface of the metal.

"I have waited centuries for this." He whispers. The circle of priests, chanting, now moves to the musical notes of a hymn. Erasmus' voice breaks. Nervously, he looks onto the Elder. His breath bursts with abrupt laughter, then silence. He shrugs a shoulder and takes in a deep swallow. (choking) "I never felt such emotions. (his eyes move to the Elder) Thank you!" The Elder removes his set of rosary beads from around his neck. Laying the beads in one hand and the cross in the other, he pulls, breaking the cross from the beads. It snaps away cleanly. The beads collect within the blessing of his other hand, while the cross remains palmed and hidden.

"Now, you will say two thousand Hail Marries and fourteen hundred Our Father's to redeem yourself. Then you would have enough time to think things over. My child this world is only a marble in a vast ocean of many more. If God truly did not appreciate you, you would have not been left to stand. The Lord as you know has a special place in his heart for creatures like you. Perhaps your destiny lies not within yourself, but within your work. Perhaps you will never see it with your own eyes. But reality is not always what you see and facts are not always revealed in one's life time." He looks onto Erasmus pleased and content that an un-life has been touched in such a way that truth and justice would prevail.

"I'll say them all!" He says confidently. But within his eyes something remains lingering. Something unknown.

"And will you stay out of sin, so long God allows?"

"I'll- I'll do the best." He squeezes the words out of his mouth. To his mind he is as truthful as un-life permits. Knowing that his mission stretches the boundaries battling good and evil, he fears that his blessing will be forfeit. Never-the-less, despite the out come of the future, he shall make this day last if only in memory.

"Now (he reaches to the dry clothes neatly stacked) take these clothes and take shelter to the rear of the church. You'll have good company there. No one to tease you. You'll share the barn with the sheep, a cow, and two horses. You can burn some wood if you feel the urge. Make yourself at home as best as you can there. You may sacrifice one animal for your cause."

"The girl?" He inquires short of breath.

"She will remain here. We shall try to locate family members. If we cannot find any she shall remain here, under the care of Father Brobova. He shall take care of her until she is of age." His answer is misleading, but for the time it serves his purpose. Erasmus understands the Elder's need for altering reality. "And this? For the sake of the safety of the confused little girl, someday the circle will be completed and a future of her destiny accomplished. For the time however she will be safely guided."

The surrounding Priests take to their feet. Their questions are in part answered, but as one question opens the doors to many others, they hope that someday they will gain the greater knowledge.

As they leave they each bestow one blessing upon the soulless creature. The blessings, he counts, are nine. He bows reverently at each one of them. Their humble shoes scuff at the floor as they elegantly walk to the door they have just replaced. The Elder also comes to a stand. Erasmus, now focusing on the Elder's face, notices that the rain has accumulated into droplets clinging to his face. His humanly aged face is rugged and seemingly impermeable to the rain. Erasmus observes his figure, as the Elder stands and takes his leave. Though he spoke much, it was evident that the Elder is of silent breeding. The slow moving Elder walks away as if the moment was all he has ever lived. There was no reference of a battle, nor joy of his victorious confrontation with one of Vigore's elite. There was no boasting. There was only a Holy man helping one of God's creatures.

The heels of his shoes lift, as they also become smaller, disappearing into the church. "How ironic that even shoes have souls. In some countries the showing of one's shoe sole is a lethal insult." Here lays Erasmus, staggering between the edge of darkness and the edge of forever darkness. If life were unfair, then un-life would be purgatory at a constant. "How ironic that humans can lift an eye and unwittingly ask the forgiveness of the Holy One and for the ones truly making the difference there is nothing there to accommodate their needs. Aye! But looking into the eyes of that Priest I see something I would never see within my own kind."

Pushing his dry clothing under his jacket, he now comes to a stand. He studies the swords still lying in the rain puddle surrounded by sand and mud washing down the flooded street. They are foreign to the soil, but for now they will not be removed. Extending his fingers beyond normal reach, he stretches until the long dark talons emerge. Silently, mystically he expands his hands as to touch the stonewalls, holding the church erect. With just barely a hold of the large stones, he begins to scale the walls elevating himself. Fixing his view on the steeple, he continues his climb. Hand over hand and foothold after foothold, his motions brings him closer towards the top of the building. The large raindrops falling on his face go seemingly unnoticed, as he climbs steadily to the top. His body glides above the wet rocky surface.

Inside the Elder walks on the tiles of a semi-ambient church, searching out the disturbed Angelica. Behind him on the other side of the stained glass, the shadow of Erasmus appears dimly outlined by way of the street lamp. The Elder, setting his view towards the first pews, sees Melonnie's outline. Staring at the candle flame she has little reason to move.

"Aye! There you are my dear."

"Oui. Je suis ici." (Yes. I am here.) She answers. Her voice is cheerless.

"What besides the mission, and the course of tonight's event, troubles you?" He inquires from the distance.

"I am missing another of my crew." She says. As the beat of a saddened melody sets into the rhythm of her heart, she exclaims. "I fear."

"It is normal to fear." He says finally reaching at her distant focus.

"No father. It is not just fear. (he places one hand under her chin) I fear that I may not complete the mission. I fear that my elite team, is not strong enough now for the powers that are to test me." Her dark eyes set themselves comfortably to his.

"My child. All good people of destiny come face to face with their fears at one point or another."

"Yes I know. But it isn't all good people. It's about me." She interrupts. Within her voice are the signs of defeat.

"Are you concerned that the way you handled yourself out there was not good enough?"

"You saw for yourself! I barely stood up to them. I am wounded. And that thing! That- Spell Maker- he nearly finished me. I am in charge of this mission. I have a great weight on my shoulders."

"I believe I must agree with you. You should improve your skills. If it had not been for my magical chant- you would have lost."

"Exactly! I can take constructive criticism."

"Constructive Melonnie- Or destructive?" He asks with a hidden sense of meaning.

"What between Heaven and Earth do you mean? Have you always spoken with such twisting words that lead to no apparent direction?"

"My dear child I am no match for you. I am just a humble servant of God. God allows me to be here, only at his will. Had he not taken care of me till this very day, I would have perished."

"God is not an Evil being- though sometimes I could question his theories." Her sentence ends underneath her breath. "What I mean is that, had he not wanted me to live. He could have looked the other way, allowing perfect time to occur."

"More riddles?" She raises an eyebrow at him.

"You mustn't always search for that clear sense of understanding on the intellectual level, my dear. You also need to understand from your heart. Allow your mind to control your decisions, but feel out with the heart. The heart understands all, for in it contains God's good principles. Your mind will then allow you to make your choices...

"*When I was a child I fell into cold water after the ice had broken while I stood on a frozen pond. Had God not allowed for perfect timing, a fellow brother of the faith would not have saved me. When I regained my strength, I asked that brother-'Why do you come this way?' He looked at me and answered me honestly. 'I over slept and was on my way to the church to attend mass.' This came from a brother that was faithful and never tardy. He had no history of oversleeping. One might ask the simple question- 'was I lucky?' Or one might see a spiritual way. I could turn to you and say that God allowed him to awaken later than he would have normally. In his hurry and in perfect timing, he found me and rescued me from drowning.*"

"I understand Father. I guess I needed for someone to remind me. I just needed to be sure. It has been a trying few days. A lot depends on the safety of what I have, for I must deliver this to the highest council member. We only hope that it will give us the knowledge of how to destroy Vigore."

"Vigore? Hmm."

"Vigore, the son of-"

"William Vigore, (his voice softens to a whisper) the noble man that gave his life to the great devil that roamed the village for a great many years. The same man that gave his life to the demon to save his son. And if he would have only realized that his fate had already been doomed. (abrupt and loud) He still lives?" The fear carries in his voice echoing down the church and drowns by the sudden clap of thunder.

On the outside of the Church and nearest the peak of the steeple, Erasmus sits leaning against a stone gargoyle. The rain still falls, yet he is motionless.

The cold frost emerging from his nostrils gives likeness to that of a fire-breathing dragon. And so, not too far from the truth, he watches carefully for the enemy to appear. Down below the bodies still soak in the mud, with the only difference being they have been buried further. He watches them, placing close attention on how the drops fall onto the pooled blood and mud. Like tiny little needles they appear to fall, at just the precise angle creating rings. The shiny steel swords can no longer be seen, as they have drowned into the mud, blood, and soil now covering the cobblestone street. But he knows that they are there. Looking down into his soaked, dark, leather jacket, there is a dark tear. From within it flows his blood. Though running out slowly, it appears not to have an effect on him. Flashes of the attack on Katia's family come to mind. It would have been easier to kill them all than to care for one. Just one.

Now regret fills his eyes and textures his hands. This was indeed a hard way to carry out the sentence of eternal life. Closing his eyes he remembers times of joy and happiness. He thinks, to the day, how he once had a wife and child. A young child- however it had been too long ago, he cannot remember if it was a boy or a girl. After all, that was when he was still human. He had been in too many battles and had taken too many lives at no discretion to either gender or age. Food was food. During wars such as these, there will be much bloodshed. 'Ironic, that the moon seems to smile at me between broken clouds, where it should be covered and hidden by the rainfall.' He was sure that the Elder had noticed. The thoughts fade in and out. Some are too far to reach them and sometimes too close to focus on them.

Chapter 4

Brahnt Vaughin

Unspeakable

She whispers in hallways
Where a pin drop echoes
Through the walls of my brain
She tends to dance
In hidden closets
Of my cortex
Like a priestess
Singing voodoo chants
Next to a wildfire.

Stranger in a Strange Land

"Damn!" He brushes off his suit. "Damn! I can't believe this!" A man waves his hands into the air, as he stands momentarily on the middle of a dark road. "Damn! Ruined a new suit!" Looking down to his wristwatch he feels the darkness around him. It is a dark night and night with an unknown hour. "Stuck in the middle of the world, again! And without a ride!" He looks left then right. There are no signs of life from either side of hell; there is only disappointment. "I really hate it when things don't go the way I plan!" He checks his body and secures his hat on his head. Setting his sights to the top of the trees, he sees the clouds have already collected and formed. There is thunder among them. He reaches into his jacket pocket. Pulling something delicate out, he smoothly slides it into his mouth. His eyebrow rises, as the wind picks up. He reaches his hand into his other pocket, this time pulling out a square box of matches. Pushing it opened with his index finger, he removes a slender stick with a red and white tip. He slides closes the box. Striking the match, it lights. The flame illuminates his coffee brown eyes, his hands, and the collar of his dark double-breasted suit. His lips move downward, as his hands carrying the flame are moved upward. The flame meets with his only addiction. "Come here." With just one inhale the cigarette is lit. Each inhale warms his face from the cool and frigid night air. Two lightning bolts cross paths in the sky colliding. They branch off choking the sky like giant tentacles wrapping themselves around sky whales. The first raindrop falls from the heavens, hitting the brim of his hat. "I tell you God must be a woman." (a crackling sound) "Is that the best you can do?" He screams at the charcoal sky.

The sound of wood splitting and a flash of light take to ear and sight. A large bolt flares, exploding through a tree near to his travel. Startled, he throws himself onto the road, holding his head and pressing his hat close to it. (the tree falls) The raindrops begin to fall, heavily against him. In what seems to be the wake of an instant, his clothes are soaked. The wind blows, lifting his hat off from his head. It lands a few feet further into the center of the street. He raises his head from the pavement and spits out his half-lit and crumpled cigarette. Thunder crackles and rattles off, leaving a heavy percussion. His eyes focus on the tree limb fallen only a few feet before him. (lightning) A reflection on the puddle underneath his nose allows him to see a bruised forehead. But like an illusion it quickly disappears. The cold rain has filtered through his suit and pants. (a gust of wind) His hat is lifted, slightly beyond hand's reach. "Fuck!" Large rain pellets penetrate through his hair touching down and cooling his scalp. The droplets collect and river down his face. Afraid of standing and feeling at a loss, he crawls to his hat. Being but inches away, he reaches out for it.

His muscles tense. (a horrid sound) His body becomes paralyzed. The screeching tires of a vehicle finally come to a halt. The sound and smell of rubber skidding toward him, wraps its fingers around his heart. The vehicle stops and his hat is trapped underneath its front tire. "Fuck! My new hat ruined! Killed by a Peugeot!" Pulling his elbows in he brings himself closer to the car. Balling his fist, he punches at the hubcap. It falls off of the rim, rolling off of the tire and blocking his view. He hears the latch to the driver's side door click open. Moving his head, the hubcap rolls off to the side. He turns to face the sound. Both of his ears fill with a deep penetrating thump and with it the large flash of light that is only too familiar.

The door comes to a sudden halt at the sound of a heavy thud and abrupt resistance. From underneath the door appears a narrow heel. The shoe, appearing too large for the foot, falls. "Merde!" The sound of a frustrated female shoots out from within the vehicle. From within comes another sound. (the sound of male mocking in laughter) "Ta gueulle!" (Shut your mouth!) The laughter increases.

"Hey? Melonnie? Speak English! You'll confuse the wild life." The male laughs some more.

"Erasmus! If you insist on speaking I will have to take your tongue and give it back to you later. That is when you are a good boy and understand how to use it." Her other foot moves out to meet the road. Her hand reaches down to the shoe and holding it steady, sliding her foot down into it. Thin, but long fingers reach for the doorframe. Pulling herself out she meets the elements. The rain falls against her skin seemingly unnoticed. The wind dances playfully with her hair and again it goes unnoticed. Her hair pulls hard and to the left, covering her face. Stepping around the vehicle door and walking towards the front of the vehicle, her eyes fill with the man. She pauses for the moment, eyeing the still body.

"Erasmus? Move the tree limb off of the road."

"Melonnie? It's raining and you're already wet." The voice sounds hollow coming from within the cab of the vehicle.

"Maintenant!!" (Now!!) She Demands.

"Ok. I see that you are pretty serious. So why don't I just go out and-" He responds. Kneeling close to the stranger, she towers over him and places her hand on his head. Her hand glides gently over top of it. He is obviously unconscious. Possibly he dreams. She reads his thoughts, as his mind projects images, small pulses at a time. The images flow to her like poetic symbols of life. She smiles at him kindly and gently, finding warmth in her heart for him. She thinks to herself, 'this is a good man'.

"So Mr.? Will I eat you?" She says out loud.

"Sorry Melonnie? Did you say we would eat this one?"

"Non not this one. He causes me humor."

"But surely in case of need-"

"I don't think we are going to run out of food on this planet."

"But perhaps we should drain from him just enough to keep him drowsy?"

"He'll be safe." She answers with her eyes still fixated on him.

"Just-"

"Non!" Her tone is a firm one.

"One bite!" (holding a finger up to her)

"Non. Non! Non!!" Her nasal French sounds dominate her accent.

"OK. (he looks to her) Don't be a grouch." He reads her facial expression. "What is the matter?"

"I'm not sure. Something about him is clouded."

"It is the rain, ma petite. The lightning is messing with your antennas." He chuckles a bit. Though finding this side of Melonnie amusing, he keeps alert. He turns to her as if to speak. She points at his mouth. Accepting the warning, he closes it. Bending down he raises the large tree limb with only a small strain and at that, it is barely noticeable. The rain soaks, searching for unoccupied hiding places within their clothes. The tree branches scratch the road. Erasmus nears the edge of the road. Within the short sight the woods are thick and darkened. Erasmus sniffs at the air, hoping to obtain a clue that may compliment his strange, but powerful, premonition. Kneeling, his eyes scan deeper into the wood line squinting his eyes so that only a fine line is visible. The rain cannot penetrate them now. Moving his head slowly from left to right and left again, he searches. Melonnie takes the man's body and lifts him onto her shoulder.

"Qu'est-ce, Erasmus?" She whispers. He lifts up his hand and holds up one finger. Melonnie unfolds the man's body into the front seat. Standing up and away from the door, she notices Erasmus has taken the form of a wolf. His red fur is dull and the layers of rain falling against it hide its color. "Erasmus!" She stares at the sky seeing that across the horizon the signs of a new day pronounce it's becoming.

The Red Wolf's eyes squint looking deeper into the forest. His mouth opens, bearing his sharp K-9's. Melonnie adjusts Brahnt's limp body carelessly into the car, but still gently. Looking over the dashboard of the dark car, she steps backwards crouching as she clears the car. With caution she turns to look behind. In the forest line there is a sight of breath captured by the stillness of the cold air. Through the woods rustles another sound. Dampened leaves and soaked twigs being to move, describing linear movement to the imagination. She tracks the sound, sighting even greater danger. Along side of the frozen-like exhaled breaths, their dull glowing eyes suspended in darkness bring terror into her soul and mind. But her fear becomes more dense, as the sound comes closer to where she stands.

Two bodies impact, but only one whimpers. The sound surrenders comfort to her ear, as she knows that the watcher is gone. She looks to Erasmus. He is no longer there. Assuming Erasmus is defending her, she cannot help but smile with relief. Pulling herself further away from the passenger door, she closes it with hurry. Quickly pacing she rounds the front end of the vehicle, reaching the driver's door. Her fingers reach the handle. (rustling in the woods behind her) Fear touches her shoulder. Her finger can feel the cold metal of the door latch. Raindrops explode crashing against it. (glowing eyes) The headlights reflect off of another red wolf, as he paws at the asphalt street underneath him. The sounds of its individual claws striking down at the street, warn her that it is not Erasmus. Her dark eyes fix themselves on the charging intruder.

Dropping her left shoulder, she prepares herself for the assault. Through the corner of her eye, she notices a red wolf has fixed itself in for the attack. As it paws at the wet ground propelling himself forward, it seems to her as if it is all in slow motion. Its breath leaves impressions of small clouds of vapor to the side of its mouth. Above her eyes the skin arcs, leaving a bony texture. She extends her hand, exposing ivory talons, slowly blackening. Her skin tone darkens. Her eyes slit, as she sets focus on the attacker. She opens her mouth. Fangs create themselves. Staring at her enemy, she warns him producing a high pitched hissing. The attacker leaps stretching out to her. It forces its neck forward and bares fangs, anticipating its deadly bite. Reaching out with both paws he insures his balance.

Melonnie's hand snatches one of its front paws.

From the side of the road, a second wolf leaps out. (a sound of two wet bodies making impact) Colliding with Melonnie's attacker, it buries its nippers into the attacker's throat. Blood seeps into both their furs, delivering their deadly threat. Both masses fall against Melonnie's body, pushing and forcing her away. She hears the sound of the dominant creature breaking the bones of its victim. The two wolves fall to the street. The victor of the battle pulls and tears at the enemy's neck removing any remaining life force. Melonnie places her hands to the asphalt and pushes her way up. Her hands are stained with the rose colored paints of life. The Red Wolf pulls and tears until he is sure that there is no more movement that can be interpreted as potential danger.

Cautious of her surroundings, she tunes her ear to the rustling of wet leaves and twigs in the forest. The surviving wolf turns its attention to Melonnie's changing face. She looks at the sky and observes its color. It is lighter now and slowly becoming even more so. Coming to a knee and extends her hand. "Come." Lowering its head, the wolf approaches her. Through the corner of her eyes, she studies the forest. "There are too many of them. The signs of the sunrise are at my favor, but not at yours." She places her arms around the base of its neck. The wolf's eyes scan the forest line. Lifting its head, it breaks free from her hold. In the forest the enemy retreats. "Hide yourself for the day. (she wipes away her tears) When night falls, travel to the nearest village. I will wait there for you, but not for more than moments, for they too will rise to find me."

Coming to a stand, and standing at height with Melonnie, the wolf howls at the forest as if warning his enemies. Standing side by side the wear-beast lunges forward into the woods. Havoc and fear rustle among the leaves as his display of power is taken with great respect. "Irony this is. That your safety is where your enemies also rest. I wish you love my sweet friend Erasmus."

The signs of the sun continue to emerge. The shadows surrender to newer shadows, these, which move by way of daylight. However, the rain continues. She opens the door to the vehicle and falls into the driver's seat. Pulling her legs into the vehicle, she reaches over to the door. With a relaxed pull, the door swings to a close. The closing the door, awakens Brahnt from his concussion. She slides the gearshift into drive position and pushes on the gas pedal. The car tires spin unexpectedly. The force pushes Brahnt deeper into the seat. Pressed back into the chair he manages to open his eyes. Melonnie ignores him for the moment. Unfocused eyes become focused on moving objects. As his eyes become familiar to surroundings, he extends both his hands in search for something to hold. His right hand fumbles its way to the door handle. Fingers fasten around the plastic latch. His right hand encounters her right thigh, fastening his fingers onto the fleshy matter. Unsure of what he has taken a hold of, he releases the seemingly unstable matter. Leaning over to the glove compartment, her fingers frantically search for a pair of sunglasses that the Priest had given her. Finding them she places them onto her face.

"Come now I don't feel that bad. I'm sure that you've touched other women that must have been worse than me." She says with a hidden smile. His eyes return to the moving objects. Taking notice of the window's glare, he concludes that he is within a car and releases his only death-grip.

"Ouch!" He reaches for his head.

"You hit your head." She says coldly and uncaring.

"Ouch!" he says more profound.

"You hit your head." She repeats as if mentioned for the first time.

"Ouch! (he turns to her) You hit your head. Right?"

"What gives you that idea?" She says sarcastically.

"What am I doing here? Who are you? And most important who sent you?" He positions his body more comfortably.

"Sent me? Hell? Heaven? In all do matters, who the hell cares? I'm here. You bumped your head pretty hard. I'll be taking you to the hospital."

"Hospital? Head? Look. (calmly) What happened here?"

"I stopped this vehicle to remove a branch that had fallen by way of passage and-"

"Where are you from?" His voice is loud and mocking.

"Sir! (rolling her eyes, searching for a word) Brahnt right? (pointing at him) I can only answer one question at a time."

"How did you know my name?"

"That is your third consecutive question in a row. Which of them would you rather I answer."

"The first one will do."

"I stopped this vehicle to remove a branch that had fallen by way of my passage and- I opened the door, heard a sound and there you were on the wet rainy ground. I felt badly for you and decided to lift you into this vehicle. I'm from France. And you talk in your unconsciousness. (her facial expression changes to a happy one) Any way, good morning."

"Good morning. (pushing his back into the seat) Been driving long?" He asks, seeing that her eyes are glued to the road.

"Actually only a few days." - Mel

"Foreigner?" - Brahnt

"Somewhat?" - Mel

"Where are you from?" - Brahnt

"Ah! Recently France." - Mel

"Ah! That's right you said that. Sorry. I love France."

"You say that like you've been there." - Mel

"I have." - Brahnt

"Oh! How long ago were you there?" -Mel

"It's been two years." - Brahnt

"What is it like." - Mel

"Its OK. Food is fine. City is beautiful. The women are women. Much like yourself." - Brahnt

"Warm and friendly." -Mel

"Mostly the friendly." - Brahnt

"Typical man." -Mel

"Hey I'm sorry. I really didn't mean anything bad by that. I happen to enjoy women. That's all." He says in a very calm voice.

"Oh! An honest pig?" She says sarcastically to him.

"Look I'm an American - (he turns casually away from her view) Spaniard. I am cursed with the will to conquer and the will for romantic strategies. (staring at the road) And when I find a charming woman like you, (his hands search for objects to fidget with) my mind wonders and my tongue speaks the matters of the heart. My words flow and I can't stop them. Frequently I know that it is better this way." He turns to her with seriousness and bewildering suspense.

"That is enough. Romeo. (she raises an eyebrow) You have courted the attention of Juliet."

"Forgive my foolishness."

"Nothing to forgive. There is no fool better loved, than a fool that speaks of love. Though human life be short and we *pray* for extension, the fool who loves will live longer than the fool who fools with love."

"How charming." He responds to her words.

"How charming." She returns her response with a loving tone. Feeling at ease with her, his tone changes to one that is friendlier.

"Are you not going to ask any more questions?" She says humored by his innocence.

"Will you not speak me the truth with entirety?" She sensually absorbs his word.

"My new found man, you *do* have a charm about you that can only be realized through selection of your voice and sight of your gestures." She comments while keeping her eyes on the road.

"Forgive me, I feel a little silly and frankly I don't know why. Typically, I am more reserved about my poetry."

"You are a poet?" She says with a bit of excitement in her voice, however, not short of leaving the tone of sarcasm.

"Well to *be* and to practice is so near and so far."

"Like the opposite sides of a magnet that dwell as neighbors?"

"Yes (coming out of her daze) something of that sort."

"So you are the real thing?" She glances at him and returns her view to the road.

"I don't know. I just live and feel." He is honest and bland with his response.

"Still your eyes have much regret." The windshield wipers are noticed for the first time. "Forgive me. I have pressed you too hard." Her attention moves to the front of the vehicle. The street slowly warms to the rays of the sun physically touching the surface of the earth.

With little warning and sudden reaction she steps down on the brakes, hard. The car leans forward, sliding Brahnt's body off the chair. His forehead strikes at the window. The vehicle rocks backwards, slamming his unsuspected and jolting body back into the chair. He sits holding his head with his hand, gritting his teeth, and squinting his eyes, absorbing the representation of pain. Turning to the driver's side, he notices that the seat is empty and so is the ignition switch. Turning his head to the windshield, he focuses beyond the windshield wipers. 'There she is.' And he cannot understand it.

Cupping her hands as if holding drinking water, she kneels before a ray of sun, breaking through the rain showers and striking down at a small wild flower. Her lips mimic the sighs of joy and sorrow and all is done while sharing the same moments. Her eyes focus and re-focus their attention on the flower and the sunlight, creating a small circle around her and the flower. Already kneeling, she motions, moving her body closer to it. She, to him, is strikingly beautiful. The innocence of her eyes and the amazement of such a small and very significant tiny life lure him into seduction. She is amazing, but he knows that there is a darker side to her. Though hard to believe, his eyes have seen it all. Or at least so he has always believed.

Fixing and re-fixing her gentle hold around the flower, she crouches closer to it like a small animal. She says one word and allows for a single tear to fall. It falls on the petal of the yellow wild flower. Brahnt is moved. Through all he has seen, he has never imagined something so pure and for the moment. Her face reaches down for the fragrance. He steps out of the car, quietly, and into the diminishing shower. His bruised heads points itself to the woman and so in that direction he begins to walk. Her nose inhales the exhaled breath of the flower. She does so delicately and repeats the same word. He steps with equal caution, coming nearer to her. She reaches down yet closer to the flower, placing a gentle kiss upon its pedals. He stares in complete disbelief. Could a woman of this age be so delicate and pure? She is by no means a hippie, a freak, nor a fanatic.

She has elegance about her, only seen in movies, and her confidence is overwhelming. Now at ear's distance, he can hear her repeat the word *La Vie*. (*Life*) Only now it sounded more like two words rapidly said.

"Forgive me. I don't even know your name."

"Melonnie. Et toi?" She returns the question.

"Brahnt. But you know that already. You love nature?"

"Oui! (she lets out a deep breath of air) Can't you feel it?"

"It's drizzling Melonnie." She reaches out for his hand. Taking a hold of it, she brings herself to a stand pulling him into the circle of light. It is obvious that she is excited. Bringing his hands close to her chest, her eyes reach up to the sunrise. He looks at her shades, able to see only a hint of the eyes behind them. They are shiny, odd, but beautiful. Seemingly they are dark and nearly solid black. Her lips are pale, as if she is an actual sleeping beauty recently awakened. He is trapped by the moment and she the same. Soft morning rays fall on her skin, as she looks up and into his eyes. There is something differently appealing about his eyes. They are coffee brown with brilliant circles trapping the color and within the color there is another circle, a darker one. One that begins the passage to his soul. The outline of her pink lips open, reaching out for his. He is enticed; drugged by her beauty, her purity. She inhales deeper. "La Vie." The meaning of the word rings in his mind, like music. She calls out "life." Moved but inches from each other, "Can you feel the sun light? It is warm like life."

"I can feel it. I can't understand this sudden passion."

"What does your heart tell you?"

"It tells me that perhaps I should kiss you." She says to him with dream like eyes.

"Will you listen and obey your heart?" He reaches closer to her. Their eyes lock on each other. His are brown. Hers are dark like a void. Completely dark and glossed by her own tears. Her fangs begin to emerge lightly, but intoxicated with her he misses that small detail. For love is blind and love is where emotions are enacted. Taking a fist full of his hair, she pulls him towards her own way. She breathes in his kiss. "Forgive me Brahnt." With their lips touching, he feels himself weakening. She pulls his breath deeper into her own. His knees turn weak and so they give way. Carefully not to disturb him she follows him down to the ground. His knees touch the wet soil and though his pants soak the moisture, he is still entranced. Melonnie, already taken to a knee, reaches underneath his body and lays him across the soft ground. Laying down he dreams of her. Taking him by his collar, she pulls him deeper into the woods. She knows that the sun will be completely at a rise.

"I don't know what you dream, (she touches his head, allowing her fingers run through his hair) but I hope you do enjoy it. I know I have never kissed a man as I have kissed with you. Regretful though, (she pulls off her blouse and begins removing her skirt) you may not live to know how I have enjoyed it." Her breasts, pale and with a few light freckles, expose themselves to the weak sunrays and diminishing rain. Her long feminine legs, now nude, hold her body upright as she stands before him contemplating her next move.

Extending her hands to her side, she releases small whimpers, as her body shape shifts to perfection. Her ears fold back and become pointed. Her fingers take the shape of talons, the highest natural weapon of a predator. At the end of her elbows and the sides of her knees sharp bone-like spikes appear breaking the surface of her skin. Her muscles twitch, as her transformation takes her over. With Brahnt to her side, she begins tunneling at the soil and packing the side-walls. Motion after motion she digs faster and further. The dark soil mixed with the water paints her skin camouflage. And with every strike at the ground, a mental image of her past appears pretending reality in her mind.

[The burial]

Fire, much fire! Fire all about her! Friends and family consumed by flames! The sounds of metal weapons. Hard steal and shields! Her kind surrounded by others that possess the same strength and knowledge. They cry. They yell! But voices are at war. On one side the Angelica, sworn to protect themselves in the name of their once creator. On the other side the Vampire, the Unnatural. And though the Angelica is near and kin to their enemies there is a distinction of purpose. They, the enemy, wanting to rule had prepared well for battle. And like history has always shown, talks of peace and movement of purpose had been used as a tool of betrayal.

Sparks! The smell of leather burning. The tunnel has reached its end. She glances the distance and is impressed at how fast she has mined the land. The claws have now struck down against a strong surface. Melonnie rests for the moment. Moving her nose to the tunnel's ends, she uses her snout to sniff out the obstacle. She inhales deeply, filling her lungs with the scent of musty leather.

Abruptly, she backs away from the obstacle using time to catch her breath. Intimidation and anger embody her sense of emotion. She is completely aware of the consequences of this book. This would bring obvious war between Vampire, Angelica and man alike. But it is of a matter that cannot be prevented. Still panting, she rests motionless. The tunnel is dark and filled with small worms and insects squirming they way out of hiding and falling from the sides of the carved walls. The walls crumble at the slightest touch and for an instant she feels the fear of closure. The feeling of being buried breaks her concentration. B*uried alive! The image of her mother attempting to save her during the war and her gentle face comes to her in the form of a vision. The Angel Gabrielle speaks to her in memory of the first awakening. Her mind echoes the order of* *business.* Her snouted face becomes solid with the emotion of determination. She paws at the obstacle. Sparks scatter leaving a miniature fire easily suffocated.

Clutching the object out of its burial and firmly pressing her fingers into it, she recalls the memory of her mother holding the same object. With a deep breath, she releases herself of her fear. Her hands become human and her body becomes calm and serene. The miniature fires diminish and the sparks are apparent no longer. Sinking her feet into the soil, she wedges herself firmly against the raw earth while facing into the earth. The cool texture fills between her toes, bringing on a temporary and childish smile. Her straight hair falls free, scraping the pit of the tunnel, as she scrapes away at the hard crusty outline pressed onto the object. There is an independent movement, coming from within the object. The shape of a goblet rises from the undefined surface of the cover.

She holds the object steady, allowing the movement to continue. Four corners surrounding the goblet make their presence known. The movement stops. Melonnie digs at the edges, bringing the object closer to its true form. Inhaling a deep breath of musty air, she blows at the surface. The light specks of dirt remaining are forced away. Behold the book, she thinks to herself. Releasing her foothold, she allows her weight to fall on her hands. Folding at the waist, she brings both her feet to the ground underneath her. There she sits quietly for the moment gathering her strength and reminded of her purpose on Earth. Raising her head she points her eyes to the top of the tunnel where there is light on the other side. Small surges of pain emitting from her lower abdomen, is clear reminder that she must feed. But first she will focus on the task at hand and so, she begins the climb to the surface. Once nearing the opening, she tosses the book upwards and onto the grassy turf. The book lands on the green grass. She pulls herself up using her hands and pushing away with her feet. She manages to lean over the top, bringing herself to topsoil. Brahnt still lays on the damp, green grass, seemingly away in his dreams. She reaches over to him. Again the sudden sharp sensation of pain attacks her lower abdomen. She grabs at it, as her fangs protrude, she turns to him.

On the road ahead, another vehicle pulls off to the side, checking their parked car. Lights flash blue, while dark uniforms step out of the vehicle. One holds a small rectangular box to his face. It is strange how he speaks into it. Melonnie observes the two men, while clothing herself.

Leaning over to Brahnt, she places her lips against his and releases a kiss, pushing her breath into his lungs. Unconsciously, he grins. His eyes come to awaken with slow movement. Placing her head on his chest, she listens to his heartbeat. She is amazed. "This heart is not a heart of a man calling himself a man, but of a man that truly is a man and by no right does he claim it his own. But are they not of the same flesh?" A thief of purity steals her thoughts.

"Melonnie? Such a beautiful name. Like music from beyond the grasp of the stars."

"Brahnt. (she twists her lip) I am here." She shoves at him. Lifting her head, she pushes away the hair from her face and places her attention to the men dressed in blue.

"I thought I was dreaming." He moves slowly, studying her attitude.

"Of another woman?" She smiles at him delicately.

"No. Of you." He is amazed at her newly found beauty.

"Thank you." (she blushes)

He sits upright. Looking to her face, he notices that her attention is elsewhere. Searching in the direction of her sight he discovers the interest. A dark blue vehicle is parked behind theirs. Two uniformed figures scan the area nearest to them, as their vehicle flashes its blue lights.

"Damn! The cops. Did something happen that brought these guys here? You don't have any drugs or anything do you?"

"Drugs? (she shakes her head) Non."

"Do you have anything they can bust you for?"

"Bust?" She asks with no apparent knowledge.

"Anything they can arrest you for?" He carefully asks the question hoping to provoke any hidden answers.

"Non." She answers quickly. His heart beats a bit faster. She feels it. Looking into his face she sees a determined look painting itself onto it. His heartbeat calms, returning to its normal pace.

"How can you turn so calm so quickly?"

"Later! Let's wait a moment here and see what it is they're doing." Brahnt watches on with curiosity and concern.

"What is he doing with his mouth?" she inquires.

"He is talking." He says, unwilling to change his line of sight.

"To his hand?" She sounds surprised.

"No, you see that? (he points) He is holding something."

"Yes. A black box, with a silver lever on top of it? Next to it are two buttons?"

"You can see that from here?"

"Yes. Can't you?"

"No. Actually I can't."

"Is the black box any danger to us?"

"No that is standard issue. They're probably going to just check out the car."

"Oh. How do they do that?" She asks him without intimidation.

"They radio in the information. And make sure it all checks out."

"The black box you mean?"

"Yes." He rolls his eyes at her.

"But are they not too far from other people at this time?"

"They'll boost the signal through an amplifier in the cop car and send it out." He says leaning his back into the mound of dirt. "Are you in trouble or something?" He asks her, noticing her grabbing at her stomach. "Hunger pains?"

"Ah ha (she nods her head quickly and sharply)." Her big eyes become wider.

"Are you running away from something?"

"(her lips curl) Oui." She bites down.

"Shit!" He reaches up to look over the mound. The cops are still there. Brahnt studies them, as they move about looking into the window using their flashlight.

Desperately her fingers work sifting through stones, picking up and dropping them as if trying to find the perfect one. Finding two flat and well-waited stones, she fists them. Brahnt keeps his eyes focused on the unwanted guests. Carefully and with stealth he observes their every movement. "I don't know. It looks like whatever you're running from is pretty ugly." One of the officer's head-cap is lifted away by a strong gust of wind. With sudden and unpronounced force the officer's head jerks to one side and he falls to the ground.

There is no further motion to him. Brahnt turns to Melonnie. She cocks her arm with another stone and launches it. Brahnt's surprise comes to surface, but for the moment he is grateful she can throw with such deadly aim. She glances at Brahnt and together they turn their attention simultaneously to the only officer left standing. She launches the next stone. The small missile breaks through the wind barely noticeable; it glides through the air. The projectile strikes and shocks the front tire of the police vehicle.

The sound of the explosion shocks the police officer. He jumps, frightened. His blood races through his body and Melonnie, though far away, can sense it. The police officer draws his weapon in one hand and carefully maneuvers towards the origin of the sound. His vehicle seems to now rest at an incline. Realizing that it must be a flat tire, he moves his blue eyes from end to end. Noticing that his partner is nowhere to be seen, he kneels, placing one of his hands on the road. Clear on the other side of the car he can see his partner lying there- still. Still without so much as a whimper. Trying to make no sound he comes to his feet and makes his way around the police car. Once there, standing near to his partner, he notices his partner's blood flowing from his head and pooling between cracks and craters of the street. A stream of blood makes its way to the side of the grass, mixing with the soil. He pulls out his black box. Melonnie draws another stone.

"Why don't you just hit him?" Asks Brahnt losing his patience.

"I need him alive." Her stomach pains jab at her, distracting her attention, but it lasts only for a brief instance. She regains composure. Inhaling deeply, she cocks her arm and throws another stone. The police officer brings the black box to his mouth and presses the button. Before a word is able to slip from his mouth, the box bursts into pieces and in its place is a blood soaked hand. His mind confused responds with inquisition and shock. How did that happen? Where did it come from? Burning! More burning! Pain creeps on into his shattered hand. He screams silently, but in his mind it is the loudest sound he has ever heard. Melonnie comes to a stand and leaps over the mound of grass that has so well hidden her. Brahnt raises his head a little bit higher, just enough to see Melonnie hiking up her skirt and running at a speed that he believes unimaginable. Watching her run is almost like watching light bending.

Her face is focused on its target. Muscle contours of her flesh molds and changes, forming her claw-like hands. Her facial features narrow developing fangs. Her feet gouge out the ground beneath her, as each step increases her speed. Still she is careful not to reveal her complete ability. Brahnt, unable to steer his attention elsewhere, stares at her transformation, while waiting for reasoning to catch-up. Though he has never seen anyone run quite so quickly, but it is still believable, he tells himself for sanity sake.

Nearing the police officer, she takes a short leap. With one hand she takes his pistol, preventing injury to herself. The other hand quickly wraps around the base of his neck. Brahnt comes out from behind the mound and starts running toward her. His feet strike on the same path she has taken, noticing the deep gouges left behind. His subconscious absorbs the information. Unlike his conscious mind, he answers himself- ‘now is not the time to wonder why’. The situation at hand must be dealt with.

She squeezes her long bony fingers together until she hears the satisfying sound of bones braking and snapping. The police officer’s face and body come to relax. “Now is the time for you to speak your mind to me. Is there anything you should tell me?” She searches through his thoughts, finding nothing more in his thoughts than confusion and fear colliding with one another. “Nothing?” She squeezes out through her monstrous face. “Your life will serve well. You should be proud to serve your kind. I have broken you, so you do not feel the pain of your life being drawn out of you. I pray you have settled your accounts on Earth.” Her mouth opens wider. Her fangs extend. With a swift motion, her fangs slither between the pores of his skin and into his veins. She inhales (leaning his body into the car), drawing in his blood. Placing one hand on the rooftop, she maintains her balance. Her other hand pushes on his chest cavity and climbs upward, forcing the veins to replenish their loss. As Melonnie inhales the liquid of substance, the talons of her other hand scrapes at the rooftop. The metal bends, giving way, and finally tears open. The horrible sounds of her feeding, enters the police officer’s ears, bringing fear closer to him.

Panting heavily and regaining his composure, Brahnt reaches the vehicle. He pauses for the moment and looks at the creature, enthralled with her feeding frenzy only a few feet away. Staggering over to Melonnie's vehicle he leans against the passenger side and places his hand on the door lever. (he lifts) The vibration carries through his fingertips and up through his arm. Pulling the door open, he reaches for his jacket in the back seat. He draws it closer to him and reaches into it, pulling out his semi-automatic. The car rocks slightly. Lifting his head out and over, he finds his view obstructed by the vehicle's trunk. Quickly! He glances to where the creature once stood; for the moment there is nothing there- no one.

Claw-like fingers appear over the trunk. With great skill, he rests his firing hand on the rooftop of the vehicle, making no sound. Holding both eyes open, he takes on the sniper position curious as to what horrors lie on the other side of the trunk. The trunk lid lowers.

His eyes widen. His nostrils flare. Appearing before him is an unknown horror. He watches the creature's face moving from side to side, placing its attention on the activities that would bring the trunk to a close. The trunk slams shut. The vibration travels through to the gunman's hand. A shadow catches the creature's eye and its face motions upward to the gunman, causing him to become hesitant. Locked eye to eye they stand for the moment staring each other down, while attempting to conceal their inner most emotion. His finger releases the trigger ever so slightly, noticing that her eyes are moving from his face and down the side of his neck. He studies her line of sight, as she constructs a visual painting of his body, allowing her eyes to continue their travel down to his chest. His finger regains attitude, hardening around the steel-metal trigger. Flexing his muscular hand his finger applies unconscious pressure, as the metal hammer slips and catches from moment to moment.

Hearing the metal collapsing between his finger and his palm, her view is cast upon to the barrel of the weapon. A silent flash! A look of surprise shadows her face. His eyes blink closed! She feels the sharp penetrating pain accompanied by the weapons blast! His weapon kicks. A burning sensation! The bullet forces her head backwards and into a spin. Two small streams of blood trail her motion in half-spherical shapes, seemingly frozen in mid-air. His eyes blink open. He fires his second shot, as so he has been trained. But much to his astonishment there is no target. In the distance he catches view of a small spark, as the bullet travels and skids off of the pavement. Perhaps the creature is on the other side of the car-dead. Now, uncertain, his curiosity mixes with a pinch of fear. Leading with his chin he peers over the vehicle searching for the creature. Strong hands finger their way into a vise like grip, pinning his muscles against his bone.

Without the pain yet able to register, his left shoulder is forcefully pulled in an unwarranted direction. He sees glimpses of her hair, her blood falling down her face, white fang, a flash of bright white, and then darkness. And for the moment he sees darkness without sound.

"Men!" The words breathe themselves away from her estranged mouth. Small droplets of blood, escaping from Melonnie's wound, come to sudden halt, as they crash against Brahnt's semi-lifeless face. Grasping his neck and bringing his limp body to a stand, she points her index finger directly into his eye. The long narrowed talon nearly touching it moves no further forward, but trembles. "An eye for an eye my sweet?" She pushes her finger forward. The wind blows carrying his body fragrance, filling her lungs with his taste. Her projected fangs retract slightly collecting her saliva at the tip. Thick serum forms into droplets. Once weighted, they fall. Her nostrils flare, extracting more of his scent from the subtle breeze and once more filling her with the flavor of his sole. Illusions of kindness.

bring to mind gentle images of him, causing her to retract her dagger like finger. Gently patting at her bleeding eye, she places her hand to her view and presses.

Staring at her own blood, she watches as the sunlight changes its chemistry. The bright red turns, deep red, deeper red and deeper still until it is brown. The breeze blows lightly against it, cooling her hand. Her wound still drips the signature of her existence. The blood on her hand dries to a dark contrast and becoming more than brittle, flakes carried off into the wind. Her face forms with the sharp lines of anguish, unable to consent to sparing the life of this creature. Looking into the sky, with a profound and sad expression, she searches for a small sign of compassion from the heavens. But there is none, today as many times before the heavens will retain its wisdom. Anguished and obviously in the hands of torment, she lets out a broken scream.

Covering her eye she lifts Brahnt from the street. Placing her hand in front of her eye, she pushes Brahnt into the back seat of her car. Her breathing, harsh and erratic, escapes within small powerful puffs. Once she has placed the body into the back seat, she leans her body against the car with her back slightly arched. She looks at the sun and how it fills the sky. Her skin is hotter now, perhaps produced from her lack of blood. Her hand passes by way of her head, forcing perspiration to collect and form into small rivers, now trailing down her face. Disguised among the tiny rivers of perspiration, is another river more meaningful and dearer to her heart, reminding of her tormented reality.

"My God? Why is it that when I do your serving, I have to suffer so much? These pest-like humans, just don't have the comprehension, that I too love and fear and...." She feels the sudden pull of death, though subtle as it may be. With its warning, she pushes out of the car. Throwing her right hand, she catches the door. It slams closed. Looking in on Brahnt she insures that he is undisturbed. With her fangs set before her lips she walks away from him. With great anger, she slams her fist against the side of the vehicle. "Merde! Merde!!" Reaching the rear of the vehicle, she opens the trunk once again. Fixing her eye into the compartment, she takes good notice of the police officer. Like branches of a weeping willow tree so does lay their wallowed, gaining only the strength to look up at the creature. "You cannot remain alive." She says to him with her expression of regret.

"Please." He says to her, through the blood crusted on his lips.

"Don't make me feel worse than I do." Her eyes squint at him with a change of anger.

"Look, I don't know who or what you are, but please. Don't. I was only doing my job." He pleads to her, while trying not to look directly into her dark monstrous eyes.

"I'm sorry. Truly! I'll pray for you." With that said, her fingers wrap around his broken body and bleeding head. Leaning into the trunk of the car, casting her dark shadow over him, her fangs clamp down on his throat. Death will soon call the grim reaper by his first name and carry yet another soul away within his concealed arms. Blood escapes the gouges brought on by her violent attack. Feeling compelled to lap up the spilling blood, her tongue glides over her lower lip. Removing her deadly bite, he feels the pressure alleviate.

"Is that all you need? Had enough?" he says hopefully.

"Non! (her hands reach down, taking a hold of his neck and head) Now stay still! (a sound of brittle bones breaking)" With but his eyes to display his defiance, he stares at the creature draining him of his own life. Slowly feeling despair and hopelessness, he thinks his prayer and hopes that it carries to God before his tomb is marked. His eyes flicker with each inhalation she makes. And as each inhalation pulls away more of his life force, his eyes flicker less and less decreasing in strength until there is no more life left. The man is now dead. The grim reaper can now take what else is left. At a full, she takes a step backwards staggering and falling to her knees. Lowering her head she whispers to the angels.

"Carry my message to the ears of God, that for this man to die, I feel remorse. Take him to where he belongs with wishes of my blessing. (a pause) Amen." She opens her eyes taking a deep breath. Spitting into her hand and rubbing them together, she cleans away at her messy hands with her shirt. Seeing that they've come cleaner, she takes in a deep breath of freshness. Trapping her breath in her lungs, she places one hand around her wrist and jabs her fingers into her eye cavity. Her lungs bring forth her pain, exhaled. Crows within the near treetops take flight, as they are startled. Trying to ignore the pain, she pushes her finger deeper into her flesh wound.

The screaming sounds, hanging from her vocal cords, increase with tension. Breaking her screams into a panting rage, there is a certain look of satisfaction on her face. Slowly and carefully she pulls her trembling, rigid fingers outwardly, removing the lodged bullet. Throwing it to one side, she presses at her face with her free hand. Sitting on the road's surface, she rocks back and forth trying to relieve the pain. Her pale skin now changes texture and color. She tears her dress, making strips of bandages. Placing it on her missing eye, it soaks red and, though ironic, it reminds her of carnations. Once her bandages are secured, she reaches up to the automobile and pulls herself to her feet.

Moving in careful time and insuring that Brahnt has not awakened, she plans the replacement of the actual scene of violence with one of fiction. She sets her sunglasses on the dash of her vehicle and walks to one of the dead men. Dragging him, she places him into the seat of the police car and so she begins to set the scene. For a moment it all seems as if they are waiting for her to photograph. And, like wise, Melonnie will remember this day as she takes careful notes of all the details at hand.

Pressing her body over the dead police officer, she reaches over him obtaining his coffee cup from the cup holder. Her strong hand takes his head, forcefully striking it on the steering wheel. She spills the contents onto his lap and pulls up on the emergency brake and places the police car in park, then walks to the rear of the vehicle. Her arms flex and muscles protrude, as she clenches at the rear bumper.

Leaning near parallel to the ground, she pushes the police car. The front tires shimmy back and forth slightly, as the transmission fights the movement. The unarguable smell of rubber burning produced by the friction makes its way to her senses. She pushes the car into a semi circle and into the middle of the street. The weight of the vehicle leaves tread marks underneath her. Stepping away, she contemplates the reality of the scene. The vehicle now seems to have spun into the middle of the road and come to a sudden halt.

Dropping to the ground, she reaches to the gas tank. Pressing her fingernail into it, she punctures the metal. She takes the cup and fills it with gasoline. The cold fluid cools her skin and she finds the sensation pleasant. Returning to the position where she attacked the first police officer, she allows the bloodstained area to cover itself with gasoline. "Thank you, Katia!" Reaching into her blouse she produces a book of matches. Lightning it, she drops the match. A puff of heat, a ball of flames, and the science is in motion. She walks toward her own car, as the dripping fuel makes its way to the fire.

Passing by the vehicle, she throws the cup into the cab of the car.

Changing her body chemistry, her figure adjusts to human form. Stepping carefully, while fixing her clothing, she makes her way to the getaway car door. The stream of gasoline behind her meets with the open flame. She reaches downward to the opened window. Her eye though not healed is fixed on the bruised man. His movement is restricted to REM. This, she takes as a good sign. 'He is well, or at least he will be well.' Reaching for the door handle she pulls the door open, finding the time to take one more look around her. "What a mess," she comments.

The ignited fuel, finding its way to the gas tank, explodes the rear of the car, forcing it to slide forward. Melonnie, faces the explosion. The percussion pushes her hair away by the shock wave. Debris slices at the base of her cheekbone. A small cut opens, allowing a few drops of blood to flow. The small wound lasts only seconds, closing as quickly as it had opened. The blood changes color and drying, it flakes away from her face carried by the wind. She closes her eyes for a moment. The breeze is warm and thus pleasing. She turns towards the car. Entering, she closes the door behind her. (one more glance at Brahnt and another for herself, by way of the mirror) She turns the key, places the vehicle into drive, and pulls out. There is no skidding, no rapid acceleration, just a steady increase, until she reaches her desired speed.

[Moments Pass]

Moments pass as moments often do, but moments such as these, pass not unnoticed. Questions fill her mind about Brahnt and his liability. "Can I afford the patience to lend towards this unknown? Is he worth that much effort? Still (she looks into the mirror catching his reflection), he is cute. Ok! And charming. Perhaps he is also a little attractive. Besides what did he do after all? He did no more than defend himself. Even *I* would defend myself. Who am I kidding? He's human and when he awakens he will want me dead. Isn't that how all humans are? They explore the unknown, conquer what is not theirs, and finally destroy what they don't understand. Still it is my duty. I am a missionary. Not an assassin. I live to protect our lives and those of humans. As long as this one is cute and poetic, I'll stand for him. What if he will not stand for me? (she slaps her head). What if he vows to destroy me? Well (she answers herself), I'll have to suck him whole. Hmm? I guess that may sound too sexually satisfying. I'll break his bones and slice his throat and watch him die without so much as a tear spent for his life." She looks at the mirror again and again. Back and forth she pushes the issues of a woman possibly falling in love with the wrong kind of man. "I'm more woman than he could possibly ever want. Oui! I can deal with him and use his soft skin leather. But I can control myself! What kind of woman do I think I am anyway? C'est le problem! That's the problem! I'm not! Je suis Angelica. Mother should have kicked that Angel. That's not fair. God forgive me. Gabriel, if you're listening-" (there is movement in the rear seat) Reaching into the glove compartment she retrieves another set of sunglasses. The silver rims and rectangular mirrored glass remarks at the parity of her life. She turns to look at him, then to the rear view mirror.

In the long distance there is nothing but trees and road. Her heart palpitates, anticipating his wakening. "What do I tell him? Enjoy your rest? I knocked you unconscious, because you shot me in the eye! Maybe he'll wake up screaming! Owe!" Allowing his thoughts to enter hers, she feels a heavy pressure building inside her head throbbing.

Quick flashes. A black car. No! Blue! Laughter. My laughter! A man, no, an older man, a woman, no, an older woman. I can't see the road. A horn! Bright lights! I can't see? (she steps on the brake. Her chest perspires) *A loud crash! Suddenly silence! Everything is slow motion.* - She breaks away.

She brings the car to a slow halt. The doors open, she steps out extending one leg after the other with the style and elegance of a lady. She adjusts her sunglasses. Taking a long glance around her, she insures, as best she can, that she is safe from any immediate harm. Her feet make their way cautiously to the rear door. The windows reflect the dark outline of her against blue sky and rolling gray-white clouds. Pulling at the door, she opens it delicately.

Once opened her emotions sway to that of a caring woman. Reaching down with her palm facing him, she carefully places her hand on Brahnt's chest. The energy flowing through his body filters to her hand, producing the same sensations as when first they met. "You are so innocent, my dear. Aren't you?(her expression drops) what is it? What is inside you? Why do you hold back these thoughts?" The link between them fades and breaks away from her grasp.

Brahnt, starting to show signs of waking, squeezes his eye shut. The bulk of his mouth widens displaying the dim reflection of his teeth. She watches carefully, as his lips spread. Softly and almost at a whisper he releases, "Melonnie, be careful." She turns away in a harsh attempt to dodge his caring gesture. Facing the sky, she allows the tears of her joy and confusion to form to the contour of her eyes and then gently fall. Her face painfully and reluctantly narrates the symptoms of heavenly happiness. 'Could he? Maybe? He lives another day! Then I can think with more clarity.'

With her new and re-found feelings of hope, she reaches down to him, caressing his face. "Brahnt?" She whispers. His face reveals the bruise, symbolic of her strike and looking into it, she realizes that life is full of surprises. To live we find that the house of life advertises nothing. The earth will crumple and the sky will shatter its mirror like beauty, with God saying nothing. Nothing. And thus to her mind comes nothing that she did not know nor understand yesterday. It is only a view of life in a different shade. Perhaps through this shade she will find strength to dream and hope.

She bites down on her finger, lightly as to allow only a few secured droplets to surface. The strands of her fallen hair, brush lightly against his face. Brahnt's eyes open. "Mel? (he squints) Is everything OK?" He reaches for his chest. Feeling that his weapon is holstered, his face shows relief and yet there is a puzzled look about him. Melonnie's blooded finger reaches out to him. "You're hurt!" He says not realizing the true reason for the blood on her finger and so he takes a hold of her hand; placing her finger into his mouth. Not being the intention behind the self inflicted wound; her facial expression falls into a state of paradox. She is neither for nor against what he has done, but the indecisive look, is interpreted. "Does it hurt?" Flattered, she blushes.

The blood swirls within his mouth leaving a tin-like taste. At first it is very strong. It must be soiled, he thinks to himself not being able to understand the taste of her blood. That's ok. She is worth it. Reading the carried thoughts, she raises her shoulder. A large smile grows on her mask of wonders. Canting her head to a side, she delicately and very lady like, pulls the finger away. "What am I doing in the back seat? Did I fall to sleep?"

"Yes, we've been driving a few hours. You must have been tired from that accident."

"Accident?" He asks confused.

"When I found you on the street. You know? Last night in the rain?"

"There was no accident." Thoughts of thoughts clash within the confines of her mind, forming a black void. 'That darkness again!' She moves back slightly. 'And why the gun?' "I was out doing a favor for someone. (he notices her facial expression) Well, (gently proceeding) let's say that the favor got out of hand and they threw me out into the street. Then drove off."

"But you were laying down. And you were out cold!"

"Oh! Did you happen to see the tree that fell next to me?" He says to her in amazement.

"Oui! But that didn't hit you." They both pause. Looking directly at one another they realize what truly has taken place. He smiles lightly, but only for a moment. The picture is clear to him now. Judgment falls against the side of his face and with this Melonnie feels a reason for alarm, as she expects that he has placed the pieces together.

Fear and his brother caution, introduce themselves to her in blunt fashion. He too feels the touch of their invisible hands pressing down on his throat, while squeezing at his heartbeat with intense energy. Her breathing changes to that of light pant, blind and unable to predict the outcome of the next few moments. Regretfully, she takes to her senses; she cannot withstand another projectile from his weapon. Her skin perspires lightly. A bead of sweat from within her dark colored hairline produces a small trail. (she swallows hard)

Although she tries to contain herself, her hands tremble while studying the man posed for death. Any sign of aggression will be his last. Her keen and focused eyes watch over him, monitoring his every muscular movement. She searches him for the flicker of an eye, a muscle twitch, or a hair follicle motioning out of rank- anything. He stares onto her, traveling beyond the shades. Unnoticed to her, her fangs protrude the silhouette of her face.

Understanding the position he has placed her in, he submits to his only option. He will have to create a bond. Without moving so much as another muscle, he relaxes is mind and body. His eyes close. His heart becomes calmer. His lips move in slow motion careful not to alarm her. "I understand."

"What?" She says surprisingly, looking slightly away from him.

"I (his eyes open slowly) understand."

"Understand? You?" As her last words leave her lips, he reaches out to the rim of her sunglasses. Being only inches away, Melonnie's fear and insecurity boils to the point of an attack. He studies the shimmy and twitch of her right nostrils. It is much like the wolves. Untrusting, but trying to trust, her teeth bare, while allowing him the benefit of the doubt. He notice's tears running down from one eye- the eye he shot. The tears seem uncontrolled. They were clearly not tears of emotion. He moves slowly.

Pulling down her shades and looking over the silver rims, he finds what he already knew to be true. They are dark! Glossy with honey, but deep as dark black pearls.

"I understand that you could have killed me a long while ago. I know that you don't wish me harm."

"And why should you live? Now that you have seen my face?"

"I don't know. (he swallows) But I bet you are not from here and need to be somewhere in a hurry."

"How do you guess so well?"

"We are not different. (trying not to move) If you wouldn't have killed those two back there. I would have." Hearing those final words she draws back and out of the cab. She releases an explosive gasp of air and within it the intentions of killing him dissipates. "Are you OK?" His voice carries concerned.

"I will be." She says lowly, "There is much to talk about."

"Why me?" He inquires calmly. He pushes his body out from the back seat.

"Because I'm alone. It's a big world out here. And I have a mission I don't know how to accomplish."

"What is that mission?"

"I have to meet with others like myself. I have to meet them because there is a greater threat well on its way. I have knowledge that can destroy Vigore."

"Vigore?" His voice is calm and soothing. He makes himself more comfortable.

"Vigore. An unnatural man, that plans to take the world by storm."

"The Nations will unite and will not stand for that. The military will stop him."

"Qu'est-ce c'est le, United Nations?"

"Military peace keepers." His voice confidently adds.

"That's to say that they are humans?" Brahnt's back falls, leaning further against the seat. He crosses his arms "Shit!"

"Oui! They don't stand a chance."

"Let's go from here. Cops will be coming to get us. I have friends that can help out a little. We'll talk more in the car."

"Sorry I struck you." She says to him with a sad smirk and a drop of her head.

"Sorry I shot you. (he extends his hand) Friends?"

"Oui, nouse sommes amis." (Yes, we are friends.) She answers back with a reassuring smile and taking his hand. "You have questions?"

"What's your name again?" He asks. The words leave a certain charm glistening on his lips. She smirks.

"I mean real questions." She says half smiling.

"Where did you get those big beautiful black eyes?"

"I'm a Wampire. (he smirks at her) Hey! (she shoves) My mother gave them to me. My turn." She inhales a small nervous breath of air. "What are you?" Her eyes carry a playful charm.

"A man." He says proudly.

"A human man?" she asks in an assuring term.

"Without an imperfection." He enunciates each word.

"You have a bruise on your head. That is an imperfection." She points out to him.

"Ah! Yes. A perfectly bruised man." Bringing her hands to her mouth, she tries to cover her smile. But her wide lips bear all. Brahnt admires her smile, as he has never seen protruding fangs such as these.

"Are you always such a clown?" She says trying to control her laughter.

"No! Only when I am nervous... Or attacked by a beautiful woman. "

"I'm not a woman!"

"Wamperes too. They look like women you know?"

"Who looks like a woman?"

"Wamperes. (he nods his head seriously) I'm sure that we can make some exception." She looks into his eyes- deep into them. Each breath he exhales has a scent of sweet. But though the aroma of romance lingers through waves of her emotions, deep within the back of her mind, she understands that she can only bring danger to him. "Tell me? What do man eat?" She interrupts her own thoughts.

"That is 'men'. A man. Two men. Same as you- we eat policemen." His voice is serious, but his facial expression leans to opposite connotations.

"That is not amusing anymore. I know that what you have seen was something not ordinarily seen." Embarrassed she looks down at her hands.

"I've seen many men die before." His voice turns a bit more serious, but never losing of his charm.

"You have. Haven't you?" She says the words as if reading his expressions.

"I normally eat dead things." He says placing his finger against the rim of her glasses.

"Like vultures?" She asks with surprise.

"No! Like hamburgers, chicken-"

"But chickens are alive."

"We kill them and then eat them." Her facial expression fills of disgust. "I mean we first kill them, cook them and then eat them."

"Do you drink blood?" She asks.

"No that is strictly out of my diet. I don't think it has any nutritional value. OK! My turn. (his mouth opens, freezing his expression) Are you on a mission?"

"Yes." She holds herself from saying anything further. With this answered, he feels safer. His experience has taught him that someone on a mission is always someone in need of a good friend. She nears her face closer to his. Tension, though slight, is still evident between them.

"How often do you feed?" - Brahnt.

"Depends on when I am hungry." Her words seem to flow from her lips like gentle caresses. It is clear that there is an attraction between them. Taking notice that her eye is tearing, he reaches into his pocket leading with no warning. She is taken off guard. (she gasps) Gently placing her hand against his, he moves with further caution. From within his shirt pocket he hands her his handkerchief. He holds her by the chin; with the other hand he pats the eye dry. Without a word spoken he knows the cause of her tears.

"I'm really sorry. I didn't know. (With an understanding tone) Frankly that's how the entire human race is, we kill what we don't understand and cannot tame."

"But that is wrong!" She exclaims.

"I know. I thought I was different. But I guess that one cannot change so quickly in just three decades."

"Decade, as in multiples of ten?"

"Uhum, why?"

"What is your life expectancy?"

"Oh! If I don't get shot, mugged, raped, imprisoned, butchered, die in a car crash, die in a plane accident, die of a drug over dose, or kill myself out of boredom, I guess about 90 years tops." He watches her expression shift and change as she tries to follow the series of circumstances.

"You have changed. There was a period of time, when men lived ten centuries."

"Yea?" - Brahnt

"Oui! Really!"

"Look we have this thing. It's called carbon testing and-" - Brahnt

"Hey until yesterday, you didn't even know I existed." - Melonnie

"Let's keep it light. Ok." He says to her not able to take any more reality for the day.

"Afraid?" She asks.

"Yes." He answers with a pouted face.

"You are funny." She giggles

"Funny looking, I hope."

"No funny speaking." She pushes his face away lightly.

"I'm sorry. Have you've been paying attention to your accent lately? I have to drop off every other word. Just to keep up with what it is you're saying." She chuckles at his remark.

"Are all *mans* like you?"

"That's 'men'. And no they are not. So don't lose your temper when you meet them."

"How will I find out about this?"

"When you drop me off at the next town you'll see." He notices a bit of sadness caressing the structure of her face, as his words leave his lips. "What?"

"I'm sorry Brahnt. I have a mission. The only way out is if I kill you."

"Wait! That's not much of a choice."

"You can ride with me, until I meet with my kind. I'll allow you to disappear then."

"I have work to do. If I don't get my work done, there will be others out to kill me. I'm sure that you'll be on their list too."

"Tell them to smoke a cigar and sign the waiting list." He scratches at his eyebrow.

"Wait! Are you running away too?" She asks trying to understand.

"Yes." His first words make her feel uncomfortable. "The police?"

"No!" He answers quickly.

"Wait! You said 'my kind'. There are more of you? And you're running? That means that someone is chasing you?"

"Moment!" She holds out a sole finger at an attempt to give him hope.

"Look if these things are going to do to me what you did to those police officers back there. Then I'm going to have to end this relationship right now, Baby!"

"I know you are afraid. But just listen!"

"Listen to what? Sitting around driving in this car, while waiting to be tortured and eaten is not my idea of fighting." He says caught in a slight panic.

"No one is going to eat you! My God you taste horrible!" She reasons with him.

"How do *you* know?" He checks himself for bites.

"It's your smell! You smell like merde du chien."

"Great now I smell like merde du chien." He pushes her away and as she falls to the street, he draws out a hidden knife tucked within the lining of his jacket. Kicking her legs she jumps back onto her feet and advances towards him.

She strikes her palm against the base of his neck. Leaning his body against the car, she presses him against the metal and pushes against his chest. With her free hand, she takes the arm holding the knife. Feeling vulnerable, he attempts to use the vehicle to push her away. However, it is of no use. She is the strongest. "If you cut me, I'll only bleed. If I bleed I'll need to feed." The look on his face changes. He knows he has been defeated. And accepting defeat is his only opportunity to live for a moment longer.

"Well Mighty Mouse? What then?" He asks sarcastically.

"Pardon?" She pushes off and away from him.

"I'm sorry. I really need to get my own work done. Or else I will not be able to live."

"What do you mean? I am telling you that I will let you go!"

"By the time you let me go, my people will be after me and kill me."

"Then I'll have to kill them too." She reasons.

"Yea? All right then. I forgot." He places his knife back into its holster. "How long will it take?"

"I'll have to find it first. I know it's here in Europe."

"Europe? Do you have any idea how big this place is?"

"Not any more."

"Do you have any idea where we are?" He opens his hands, palms facing up.

"No. I have a map- hand drawn. Look!" She explains to him, with certain affirmation.

"Hand drawn?" He realizes that he is a bit angered. "Look. I'm sorry. It's just that, I don't like the feeling of being locked into a situation that has no way out."

"You'll have your freedom. You will be able to go, when I finish my mission. I promise you. And it will be the adventure of a life time."

"You mean if you are not killed first!"

"You don't have faith in me?" Her perception of his trust leaves cold trails of bitter despair.

"No! I've seen what you can do. But...but- well, if you are such a bad ass, for lack of a better word (holding his hands up) then I hate to see your enemies." His view turns to the sky.

"Look. I'm sorry. The only thing I can do is end your fear now!"

"No. I'll come along and prolong the agony." He says not accepting the resolution.

"All right then. I'll need to find a place where I can stand and rest until sunset."

"Where are we?" He asks trying to figure out his location.

"A few miles east of where I picked you up from."

"OK. That puts us-. How long did you travel before coming to this stop?" He asks realizing the great distance traveled.

"I'm not sure how to measure the distance."

"Well, you've traveled since-"

"The sun was breaking. It must be some time near after noon."

" Somewhere about 2 PM." (looking into the sky) He responds.

"Noon." she murmurs.

"Noon?" He asks in low sounds of inquest. "Oh! The lunch thing? Yeah noon." Brahnt's mind becomes focused on the task at hand. "My guess is that we need to get rid of this vehicle."

"Can they find us with this vehicle?" She asks with surprise.

"Yes."

"Is it by its color? Or is it this? (touching the antenna) Does this tell them?" She asks remembering the police officers' radios.

"No this is only a receiver antenna." He glances at her, "You're really not from here. Does that mean-"

"No! My enemies have been walking the world a longer amount of time." Her voice is despairing.

"There goes the advantage." He peeps at her, noticing doubt on her face. "What? I trust you. It's just that maybe I had it over on them when it comes to the technology." She reads his next thought in part, but says nothing, as she starts making her way to the driver's side of the car.

"I believe you said it was a good idea to leave the area." She says in the attempt to remind him.

"Yea! You're right. Well have to get rid of this vehicle at the next stop." He says following her into the car. They open the door and they close them simultaneously.

As they both sit in the vehicle doing whatever is necessary, she feels the black cloud that surrounds him, once again. She is uncomfortable with it, but says nothing and displays nothing. He reaches over for the seat belt, fastening it around himself. And if not for that, he would have been still engrossed with his own conceptual thinking and subtle emotions. She turns the key carefully listening to the engine turn and roar to a start. Shifting into gear and pressing down firmly on the gas pedal, the tires spin. The skidding sound of rubber breaking friction shoots dirt out from under the car. Brahnt sits still, almost non-caring. The car slides from one side to the other, until the both tires catch and they are able to drive off. She smiles at the sound and so does he.

Chapter 5

Finding the Book of Vigore

Shadow from within without

I will wake from within and quietly inside I cry.
Believing was foreign to me.
Nothing I have ever seen could have prepared me,
For the tears yelling from her face,
I could tell she hated me with love and regret.
The time had gone by.
"Just yesterday I picked you up and now I let you go."
"Three weeks were full of fun for me"- the glass is half full.
"I can't let you go-" That glass is half empty.

Catch me if you can.

The sun sets in the distance. It paints the sky with its beauty and mystery. Brahnt feels the discomforts of a long ride without the benefit of having a meal. Long moments of silence come to a break, as the two begin to speak once again.

"Hey you? Brahnt?"

"Hey you? What?" He returns the sarcastic humor.

"Why are you so quiet?" She asks with concern.

"I'm thinking about who is going to kick my ass first."

"Oh! That again?" she answers.

"Yup! That again!" He reaches up and scratches the itching at the top of his head.

"I'm sorry, but look at it this way. You would have died, if I would have left you back there on the road."

"Maybe." He says uncaringly.

"How are you so ungrateful?" She is at opposite with his way. Glowing lights surrounded by a light mist bring their attention to a fueling station. Along side of it sits a motel. It all looks brown from far away. Maybe it's because of the dusty area, maybe not, but it will be their first stop. Her smile widens, as her lips begin to spread. "You will help me?"

"With what?" He says not taking notice of her.

"You know?"

"Yea. (his character softens) I'll help. Besides I could use a good hamburger."

"What is that? Is it made of ham?"

"No."

"Then why do you call it that way?"

"I think a guy by the name of Hamburger decided to call it that once upon a time."

"Still the male ego lives."

"Mel!" he warns her.

"Mel? Isn't that a boys name?" She replies ignoring his warning.

"Sometimes." He smiles back at her, quietly.

"I like Mel. What was your question?"

"How old are you?"

"You wouldn't want to know. But feel free to ask me anything else." She says confidently.

"Ok. Where did you come from?"

"The last place I lived in was France. A small place called Strasbourg."

"How long did you live there?"

"You wouldn't understand. Would you like to ask any other questions?"

"No. Thanks. I don't think I could handle the rejection." Brahnt's attention steers off to the distance.

"I'm sorry. I lived there for a long time. About seventy years."

"But you look so young. How can you-" He is interrupted.

"See?"

"See what?" He questions back.

"You don't understand." Her tone is one of confirmation.

"Is it because you drink blood?"

"Non." she says to him as if singing a musical note.

"Wait! Its monster magic." He mocks at her.

"Non. What does 'monster' mean anyway?"

"Ah! Then how do you know that isn't the reason?" He reasons against her.

"Because I know what magic is."

"And who told you that?"

"Katia." She says as though Katia is an authority of the subject at hand.

"Katia? Another one of your kind?" He asks.

"A young life that I spared." She snaps at him and then looks onto to the road.

"Spared? Now don't tell me, I wouldn't understand. You know? As much as I am concerned about you and what you are up to, I can't *help* but find you *irritable*." Looking forward and onto the road, she smiles at him. He watches her lips curl, expressing her gratitude.

"Hey you?" She calls out to him.

"What you? (smiling)" She glances at him.

"I'm tired. We should rest here."

"I was planning to rest till sun. All these people will be dead if we are not out of here sooner than that. The sad part is that they will possibly be killed anyway."

"Who's going to kill them?" He inquires seemingly without interest.

"I believe- it's the Red Wolves."

"They are the bad guys- I hope."

"Yeah they have taken out my team, one by one. If it weren't for Jacques- well- we wouldn't have come this far."

"Who is Jacques?" His interest peaks at the sound of another male's name.

"My mate. Well, he was my mate." Her tone saddens at the sound of his name, but she continues to keep it light.

"Remind me not to look at you that way again."

"I'm flattered. (holding her hand to her chest) Really! I think you are very charming." She bats her eyes at him.

"No I'm not." His voice is monotone.

"You are. Really!" She reassures him.

The car pulls up to the rest area pushing the dried powdered soil into the air, clouding it. Brahnt studies the place carefully, finding a few vehicles that might suit his purpose. Observing the location, as the diner is set off to the side of the road and near a gasoline station, he notices that there are many other vehicles parked in the lot and that none of them is a semi. Not seeing anyone standing at the pumps, he drives towards them hoping to fill the car. Melonnie steps out soon after him.

"I'll go in and wait for you there." She says to him with a diabolical smile.

"OK," he responds. He watches her leave while rubbing his hands, and blowing warm air into his palms. The night air is frigid and subtly cool. "The days have got to be warmer than this."

He turns to the pump and leans his back onto the car watching the numbers increasing the value of his purchase. His eyes are taken by the dull glint of the door, as Melonnie makes her way into the restaurant. "And so enters the fox into the hen house," he sighs rubbing his forehead with surprise at the words he has just mentioned. "I can't *believe* that I just said that! She's the most beautiful and emotional woman I have ever met," he answers himself as though split down the middle. "Look at yourself, you sound like a fool in love. Is a baby also not a fool knowing that he shall fall against the Earth and yet he continues his dream to walk like those around him?" "Yes but, he doesn't have but two feet to fall. You are an adult and well close to six feet. Ask me and I would say that is a far way to fall." "If we do not look at the new with the eyes of the innocence we cannot see its potential." They both come to agreement, "To love, that wonderful feeling of man so that he can touch the sky or maybe even the stars!" The gasoline reaches full and the nozzle's auto-shut off is activated, spurting onto his hand.

"Damn it! Sometimes a dreamer must be awakened from his inner melody, but this is ridiculous." He restores the gas pump to how he originally found it. Taking a paper towel from the dispenser, he wipes his hands clean of the cool and quickly evaporating gasoline, however, the smell persists. "I can't wait until those new Galantras come out. It'll put an end to this fueling business. Then maybe I wouldn't spill this crap on me." He smirks. "Yea? With my luck I'll probably end up short circuiting myself." His attention veers to the glimmer of the diner entrance, caught by the parking light.

An unexpected breeze gently caresses his body, lifting his hat and blowing it off of his head. He turns to it, instantly trying to snatch it from the air. However his attempt is defeated, as the wind takes it around to the passenger side of the vehicle. His body comes to a light and quick jog. Stepping up to his hat and bending down, he extends reaching for it. The grip of surprise touches him, seeing that Melonnie sits within the passenger seat. There she sits as if having been there all along. Brahnt admits to himself, that she has personality. Carelessly, she looks over to him.

"Brahnt, will you please move the car over there?" She points using her index finger as a guide.

"Sure (gasping). I mean (he clears his throat) sure."

"I didn't startle you did I? Socrates would have said-"

"I don't want to know," he starts to drive in the direction her finger points. "May I ask why park in that spot and not closer to the door?"

"No," her word is quick and followed by other words, "Look! You're going to miss it!" Her eyes express every letter of her words with subtle complaint. He reluctantly pulls into the yellow slotted parking spot and turns the ignition off.

Pressing the key into his pocket, he glances at her with a concerned look in his eye. Thinking nothing more of it, he opens the vehicle door. Stepping on the accelerator and passing a Suzuki Motorcycle, she leans over to Brahnt. "What will you have to eat? One of those delicious, but generic, hamburgers? Then will you request a side carton of those frozen French fries? (she excites) And will you then follow your course with a milk shake or with coffee?"

"Melonnie you do have a way with words. You make a meal seem more appetizing than I imagine it to be. A hamburger (he opens her door of the car) is more than a dead cow. It is a work of artistry. "

"Artistry? Is that a word or did you make that up?" Her question is innocent, yet bordering insult. She moves her body outside the car and rushes to catch up to him.

"Are you going to listen to the definition of a hamburger or not?" His voice carries lowly to her ear, as he opens the door to the diner. Taking a glance back at her, he takes notice of her beauty. Having the door completely opened, Melonnie rushes quickly pass him. Now on the other side she is satisfied that she can hear him better.

"OK. Boss. " She stands up straight, holds her head high and chest out.

"Are you sure you're not human?" he asks rhetorically, observing the beauty and lure of her bosom.

"Never. Why is that part of the meaning of a hamburger?"

"No! A hamburger is a device that captures the sensations of many people in where I come from! Women, men, children, *that's* boys and girls alike, enjoy the idea of searching for the right restaurant that will serve them the best hamburger in the world. Of course 'THE WORLD' is merely an expression producing an exaggerated effect," he walks proudly over to the booth.

"I don't know Brahnt. That sounds like a very large definition. Give it to me straight." She slaps her hand at his back

"All right! A hamburger is made from a cow. Not a whole cow, just a little portion. One cow produces a lot of hamburgers."

"So then things are the same?"

"What is the same?"

"You eat meat!"

"Of course. Didn't you ever hear of eating meat?"

"Yes. But I just wasn't sure what a hamburger was. You've placed so much emphasis on it, when it is just a slab of dead cow flesh."

A woman with a soiled apron and pink shirt walks over to the booth.

"Don't you worry there none missy and you neither. We serve a pretty good burger here. Can I git you somethin'?"

"Yes. Some fresh cow juice." Brahnt sarcastically remarks.

"Pardon? Est-ce que vous parlez français?" Melonnie asks.

"Excuse me?" Returns the waitress with uncertainty.

"Milk!" Answers Brahnt abruptly, "milk will do her fine." She pencils in the order and turns in the direction of the kitchen. With her at a safe distance, he begins. "You can't assume that people speak French everywhere you go."

"Anything for you sir?" – The server

"I'll have the Golden Gate." He says while pointing at the menu. The waitress pencils in the order, waiting but a moment longer, she leaves. Now in confidence, he leans to her.

"Mel. You can't assume that everyone speaks French." He says to her, with a concentration of espionage.

"Why not? It's the most important language on the globe." She returns at him bluntly.

"Melonnie that may have been a long time ago. Not anymore! The most important of languages today is English."

"The queen's English?"

"Well not exactly. But it will do? Just so anyone else can understand it. (he takes his napkin from the table) Melonnie? Just how did you get here any way?"

"It will take too much time to explain."

"I have a feeling that you are not too worried about time."

"It's probably something that you don't want to hear.... it's too long. Really!"

"Give me the short version."

"It's sinful."

"I'm not deeply into religion."

"It's painful! (she stares into his eyes) All right. (she waves her hands frantically) It's something I just don't want to talk about." Picking up the menu, she hides her face from him.

"I'm sorry. I shouldn't have pushed."

"That's right! You are only a human! (a tear falls from her eye)" She picks up her napkin patting it underneath her shades to dry it.

"Comprised of superstition!" He consoles her.

"That is right!" She snaps back him with a pout.

"Never searching for the truth, but settling down with a compromise for lack of understanding."

"Yes! You should all go back from whence you came."

"I'm not Adam."

"You might as well, be. You and your self-righteous thoughts and ideas! Governing the planet and destroying all the beautiful things that were once ours as well as yours."

"Is this where you're going?"

"Escussie?"

"To your kind? The castle? The place where you're going?" He asks. She inhales deeply but no answer is given. "I've been meaning to ask you?"

"Yes." She answers his previous question, giving him her attention.

"What does that word mean?"

"Escussie?" She says searching for a word

"Yea, that's the one. (he lifts his chin and squints) Is that a word or is that something you made up?"

"It's something my mother made up." She smiles.

A glass of white creamy milk makes its appearance, breaking their concentration.

"I thought maybe your taste buds could use a different texture. Copper can not be your only flavor?" He sarcastically asks.

"It's actually a little salty and the copper is all in the smell really." She pauses at the waving of his hand.

"I don't want to know right now. Thank you. As a matter of a fact I don't think I ever want to know." As his words deny her,

her eyes sadden and drop to the tablecloth underneath the glass of milk. "I would like a Pepsi with that Golden Gate.

"We don't have Pepsi." She responds.

"Coke then." He says without giving it a second thought.

"And will the lady have anything else?"

"Ah!" Brahnt's eyes turn cold. Not being able to grasp an answer and afraid of what Melonnie might say. Melonnie interrupts-

"No thank you. I'll be just fine." Melonnie answers with a smile. The waitress, now looking at Melonnie, smirks and winks her eye. She walks away, as quietly as she appeared. "You may be of a new world, but you're still a man." She smiles.

"What does that mean?"

"You lack charm in your tact."

"You!" (he raises from his seat), he leans over to her and she to him as if attracted by a magnetic impulse. "Are right." (he pecks her lips with his) A flash! A paradox of time produces the question; 'Could I love him? Would he love my children?' She is astonished by his affection, but reacts not. 'No', her mind ignites the answer. Surprised by what he has done he stands away from the booth. "I have to go to the little boys- room." He walks away, touching his lips with the tips of his fingers in amazement and perhaps also the feeling of his attraction to her.

Sitting there alone, she glances at the people around her. The diner looks casual and neat, however there is an air of uncertainty. A sense of carelessness. The people sit before their meals eating with haste and showing a lack of proper etiquette. It is as though they have taken for granted their meals, the plates they eat upon, and the services that came to play as their meals were presented. 'Such a self-egoistic race you have become.' Her attention veers to an obnoxious man flagging down the waitress. Her ears become pointed, slightly protruding through delicate strands of her hair. With them she is able to capture his annoying voice.

"Hey honey? This steak is not cooked well enough! I'm not paying for this. It hasn't been cooked enough." The waitress looks down at his plate.

"Sir, you've eaten most of you meal." She points out to him the obvious.

"I don't care. It's not healthy to eat raw meat. What are going to do about it?"

"Well sir, since you've eaten nearly all of your meal-"

"I'm not paying for this! It was your responsibility for assuring this meal was digestible. I'm going to the bathroom. 'Clean up and all'. When I come back I expect this matter resolved!" He throws his napkin down onto the plate and stands away from his chair. Briskly, he walks towards the bathroom. Passing Melonnie, he notices her stare, but places no importance to it.

A gentle hand presses on her shoulder. Brahnt's scent fills her sense of smell, instantly removing her anger. He sits in front of her. Casting her head to one side she takes a look at the waitress. Frantic and filled with uncertainty, Melonnie excuses herself from the table. Brahnt looks behind his shoulder, hoping to spot the answer to his question. He notices the nervous waitress. Returning his view in the direction of Melonnie, he looks at her shoulders and down to her thighs. 'Hot!' He thinks to himself. Melonnie turns facing him and smiles. His expression draws inward like a boy who has been caught staring under the teacher's dress.

Approaching the restroom, she sees the symbol for "**man**" and "**woman**". Disregarding them she pushes the men's door, swinging it open. Her eyes fix themselves, on the same man with the same annoying voice now standing at the urinal. However, confident, he stands about his business, taking no immediate notice of her. The door slams closing behind her. The sound forces curiosity. Against the corner of his eye, the female silhouette surprises him. The door swings open once more. Canting her head, her eyes roll towards the sound. An older man places a foot inside the doorway and startled, notices a tall muscular female standing before him. Melonnie's look is one of complete rage. He takes the silent warning and removes his presence. She reclines herself on the urinal nearest the annoying man. He glances at her and then back again.

"Excuse me sir?" She says as politely as she can

"What are you doing here?" He says with much surprise.

"That's *not* the important question here."

"I'll call management!" He says, threatened by her tone of voice and fumbling with his zipper.

"I am the management now!" She says stealing the authority from his voice and watching him zip his pants. He points his finger at her, as if attempting to gain control of her fear. Before even a whisper is released from within his demeaning behavior, she snatches his finger from the air, bending it backwards and forcing him to fall onto one knee. Her vampiric eyes, show themselves as a predator, slitting down the center. Reaching across with her other hand, she points her index finger at him. "The only question you need ask, goes something like this, 'Do I want to leave this place alive?" Breaking the contour of her femininity, her hand extends a single talon. Reaching its full length, it hardens and takes the appearance of onyx. The nail comes to a sharp and feared point. "Now! Can you repeat the question?"

"Do I want to leave this place alive?"

"Can you say that backwards?"

"Ah, Alive..(she places her talon between his eye, lifting his eyelid)....place this leave to want I DO.....I DO! ....I Do!"

"You will pay your meal and apologize for your rudeness. You think you can handle that?"

"Yes." (she removes her finger and her hold of him) He stands, trying to erect his limp body. She walks to the door.

About to leave, she challenges his integrity. "Did I understand that you *think* you can handle this?"

"No! I meant I will handle this. Right away! Thank you."

"By the way (still turned away from him) was that meal honestly bad?"

"No!" He stumbles.

"So why did you do it?"

"I thought I could get a free meal." He says nervously and with a greater appreciation of life, his own life.

"I thought so." She confirms, squinting one eye and nodding her head. "À toute à l'heure."

Opening the door she leaves the men's room and makes her way back to Brahnt.

Brahnt attempts to ignore her beautiful sexuality, he looks away from her, but her long white dress makes it seemingly impossible, as he peeks at her every moment he thinks he can get away with it. She sits across from him. "I see that your compromised 'Art' is here."

"You just don't understand. Life is not the same as it was back then." He glances at his burger and takes a bite. She reaches over and removes the burger from his mouth and cradles it to the plate. "What are you doing?"

"There! There is your God! Bow down."

"Mel-" he becomes silent.

"Bow (steadily focused at the burger) Bow down to your God!" Brahnt looks down at the burger. The grease flows from the burger and onto the plate. He feels shame. Her lips curl, her expression saddens and her body shifts away adjusting for her mood. "Brahnt you just don't understand! We are not a cult, a clan, or a sect! You just can't make a category and reduce us to a religious superstition! We have a history. We have a need. We have a reason to be here!"

"I don't know-" he shrugs and pushes off the issue with lack of understanding.

"What the hell do you we think we are?"

"Ah, (a pause) servants of evil?" He carelessly subsides.

"Evil! Evil Brahnt? When (she reaches to his mouth) have your lips touched evil? And when have you ever touched evil to know what evil is?" She reasons with compassion, for compassion.

"That's easy. Evil is anything that opposes God's will."

"What may that be?" She says softly. Painfully. A moment ago she was kissed by one she could learn to love. Now she finds her emotion betrayed.

"Thou shall not kill?" For the lack of a better response.

"Come now! (accentuating) *Man*! When a tiger hungers and feeds from a man, woman, or child in neighboring villages- is that evil?"

"That is *so* different." He says shaking his head.

"Oh! How?"

"That is the way things are because of nature."

"Oui! And we are not natural?" (waving her hand at him)

"How (he starts to whisper) can you call yourself natural, when you're seemingly immortal (he flickers one finger), you have no religious boundaries (a second finger), you defy gravity (a third finger), and you prey on innocent people." (the fourth) With his hand now opened, he extends reaching for the burger. About to grasp it, Melonnie slaps down with her own hand, stopping him.

"The tiger comes when you least expect it. But always obtaining its goal."

"And what does that mean?" he questions her action.

"No Brahnt. What has that meant? You eat helpless cows."

"For substance, (with haste) so leave the hamburger out of it." He reclines back into his chair and crosses his arms. He broadens his mind, expanding his lungs and proceeds in a gentler tone. "Melonnie the books? The stories? I read Bram Stoker's, "Dracula!"

"Yes and when the Spanish Inquisitions started? WWI? WWII? The search for religious righteousness? The witch hunts? These things don't happen because humanity has the answers to all questions asked. *Comprande*?" *(Understand?)* She catches her breath.

"And what you do is so different?"

"What we do is all to survive and to save your lives." She expresses the meaning of concern.

"Vlad the Impaler?"

"Other famous leaders? Besides Vlad was an idiot. He wanted to be what your society thought we were."

"You make it sound as if you're part of the eco-system. And you pose a good argument." He stands from the booth with nowhere to go.

"Brahnt sit." She points her finger.

"No thanks!"

"I can make you sit, you know!" She says tapping her fingers on the tabletop.

"On second thought, thank you very much. Is this chair occupied?"

"No. (she starts with a more forgiving tone) Actually the unkind gentleman sitting has removed himself." She smirks at him quickly.

"Brahnt when God created your world in seven days. He had no idea of time. And we also did not. We could have been there for centuries before the beginning of the next day. Days are in linear time."

"In other words, time exists because we begin and end." Brahnt contributes.

"Yes, and when you lived among the first creations there was no death. No pain. No hunger."

"No time." He whispers to himself, marking the first moment of understanding. "And where do you tie in this?"

"We were there before man. We had these (her face lightens) wings, gloriously expanding, twice the length of one man." She says leaning over the table and coming closer to him.

"Angels?"

"No." She says. "Just creations with no names. We played all day and danced in the skies until morning. Then came Adam, giving everything names. He named the dances we sang to with our most comprised joy. Then shortly after, came Eve."

"So what happened?"

"Eve was good. Oh Brahnt, close your eyes now and be mortal for just a small ripple in time."

"It's just a lot for one day."

"1969's just a moment before man made his first journey to the moon. Many people did not believe." She sees him shaking his head. Nearly giving up, she asks herself, 'Can he ever love me?' *Will* he ever love me?' His head lowers. His eyes shut. A moment passes. And as if reading her thoughts he answers her question-

"I can love you." He looks up to her, staring into her sunglasses and imagining her beautifully dark eyes. Her chest rises and then falls, absorbing hope. "But can you find a way to love me?" Speechless and tearful she slides the hamburger in his direction and takes a sip of her milk. Her sorrow turns to that of a sullen joy.

"I can't feed on milk, but it tastes good." As if looking at a Norman Rockwell, her look is so human, how could she ever be anything else?

Lifting the burger, he sinks his teeth into his meal, bearing the smile of a satisfied and wanted man. Behind her, she sees the obnoxious man paying his bill, nervously, but careful to display his good intentions to Melonnie. The waitress that served him stands from afar in amazement. Noticing her, the man approaches her, holding out the tip. Passing by Melonnie, he holds it out. Placing it into the waitress' hand, he smiles at her and excuses his behavior. Melonnie glances back at him, demonstrating her approval of his behavior.

"Good night Richard!" She says to him, taking him off guard. Fumbling with his words he gives the greeting of the day.

Brahnt, having finished a good portion of his hamburger looks at the two with a bit of confusion. But the moment passes as quickly as it appeared.

"Do you two know each other?" Asks Brahnt watching the man waddle away.

"No! We only met briefly." She answers with hidden meaning. Remembering the waitress' tip, he recalls leaving his wallet in the pocket of his jacket still laying in the back seat of the car.

"I think I left my wallet in the car. I'll fetch it." He says to her. Allowing him to walk out to the car alone is truly a form of trust. But she knows his intentions mean well.

"Okay, I'll wait here." He excuses himself, making his way out.

Once outside, he takes a moment to reflect and compose himself. Leaning against the building, he takes a break from the world. He hears the distinctive roar of motorcycles leaving the pumps and approaching him.

'Can I? Really love?' He considers the possibility of their relationship. 'But what to do with my humanity? How could I compromise? *How* will I compromise?' Pushing himself off, he answers- "I guess I'll just have to learn." He makes his way to the car, now surrounded by bikers. Brahnt makes of little notice and opens the door of his vehicle. Leaning over the back seat, he retrieves his jacket and climbs into the soft cushion.

"Hey you guys smell something?" One of them calls out, but Brahnt pays no attention.

"Yea. I smell something rank!" Brahnt can smell the trouble. He glances at their apparel, he notices that there are no obvious bulges or slight of hand. 'This is good. They probably don't have guns. Knives and chains maybe, but no guns he mumbles under his breath.

"That's funny I see something rank!" Says yet another. Brahnt glances at them and counts four. Ignoring them and fitting his jacket, he moves to leave. As he passes one of the last one nearest the diner, Brahnt feels the spit from one of the biker's fall heavy on his boot.

Looking down at the saliva rolling off of his boot and onto the dusty ground, he assesses the situation. From the pumps, the final motorcyclist brings his bike to the rear of the pack. Brahnt lifts his view staring directly into the eyes of the long dark haired man. His experience had taught him that one who backs down too many times, will lose the fight. Therefore, he should prepare himself for a confrontation.

"Could it be that what you smell and what you see is the same thing standing here in front of me?" The fourth one calls out. To Brahnt this is the typical pattern. One brave soul, who believes he can act a fool while the others slowly gain their courage, as if giving themselves doses a little at a time.

"Yea! (the first three) Yea! (the fourth)" Brahnt looks at himself and then at the motorcyclist. Brahnt ignores the chorus line and moves toward the furthest one away.

"You know, I ride bikes too." He mentions in polite conversation.

"You know what kind of bike this is?" Calls out the second biker.

"It's a Harley." Brahnt says without much stimulation in his voice.

"No it's a HOG, a FXSTC1997" He answers back at him with rude intentions. The driver's hand caresses the brilliant, blue fuel tank. The bike, though indeed beautifully decorated with shining chrome and chrome instruments, causes Brahnt to look away. His glance is taken as intended, rude and sub-ranking.

"Well a bike is -" Brahnt snaps back at him.

"What type of bike do *you* ride?" Calls the fist one.

"Well, now that you ask-"

"*Rice* burners oh!" Calls out the third.

"Kawasa-" Brahnt says coldly

"Yea? What's that a cow with socks on?" The second spoken calls out. These were not the words of professional thugs and for this reason they are probably more dangerous.

Brahnt directs his attention to the fifth one. The biker, looking down at the rim of his speedometer, runs the tarnish off with his index finger.

"Smart boy." -biker leader.

"Smart enough. So how do you want to end this?"

"Very smart boy!" - biker leader.

"The name is Brahnt." He says coldly and seemingly without emotion.

"Look I don't give a rats ass! OK?"

"The funny thing about this is? Very few bikers are as big an asshole as you and your friends here!" Brahnt's insult threatens him.

"What do you know about bikers? You little fuck!" He enunciates each word with rage and perfection.

"Just because your family life and social life has made your heart as cold as the road you drive on, doesn't-"

"Hey Joey," he interrupts, "take care of the light weight." His voice is more than confident.

"OK Frankie!" Joey, the first to have spoken, steps down from his hog attempting his hand at intimidating Brahnt. Joey, sliding his hand off of his bike, grabs a fist fill of his chains. Nearing dangerously close to Brahnt, he swings the chains. The chains arc toward Brahnt. Sighting the threatening chain links swinging toward him, Brahnt dodges, bending at the knee. The chains cut at the wind above him as they clear. Kicking out at Joey's legs, Brahnt's heel pushes into Joey's solar plexus. Letting out a suppressed yell, Joey's body is forcefully pushed against and over his fellow biker. Joey, his friend, and the bike fall onto the dusty ground. Hardly able to move, Joey grabs at his chest trying to catch a better breath of air. Obviously doing the work of a professional, Brahnt comes to a stand without so much as skipping a breath.

Two other bikers push their bodies off of their hogs, jumping down from their bikes and approach Brahnt from each side. To Brahnt's left the taller biker swings his fist, aimed at Brahnt's face. Seeing only a blurb of the mysterious stranger, he watches Brahnt showing instructions on how to defy the odds. Spinning swiftly, Brahnt back-fists his opponent's punch. Landing his strike on his forearm, the taller man squirms. Striking once more, Brahnt punches at his elbow, forcing the arm to hyper extend.

From his opposite side swings the other biker. Hip to hip and slightly behind, Brahnt allows the biker's punch to approach deathly close. Slightly shifting his weight, the biker's fist brushes against the cheek of his face. Brahnt's sacrifice pays off, as he takes advantage of the biker's position. Reaching across with the full length of his arm, Brahnt trounces the biker's throat. Surprised and defeated, the biker gasps and chokes. With no air able to fill his lungs and the burning sensation pulsating at the back of his throat, he falls to his knees wheezing air into his lungs.

Brahnt's focus shifts to the leader of the pack. Still sitting comfortably, the leader displays little fear. Brahnt has seen men like these before. Reaching into his jacket, Brahnt's fingertips make contact with the handgrip of his silencer. Great pain intervenes, as one of the biker thwacks Brahnt's kidney.

His back arches, feeling every inch of the chain links penetrate. With no more to exhale, his body folds, falling directly onto his left knee. Joey draws his knife from the small of his back and presses the blade into Brahnt's neck. The deadly edge and the throbbing pain coming from his bruised back, force him to hold still. Forming at the sharp edge of the knife, Brahnt's blood flows and pools at the base of his neck for a brief moment. As it over flows, soaking into his shirt, Brahnt breathes in slowly, cautiously, as he has been here before. Reaching into his jacket he prepares to draw his silencer.

"Pretty smart boy! Now let me tell you how this will end." The other men stagger to their feet and join, forming a semi-circle around the seemingly defeated Brahnt.

"Escussie?" Another voice shoots out from the near distance. Her voice ensnares them to momentary captivity. Surprised and bewildered, they turn to the woman's voice. "Would you mind letting go of my boyfriend?" Her delicate notes project innocently from behind an ice cream cone. She licks at the cold paste.

"I (Brahnt's throat squeezes, stretching his eyes towards Melonnie) would do as she says."

Frankie, the biker leader, smirks and in an uncaring gesture, he closes his eyes to blink. His insulting demeanor sets Melonnie at rage. Instantly and without further hesitation, she attacks the first biker by driving her fingers through the biker's mouth as if each digit were a portion of a steel lance. In an explosion of blood, bone and cartilage, her digits burst through the back of his neck. Taking a hold of his chin with her thumb and with demonic strength she jolts left then drives his lifeless husk to the ground. His neck snaps, as small brittle bones pierce and protrude from within his neck. Ghost like and imperceptible to the human eye, she glides to the second biker standing nearest to her. Frankie's eyes blink open. He watches his friend's dead weight fall to the ground, able to catch only a blurred image chasing way to another fellow biker. Turning his eyes towards the movement of the phantom, and unable to focus on the assailant, he witnesses the second victim's chest cavity explode. Small specks of blood attach themselves to the speedometer of his bike, but his attention moves about with frustration, as the phantom has captured the life of a third victim. As he observes the path of the unbelieved creature, his third friend also falls to the ground missing what seems to be an arm.

A flash catches his eye. Swaying forward and back, swings a familiar necklace, pinched by the meters of his bike further convincing his mind of the weight of the situation. A thump against his boot draws his attention to a beating heart, (a cloud of dust) still pumping, unaware it has been relocated from its host. A small quake awakens him and for the first time, fear becomes him as he sees his friend's arm draped over his front fender, unnaturally bent at the elbow. Frankie quickly draws his attention to Joey. Joey is motionless. A tear flows down his cheek as he stares at his little brother's lifeless body.

"How do you feel?" Inquires Melonnie.

"Afraid." Frankie's mind whispers unconsciously the fear of what may yet come. Brahnt pulls himself from under Joey's frame, showing Frankie the damage wrought forth by his own discourteous behavior. His brother's head motions backwards and off from his shoulders. (Brahnt comes afoot)

Melonnie motions her hand forward presenting another hand within hers holding Joey's knife, "I think this also belongs to you?" Joey's body falls. She pulls the knife away from the dead hand. Cocking her arm she brings the knife to her ear. With a powerful thrust forward, she impels the knife towards her final victim. The silver like metal cuts through the wind with a horrific chime. Unable to react to her speed and deadly accuracy, the blade stabs itself into the biker's throat throwing him from his motorcycle. "And then there were none." She says proudly. With its companion slain silently and resting on the dirt ground, a solitary motorcycle is left in solitude, glinting beneath the halogen lamps of the pumps. "As usual, blood adds to the beauty of anything." Melonnie comments as she notices a single drop running down the forks.

She kneels down next to Brahnt. "You fight very well. I enjoyed watching you move. Where in the world did you learn to move like that? Wow! (she looks at the blood) There's enough food here to last for weeks! No insouciant people died here." She kneels down and laps the pooled blood from the dirt. Carefully, she laps avoiding ingesting the impurities. She places one of her bloodied fingers into her mouth and turns to Brahnt. "Oh! My God! This one was really angry. I can taste it! (she points her finger at him) Do you want to taste it?"

"No!" he falls to his hands. Squeezing the ground, he explodes into a vomiting fit. The sloppy wet sound disturbs even Melonnie.

"Oh that's sick! Couldn't you at least hold it in?" She abruptly asks.

"I'm sick!" he whimpers and points his mouth to the ground. "I don't lap up blood like dogs." Feeling a shadow over his face, he glances up.

Melonnie, now face to face with Brahnt, lets out a fiendish roar. His eyes open widely, his heart freezes, and she motions forward and attacks. Landing on top of him, she pins his body to the ground. His eyes focus on the horror of her face and yet he finds beauty there. Beside him, as he takes a quick look, Joey's blood pools. Melonnie raises her hand exposing her razor talons.

"No! Melonnie!" He pleads.

Both their eyes turn to the flashing of blue.

"Shit! The *cops*!" He grunts. Melonnie reads his expression. She crosses her arms and swings her fist down across Brahnt's face. His nearly healed cut opens, as his head is violently forced to the left. With her opposite hand she grabs at his shoulder. Digging hard into his muscle, her hand talons while her skin conforms to a pale scale like texture. Her eyes peer at the approaching spotlight, now exposing her position. Glancing desperately for an escape, she finds no shelter.

The car comes to a hard and sudden halt. Among the focused beams of light lifts a clouded dense air, much from the dusty territory. The driver's eyes notices that a woman towers over a man, but the instant is brief. Too brief. Propelling herself off of one leg, she lifts herself from the slaughter carrying Brahnt's deadened body with her. And much like searching for an image through water-ripples, their images bend light becoming suddenly invisible. Not finding logic to his witness, the idea is passed for a reflection of dust particles within five unmoving objects.

The police vehicle door opens. Out from and underneath the door drops a boot, followed by a large hat rising above the door, a shoulder and finally the complete vision of blue justice appears. Melonnie watches hovering over the area, as if suspended by the stars. Giving each other the signal, one police officer stays behind as the other approaches the slaughter. The scout reaches into the center of the crime scene. Placing his index finger underneath his nose he breathes in as little as possible. Taking a look around and observing the crime, he realizes.

"These men never had a chance." His voice is low and muttered. Melonnie's ears triangulate capturing the small sounds beneath her. Looking down at his feet, he observes the wet ground, wet from a dark substance. "It smells like copper. Blood!"

Overhead, Brahnt begins to wake. Melonnie glances quickly at him, while his head takes its first motions, but returns her view to the action below. The little man dressed in blue and semi shiny metals turns his head in all direction searching for answers, however he finds nothing. Unable to see clearly down below, Melonnie's eyes become slit and glossed with a yellow haze. Doing so, her mouth protrudes much like the snout of a wolf but not quite yet breaking her complete human silhouette. Brahnt, becoming restless, opens his eyes with fatigue. Bringing his hands to focus, he becomes overwhelmingly curiosity by them, as they seem dead and hanging. Below his hands is another curiosity. 'My feet?' As his eyes further adjust and focus, he sees that below his feet is a little man holding his hands near his mouth. His feet swing loosely. Realizing that the ground he once stood upon is now several meters below his feet, Brahnt takes a deep inhale. He gasps again.

Melonnie lifts him higher adding to his fear. Reaching over his head and clumsily taking a hold of what feels like her arm, he feels an odd expression of relief. Not a grasp of the situation, he lifts his head searching for the crude explanation. She turns curiously to face him as a means of further understanding what it is he is doing, to find his expression less than cordial. His mouth opens wider, gasping for small breaths at a time. His breath commences to exhale preparing for the scream, but only a shortness of sound is permitted to release. Melonnie presses her enlarged hands against his lips and wraps her elongated fingers around to the back of his head.

His eyes peer at her snout, he reads the mimicking sound "Shhhh." Frightened and shocked even more by the creature's razor like fangs. His stomach squeezes together and with one heave he vomits.

Slithering its way between her hand and his face the mucky matter makes its way down below. A wet, yet hard sound creates itself from behind the officer, alarming him. Turning, he draws his weapon. (Melonnie caresses Brahnt's face inquisitively)

Taking another step in the direction of the sound, the policeman's foot presses on the slippery blood. He slips on the dark blood, falling and landing on his back. Striking his head on the ground beneath, he is forced into looking into the night sky. Now looking straight up he sees the two figures dimly lit by the reflective illuminating street lamps.

Feeling the depth of her desperation, Melonnie's arm muscles Brahnt, throwing him in the direction of the rooftop nearest her. Witness to his few moments remaining of his existence, Melonnie's victim quivers his mouth to an open. A portrait of fear and doom. But no scream will escape his breath tonight. His partner observes him not able to understand his sudden paralysis.

Swooping down, the bird of prey disfigured and now barely recognizable, descends over the policeman's chest, puncturing through his ribs and wrapping its claws around his heart, leaving to pant to his death. To the near distance both, the lone policeman and the creature, exchange glances. The officer left standing, stares dressed with pale colors as the beast hisses and bares its teeth. Moments of his consciousness slips through the delicate fibers of time, as he stands frozen by the impact of his denial and disbelief. With but a seemingly effortless jolt, the creature leaps into the brisk night air, carrying policeman's heart in the claw of her foot. In his hypnotic state, he watches the creature reaching for the man it has just thrown. (she opens her foot, releasing the human heart) With great agility the creature catches the falling body.

Having captured the man in one arm, the creature's body absorbs the shock of his falling weight and regains momentum forward. Her body twists grappling with balance, struggling to regain control of her descent. Nearly missing the edge of the rooftop, the creature extends an arm snaring her talons into the brim of the roof's ledge (the heart strikes the ground) while the man's body hits against the building, as so does the creature's. Breaking the spell of his hypnotic fear, the policeman unholsters quickly, accurately. Taking quick and professional aim, he fires his weapon. The projectile is jettisoned, penetrating into the creature's body. He regains aim, sighting her as best as the obscure night allows.

Vigorously, she pulls both of them over and onto the rooftop, missing further opportunity of being fired upon.

Both of them lay side by side. Both of them lay injured.

"Are you OK? You really should avoid those." Whispers Brahnt, out of breath taking a short glance at her wound. She says nothing. She, for the moment, only pants while looking at him with projecting terror. She inhales her breath quickly and just as quickly does she release it. Blood from her wound stains her clothes as so it does her hands. Small beads of sweat proclaim their presence at the edge of her brow. Her opened eyes panic even Brahnt, pain stricken and glossed, they express a sense of regret to come. Brahnt fears the worse. With one hand on her wound and the other on his face, she slows the bleeding. Leaning down to him, she extends her pure white, shimmering fangs. Forcing his body to hers, he has no time to struggle.

"AWWW. No." Tears filled with the texture of nostalgia run down her face. "Please don't. Not me! Not now." His eyes close gently with each weakening pulse of his heartbeat. His voice silences as his rapid breathing slows.

Filled with the strength of his blood and his vitality, she releases her hold of him. She pushes her finger into the wound removing the bullet.

"What's this?" She inquires observing the retracted bullet within her fingertips. Squeezing it between her fingers, as if it were clay, she hisses at her wound. Drool mixed with Brahnt's blood oozes from the side her mouth, falling onto her wound. Coming onto all four limbs, she magically and swiftly crawls across the rooftop bearably placing her weight upon it. Focusing her eyes on the roof's edge and her ears attentively set for what lies below, she reaches the edge and pulls herself slightly over it. Staring down into the alley, she stalks like a tiger waiting for its prey. To her left, in the narrow passage, she can hear the alarmed restaurant patrons screaming out their fears and chaos.

The police officer looks down the dark alleyway, blocking out the sounds of the crowd. Melonnie's nerves begin to pump out hatred and destruction, poisoning her mind. The policeman, entering the unknown, points his weapon and inches his way through the thick darkness. Melonnie leans over the edge. Climbing down the brick wall, she maintains her stealth, keeping a low silhouette. Walking the side of the wall, face down, she claws at the side of the building descending down to her prey.

The officer looking into the purple sky, notices Melonnie's unorthodox form braking the contour of the building. Lifting his flashlight he brightens the area of immediate concern, revealing only the fading bricklayer. He is fooled believing that what his eyes have seen is merely an illusion of fear. His ears catch the sound of small scratches echoing down the alley. Not being able to focus their origin, he continues on slowly down the uncertain pathway.

"Shit. This is not supposed to happen. This is impossible." He wipes his nose and eyes with the cuff of his uniform, removing sweat. Still moving forward he tilts his revolver.

Finding him out of reach, Melonnie jumps to the wall opposite him. The policeman takes a few steps further, leaning his shoulder against the brick. Not able to see up the dark wall, he brings his flashlight up to his cheek. The beam of light scales up one wall. Behind him, Melonnie's vampiric eyes shimmer in the light's reflection. Cat-like, she leaps from the wall plunging her fangs on the side of his face. The weapon fires once more. Pulling vigorously, she severs his hand from his body.

It falls to the ground beneath still holding the revolver. Screaming, he waves his arms. She pushes her body against his, slamming him forward against the brick building. Disabled and bleeding profusely, Melonnie punches her hand through the policeman's back. Her hand closes around his warm spine. With a sharp and attentive movement she rips it out. The sound of bone snapping insures the victim is powerless. Melonnie sinks her teeth deep inside the veins of the food robbing its of all it vitality. His thoughts become hers as his life flashes before him in a rapid fire of a chain of memories. The skin on his face molds, plastic-like, conforming to the exotic curvature of his bone structure. She draws his blood with each inhaling breath. In desperation, she tears at the flesh with her teeth sinking deeper into the wound. Every drink regains her vitality. The sounds of spectators coming from beyond the light at the end of the alley enter the darkness.

A dull light pulses its energy against the feeding creature. Her attention diverts to the new light displaying vicious intent. Adjusting and focusing beyond the light, her eyes make known the presence of a small child standing. Her eyes shift, molding to a semi-human form. However, unable to differ among colors in predator-like state, she knows only that the child's hair is long, seemingly dark. Her eyes are light colored and her expression is fearless. Melonnie tries to smile, "go to your mother."

"She's not here." (hand to mouth) She whispers.

"Where is she then?" Melonnie's words become as whispered as the little girl.

"She is calling the police." She says to the creature in secret:

"Well run to her and tell her that I will soon be out of here, she needn't worry."

"OK." The little girl nods with a smile and Melonnie returns the gesture and turns to leave.

Sinking her scale-like feet into the alley, Melonnie takes a leap. Landing on the rooftop, she looks at Brahnt. (she inhales deeply) He is completely motionless. "There is still some blood left in you." She grabs him by the jacket collar and drags him to the edge of the roof. Her strong muscular legs bend, leaping over the quarter-height brick wall.

Her massive, beastly body lands on the ground beneath. With her free hand she leans down and takes a strong grasp of the withered and boneless like policeman. She inhales collecting her strength and throws his cadaver.

The on watchers are taken by sudden surprise, as the policeman's body blurs passed them from within the darkness of the alley. His body smashes against his own vehicle, exploding the rear passenger window. Clear shards of glass burst into many directions, as the vehicle rocks absorbing the impact.

Advancing from within cloaking shadows, steps forth the creature. Tall and muscular. Behind her drags a lifeless man, pulled by a limp beastly arm. It approaches the vehicle in its massive structure. As if in slow motion the figure of a barely recognizable woman's torn clothing and untamed hair mimics her motion. The wind blows gently, playing with the loose portions of her vestment. She walks over to the passenger side of the police car and pushes the limp body into the seat. Motionless and very still, she places the safety belt around his waist, capturing his arms. Melonnie stares into the crowd once more spotting a glistening object in the hands of a crowd member. (a pause) The silence among the people is instant and without flaw. The man wipes the knife against the breast of his shirt. Melonnie's head shakes inquisitively. The man realizes that she is staring at him directly. The knife! His hands open wide. It falls. The sandy ground indents, nestling the knife. She releases a grunting sound. Opening the driver's side door, she climbs in and twists at the key. The engine turns. Placing the vehicle into gear, she presses down on the gas pedal and drives off. Looking into her rear view mirror, she assures no one is following. The seemingly large crowd groups and gathers, fading into the dark background. The tires squeal hitting the paved road. And for a moment a sense of relief, blankets her.

Looking ahead of the dark yellow striped road reminds her of a beacon, a trail of crumbs for authorities to follow. The headlights are turned off, using nature's camouflage. She searches from left to right, hoping to find an alternative route. Another road. Perhaps an escape. Brahnt's body is motionless and unconscious. For what it's worth, it is better this way. Looking ahead she comes upon a fork in the road. The tall trees bend with the bending of the road, serving as further cover. For the moment there are no other lights traveling the path. Looking ahead she steers the vehicle to the right.

Driving too close to the edge of the road, her attention is ruptured by an oncoming car. Jerking the steering wheel, she crosses over the uneven pasture. "Merde!" Uncontrollably, the car rolls down the hillside. Scrapping sounds scratch at it. A loud clap of thunder! The car falls into the wood line.

•

The rolling car throws Melonnie's body out of the front windshield. Catching the tree with her right shoulder, she feels the crushing of her bones. Her legs come open, rotating her torso, and she lands with her face buried into the damp cold ground. Frustration and pain fill her senses, "oooowww". The pain subsides becoming a memory of pain and laughter engulfs her mind. Mad laughter. Ironic laughter. Laughter nonetheless. Like a tide, the pain rushes swiftly back into her head. Her eyes fill with horror. This time the world becomes black and lost in a misty array of gray colors. She pulls at the ground beyond her, with no resulting motion. A small popping sound produces a small glow. Turning her eyes to the light, fear deepens further, as flames rise from the hood of the car. "Brahnt" she whispers out of breath and out of hope. The fire begins burning brighter. Another sound catches her ear, but it's to late. She slips into darkness.

Chapter 6

Thulis Ruchanka

Fatal Blow

The wind caress like,
Gentle fingers of a love unseen.
The moon shines,
Within a heart of cold.
Love's name rapes
An image of a savage beast- untamed!
But I know!
Love's touch is the fatal blow

The Guest and the Fool

Smooth caresses of a gentle fragrance fill his senses. His eyes open at once, however gently. "Hi there." The figure of a young woman, blends and meshes with obscure and unfamiliar surroundings.

"Melonnie?" He inquires.

"Father? I think the gentleman is waking!"

"Melonnie? Father?" Repeats Brahnt, meshing thoughts that should not combine.

"Hold on there feller." The voice was manly and compassionate. "I'm not your Father. (he says facing the young girl) You were brought to me by a woman." He pulls a chair over to his daughter. "Do you have a name?" Trying to change the subject.

"Brahnt. I think. (touching his head) Where am I?" He asks confused.

"You're at my house. The hospital was too far of a drive. I though it best to let the local town doctor see you. (he tugs at his covers and with care searches out the wounds) Well- she did and said you needed rest. Samantha?"

"Yes Father?" She answers. The father may have not caught on. But Brahnt's trained ear twitches silently, catching the playfulness of her words.

"Get this man a drink or something comparable. I'm sure he should be thirsty."

"Yes Father." She excuses herself, running off to the kitchen.

"You wouldn't happen to be the feller that got dragged off by that monster a couple of days ago, would you?"

"What? Monster? Please don't call her that." His voice is soft spoken.

"Yea.... Don't worry none. It's just that some local boys got... Well (Brahnt sits upright) got torn up about twenty miles from here and it seems that every one described some creature.

Some waitress said that a poor gentleman was drug off too. I don't believe it or anything, but for *all* of the town folk to be talking about it just seems odd. It sure seems funny. (he pushes Brahnt's shoulder) Are you sure your OK?"

"I feel tired, but not sleepy."

"Well you shouldn't feel sleepy. Sore? That is another matter though." He says reassuringly.

"How did I get here?" Asking, unsure that the question has been asked.

"Your friend brought you here, she said that you were traveling through and got injured." He mentions quickly.

"Where is she?" He says to him directly, knowing that he is hiding something.

"What did you guys do out there?" He questions with a more relaxed tone of voice.

"How long?" He asks, he asks relying on his own strengths.

"How long?" He returns not sure of the best answer. "Oh! A couple of days?" He breathes outwardly giving away to defeat.

"Excuse me?" He says moaning a bit. He removes his covers, leaving himself naked.

"A couple of days! (Brahnt checks himself for wounds)"

"You said a couple of days?" Brahnt's voice displays amusement at the situation with a bit of sarcasm. His voice is calm and surprisingly with new energy.

"I'm sorry. *My* name is *Erasmus* (the girl enters), this is the priest's daughter Samantha. Her eyes inspect him from head to toe, while holding his pants draped across her forearm. "Don't stand there, young lady. Bring the drink." He sends out the command, with a bit of sexual tension. Erasmus focuses heavily on the bottle and glasses temporarily defeating gravity, by way of a polished silver plane.

"I'm sorry Erasmus. I've never seen a human before." She answers with an apologetic tone of voice.

"And good that you haven't. You may have been mislead!" Erasmus rolls his eyes at her. "Bring on the drink." He calls out again, but the young woman doesn't move. Brahnt glances at the small woman while reaches for Brahnt's clothing. "Come little flower. Blossom and blush later. Bring the drink!" The melody of his words is as rapid as it is sarcastic, but never lending to anger. Having taken the clothing draped around her forearm, Brahnt fastens his trousers. The drink liquid filled glasses move just a bit.

She begins to walk forward. "It's (sings the words with sarcasm) about time. I've been waiting so long, I feel of thirst myself." He takes the bottle and removes the cork. Placing his mouth to it, he takes the health drink. Without even drying his mouth or the bottle, he removes the two glasses from the tray.

"Thank you, Samantha." He lets out, while pouring two drinks into the glasses.

"You're welcome." She says, twisting her mouth in disapproval of his manners. But within her is the key to understanding the ogre. She reaches out touching Brahnt's chest. His muscularity fascinates her. "Wow! Our kind is not quite like this." Her touch is slightly frosty. "You are so warm. Like the sun."

"Wait! *I* have muscles!" Erasmus clowns at her.

"Hurry, Sir Brahnt, we haven't the time now that you are well. Melonnie has kept you alive for the while. It is to my suspicion that she enjoys your company."

"And I do hers."

"Love? Is that love in your eye?" He steps forward, for a better stare into his eyes. "No! Didn't think so." He walks off with Brahnt's shirt. Samantha takes a few steps back and discontinues her admiration. Melonnie will wake soon. Be on your best behavior, she is not very pleased with anyone right now. There is much to do and so little- well my newly found friend, you know the rest."

"Fiend?" Brahnt questions Erasmus' intentions.

"Sir? I beg you repeat yourself?" His attitude is prissy. He pulls his own ear to Brahnt's mouth. Brahnt grins.

"Sir you've called me fiend." Brahnt repeats with more description.

"Ah! (a pause and a thought) No doubt, I did. Slip of the tongue. Yes! (another pause and thought) Yes. I am brilliant. That is what it is! A slip of the tongue!" Brahnt smiles at this move. "Why do you laugh?" His look displays an inquisitive curiosity.

"A clown who clowns in clowning. Seeks to clown the clown he is clowning, but finds the clown he has clowned is truly the image of himself." Brahnt snaps back with a force of wisdom.

"Ah! (he sticks his finger in the air and Samantha pulls the shirt from within Erasmus' hands) A man who understands the use of words. You and I won't be as good as the enemies I thought we'd be."

Samantha mimics laughter, trying to maintain herself within disciplines. Turning to her, Erasmus frowns. She takes the shirt and holds it to the air, allowing Brahnt to slip his muscular arms into the shirt. "Now button up, Melonnie will want to ask you of some affaire."

"Is she OK?" Brahnt asks, while buttoning his shirt.

"Very much so. She is a strong woman. I heard you shot her in the eye?" Samantha asks him, taking a few quick glances at Erasmus. It is of no concern to her that Erasmus knows of her discomfort.

"Does every one here know?" Asks Brahnt.

"Well let's see (he counts his fingers). Ah- YEA" Erasmus starts again, finally lets out the more resentful emotion. "Embarrassed? Don't be. She's been through worse. I just can't believe she didn't take one of yours." He searches

Brahnt's reaction. He finds none he can manipulate. "She's just that way. But loving to the last."

"You used this?" He pulls out the pistol, with the extended silencer. Brahnt can feel the tension building, but this tension is unlike any other. This tension offers friendship and alliances in forms disguised as threats and deceptive maneuvers within the meaning of secret dialogue. They judge not by actions, but by the measure of intent and meaning. Brahnt feels Erasmus' bitterness. And would anyone be bitter? Brahnt asks himself.

"Semi-Automatic, there is only one safety."

"Semi-Automatic? I know what this is." He says to him holding the weapon loosely and canted facing Brahnt's direction. Brahnt makes no sudden moves. He stands calmly."

"Erasmus!" Samantha calls out, stepping in the way between the bullet and Brahnt. She reaches out and takes a hold of the wineglasses. Staring into Erasmus' eyes she bows her head carefully, playfully and sips the liquid. Her wide lips cup the front edge of the glass. Her blue piercing eyes penetrate beyond Erasmus' attention. With a sharp motion she spins in place and turns to Brahnt. She reaches out with the glass of wine in her hand. Brahnt grips the glass. She watches his fingers casually and places close attention to his fingernails. Looking just slightly down to her he looks and is absorbed by her eyes as well. Truly a spellbinder. He thinks to himself, but his mind floats off, wondering about Melonnie.

Bringing it to his lips, he sips at it. The wine is very well fermented. The taste is exquisite. He swishes the wine and lifts the glass up to his mouth, he allows air to mix the flavor. Her chest comes close to his, as she pushes him slightly away from Erasmus.

"I'll take it from here, Erasmus. Go cool off!" Her words enter his ear and he knows that to be the best thing he can do at this moment. He turns away from them, taking a hold of the wine bottle. Over his left shoulder, he throws the weapon. Brahnt, almost motionless, snatches the weapon from its passing flight. She is impressed by his coolness, unlike what she has seen of her kind. The pistol half-spins within his grip and he places it on the backside of his pants. She smiles back at him with amusement. "They'll be a meal prepared for you by order of the Priest.

"I'm in a church?" He asks a bit confused.

"Not exactly. You see Erasmus? There! (she points behind her) He couldn't enter a temple." He looks behind her, seeing nothing more than an open window. Beyond the window there is darkness with a tint of sunrise. Brahnt looks down to his watch. "Its true. He'll burn with the rays of the sun."

"But-"

"What about Melonnie? She's natural. That's different. I'll let her talk to you about that." She says to him. "Don't worry you'll be OK. At least that's what I think."

"Oh? And what does that mean?"

"Woman's intuition. Though, I don't know. She can be difficult and unpredictable sometimes."

"Aren't all women?" He says to her, as she moves away and into the doorway.

"I don't know. I've never met one." She says looking over her shoulder. "Coming along? You'll be expected." She stands facing away from him, mystically. His eyes ride the mesmerizing contours of her body. Her mid back length hair is shiny and brilliant. Her robe fits her well, neatly gathered at the waist by method of stylish rope and tassel. Her hips gently curve surrounded the cascading light against her pleats. She turns away from him, absorbed in the complement. She takes a few steps further and is suddenly swallowed by the darkness.

Though slightly at odds and dazed, he presses forward into the unknown. 'A delicate matter though', he thinks. He has been in worse situations before. The air is filled with small pockets of cold air, mostly noticeable with each inhale. The doorframe is an older one. He knows this much. He is not in the city. City air is nothing like this. Beyond the door he watches her fascinating figure stretching to her toes, as she leans to light a lantern. To his right, he leans his hand on a long wooden rail. It extends to her and beyond, wrapping around a wide stairway and leads down to lower levels. Finished with the light, she reaches out her hand to him smiling. Looking at her smile he knows she is pleased with him. He smiles back at her. "You must be an awfully nice man."

"What brought *that* on?" He asks with less than an inquisitive curiosity.

"You say the nicest things." She walks over to him. Her feet are light, almost unheard. If not for the way her rob kicks out at the bottom, one might think she is gliding. He looks down at her and admires the impression of her breasts against the cloth she wears. "You see? There!" She says spontaneously.

"There what?"

"You admire things, rather than desire them for you own personal- how do you say. Own personal- Personal-"

"Pleasure? Use? Abuse? (he searches for more common words)"

"You give compliments well." She reaches towards his cheek and places a kiss. "Thank you," she says with her eyes closed and pushes away. He can feel the meaning of her words, but says nothing. He realizes that his intellect though appreciated, is nothing in comparison to that of theirs. Who ever they are. "Come now, the food will be cold."

Down the long wide stairs they descend. From beyond the soft red colors, pleasing to Brahnt's eyes, are sounds of utensils being toyed with. But, perhaps they are being strategically placed. The side of his lips curls slightly. "Familiar sounds?"

"Yes actually they are. Though I've not heard them for so long."

"I realize that you are a strong man, in the human world. (the word human ears curiously) Tell me? Do you believe in God?"

"Not really. Not much any way. Though I find myself respecting the people who involve themselves with Him."

"It's just as well, you know? Once someone has their mind set a certain way, it takes a few centuries to convince them otherwise. But you wouldn't know about that."

"I wouldn't?" Brahnt calls out.

"I'm sorry. I didn't mean to offend you."

"I'm not offended." Hearing his words, she stops at the stairs, half leaning over the rail.

"That's right (she feels out)! You're not." Her head cants to her left and so do her eyes. With a touch of high aristocratic rebellion, she smirks and kicks at the railing, continuing her descent. Though armed, Brahnt doesn't feel the normal comforts of safety. He understands that the safety of his life relies heavily on his ability to be intellectual and open-minded. It is obvious that these people are not what they seem, but something else. However, that is his perception. And being solely his perception, he cannot judge them. Perhaps they are human and just out of circulation. But how does he explain their seemingly powerful and mysterious presentation.

Descending to the base of the stairway, he dissimulates his search for clues for disorientation.

"That's not important at this moment." She says to him. He is surprised at her ability to out think him. Though first a suspicion, he finds that her answer is totally unrelated to his mention, but is indeed regarding to his thoughts. She turns to him and places her finger to his lips. "Shhhh..." Her lips fill with the word, making her Asian appearance a hint more European. "What matters today is that you show your pure heart. Do not doubt our ways, but mostly do not show yourself as a threat to our kind. Don't forget you're human and the cause of our fallen race. There is much prejudice to your kind, being so close to us. Melonnie is not here to defend you and she is the only one that can. Her influence and sacrifice is well known throughout the underworld." Taking him by the belt, she pulls him forward, completely leaving behind the emotion just displayed. In the light of the next room, she enters with a fire in her eyes. Motionless, and staring upwardly with a tinge of fear, the server stares at Brahnt. Brahnt, not having the time to digest the warning just given to him, looks directly at the men and women sitting down at the table. The man at the head of the table brings his fist to his mouth and clears his throat. The attendant continues forward without hesitation, bringing to notice the human.

"Welcome" with a smile, the man at the head of the table lends the first greeting.

"Thank you." He reaches up to his head. "Thank you for your help." The Head master smiles back at him, while nodding his head. Brahnt reaches behind himself, taking a hold of his pistol. All at the table sit back, waiting in anticipation. Holding the weapon in a non-threatening manner, he offers it. "Where can I set this? Erasmus was kind enough to return it to me." The waitress looks at the head master waiting for a signal. He nods his head displaying his approval. Immediately, she unfolds a small towel and pushes the tray up and towards him. Brahnt places his weapon respectfully upon it. The waitress folds the towel and makes away with the weapon.

"You are much welcomed." Says the man at the head of the table.

"Here, here! (say the others) Welcome!"

"Have yourself a seat. My name is Thulis, this Samantha, Bianque, Michelo, and Farel." Samantha's smile merges with relief. She reaches over and pulls out the last seat opposite Thulis' right hand. Brahnt smiles kindly at the young girl. Taking his place and carefully looking for hints, he looks into Samantha's face. She denotes a sign of praise. Through the large stone-framed windows, more signs of the sun are visibly making their appearance. She walks quickly opposite Brahnt, seating herself comfortably. He watches as she suspiciously tucks herself in.

"Brahnt?"

"Yes Thulis?" He answers back politely, trying not to sound too much like a child being called by his father.

"I know you have questions. And perhaps after you understand us more, you'll understand your discomfort." Brahnt's sight reaches toward Samantha.

"Go on." Brahnt says calmly.

"Why do you suppose that we are sparing you life?"

" (squinting) Because this is a battle that is larger than I am."

"What do you suppose that struggle revolves around?"

"I'm not sure. I wasn't awake long enough to find out!" He sounds of bitter resolution. The others focus carefully on their meals, seemingly uninterested. Before them is deep dish of dark red liquid and meat that seem to act more as sponges that the diner. Though careful and well mannered, Brahnt feels a sense of disgust. The waitress re-enters the room and places a cooked portion of meet well seasoned. A clear freshly picked dish of vegetables is placed to his right.

Smiling at the waitress he takes from her a tall glass of the same deep red wine, he so much likes. She returns his smile with one that fills his sense with appreciation.

"That is not the question asked!" Thulis says.

"That is the answer. Whether you like it or not. It's the answer I offer you." He says too firmly, but without any loss of respect. Among the ones eating, there are small snickers of laughter.

"Do you know who we are?" He asks, taking a spoonful of stringy soup.

"I have no idea. But I don't sit at tables willing to agree to a game of verbal manipulation."

"Here! Here! The table adjourns." Brahnt looks to their faces for the sincerity of the argument. Much to their surprise, he can see that they are of agreeable stature, while pushing their spoons into their mouths. Brahnt reaches down to the table and takes hold of his fork and knife. Without uttering another word, he cuts a portion of his cooked meat. The meat separates at the gentle strokes.

Pressing the fork into the meat, he dips it into the brown sauce. As he places it into his mouth, he can't help but wonder what it is they eat. Like-wise they share a similar curiosity. 'How could that meat be a meal? Dead meat with no real substance? How disgusting!' Brahnt feels the weight of their stares fixated on him.

"Listen, (half way chewing) I know that I'm obviously not eating the same meal that you all are eating."

The waitress stands by, with anticipation. "And not that this meal is bad, it's more like one of the best that I have ever had. But I can't help but be curious as to why you all have other dishes. Is this a family dish or something? I can probably eat that. Going through all of this trouble just to prepare something for me? Like a special dish." Pointing out his finger as if asking the spoon to come his way, Farel, sitting directly to his right, dips his spoon into his own dish and carefully brings it over to him.

The spoon is made from dull and dingy silver. Light to medium scratches, are visible and Brahnt realizes that this spoon has seen action. Farel smiles. Brahnt realizes that his thoughts are being heard. With such old grace, old like an experienced combat veteran offering food to his prisoner. Brahnt reaches out, completing the role, taking a hold of the hand that is about to feed him. Opening his mouth, the smell of the meal is not bad. The spoon falls into his mouth. The contents are emptied and the small crowd watches with respectful silence. Brahnt absorbs the taste. This dish is served luke-warm, its seasoning is raw. It still had a taste though, nothing extravagant. Actually it tasted like watered down meat. The deep red sauce is less dense than anticipated. All in all, it is awful.

Watching him gracefully eating the soup, he feels he has gained something of a comfortable stance. If anything at all, he has shown the willingness to understand and settle this feeling of being an outcast. Farel reaches over and points to Brahnt's dish. "I don't think you'll like it." He tells him handing him over a piece of his meal.

Nonetheless, he takes a hold of it with his teeth and begins to chew. Not being able to look as graceful as Brahnt, he makes faces of disgust. The others begin to laugh at his inability to disguise his discomfort. Brahnt smiles nervously, as Farel's face reminds him of how he feels.

"Would you like to know?" -Thulis

"No. Yes- No! No! Forget it." Brahnt stumbles on his own words. The others though smirking and snickering, continue with their meals. Their meals are devoured, as if their lives depend on it. He glances hastily at Samantha. Catching the glance, she blushes unexpectedly. Not minding her actions well, her spoon tips allowing it to drip onto the black glass-like table. As if synchronized they halt their gorge. All eyes turn to Samantha. Brahnt's fingers tighten their grip on his knife and fork. Still looking at her face, he notices her swallowing hard. Using her finger she scrapes up the drop and brings it to her mouth. Knowing that no one could observe her right eye, she winks at Brahnt.

There is little table talk and Brahnt makes no further effort to break their silence. Not having his gun brings to him a feeling of insecurity, but having it would have probably secured his death. And what of Melonnie? Though perhaps he is not of their kind. He did regret some of what has happened to him. Brahnt can see the signs of gratitude painted about their faces. Samantha too, though charmed and intrigued by the guest's presence, concentrates on her food. It is almost like a ritual of total enlightening. Each spoonful is carefully dipped into the soupy meal.

Observing their behavior, Brahnt feels the intimidation and their strength. However, the thoughts are blocked from consciousness. Replacing his fears are the thoughts of Melonnie. 'How is she and what is she doing? Is he here because of her? Or has he been rescued from her? And what is all the mystery?' Thulis sits within good grasping sight. He seems a powerful man, and though bulky strong, he seems to have speed.

The room is quiet and still as they eat the meal. Most of them move forward to the bowls as the spoon makes its way to their mouths. Though their customs are not those that were familiar to Brahnt, they are calculated. Samantha, the most refined of them all, delicately navigates her utensils. Her hair, pulled back behind her right ear, allows Brahnt to view her beauty and motions. Widening her lips and gently placing her spoon into her mouth, she inhales. Sealing her lips around the spoon, she pulls the spoon outwardly looking as if she were smiling lightly towards him. He can feel her interest, and though it would make any other man feel threatened, he feels comfort knowing that she is on his side.

Brahnt's smile collects at the corner of his mouth and he continues his meal

[Time Passes]

Feeling satisfied of the meal he's eaten and the experience of meeting these people, he paces slowly across the stone floor of his room. There, he knows that he is waiting, but he is not exactly sure why he waits. Still the sense of fear like tiny spiders crawling across is back remains. His fear is not complete. There is yet another feeling. One, that is filled with concern and regret. 'Melonnie? Where is she? How is she? Will she return for him? When? Is this what we are all waiting for? And is this the only reason he lives?'

It's rather quiet inside the walls created from thick stones. Rubbing his face and pushing back his loosely fitted hair, he walks over to the window and opens it. The breeze enters his comfortable prison and reminds him of how steep the climb would be if he fell out. He looks at the horizon. The trees give him a sense of pleasure and their smell of freshness enhances their appeal. He leans over to the stony ledge, carefully inspecting it. Leaning, each groove and pit presses up against his hand. The view is spectacular and he absorbs as much of it as he can. Bending down, resting his elbows, he reaches a comfortable position to enable his eyes to search out the territory. 'Normally', he thinks to himself, 'I would be searching for a method of escape. I don't feel that way. I don't feel that way at all. Is it because underneath their skin there is something more? I know that they are not human. Melonnie has already proven that to me. But, I can't shake this feeling that there is more to this than I can understand. There seems to be a plan here. A direction. Something... something tangible, but what?' He loses his thoughts to ghosts of his past. And like the very phantom, the wind caresses its delicate fingers crossing his hair, as if toying with the idea of physically entering his mind.

First his mind enters a void of darkness, something there stirs in the void of forgetfulness. Though he knows it is there, he treats it like a wrapped present that has not been opened in a long time.

And, as that is the fact, he questions himself as to why he allows it to exist that way. He doesn't have the answer. Further into his mind he enters, allowing him to think more profoundly.

He sees a picture image of his pistol, very much like a motion picture. He sees a rock suspended in the darkness. *It floats past him. A car- his first car, no! It's his family's car. Inside he sits there swishing from one side of the back seat to the other. Sounds slowly come to the forefront of his thoughts. The window of the car is down, allowing the wind to fill the rear seat and caress his hair. He can feel his hair dancing in the wind. And this adds to his sense of joy. The sounds are clearer now. It's about singing, no-wait! It is singing. Singing a song, ("....there was an old lady who swallowed a fly. I don't know why she swallowed the fly. Perhaps she'll die. There was an old lady who swallowed a bird. She swallowed the bird to catch the spider. She swallowed the spider to catch the fly. But I don't know why she swallowed the fly. Perhaps she'll die. There was an old lady who swallowed a cat. She swallowed the cat to.........")*

The song plays in his mind as the motion continues. *His father looks at him through the rear-view mirror. Brahnt enjoys the attention. To his left is his mother. Noticing that his father is staring at him through the rear-view mirror, she too turns to take a glance. Brahnt focuses on the large red surface clearing the hill in front of the vehicle. Silver strips break the plane, then glass. He realizes that it is a very large pickup truck. And it's on the wrong side of the road, set for a collision. His eyes widen. His father loses his smile to concern. Caution and fear turn his father's head towards the windshield. His mother jolts her neck forward. There is silence. No more sound. No singing. No sound of the wind, once blasting through the window.*

His flesh is numb. His mind plays all in slow motion, hoping to prevent what is about to happen. *His mother's hands raise themselves face level, their muscles stretch to the point of violent shaking. A dull sound of metal bending and folding, as the front end of the vehicle crumples like a piece of shiny paper. Darkness- nothing more than darkness. He feels his body falling, tumbling--everything but resting. Then he feels the sensation of falling... falling... Falling like the image of a small crumpled piece of paper. On it the scribble of a large pencil. With the word soul... Images of blue flashes. Red Flashes. More darkness. The sound of his heartbeat.*

Louder and louder, he hears the heart beating. His dry mouth forces his tongue to move about accordingly. He licks his lips. The countryside comes into view. The landscape is beautiful. The fresh air refreshing. As distracted, as he may seem, he knows that he is not alone.

"Hey. (softly) How are you?"

"Fine." She releases, ending on a high note.

"So? Did I make myself look horrible downstairs."

"Non! Oh lá lá, you have impressed everybody." Her accent is stronger. Or perhaps he can hear better now that he is awake. "You even got Farel to eat from your plate. He'll have a time digesting it. But it was fun."

"You have a nice accent."

"Merci."

"But you're Asian."

"Oui –er -(she interrupts herself). Yes, of course. I am many things- many accents." She walks over to where he is standing.

"You are also very rebellious." He points out clearly to her.

"Perceptive! I can see why it is that Melonnie enjoys keeping you alive."

"She's not like that."

"Neither am I. Nor the rest of us, for that matter. (looking out the window) Actually, I'm here to invite you to a sunbath."

"What (smiling) is a sunbath?"

"Where we all go to the edge of the lake and bathe."

"Who will be there?"

"Thulis invites. If you want to know. And I will be there. Usually we all go." Samantha's voice comes across playfully.

"How many today?" Unlike her, his voice carries a sarcastic tone.

"The same people that were at the table."

"Sure, sounds like fun."

"Bon. By the way? (she leans over the edge of the sill) You're not a prisoner here. But, you are pretty deep into the woods. And there are wild animals out there."

"Like wolves and bears?"

"No. Wild ones. You know?" She smiles at him and takes his arm, acting as if he should have been forewarned and is simply teasing.

The sun filling the sky is not as hot today. Perhaps it is the canopy of trees that cools the lower level. Perhaps. Pushing off of the windowsill, he takes her by the arm much like a gentleman would. She is honored by his hospitality, and so she marches off with him hand in arm.

They walked together hand in hand through the doorway and outwards toward the stairway. Brahnt wonders if he is being taunted or if he is being tested. Perhaps, he comes to resolve, she is just that pretty. Perhaps she knows it. Perhaps she is as curious about me as I am about her. He admires her hips carrying her body down the stairs. Her beauty and grace bring to mind his first girlfriend. He wasn't in love then and definitely not now, but if he had a camera he would take a picture. 'If I were that kind, I would-' he says to himself. He hears the seal of her lips breaking. She must be smiling. Her hand rises upwards and to her face, but he cannot make it out for sure. But she is definitely smiling.

Together they reach the doorway leading to the edge of the wood line. Covering her head with a hood like extensions of her vestment, she shades herself from the strongest sunrays. But it is pretty cool out here; the canopy overhead is strong. Brahnt continues forward, taking her beauty in as it is reflected from the sunrays. Looking at him through the corners of her eyes, she smiles, bashfully. Brahnt's curiosity takes the best of him. Still keeping time with her, he moves allowing her to lead the way to the water.

Barefooted she steps overtop of the earthly soil, seemingly unaffected by the detritus didn't seem to make much difference. Making it look easy, Brahnt wonders what her foot is made of. Side by side they keep in stride, with few words passed between them. Approaching a small hill, Samantha sways her body slowly. Brahnt continues a few feet further. Placing his foot on top of the mound, he admires the steep and sudden drop and wonders how he would reach the bottom.

Again she smiles.

"Why are you smiling at me like that? (her grin becomes cocky)" Before he can respond to her sudden lunge, he feels her strong hands firmly securing his arms.

Her body crashes against his lifting his feet off of the ground. Pushing him over the edge of the cliff, his hands cling to her shoulder and neck. Clinging to his body and lifting her feet, she wraps them around his waist. Flexing her muscular abdomen, she leans her body close to his.

Face to face, she presses her mouth to his. Confused and pumped full of adrenaline, his hands pull her kiss into his. Strands of her hair flailing in the wind, while the cliff behind her grows further away, seduce him to believe that it is only a dream. He can feel her excitement pulsating through her thin layers of clothing.

Fear and adrenaline pump through, rushing against the walls of his veins. Holding him, breast to breast, their chemistry and energy intensify. She envisions each drop of blood wayfaring though his them. Her fangs jut out swiftly accompanying her bewitched smile and laughter. He does not notice. She presses her nose to his neck, as his excitement excites her. Hard pressed, her hands hold him clutching his body absorbing the sensation of his pulsating veins.

Falling… Falling… Her concentration is unexpectedly broken away, as the scent of fresh water enters her nostrils. A large splash! And nature swallows them. Bubbles! Lots of them! He pushes up with his hands while holding his breath. The suddenly felt water, helps him come to, cooling off the adrenaline rush.

The surface of the water bubbles and then explodes, giving birth to Brahnt. He swings his head to the side clearing most of the water retained within his hair. His heavy body submerges. Gasping for air his body comes to a slow bob, as he attempts to tread water. The water streaming down from his hair blurs his vision temporarily. His hands swim across from the water, maintaining the barely recognizable characters in sight. The area is silent for the moment. Remembering Samantha, he searches for her. Looking up at the cliff, he smiles thinking of himself a superhero.

Behind him, Samantha emerges. Her body pushes out of the water and into an aerial somersault. Figure and shape is now better described. He, for the moment, is amused at her ability. "Any more and you could touch the sky." He comments to her smiling.

Falling back into the water with minimal splashing, she turns and rotates surfacing and treading the water next to him. Aside from that, her Asian smile appears to be still painted on her face. Brahnt can't help but smile back at her. 'She is truly something to be looked at.' Her deep-layered eyes show off more than she could possibly realize. Brahnt, impressed by the height of the jump, suspects that she is trying to encourage a friendship. She swims up to him closing any possible distance between them. Letting out a delicate and playful glance, she pecks at his cheek with her lips.

"Did you enjoy you fall?"

"I like falling very much. Thank you." His tone is one that hides an inside joke. However, her tone carries an invitation to dance with the devil. A dance that feels closely familiar to his line of work. Still, she could have easily killed him so much earlier in the game. She takes a hold of him and motions towards shore. She is obviously a strong swimmer. A stroke at a time they move closer to shore.

Brahnt looks at the shore, trying to spot them all and gain recognizance of the area. He can see the figures that were part of breakfast, but there is no Erasmus. And worse even. No Melonnie. 'How long would I have to wait?' Treading the water and moving closer to shore, his attention moves to his immediate surroundings. Swimming slowly and uncomfortably towards the shore, he sees nothing more than the calm cool water. The water moves around inside his shoes. Finding this uncomfortable, he sinks into the water and reaches down for his feet. Sinking for the first time, the shore creatures lift their heads and turn to Brahnt in a unified manner. He ignores them. Quickly and with great detailed agility, he unties his shoes. 'Again' he thinks to himself, 'this is something of a familiar task'.

Coming to surface, smiles come across each of their faces noticing that he has tied his shoelaces together and has draped the shoes around his neck. Calmly, he fills his lungs with a fresh breath of air. He is comfortable with the attention. No longer seeing Samantha, he pushes off with his feet he makes his way to shore content that his feet feel free. (a glimpse of white) Below him is a distortion much like a white shadow. His toes tingle with the sensation of fear. Though out of his element, he remains calm, cool and collective. His swimming stroke slows. Preferring to see his death rather than being surprised by it, he inhales deeply burying his head underneath the crisp water. Expecting the worse, he finds the sigh of relief. (he remembers the water is fresh)

Swimming below him, Samantha's figure slithers as if a native to the environment. 'But how?' Strands of her clothing drift about her leaving residuals of ghostly impressions. Enthralled, he is unable to look away. As if having been given a queue, she turns, swimming onto her back, with her eyes wide open. Looking directly to his face, he feels his muscle squeeze the air out of his lungs. Out of breath, he lifts his head for a breath of fresh air. Submerging, he finds her gone without a trace. Eager to meet with her again, he continues his journey to shore. Allowing the bubbles to trail out of her nose, she smiles as if amused and changes her attention to the event. "Always one step ahead of me, as so it seems once again." He mutters approaching shore and remembers her deadly beautiful smile.

[Reaching shore]

Having reached the shore, Samantha leans forward offering him a towel. Along the blade of her shoulders, Brahnt's eyes come across strangely noticeable markings.

"These are scars. There is a lot of knowledge to fill your mind with!" Thulis' eyes, along with the others, stop their tasks. Lifting their heads they focus their attention toward Brahnt, examining her symmetrical scars. Realizing that he is staring, he reaches for his belt and unties his shoes. They fall onto the sand, leaving their pale impressions. Without much else said, and with a subtle tone of sincerity, he begins removing his clothing. The others smile, showing their discomfort removed. Thulis' smile is the most pronounced, and places his masculine hand against the base of Brahnt's neck. Behind him Samantha removes her clothing, joining the ritual. No further attention is given to the members. Brahnt however looks at her from the corner of his eye, unable to deny her remarkable physique. Her face blushes subtle, as she removes her robe. She realizes that the attention of the new comer has been being offered to her. Brahnt agrees. She is definitely different, perhaps a bit on the mystical side, but definitely perfect. A woman could not be so lucky. It's always the farm girls, he thinks to himself.

His ears are startled by a burst of laughter. As sudden as it appears, it dwindles to a light smile and a few chuckles. Brahnt's cool attitude allows him to move about freely. With his shirt on the floor and pants already down, she takes her turn looks at his body. 'There are obviously some differences. Casually, she walks over to him. His eyes catch each step sinking into the sand. Her eyes remain focused on the center of his body. The others also take notice to him, with great equality. He has eight ribs on each side, his muscularity is well defined, hair on his chest has strange fur, but most strange is Brahnt's semi-oval indention at the pit of his stomach. Thulis, amongst all of them, pays little attention to the curiosity at hand. But within their curios gestures, Brahnt feels their jealousy. However, not being the kind of jealousy that promotes violence or deception, there is deeper meaning.

The touch of her cool hand, produces goose bumps. This is much to their amusement. "Is this a defensive mechanism?" Asks Farel.

"Will it excrete poison?" interjects Bianque. Samantha's wet, cool hand glides over his muscular chest, inspecting each turn, bend and pit.

"My hands are cold." Samantha's words slip out slowly and deliberately. Her attraction to him is obvious, but the reason is the mystery. The men keep their distance, still untrusting of the human's body unlike Samantha pushing the boundaries of his personal space. Brahnt, however, makes no gestures lending to his conviction. Actually, he is as equally interested in them.

They seem similar, and yet different. He wonders if Melonnie is of any difference. Taking his hand, Samantha places his palm against her chest. Proudly and nervously, she inhales and flexes her strength.

Amazed, Brahnt's facial reaction is stirred. He finds it unique that her skin is pillow soft and smooth, while deeper within it is a strong barrier. It is as if soft fatty tissue has cleverly masked a layer of muscle several inches deep.

"Am I like as good a woman as any other you've met?" Brahnt's mind wonders off for a moment. She smiles proudly and pushes away with a stronger sense of pride, she walks to Thulis' side. One by one the others line up, taking turns at placing Brahnt's hand on their chest and asking similar questions.

"What's the matter? Do you not want to touch the man and explore him?" Samantha asks Thulis, kicking at the ground with her big toe.

"My dear little young child. I've been to war with his kind." His look is one of sadness and at the same time displays signs of unforgiving madness. Samantha bows her head, slightly. "He is pure of heart. Yet he is a powerful man. There is much of him and of his mind we can benefit from."

"So he lives?" She says with optimism.

"Yes. For the time. We must wait for Melonnie and see what she has to offer. I must understand why she has brought him here?"

"Are you questioning her judgment?" Samantha asks confused.

"No. Just her cause."

"Has she found the book?"

"No." - Thulis

"You have spoken with her? Where is she? Where is my cousin?" She sounds of concern, but insures no disrespect.

Chapter 7

The Cloak and the Dagger

Thief of Moments

Ghost like, she moves across tiled the floor.

Mystic colors collage, meshing with the mystery of her Delicate motion.

And the only reason I know she moves, is because I can Feel the wind gently shifting as she passes.

Beauty is no stranger to her,
For beauty is jealous.

For beauty has seen her graceful dance by the light of The pale moon.

And the poet is the sinner.
He watches with attentive intent,
Though his reason not be known.

So in his plea for pardon,
He writes- I have captured you on sheets of stolen time.

I return what I have stolen.
I return this leaf to the owner,
Who so inspired me.

The Cloak and the Dagger

The netted fabric scraped up from old sheets and, what seems to be potato sacks, barely suspends Brahnt's body from falling to the ground. Swaying back and forth from between the two trees, He looks onto the horizon. Able to feel the peace that surrounds him, he thinks clear thoughts of life, love and the questioning of his existence. For that matter, he questions the origin of man and how we have become the individuals we have.

A few minutes into these thoughts he finds some resolve and contentment. He is more than aware that this conundrum has quizzed humanity since the beginning of time. Thus, what would one more or one less question change? Would it be answered or not? Some how, he thinks deeper into thoughts, perhaps this place and these people will bring to light something better to this decaying world.

Feeling the gentle fingertips of the cool morning breeze lightly brushing against his ear, his mind travels to thoughts of a time when it was a safer world. The hammock rocks peacefully. Above the treetops, birds sing concealed within the small canopy. There is movement among neighboring branches and leaves. 'Perhaps squirrels? Monkeys? Who knows?' He thinks to himself letting the thoughts pass, as he isn't much of the outdoorsmen. The sounds though unfamiliar are somehow familiar.

The day had spoken and the night for that day, then the night again. The dew of morning and the cold of midnight had visited him twice before even the thought of rest had passed his mind. Still, he knew he had been through worse. Having made provisions, by digging the proper trench, he was quite comfortable in his fall leaf suit. At least that is what he called the sniper uniform he made. Now having to sleep in it for the

13th time, he was thinking of corrections that needed to be made for it. Some, he admitted, he had thought of before. It was best always to make things yourself. And purchase from several different areas. It would be harder to trace. And credit cards were of no use. They could leave a paper trail miles long. Well money wasn't always the best choice either.

'Nope! There's not much to think about out here. Except that for a moment all seems peaceful. All seems quiet. Too bad I have to kill somebody here sooner or later. I remember that face.. of that man... that man.... that round faced man. What the hell was his name? Anyway. The nerve of that guy! Asking me if I ever killed anyone. He had his body count all set up neatly. If I would have pushed him, he probably would have named them all. What I really felt like asking him was if he could count that fast in the middle of a firefight. Ahh! He was truly a rookie. Charm? He had some of that too. He was really quite popular with the ladies. Too bad I have to kill him. Frankly I'm tired of pissing on myself here. After I shoot him from here, I can go on the hike and get my stuff from the top of the hill. A nice set of clean clothes. Still I can wait. I mean, whom do I have to see. Mr. McCormick? That old man has so much of my money that I don't know if he loves me or if he loves my money. What the hell? The money is good. Yea,(softly) that's right. That is what I do and why I do it. (he wipes the sweat from his eyes and looks into the scope. Without moving the muzzle of the rifle) I think I'm going into town and to Allison's for one of those deliciously greasy hamburgers. I'll have some of those mushrooms and onions and- Onions? Hell no! I'll change my mind on those onions. Last time I had them they gave me some serious bad breath. Wait! But I don't have anyone to impress. What the hell I'll have the onions too. Then it's off to Germany. I'll visit my relatives and have a blast. I'll listen to my stepsister talking about how no one single woman in the world is good enough for me. She'll question me about why I don't get home very often. Then she'll ask me to marry some girl

that she met at a local disco. Typical, but that's what my profession has brought me to.

'Now if he would only come out of the fucking house, so that I can have that burger. "Darrel!" Darrel Martin! That's his name! That's all I need too. I'll feel bad for his family. But she'll be better off. After studying the situation carefully, I found him to be poison in her cup. The kid will never let it go, though. Never. He's as stubborn as he is. I guess I'll have to add him to my list and then check up on him every few years. That's if he doesn't check up on me first.' He looks down the scope and focuses beyond the cross hairs, finding them more annoying than useful. At the bottom of the hill and beyond the trees he sees his target walking naked about his house. Brahnt pays his body no mind.

[Waiting]

"Hey there?" A soft voice. Brahnt stretches up looking around, as his daydreams blends with reality. (a pale dress)

"Hi Samantha." He says only at a glance.

"Samantha! Hunh! Has my cousin been teaching you how to tease me?" The voice is more familiar to him now. And though familiar, it displays a bit of aggression.

"Do you know where Melonnie is?" He asks in the same sleepy tone of voice, as if disregarding the sounds of aggravation.

"Brahnt?" She raises her voice just enough to demonstrate her disapproval.

"Look, I can't sit here and wait for her. I have a job to do. And you guys are friendly and all- Well, that is all but that stiff neck Erasmus, who sees it humorous to bother me at night." Mimics of Erasmus' way of speaking accompany his statement.

"Tell me more about it." The female's voice changes tones, as if now curious of what the human will say next.

"Well, the way I figure it, she has the hots for me and if Melonnie doesn't want to come by and admit it to me then perhaps she doesn't like me. Now of course, you know it has *been* a few days? I am just a man-"

"Are you?" Asks the woman, while crossing her arms and leaning against the tree. "A man?"

"Besides Melonnie is probably old. I heard the guys talking about her." He looks away from her, leaning his body further back into the hammock.

"Which ones?" Her voice is now more than aggressive in tones, as she is seemingly offended.

"The guys! You know?" Brahnt, not being able to hold a straight face any longer, breaks out in laughter. Though he struggles to reduce it to a smile, it seems impossible. Melonnie leaps over to him and looks down and into his face. Seeing him smiling and content, she looks to him with concerned eyes. Changing his tone of voice, he questions her. "Are you OK?" She nods her head. Catching his image between strands of her hair, she seems relieved. And he is not certain why. Still, he is happy to see her well and it shows well enough "Was it my fault?"

"No. It wasn't your fault." Her finger reaches down to his face, absorbing the radiating heat from his body.

"Did it heal?" he asks her in a quiet voice.

"Oui. It's OK. Really. It has a little pain still. What was that you used?"

"It was a gun shot. (lifting his head) Glock!" His voice has the delicate note of seriousness and genuine concern. "Most cops are using them these days."

"How do you know these things? Were you a cop once?" Her voice becomes more comfortable.

"No. But if I want to stay alive, I need to know things."

"The guys think your most amusing. They think you're funny." Her eyes lighten up, each filling with sparkles inside them.

"Yea, I know they said so." He says very seriously.

"They do! They just have problems with having human friends. That is all."

"That brings me to my next question." His eyebrow rises.

"What is that?" She squints her eye at him and moves down a little closer to his face

"What the hell, are you- you- people?"

"Yes, we too are people. But with a very different background." She extends her hand to him. "We bleed. We eat. We hurt. And-"

"And what?"

"And-"

"And what Mel?"

"And (his eyebrows raise) we are at war." She says sadly.

"At war?"

"Oui. We have been, since the beginning of time."

"How long?" He says confused.

"Since when you were born." Her words come out with low tones of disappointment.

"Melonnie? I don't know anything of a 27 year old war?"

"27? How did you come to that number?"

"You said since I have been born. (he realizes the depth of her words) You mean since.... (her head drops) since Adam and Eve?" She nods upward.

"Melonnie how old are you?" He waits for her answer impatiently, not knowing what to expect.

"Not as old as Adam and Eve, (rambling) but quite older than you are. And the way we measure time, actually I'm pretty young. (changing the subject) Tell me about this gun shot."

"Well those policemen- the people in white and blue- they shoot at people when they think it is appropriate."

"But those guy were, worse than me. They were the bad ones! After the way that they went around, treating you like as if you were-"

"What did you say?"

"Attention s'il vous plaît! (Your attention Please!) You were my responsibility. And I needed you alive. Who else will explain to me these things, called policemen and driving signs or even those things you call ham-boorgers." She mentions to him as if trying to convince herself.

"Burger." He says to her lowly.

"What?" Still agitated.

"Hamburger. The word is Hamburger. It's something you eat, not something you pick." He says to her with easy politeness.

"Brahnt?" Her tones comes submissively.

"Yes?"

"Why do you like this thing again?" She says making herself more comfortable, while sitting closer to him.

"You might not understand." He leans deeper in to the hammock, allowing himself to reconnect with his feeling of comfort.

"Give me the chance." She says waving her hands to him as if inviting the words to physically arrive.

"Mel. What do you eat?"

"Well, I actually don't. I ingest blood and break its components through a complicated cycle we can pho-"

"You see?" He points lightly into her direction.

"See what?" She questions lightly.

"You don't understand. (she frowns at him) Were you ever." He hesitates.

"Ever what?" She asks with pure curiosity.

"You're not going to punch me are you?"

"Unless you call me a dog again?" She says to and waves her fist. There is a sense of relaxation within her. Watching the symptoms, he continues his playful quiz.

"- Ever human?"

"What? (he lifts up a fist in defense) What did you call me?"

"I was just asking." (still holding his defensive position)

"No! And it's not fair that you have to compare everything to what seems to be humanity. There are other things out there more beautiful and charming." She crosses her arms.

"Exactly my point! And so are the Hamburgers. Ever since I could remember. When life was simple. You know, before the fighting and the 'having to find and work' for your own food." A glimpse of sadness appears painted on her face. He finds it disturbing, "You didn't have it so easy? Did you?" he asks waiting for her answer. She only shakes her head slowly. "I'm sorry Mel."

"No don't be. I really want to understand what this Hamburger thing is."

"Well if it is important to you. It's not the meat. God! We don't even kill our own cows. It's a massive slaughter. That doesn't seem the same. It's just that we humans in America get together on a day where we say that nothing matters. Nothing but you and the family. Mom doesn't have to cook and dad doesn't have to go to work. We all go out to the park, but on the way we stop over to the burger joint and get and buy hamburgers."

"Only hamburgers?"

"No there's fries and soda. Sometimes maybe even a milk shake. Any way, we all go out and together we have a good time eating. It's a way of life here and-" Unable to hide her pain she begins to cry. Startled by her sudden burst, Brahnt feels helpless. And feeling helpless he discontinues. "What's the matter Mel?"

"I have only dreamed of such things. Like a moment of peace. I must raid and kill often. Hunt for my food. I cannot remember when was the last time that I was able to sit and eat a descent meal or develop scientific solutions for our dependencies. I can't remember one day we have not been at war. The first battle was with the Angels. We didn't understand what was happening. We were so confused and thrown off balance. Then we fought with our own kind. The Fallen ones gave our kind great immortal powers and weapons called magic and technology. There was a time when most of my kind was slaughtered. There was carnage spread out miles wide and I thought that our kind would become extinct from the face of the world and possibly the book of life. We had to learn the art of war. And overcome our opponents. Alone and abandoned by God, we sought power from the humans. But humans were hard to trust. After those simple conflicts, came a great warrior. Vigore! He greeted others like him. We thought that we were winning finally. But he and his men took over by storm. Oh and let us not forget the people who started all of this mess anyway. You see, they say that only for the dead-"

"Who's slaughtering your people?" Brahnt asks quietly

"Well- You. I mean not you, even though it was your kind. Humans and their constant witch-hunts and vampire chases. What the hell (she pokes her finger into his ribs) do you think we're made of?" Her chest rises and falls, with it her head leaning down onto her chest.

"If it's any consolation, my kind has warred for many years at a time. As a matter of a fact, there is war in the Middle East. Shit, there used to be slavery and for all I know it is still going on. I guess as a race, we have an inferiority complex. Maybe that's why little men have to hold their hands to their hearts and claim war against the world. Our kind tortures itself. There is really no one-way of determining the solution. We each choose our own way."

"What is your way?" She asks, watching him brush his eyebrow.

"I rather not say."

"Brahnt, it's not your fault your parents died. It isn't. I know you can't remember." She places her hand on his head. His eyes rotate to her direction and she feels his forehead has become hotter.

"How do you know this?" He asks cautiously.

"Didn't my cousin explain it all to you?" She says blowing on his forehead.

"No. Well I think not. Explain what?" His voice is steady and quite calm.

"And didn't Erasmus explain it to you either?"

"No! Actually, I thought I was supper for a while there."

"You poor soul." She says to him with an overly concerned tone of voice.

"Poor? I'm not too sure of that. But confused is definitely a sight of injustice." His sarcasm calls out for attention.

"They should have told you. (she shakes her head in disbelief) Humans have very simple methods of thinking. You see? Your entire body is powered by the breath of life. This is a field of energy, much like electricity. And when you think... well, when you think you produce areas of concentration in your brain. So whenever there is thought produced, we can pick up on the images. Some members of our kind have been known to be what you call psychic."

"So you can read minds?" He asks still not sure of what she is saying.

"No! That's not what I said." She responds with a bit of agitation.

"What *did* you say then?" His voice sooths her. It is a gentle and understanding sound.

"You see? Your entire body is powered by the-"

"The shorter version.... Please?"

"When you think, we can read your thoughts."

"Oh! Just the thoughts as they are being created?"

"Oui!" She claims out proudly. "Just now you are amazed... Now you are thinking if I'm right. (a pause, a frown. She reaches out and slaps him across his upper arm) How can you think of me like that?"

"I just wanted to be sure that you were telling me the truth."

"Listen *hu-man*. I am still a reputable creature. A lady, if you will. I don't go around with men that are not my kind." She stands up, grasping the hammock. Her fingers come together making a fist, arresting the strands of hammock within her fingers. The hammock strings pull away from underneath him. She pulls harder. His expression is comical, as so she laughs at him.

Fallen to the grassy floor, his body lays motionless. He inspects for bruises. Finding none, but the soreness of his hind side, he smiles thinking to himself that at least he has asked for it.

Bending at the waist, chuckling, she smiles down at him and extends her hand to him in a gesture of friendship. Agreeably he accepts her gesture and allows himself to be pulled up to her level. The wind plays lightly with her hair. "You read my thoughts well." He tells her. "Is there a way that I can prevent you from being able to do that?"

"Oui!"

"What is it?"

"I'm not telling you." (smiling) Still not having forgotten that he claimed his parent's deaths, he reaches out with her the back finger dragging them across her face lightly. Her eyes close slowly accepting his soothing caress. In the back of her mind she knows, that the others would not agree to this. But she holds prestige among warriors and being that her mission is more important than the feelings at hand, she will chance at the pleasures a man can submit. After all, as she recalls, the males have often boasted about how human women would squirm like worms in their hands. Melting from the inside out, ready for the embrace. Then of coarse! The subtle seduction, which would lead to their deaths. This is no different. Except, maybe, that she would prefer to see him grow old and by her side.

"I'm-" he begins, but finds himself interrupted by the gentle pressure of her lips. She places the delicate kiss onto them. He is taken by surprise. The kiss is short lived and Brahnt feels her cool breath escaping her mouth. Cooling to senses, it leaves behind only the moisture her lips. Looking deeper into his eyes, she is flattered.

"I'm flattered Brahnt, but I'm definitely not your type." Her tone of voice is one that is both pleasurably sexy and yet defiant.

"I don't- I mean I know." His voice stutters.

"You are a sweet man Brahnt. If I could remove your pain, I would."

"If I could take your hell with me, I would." Brahnt presses his hand onto her face. It feels cool and pleasurable.

The wind blows with its generous collection of night fragrances stolen from those, whose breath is released and surrendered to its many hands. The stars each show their brightest faces, hoping to enlighten the world with their subtle knowledge and their deep sense of emotion. The moon's glow creates images of softness and draws their attention.

With all of the elements surrounding them, perhaps they cannot be united by the road of pleasure a man and woman can feel, but they know that they have bonded for the while by means of their hope, their dreams, and their compassion. If not carnal love born, then spiritual love will come to rise and pronounce itself the sole victor of this evening. Slipping his arms around her, as she stares into the moon she feels a sense of safety. Not safety from the evil villains that may be planning their death or safety from the unknown dangers that will lurk in their adventure, but one that allows her the escape from the pain and suffering she has known since birth.

Two lost creatures, one soulless by art of birth and the other who has lost his soul, tonight, share and fill each other with what each has longed for. Though many secrets still pass between them, one key has unlocked the magic that holds the universe together. Both knowing that moments are to be cherished and maintained for as long as they are beautiful, they sit there with barely a word to say. For moments like these are seldom expressed not with words, but with feelings.

Much like a candle dimming it's life into darkness, the night fades into darkness sealed with a kiss.

Chapter 8

Watching over Brahnt

I Can

Because of your strength,
I can see a better future.
Because I can see that I can rely on you,
I can plan for the future.
Because I can speak to you,
I can I know you are real.
Because I can rely on you,
You are my friend.

The Calm before the Storm

Subtly, steam rises from the trees. Droplets of water, collected throughout the night, fall to the ground, gracefully and unhurried. Birds rustle within the leaves of the trees, singing their morning songs. The wind carries a sense of life and though it moves delicately, all of life is aware of its presence. Warm delicate fingers spreading their gentle caress. Between strands of hair and loose clothing, both Melonnie and Brahnt move about slowly, suspended in the air by the hammock, they rest still and lifeless, much like most of their sleepy surroundings. Her body gently presses against his and as they both move closer together, comforting each other, she awakens slowly. Her brow presses downward, while her nose twitches almost unnoticeably and she stretches her hand over his body for a firmer hold. Coming to life, she opens one eye at a time.

Blinking twice, she focuses on the figure before her. A smile breaks the mold of sleepiness and brings new meaning to a new day. This is the first time she has smiled from the heart in a long time. His scent is raw and undeniably attractive. But she does not forget, that he is not of her kind. Inhaling a deep breath of morning freshness into her lungs, the expanding of her body cautions Brahnt to awaken. Quickly she closes her eyes, pretending to sleep.

He, unlike her, awakens with all of his senses alerted. His eyes are ready and focused. There is very little muscular twitching. In fact it would seem that he is only idling instead of truly sleeping. However, this could be furthest from the truth. The truth of the matter is, he feels more alive than ever. He has never rested with such peace. Inhaling his first deep breath of air. He releases the words-"Good morning Mel."

"How did you know that I was not asleep?"

"Your heartbeat. Your scent, the relaxed sensation of your hands. Need I say more?"

"No. What is your trade Brahnt?"

"Do I really have to tell you?"

"Non. Are you a policeman?"

"No. Why do you ask?"

"Well. You carry a gun." She says to him making firm eye contact.

"No. I'm not a policeman."

"Alright then. Why do you have a gun?"

"My job requires it." His tone of voice is matter of fact, as if having no importance.

"Bon! My curiosity has been satisfied." Her eyes move down his arm and notice that his hand is resting lifeless on her hip. "How close do I feel to the real thing?"

"Excuse me?" he says caught off guard. (looking down at his hand) "Very close. As a matter of a fact, so close that I couldn't tell the difference."

"You toy with me?" She shoves at him with her elbows. He smiles at her tight-lipped.

"No I'm not. You feel just like a woman. Actually, given all the (his finger tips travels up her back and down to her waist) muscularity you have. You are a hell of a lot better than most women."

"And how many women have you been with?" She asks.

"Many. But I'm a vampire virgin."

"Bon. I'm a human virgin. (realizing he is teasing her) What are we talking about?" Kicking up with her right leg, she twirls and flips out of the hammock and onto her feet. Brahnt is impressed.

"Neat acrobatics!"

"Physics my friend and a few hundred years of practice."

"Wait! No magic or supernatural powers on that one?"

"Nope! One hundred percent natural. (she whispers) But don't tell the others. They really hate it when I do things the hard way."

"Why do you do it then?"

"For the thrill of defeat!" She says proudly. Fixing her clothing, Brahnt contemplates what she has done. He kicks up one of his legs and leaps much in the fashion she has. Landing on his feet, he too feels proud. Turning around, she looks at him with greater pride. She smirks. Then grins. The corner of her mouth icons the seal of approval. But they know that there is business at hand that cannot rely on swift acrobatics.

Dried leaves and tired twigs break, bringing sounds of caution to their ear. The sounds seem to be coming from a four-legged mammal. Brahnt studies the timing each footfall. Melonnie's attention diverts to the end of the hammock. "Did you make this?" She asks, ignoring his concern.

"Yes. I did." He answers quietly. The shrubs before him open and produce another being dressed in a white dress.

"Good morning, Cousin!" Melonnie turns to face the woman's voice.

"Good morning, Samantha!" She yells. They run into each other's arms embracing one another with great energy. The sounds of bodies pressing and lips kissing, brings a feeling of joy that even Brahnt can understand.

"It's been so long! (Samantha pushes her tears away) How long will you be staying?" She asks.

"Only a few moments. I'm on a mission."

"When will I be old enough to mission as well?"

"Next session. I promise. (placing her hand on Samantha's head) I will teach you myself."

"I wish it was now." She says almost pleading.

"It's not you. It's the mission." Her tone is regrettable and yet happy. Brahnt stands by, collecting the pieces. "And you? You didn't explain anything to him?"

"It's only a joke. He says such nice things about all of us. (reaching over to her and whispering) But I think he has a crush on you." Samantha leans back. Melonnie looks at Brahnt (he smiles back at her) and then to Samantha. Swinging playfully, she smacks Samantha's shoulder.

"We will leave soon." She says still with a smile on her face.

"Sure thing Melonnie. We have acquired a vehicle for you."

"Oh?" She questions.

"Oh! Yea! You'll love it! You do know how to drive? Or has this charming man been your chauffeur?"

"No. I can handle a car."

"This is no car ! This is a CAR."

"Quit! Show me what you got." Melonnie fills of anticipation.

"Come on I'll show you!" Samantha leads the way to it.

"Melonnie?" Asks Brahnt. "How much time do we have?"

"About two days. Why?"

"I'd like to take you out someplace familiar to me. Maybe get you a nice dress. Maybe go see a movie. Just something to give you a taste of my world." He looks onward, as if uninterested in her answer.

"Are you asking me out?"

"Oui." He says to her. "I know where they've built this mall. It's not like back home but, it's close enough and who knows you might like it."

"I cannot believe you!" Her mouth still open, she pokes at his shoulder. "You might think that you are trying to impress me." She says out loud.

"He's good at that!" -Sam

"Stay out of it Sam." He shoots back, slightly embarrassed.

"I'd take him up on it. One of you might get lucky." -Sam

"Sam!" Both Brahnt and Melonnie yell out. Looking at each other. All three laugh. Samantha touches her nose and winks her eye.

"We can spend an hour or two there. Who knows what will happen shortly there after?" They continue to walk muttering, laughing.

[The Drive]

Having driven many miles towards the nearest city, Brahnt wrestles uncomfortably within the restrictions of the passenger seat. Melonnie looks at him with great curiosity. But for now, she feels the frustrations of having called his name several times. Consumed by the dark cloud that incarcerates his soul, he moves about struggling to awaken.

"Took you long enough to answer! I thought you were still in a coma. (she takes a breath) Look, I'm sorry! I didn't mean to drag you into this as I did. I have been under a lot of pressure to do the right thing. And frankly it is your own fault. You humans are so complicated. The wars I have been fighting will never end. These wars have been happening since the beginning of time and will until the end of time."

"My hat!" He screams out spontaneously, startling her. In a panic, she presses hard on the brake and clutch. Sliding off of his seat by the force of the vehicle, Brahnt's body jerks forward. His head strikes the window and in the same motion the weight of his body falls back into the passenger seat. The throbbing pain prompts his hand to cover the pain. She on the other hand does not move, and remains frozen in place. Her arms are locked into place and are frozen of all motion.

With fear and apprehension, he reaches over to her sculptured like body. With barely a touch of his fingertips, she explodes. "It's in the back seat! Look I don't want to hurt you.

You are a nice guy and all. I really didn't mean to run you over or even to bite you on the roof. I mean, maybe if I were hungry. I mean..."

"It's OK. I'm OK. You're OK. (reaching behind the seat and taking his flattened hat) My hat is...OK?"

"I'll take you to the nearest town and drop you off. But I won't be able to be with you- I want to be with you."

Taking her hand into his, he whispers poetry to her ear.

"There must have been a million and one ways to create a
Woman during the beginning of time.
And when God controlled all there was,
He could not make his mind.

I know this!

For since man seems to be of a general kind,
Woman could never be figured.
Though there are many beautiful flowers adorning the world,
Mine is the most blossomed of all.

And let us consider that some flowers may bloom for a shorter while than others may.

My flower blooms longer than all.
Truth being bare and unharmed, the flower's bloom is not tangible to reality, but to man senses

His words enchant her as if medicine has been spoken from a mystical healer. She calms to the tone of his voice, while looking into his eyes, spellbound.

"That (she chokes) is beautiful. I haven't heard something like that since France, 1848." She says still taken by the moment.

"France? 1848? Just how old do you think you are?"

"Twenty-nine?" She brazenly snaps at him.

"Why you don't look twenty-nine." Taking a deep breath, she anticipates his next phrase.

"Well I'm not thirty human years either!" She slaps his arm.

"I didn't say anything!" Amazed.

"You thought it! And that's bad enough. (looking at the window) And just who do you thing you are breaking my window?"

"I'm not sure I caught that!" He snaps back at her.

"You broke my window! Look! There. (pointing) See?"

"And what did you do?" He asks with sarcasm.

"You shouldn't push it! I'm on cycle!"

"Your nuts?" He says pretending to have asked a serious question.

"No really!" She says equally as serious.

"You're really nuts?" His voice fluctuates nervously.

"Look you! Men don't have the knowledge to understand these things. I don't care how unnatural they are." She presses on the gas pedal.

"You mean your menstruation?" He speaks to her, but she is too busy to give her full attention.

"Oui!" She says unaware of the question.

"I thought you were going loony. (he pushes the hair from his face away from his eyes) Though who knows it's probably the same."

"What? What are you muttering? For your information I picked you up. I saved your life!" She says, concentrated.

"You ran *me* over lady!" He reminds her.

"You were probably already road kill!" Her voice is settling but obviously upset. There is immediate silence in the cab. The mile marker passes them by, one at a time.

Realizing she is being too aggressive, she looks over to him with softer eyes and a kinder expression. "I'm sorry." A pause.

"What?" He says still ill tempered.

"Let's make a new start? (she inhales deeply) Melonnie. My name is Melonnie. I am a vampire on a quest to take the Book of Vigore to the Vampiric Council. It is said that the Book of Vigore may show us how to defeat him, before he enslaves humanity. I was born under the Aries constellation. How do you do?" She says politely. Brahnt smiles at the sudden shift in mood.

"My name is Brahnt. I work on international backgrounds. I am what you call an international assassin. I am also an Aries. I was born April 4th. I think I was born under a full moon." He taps the window with his knuckle. "Maybe we should park the car here and chat. We could enjoy the rain for a minute." He receives no immediate answer.

"How about the car?" Her voice is spontaneous.

"Oh the car won't mind. It's wet too."

"No stupid! (pushing at him) Can we sit in this dry car? Besides you might catch a cold and I really should help you to the next town. You perhaps have human needs to tend."

"Does it look like I need to go to a hospital?"

"Well you do have that bump on your head which could use some attention and you do look feverish." She says with a kind gesture, watching him wipe the mixture of sweat and blood off of his forehead.

"All gone. Besides, it's nothing that some good (she anticipates a sexual remark) conversation and exercise won't handle." She exhales with the sigh of relief.

"Sorry!" She smiles remembering his bruised head. He holds it as her look reminds him of it too. The lightning illuminates the clouded skies, the soaked trees, the drowning streets and their faces within the vehicle.

Taking a closer look at her beautiful eyes, he releases his frustration. The raindrops fall heavy against the car, drumming their way into their hypnotic silence.

"What are you thinking?" She asks him.

"Nothing."

"Something is inside that mind of yours."

"Yes there is."

"What is it then?"

"Just stupid words."

"Napkin poetry?" She asks wide-eyed.

"Yea."

"Say it then. Don't you know that women are attracted to intelligently beautiful words?"

"You really like the words?"

"Oui. Beaucoup." (Very much). He takes a moment of composure and with a single slow and seductive breath he releases the words.

"Soft are the words
Spoken from your eyes,
Violet is the flower
Your words reflect.
And to this I say
I see kindness
Glowing from your heart.
This is rare
And this is beautiful,
It is kind and it should be what
The world be made of."

"That is just so beautiful." She says with slight tears in her eyes.

"It is napkin poetry." -Brahnt

"It is passion."

"It is paper and ink."

"It's living."

"It's dead rejected tree parts."

"It's... it's... romantic."

"It's true. (her mouth opens and closes quickly) No, it's true. I'm a hopeless romantic." He says finally surrendering to her.

"Hopeless? Helpless is more like it." She smiles at him and he receives it in good humor.

"Yea.. yea.. I never get passed first base." Hearing his sentence come to an end, she slows the car to a stop. There is a little abruptness to the halt; he grabs his forehead. "With the whole world singing to a song that has no rhythm, I can only feel the despair left as residue from their- so called enjoyment of life."

"You're not telling me you haven't had sex before?"

"God no! Not at all, I've just never fallen in love before." His tenor is witness to obvious suffering. Once again Melonnie senses the dark cloud that looms within his head, like a void of a memory long forgotten. Perhaps he even doesn't know that it is there.

"You're cute. Tell me about your up-bringing."

"Well I was born a poor boy. But in France, aren't we all poor? (he sighs) My father moved to America to find a good job. But he drank more wine than I care to mention. Doctors say that wine is good for the heart. But it was his liver that gave way in the end. But he was peaceful. Of course there was the time he set fire to the neighbor's garage. He does claim, however, that it was an accident. Knowing my father, it probably wasn't. He worked at a factory on the assembly line. And though he made lots of money, no one ever knew where it went. He said that a dime here and a dime there was chewing away his trying to save" They look at each other, simultaneously saying "But it was that old pink elephant, singing to him. 'Let me be, let me be."

"You've heard the story before?" He asks her.

"Non. Non. Please go on!"

"Now mom, on the other hand, was the worlds greatest mom! She knew how to cook, though whenever dad wasn't busy sitting he could stir up some mean grub."

"That's funny! 'Stir up some mean grub.'" She laughs.

"Oh! Yea, she was a good cook. That's until I was old enough to make my own money and have a girlfriend. I started taking myself out to hamburger joints. Then I looked at mom's cooking a second time."

"You don't mean that?"

"Oh ye'per mam. I started hitting me Kentucky Fried Chicken, Wendy's, Taco Express and all that fast food. That's until mother died." His tone becomes gloomy.

"You didn't grow up in France?"

"No. I grew up in America."

"How did you get to France?"

"I told you. I'm a man of international mystery."

"So please continue with your story."

"She died. Then dad died! They were good folks all the way around. I ended up going to a juvenile home and finally a family adopted me and gave me a chance to live again. It wasn't the same. But, it was all I had. All the reality I could hang to, at the age of nineteen (she smiles lightly remembering her youth). I remember one day we decided all to go to the amusement park. It was quite a ways. But, my parents didn't mind. I was twenty-two and they were on their second child hood. We were singing cartoon songs all the way through to the next state. We came up over a railroad crossing. The tracks were on a small hill and we couldn't see the other side. We cleared the hill and when we came over we met head to head with another vehicle. (closing his eyes and covering his face) The two cars were lifted from the ground and I was thrown from the rear window. (looking into the rain) I shook myself from the gravel and stared at the two falling cars. They hit the ground at the same time and out of nowhere they both caught fire. The concussion threw me off a few feet. I went into a coma for one-hundred eighty days."

"Tell me no more." She places her fingers on his lips.

"Well it doesn't matter. I lost at least fifteen years of my memory. Most of my life, after that, I've spent putting my memories together out of scraped up flash-backs and stories told to me by relatives." He rolls down his window. The rain passes the once barrier. She turns to face him and catches the back of his head. He jumps out of the car and runs in front of it. Starting to dance, he attempts to sooth his pain.

"Êtes-vous tombé sur la tête?" (Are you crazy?) She asks with great enthusiasm.

"No! I'm not food!" He says misinterpreting her.

"No! Man. Are you crazy?"

"Crazy? You're the repressed woman! Don't you know nature?"

"Only too well! Get in!" - Melonnie

"I want to dance and feel the tiny feet of swelled cloud tears to fall on my skin. Kissing my body with their small blessing."

"Look you! I'm in a hurry!"

"OK. OK. Let's go find a place to eat." He runs to the car, bends and enters."

"Rest!" She snaps.

"*You* can rest." She steps on the gas. The car begins to move once again. The rain changes to drizzle, but the lightning continues dominating the sky.

What's the hurry?

"It's about that time and I don't have the strength love."

"But it's that special moment when all poets feel talons tear out the saddened heart and for a brief moment we die into the hands of hope and a new day."

"Sun light just kills me!" She says sarcastically. "There should be a motel about three more miles from here. Look it up will you?" He looks around aimlessly.

"The map is in that compartment. (she points to the glove box)" Opening the glove compartment and searching about, he finds it. She watches him amazed at what he's done. She reaches under the lamp as if exploring it.

"It says you started your journey where this 'X' is, but there is nothing there. No town. No village. Melonnie, this is an old map- (looking up at her he catches sight of her seriousness. There is a light mist forming on her skin.

"Just find the room and board!"

"OK! Relax a little. OK?"

"OK. Sorry. Tell me now, where is it? (kindly and patiently) Sweetheart I haven't fed yet. That means that if the sun rises, I will become ash unless I find someone to kill. Get it?"

"Shit!" He gives her directions, as the purple, red, orange, and yellow glow of the sun's rising, warms the clouds and begins to converse with the land. The land responds releasing captured vapors. Reluctantly, it rises, evaporating into nothingness. He contemplates the settling as she pulls hard to the left and into the motel lot.

"Ow! (holding his head)"

"Pay for the room (she throws him a wallet) and don't disturb me. Make it separate rooms. I don't think you'll like me in a few minutes." The car comes to a skidding halt, inches in front of the management's office. He looks over to the driver's seat. No one is there. His door opens. He feels a tug on his right shoulder and suddenly finds himself afoot. She rushes him inside, to the registration desk. Frantically she slaps down on the bell. Stepping out from the back room, an elderly man comes forward slowly making his way behind the desk. He opens the registry book with equal care.

"You have a room for us. (she says confidently) Room 27 and- the next available.

"I'll take the one next to that." Brahnt says with a tendency towards doubt.

Turning to where he believed her to be standing, he is surprised that she has gone. With no one else to turn to, he lifts his head to the clerk. The attendant responds with an inquisitive raise of the eyebrow.

Opening the door to her room, she walks towards the bed and takes it by one of its posts. Dragging it to the window, she lifts the end opposite the window. The bed serves as a blockade. Her back slams against the door, with gestures of relief. Feeling her knees shake, she slides down from the door and onto the floor. Her face and hands become clammy. Sweat makes its first appearance. Remaining on the floor, she crawls to the center of the room.

Outside her door, Brahnt hears her screams along with the sound of something else.

"Melonnie?"

"Get out of here (crying). Get the hell out of here! Merde!"

Without another word he turns to leave. With his feelings obviously injure, he walks away while reaching his fingers into his pocket for his room key.

With keys in hand, he reaches the door to his room and pushes in the key. The warm key slithers into the lock, but his mind is numb to the matter. He is more concerned about the charmingly strange young woman in the next room. He shakes his head, turns the key, and pushes the door inward. Darkness. A bit of light from the drawn window shades. His eyes still unadjusted to the light, guide his body to the wallpaper. Leaning closer, his tired and bruised head leans to it.

The sound of running water masks what seems to be wood splitting, in the next room. 'Wait! Water? That sound is not coming from the wall', he mutters. His hands pass by way of his waist and into his shoulder holster. Feeling the weapon secured around his fingers, he walks towards the bathroom as quietly as he can. Each step moves with precise accountability. Stepping on the sides of his feet and rolling onto the ball of his foot, his movement becomes stealth like. There is a dim light coming from underneath the door and its boarders. Once at the frame of the door, he pauses. 'I'll wait for him to come to me.'

Another sound catches his attention. He decides to surprise the intruder, instead. Reaching down he opens the door suddenly. A flash of white, flesh, and dark hair. A woman! She lifts her eyes to meet with his. Realizing she is sitting on the toilet with her thighs exposed, she stretches her skirt and blouse over her exposed skin. Her dark coffee brown eyes meet up to his, catching a glimpse of his embarrassment. He pulls away from the door. Placing his back against the wall, he takes a deeper breath and releases the hold on his pistol. He can hear her wrestling in the bathroom.

Stepping out of the bathroom, she lowers her head and walks up to him. Collecting her pride, she realizes that this is a good-looking man. And an elegantly dressed one as well. She raises her eyes to him.

"I'm sorry sir. 'Didn't know this room was rented out to-."

"It's OK- I should have knocked." He says to her allowing her to escape her comment.

"We don't receive a lot of day or early morning-" She says making her way to the exit door.

"I just naturally assumed-" He interrupts.

"And-" She opens the door and takes a glance back at him. Her eyes lock dead into his. Her mouth opens slightly lowering her jaw line and so does his." But the moment is too brief. Their recognition ends. She bows her head and makes her way out the door. Entering the bathroom, he too escapes fleeing his embarrassment.

Stopping at the door just before closing it, she comes to a dead stop and contemplates the event. 'I didn't do anything so bad'. Her eyebrows lifts remembering his facial features, but even a novice reader could read her changed expression. (the toilet flushes) "Damn!" She grits her teeth, bringing the door to a close. He on the other hand is able to erase his blushing face with soap, water and a washrag. Facing the mirror and clearing the soap residue, he takes a short recess while dragging his comb across his head. Realizing he is tired, he determines a nap would be a good idea…

[Waking]

The ticking of a clock. A warm muggy feeling. A sour taste in his mouth. Light. A deep breath fills his lungs and with it the feeling of a comfortable stretch. Mental images of his whereabouts. Rubbing his eyes and passing his hands across his chest, he feels the subtle sensation of a burning stomach, yearning for a good meal. The thin, smooth blanket covering his otherwise naked body is barely noticeable to him. Throwing it to the side, he rolls over to the edge of the bed. Observing only one hand in front of him, he searches for the other. Finding it and securing his holstered pistol he smiles at himself "I can't even sleep without being paranoid." He bends his knees, and lunges his weight onto the hardwood floors.

With them firmly planted on the floorboard, he stretches his body upwards flexing his muscularity. Shifting his weight he moves slowly toward the bathroom. Naked and aware of his surroundings, he moves his eyes about searching for anything of an inconsistency. Moving his eyes up towards the clock, he realizes that he has hours left before Melonnie is able to come out of hiding and the thought of that scares him a little. As he didn't understand her hurry, he wonders if perhaps she'll need to feed. 'Perhaps this will be my last day on Earth. Perhaps it will be the beginning. Whatever the case it will be a complete surprise.' And he is not the kind of guy to up and leave. 'Besides, I can run, but I can't hide. Not if she didn't let me.' He rubs his eye and enters the bathroom. Remembering the innkeeper, he shakes his head and smirks. Reaching down he takes a hold of a complimentary package. There within the plastic is soap, toothbrush and a tiny squeeze of toothpaste. Washing his face and brushing his teeth, he can't but feel the redundant efforts of human life.

The palm of his hand cups the larger towel set aside on a plastic rod, he wipes his face. Then looking into the mirror he admires the jail that keeps him prisoner of the planet. His body is truly the ultimate killing machine or at least so he thinks for the moment. If he were Melonnie, he truly would make the difference to the planet. He would kill all those who caused harm and control the safety of the world. But perhaps that would be too ludicrous. As in his profession, he is sure that she had enemies of her own. And worse yet, he would probably meet them soon. 'So let's eat while I still can.' Walking over to the clothes rack, he pulls his clothes from the hooks. Slipping on his dark pants, a leg at a time, he inspects his muscular legs, knowing that they will be of use to him later. Lifting his pants above his waist, he allows the pants to rest while he reaches for his white shirt. Tucking it in, he fastens his pants and then finishes buttoning it, securing his automatic into its holster and then underneath the dresser.

Lending a glance at his jacket, he decides to take his wallet and keys and leave the jacket. Closing the door behind him, he stares at the distance for a moment and remembers the beautiful colors that make the day have its glamour. But it will be night soon again and he can only imagine what mysteries Melonnie will reveal to him this evening. He turns his head towards room 27 one more time. Not understanding much else, he turns to the restaurant and continues his walk. "At least I won't die hungry." He smirks at fate.

[Evening falls]

Brahnt has eaten his meal. And now sitting in the small confines of his room, he waits for the next event to take place. Watching time pass him by as the sun slowly sinks into the horizon, there is a feeling of anticipation. On the table is coffee and bread, which he dips slowly. The door creaks open, and carefully placed footsteps press on the wood floor. Though his back is towards the door, he can sense that it is her. He questions his feelings for her and he smiles thinking of her. Her gentle manner is one that intoxicates him with feelings never experienced before. Once at his shoulder, she touches him lightly. Without looking at her, she speaks to him.

"Brahnt?" She calls out to him, searching for a sign of invitation.

"Yes?" He responds to her with a relief.

"May I sit?"

"Yes please." His words are carefully pronounced.

"I'm sorry for being abrupt, earlier today. It was rather urgent that I left the area. It's still not safe."

"Why? What's the matter?"

"I have not eaten for days. I get weak if I don't eat for long periods at a time."

"So why didn't you eat?"

"Brahnt you just don't understand! We are not a cult- a clan- a sect! You just cannot make a category and reduce us to a religious superstition! We have a history. We have a need. We have a reason to be here!" Her words are compassionate and he knows them to be the truth.

"I don't know." He replies honestly.

"What the hell do you think we are?"

"Servants of Evil? (he sits deeper into his chair) I don't know." He closes with an apologetic tone.

"Evil Brahnt?" Brahnt raises an eyebrow and watches as she rubs her face and pulls away her hair attractively. "And when have you ever touched evil to know what evil is?"

"I know about evil!"

"What may that be?"

"Thou shall not kill!" He says reaching out for an answer.

"Come now! Look who's talking! If that is the bases of your argument, I may as well let you go here." She pulls herself out of her chair. Reaching out to her arm, he prevents her from leaving.

"It's not what I meant."

"When a tiger hungers and feeds from a man, woman, or child, in neighboring villages is that Evil?"

"That is *so* different!" He says to her hoping that her next words will convince him.

"Oh! How is that so different?"

"That's the way things are because of nature."

"Oui! An ant can lift ten times its weight. How much weight can you lift. Are you saying that we are not natural?"

"Mel, how can you call yourself natural when you're nearly impossible to kill, you have no religious boundaries, you defy gravity, you pray on innocent people."

"That's not true. You have been mislead. That, is the weakness of your kind. If you are not on top of the food chain, you panic like little children. I do what I do to obtain my needs. Pas rein!" (Nothing more!)

"And what is that to mean?"

"No Brahnt 'what has that meant'. You eat helpless cows!"

"For substance. And leave hamburgers out of it! (remembering his previous hamburger battle)" He rocks back into his chair and crosses his arms. "Melonnie, the books, the stories… They come from some place?"

"Yes and when your kind went through the Spanish Inquisition? What of WWI, WWII? The search for righteousness? The witch hunts? These are only a few of the things your kind is responsible for. These things don't happen because humanity has the answers to everything. You know that. What we do is no different than what you do to survive."

"Vlad the Impeller?" He shakes his finger at her, taunting and realizing that she has long won the argument.

"Gangues Kahn, Mussolini? Besides Vlad was an idiot. He wanted to be like us. He never even had a clue."

"You make it sound like you are part of the Eco system. You pose a good argument!" He stands up and motions to the door.

"Brahnt sit." She points her finger at the chair.

"No thanks!"

"I could make you sit you know!" She waves her fist at him.

"On second thought. Thank you very much. Is sitting here OK?" His sarcasm accompanies him, as he re-plants himself. "Yeah Sure."

"Brahnt. When God created the world in seven days. He had no idea of time. And we also did not. We could have been there for centuries before the beginning of the next day. Days are in linear time."

"In other words time exists because we begin and end." Brahnt nods back at her, showing her that he understands the concepts.

"Yes, and when you lived among the first creations there was no death. No pain. No hunger." Her words sink into his heart, while only one thought comes to his mind. The thought that only a fool in love would dare dream.

"No time! And does this tie in somewhere?" He says trying to mask his thoughts and feelings.

"We were there before man! We had these glorious six to eight foot wing span."

"Angels?"

"No. Just creations with no names. We played all day and danced in the skies until morning. Then came Adam, giving everything names. He called us Creatures that dance with the angels, Angelica as we have become to be known. We were happy! Then shortly after came woman and woman was *good* for Adam."

"I've heard enough!" he exclaims.

"Brahnt close your eyes now and be mortal, filled with superstition for eternity or open them and at the very least walk on the Dark Side of truth." She leans over the table, taking in a closer view of his beautiful eyes. A few strands of hair fall to his forehead. "Don't forget ancient history! Just a moment before Apollo made its first journey to the moon. Many people did not believe! Remember? Remember Mathew?"

"Mathew who?" The name sounds distantly familiar.

"A small island near Korea."

"You?" He says remembering the story told to him by his foster parents. It was something about a woman that saved his grandfather's life.

"No but someone like me. Most of our kind, do not want the human race to disappear. Watch closely. I will be able only to hold this for a little while." She takes a deep breath of air. Holding it, she begins to change. Her hair turns to a darker black showing blue highlights. Her complexion becomes lighter. The shape of her beautiful eyes turn Asian. Sitting still and bewildered, he says nothing. He admires her powerful ability. Speaking to him in Korean, he understands not a single word she says. However, he is marveled and entranced, as she grins at him with a devilish smile. She can feel his heart throbbing with excitement.

"How do you do that? How do you know?"

"We have many different talents." She tells him.

"Oh yea. I forgot how old you really are!" At that remark, her body changes to her original form. Startled by her abrupt behavior, he is forced back into the chair. Splitting the wooden backrest.

"Oh Brahnt! (her eyes gloss) Vous-êtes impossible! You are an impossible little man! (her fangs erect slightly) Why? (her view becomes keen) Get out!" She says stopping her foot down and pointing at the door. Brahnt stands, but makes no immediate motion to the door. She stomps her foot down again and insures that he sees her finger pointing at the door. Taking a step forward he glances at her again. Again she stomps her foot and points at the door.

With nothing left to say, he rushes to the door and slams it behind him. Pressing his back against it, he breathes deeply.

The old custodian approaches his way making his way to the cafeteria. Without effort, he allows his rusted grin to appear on his face. (Melonnie's hand paws at the top of the dresser, swatting at the night lamp. It crashes against the door and Brahnt feels the blow) His eyes close expressing his uncertainty. As the Elder passes Brahnt, he holds his finger to the air. "Women are men's route to evil." Normally Brahnt might have agreed. But it was obvious that the old man didn't know this one. Or did he?

"You haven't the idea, old man." He replies softly, staring into the cold beginnings of the night.

Tracking the old man, as he walks in the direction of the cafeteria, he notices another figure standing at the edge of the railing. He is almost motionless and has cloaked himself with the darkness. His wool jacket and wool pants, make him seem slim and tall. His hair pushed back tightly to his cranium hint subtly at the rays of the moon. Brahnt pulls the door closed. As if guarding it, he places his broad back against it.

"Tell me?" his words catch Brahnt's attention.
"Is it to fantasy or reality?
That should have been Hamlet's question.
Of a blissful and ignorant life!
I cannot be Hamlet or he I.
"Aye!" But one thing we do share in common! We are both the shell of a man intending to be.
That is his 'to be or not to be' soliloquy.
Tell me Brahnt
Can God or man say what should the statement of truth be when he a king crowned of kings lives not among man and has a voice not heard!

And as to man what can puny man-describe when his eye is smaller than the universe, smaller than the moon, (he points to Melonnie's room) smaller than the shelter of this room."

He walks away and Brahnt is left to his own solitude, at least for the time, his mind wanders into the universe of words and meaning.

"And so I leave my chamber to enter the world, to find that the world has entered me." Brahnt turns to the door and walks towards it. Placing his hand against the doorknob, he pushes it open. The lamp lies still on the floor. Noticing a dark shadow against the corner of the room, Brahnt reaches down for the lamp. He places it to its original resting place.

Melonnie turns away from him, hiding her face in the corner. "You make me feel like a monster."

"You're no monster. I am." He answers

"Yes you are."

"I don't mean to offend you. I'm just afraid. I am only human. You are so much greater than I could ever be." His voice is soothing to her hurt emotions.

"You fear me?" She asks carefully.

"I fear that I will not be able to defend you against your enemies and against this great battle. I fear I'll let you down."

"I'll protect you. And if I die it will be your fault. I just want you to accept me and my fate, just as we are. Death comes to us all." He opens his arms.

"How can I say that I'm sorry?"

"Like this." She walks over to him and embraces him. The moment lasts forever.

Chapter 9

Melonnie's Rage

Soon to Victory

The arms of darkness soon cover the land
In as fury and rebellion against the light day.

The moon defies its total victory.
It is here, in the shadows,
That live most men.
Torn between good and evil,
Between love and hate.

Squeezed between the arms of fate!

L'eua de Toilet

The air is dense and heavy. Again it looks like it may rain. Brahnt turns to the road leading to the mall. The parking lots are divided by a bed of large rocks, framed by a layer of cement and Melonnie takes notice of it. Brahnt cruises by a few empty lanes of parking. "This is the fun part of the mall. People try to find a parking spot near the entrance. I don't get it. Park and walk is all I need. Look at that one there, Mel." He points at a white Oldsmobile. Inside there is an older man and as they pass them by, she looks inside.

"Do people actually wait there?"
"Like walking is a crime." He says sarcastically.
"Here's a parking. B4!"
"Before what?" She asks
"Just B4. Melonnie." he says assuring her.
"I know. But before what?"
"There's (he points at the sign) our parking spot."
"I knew that!" She says proudly.

Smiling he opens his door and rushes over to unlock her door. She watches as the romantic fool, rushes to open her door. "Well look at you. Monsieur! S'il vous plaît!"

Melonnie steps out of the car. She looks up at the tall brown metal lamps, "electricity right?

"Yup. Very common today." - Brahnt

"I knew this would happen. Can you imagine what it will be like in another hundred years?"

"I should be so lucky." He says sarcastically.

"I'm sorry - Human."

"Human?" He inquires, taking offense.

"Yes you are human."

"I used to think that was a bad thing. Today I think it is a wonderful thing. You're (he pulls her closer) the odd ball lady." He looks on to the structure ahead. Looking on she notices the blends of stone and metal together. Protruding from the stone, like a glass canopy, is a structure never seen to her. Glass is suspended by more brown metal, riveted in place, softening the glow of light spinning. Within the spinning carousel she sees children, parents, men and women, and possibly lovers.

Melonnie and Brahnt, hand in hand, make their way to the Eastern Mall. The glass doors, framed with their aluminum alloy, respond to Brahnt's push. Melonnie's eyes open large. Ahead the doors there are still other doors, but the images are clearer. Lights of many shapes and subtle illumination make for an excitement never before felt. Plants are strategically placed - a self-contained habitat. The sounds of laughter and confusion fill her ear not of war and death - but of life and joy. "This is fantastic." Her hands meet and together and both of them meet her chin. The glossy eyes become more reflective. The tears of excitement are more noticeable now. "I can't believe all the food here!" She looks at Brahnt's twisted and confused expression.

"You're not thinking - "

"I'm kidding Brahnt." He shakes his head (reaching for his jacket pocket) giving her his pair of Gargoyles Sunglasses.

"What are these for?" She says looking into his eyes. Puzzled, her eyes flicker back and forth for a brief moment, looking at each on of his eyes. "Oh! Yeas of course!" She puts them on. (the second doors open) She gently strikes her head with her hand, "that's right! He is a human, round eye and all- After all I can't show my deep black beautiful eyes. Oh! (she steps into the mall) and he- (she lifts her head) WOW! (she pulls down her sunglasses) This is beautiful!" Raising her body up and down like a young girl, Brahnt smiles at her innocent pleasure.

"Mel? Your shades." One young man passing, staring, notices her eyes, as she sets her eyewear into place. Brahnt snatches a magazine from the hands of a man standing near. Rolling it up, he delicately smacks the boy on the head with it. "Young man? Put your arm around your own girl." He tosses the magazine back to its owner. "Sorry."

Melonnie's eyes come around in time to catch his girlfriend smacking his young man's head. His hair becomes a mess as his girlfriends hand motions back. The young man opens his hand and arms, as if within them is the explanation for his behavior.

"Good for you!" says the man with the magazine. "Protect your beautiful wife." (he opens his hands) Brahnt's eyes recognize the large gold ring on his fat stubby finger, as one from a prestigious country club. He retracts his wrinkled strong hands.

"You see? (Brahnt puts his hands around Melonnie shoulders) We make the perfect couple. But only if they knew." They smile together and walk on.

"Did it take years to build this?" She marvels at the structure.

"Non, ma petite?" (No, my petite) He responds with a bit of flair.

"Where did you pick up that bit of *Français*?" She inquires delighted at his attempts to comfort her.

"TV show, some clown said to a woman with a Valise Verte." (Green suitcase)

"What TV show might this be?" She pokes at his ribs.

"Ah! La vie de Brahnt." (the life of Brahnt)

"There is no show! You like to tease me?"

"I enjoy being with you, Mel. I think you are - Hey look at this!" They walk past the carousel and she takes another glance.

Nothing is said for a moment, as they pass the food court and make their way to the center of the mall.

"Wow this is really beautiful. (standing before a large waterfall)" The sounds of rushing water take to her ear, as would music to a musician. "Can we sit and just enjoy this?"

"Yes."

"It just sounds so perfect. It is so safe. It brings back warm feelings. Pleasures that bring back memories."

"I have a question if you don't mind me asking."

"Go ahead." She says still captured by the sounds.

"Were you there at the beginning?"

"Of what? (silence) Was I the Angelica?" He nods his head lightly. "No I'm much too young. My ancestors had written it and passed it down."

"You have books written?"

"Some of us do. Mostly it was left to the poets of our time. The warriors have other writings." She leans over, placing her elbows to her knees and looking, maybe even examining the floor tile and all of its complicated grooves.

"So how do you remember what happened and how it happened?" She rotates her head to face his.

"It's (pointing to her head) in here."

"Like a story?"

"No like writing. Stored memories. Passed down from mother to daughter from father to son."

"You can have children?" He speaks surprised and with a hidden pride.

"Why are you smirking?"

"I'm not smirking."

"You are too!" He smirks further, hearing her voice and accusation.

"I am not, Mel."

"What do you call that? Tu le fait! (You're doing it!) That is a smirk. Regardez!" (Look!) She says pointing at him.

"OK. So I smirked."

"And what does it mean?"

"I thought you wanted to walk the mall?"

"I'm sorry to embarrass you." Her lips come together, twisting at one corner. "So you are an assassin." He looks at her and then to his surroundings. His lips twist at her verbal freedom.

"Mel. I can die very easily. And you need to remember this. For me all it takes is a bullet, a fall, or a virus. For you it takes an act of God."

"Actually. One sharp cut (she mimics) across my neck like this." He bobs up and down.

"Really?" he asks surprised at the way she drags her finger across her neck.

"Really!" She says mocking his expression.

"Do you like me or something?" He asks her sarcastically.

"I'm in love with you." Her tone is serious and direct, almost expressionless. He swallows hard and sits himself further back in the chair.

"No one's ever had the time to love me, before," he whispers.

"I know! That's because you're an assassin." She makes a gun gesture with her hands.

"Mel? (his mood rises) About my work-"

"J'aimerais te faire l'amour!" (I would love to make love to you!) She says just as seriously.

"You - can't (distracted) tell people that (he brushes his brow), I'm an assa-"

"Maintenant!" (Now!)

"Me too-" he agrees to her. He takes her hand, bringing it closer. Leaning over to her, they come nose to nose. She takes in the sweet scent of his breath. Her face becomes slightly irregular and for a brief instant, there is no clear definition of race or form, revealing of her culture. He anticipates the reception of her spiritual essence. Her red lips widen, blossoming the birth of a Rose. And time stands still. For love knows not time, but only hints at shadowed memories, leaving futures uncertain.

Looking into his eyes, as if seeing beyond, she contemplates the universe while engaged in a moment of stillness. She believes that the gateway to the soul is truly the eyes. His eyes! Their lips near each other. He can feel her cold breath cooling the surface of his skin. His gentler, warmer exhaling breeze, on the other hand, excites her. Glazing her lungs with a hint of life. His life.

Is it her vampiric sense allowing her painting of him to exist within her inner walls? Or the feeling of his pulse, pressed against her face by way of his hands. Her lips tremble. His body comes forward. The wind barrier between them collapses. Life exists no more, as their emotions come together. Time is paused, breaking away from the carnal reality. The lights once illuminating their way, like a sunset, dim and disappear. A moment of stillness as pressing lips collide, his soul into her and is captured. His taste is now permanent within her. The bodies become incorporeal. All that exists is the contact of their lips.

The moment fades with the same gentleness as their engagement.

"Why?" Still lip to lip, her eyes frantically trace the lines of his face. "Parce que je t'adore."

"Pourquoi?"

"Love never has reasons we can understand. Maybe, because of you I can see man in a different way. Unfortunately, I am at war with everything and everyone. It's nice that I have someone at my side. Brahnt, my love, this war is bigger than the casualties at stake. And believe me there have been so many."

"So you have regrets?"

"(she corners a her smile) Yes. Many."

"The only things I do not regret are those of my cause and of my love."

"You are an incredible woman."

"You can call me that?" She laughs, spontaneously.

"Humor me." He says remembering her species.

"When I love, I love for ever."

"And what do you like about me?"

"Well you're strong. You are very nice. Very intelligent. But most of all I love the way you love."

"What do you mean?"

"Your love is like nothing else. You love from the inside first and then it slowly (she runs her fingers down his jacket) it comes outward."

"Slow like, sounds coming from distant halls,
doth love travel and creep to you like silent thieves.
They do rob us of all ill,
And thus love is the food for the souls of man woman and beast a like.
Fools are those wise enough to contain it,
For love brings knowledge of heaven to our hearts.
Ignorant are those that reject it,
For love brings piece and piece can only be measured by moments.
But at last there is the dreamer;
who during his existence he doth chase love;
and once captured he allows its passion to overwhelm him and guide him.
To this dreamer does love have truth of value.
For love loves him best
and loving him doth he understand the elements of emotion."

He tells her, watching a teardrops fall from her eye.

"I only wish that I could be the woman that those words spoken to, and not the Angelica." The right corner of her lip moves slightly upward. "You are a doll. She makes herself more comfortable in her chair, resting in his shoulder.

But her comfortable feeling is soon diminished, as she detects unrest within the crowd. Melonnie grabs Brahnt's hand, leading him into the crowd of moving people. Reaching the rim of her glasses, she pulls them down enough to have a view. "Brahnt, I'm afraid for you."

"What do you mean? For me?"

"I have lived a long and productive life." She whispers making her way through the crowd.

"Mel, I think I know what you mean. But you're not so invincible. How many?" He asks.

"I don't know."

"Can they detect you?"

"I think they can."

"How?"

"I don't know. Smell maybe?"

"Wait I have an idea. Try to walk close to these women." She looks on carefully and steps in time with the group women walking. "Oh là là! Merde!"

"What?" he whispers to her ear.

"These (reaching her lips to his ear) woman smell terribly, like Merde."

"Merde?" he questions.

"Oui. Like shit." she nods her head and continues on walking. He focuses on the Sears display of perfumes. He pauses for a moment, grabbing one of the testers.

"Mel, come here." She walks to him. She hears the hissing sound of the bottle, as it releases its fragrance. Instantly, she feels the cool perfume droplets settling onto her skin.

From underneath his eyebrow, he looks behind him, scanning the crowd for obvious danger. Within it he spots men and women wearing long leather coats. The black shine of their jackets glides with them. With their noses in the air, they walk cautiously within their surroundings.

"Where the hell is security?" Brahnt says aloud.

"Brahnt my dear don't think! Remember they can hear your immediate thoughts. (whispering) Just behave like you didn't notice them." He starts laughing and picks her up by the waist.

"I love you." He explains, facing the cashier and snatching a bottle of perfume. "I'll take this one."

"Excuse me sir?" asks the cashier.

"I'll take one of these bottles of perfume for this beautiful and sensual woman." The cashier looks at Brahnt and grins. Melonnie takes the bottle from his hand and sprays the mist. She sniffs at it. With the bottle in her hand, she presses down on the button spraying producing another cloud of fragrance.

"I'll take from this one instead. It reminds me of our first day together." The cashier moves towards the back, opening a cabinet containing more of that brand. "Honey! You're just so thoughtful. You really don't have to you know?"

"Oh but Mel, I want to. I feel (he points his fingers to his heart) the need to reach down into my soul and capture this moment with you (he strokes her face) as if it could be my last." This he says with passion, as she reads the deep emotion in his eyes.

"You should go! Run! Please! Away far away!" she pleads with him through her soft-spoken words, while shoving him away.

"Cash or charge, sir?"

"Charge it. (a pause) No. Cash!" He removes his wallet from within his breast pocket. "I want to be responsible for this moment."

"$73.67." The cashier confirms. Brahnt pulls a few twenties from his wallet. He returns his glance towards her, looking over her shoulder. The expression on his face is one of a man in love for the first time. "You are just so lucky, and he is so cute." The cashier says in secret to Melonnie.

Brahnt's attention moves to the mall crowd, trying to ignore the two passing Black Coats. (one a man the other a woman) He reaches for her shade and snuggles closer her. Behind her shades is a pair of frightened eyes. The two dark coats pass them by.

"Oh look it says 'L'eau de Toilette'" she remarks.

"What does that mean?"

"It wouldn't be the same."

"It sounds pretty." - Brahnt

"It is. (she hesitates) In French." The cashier looks at them with romance gleaming from her eyes.

"You two are just so perfect together." She smiles, "here is your change." - attendant

"Keep it. By yourself a gift." He pushes away from the counter, pulling Melonnie with him.

"Do you have that effect every where you go."

"Only since I've been with you." He says to her proudly, as he walks towards the center of the mall. Three Black Coats are positioned themselves directly in the center of the mall.

One of the dark coats stops to clean his specs, using his deep burgundy shirt. Brahnt pulls Melonnie towards the sight of danger. She is confused, but not being able to concentrate, she is forced to follow. Brahnt carelessly swings his new purchase.

The bag smacks the corner of his glasses, forcing them off of his face and destined to crash against the floor. Brahnt releases his hold on Melonnie and reaches for the glasses. He catches them only inches from them hitting the floor.

Looking into the glass he confirms his suspicion. High above them, on the other side of the triangular glass roof, are more Black Coats running about and searching for Mel. Looking slightly underneath the blonde's jacket, he can see what seems to be the tip of a saber. They've come prepared says his inner self, but his mind is set on apology. Standing erect and coming face to face with the blond. Brahnt smiles and says, "Excuse me. I didn't notice you standing there."

"Ya ist OK?" her blue eyes meet with Brahnt's, her more serious than Brahnt's. Brahnt takes Melonnie by the arm and begins to walk away, briskly."

A moment of silence surpasses. The rush of blood travels through his veins, bringing the sound of his heartbeat to his ear. Steady. A sense of danger. A small shard of glass brakes against the hard tile. Then a sudden crash, as the glass ceiling, high above is broken and shards now fall to the floor, pronouncing an even larger arrival.

Brahnt spins around, whirling Melonnie like a whirlwind. Melonnie is now left standing behind him alone and uncertain of Brahnt's action. Now facing the enemy, Brahnt takes a hold of the female Black Coat, facing away while removing his semiautomatic from within his jacket. He pushes the Black Coat. Stumbling around his back and crashing into Melonnie, the Black Coat is disoriented.

Melonnie's hands talon, like protruding black daggers extending from her fingertips. She pushes her talons into the female's chest and pushing through to the other side, removes her heart. There is a look of surprise left on her face. Her eyes close, never having released her last breath.

Brahnt's pistol takes aim, sighting another Black Coat. A flash. The shell projects from the chamber, leaving a small trail of smoke. The bullet, at point blank range, is too much to take, even for an UnNatural. The Black Coat's head vigorously jolts backwards, giving Brahnt enough time to reach for the enemy's sword. (the public screams) Taking a hold of the hilt and kicking into the chest of the enemy, the sword is freed.

Another Black Coat drops down in on Melonnie. Brahnt spins around, extending the reach of the sword. (glimpses of white and black) Estimating the distance of the Black Coat now before Melonnie, he allows the swords sharp edge to hack down her head. The blade penetrates. Strands of blond hair, separated by the swords stroke, fall to the tile floor. The sound of bone snapping vibrates the blade and into the hilt. 'It feels good.' He thinks, continuing the motion. Melonnie's cheek is grazed, allowing blood to fall from the wound. The sword clears and using the same momentum, Brahnt continues the attack. (the severed head hits the floor with the body at a stand) Melonnie reaches for the head-severed coat's saber and arms herself. A flicker of light escapes at the heart and neck. The body falls, lifeless.

Still spinning Brahnt bends his knees, ducking and unknowingly missing the blade driven by the male Black Coat, now bleeding from the bullet wound (a strong authoritative voice from the back round). Over top, three bodies glide down to the mall floor. (the sound for the carousel bells ring. The music still plays from the loud speakers. And the voices still yell.) Brahnt swings his blade catching him at the knees. Again the sound and vibration of bone travels to the hilt. 'This is good!', Brahnt tells himself. The Black Coat's blood falls to the floor, along with the blonde he's just slain.

Staring into his now vertical blue eyes, Brahnt twirls the saber and severs the male's head. (bone snapping) A flash of light, almost barely visible. The three other bodies touch ground. Brahnt now turns to the black and white colors- Police. "Shit! You just can't have any fun around here!"

Melonnie hears the sound of a sword being drawn. She turns. (a glint. a faint flicker) She feels the other side of her cheek slit. This one is deeper. Blood now falls from both sides of her face. The coat prepares to return swing, twirling his blade underhand and wheeling for an overhead assault. Melonnie raises her sword and hilt, blocking. The sounds of the two metals chime upon impact. But, at a slight disadvantage, her sword is pushed down absorbing the raging force. Another vampire lands in front of Brahnt.

The voices of the police are barely noticeable over the strikes and the crowd. From their position, it is obvious to Brahnt that they will soon open fire. The captain's hand is motioning the crowd out the way. As soon as they are all gone, the bullets will rein.

Behind him Melonnie takes the blow and guides the sword down. Both women now stand shoulder to shoulder. Both swords touch at the ground with their tips chipping away at the tile. Melonnie angles her elbow and strikes the Coat with it. The Coat's nose breaks and her head is forced backwards. Melonnie, taking a step forward, while on the same foot, pivots her body in a circular fashion. Extending her reach within her spin, the tip of the blade slices her opponent's neck. Deep enough to cause pain, but she has missed the kill.

Brahnt, throwing himself onto the floor, sweeps the vampire's legs from underneath him. The vampire falls. While on one knee, Brahnt holds his saber vertically, and stabs (a grunt) the vampire's right shoulder to the tile floor. A sharp sound of metal cutting through tile. Brahnt moves away from the other group and moves towards Melonnie. The coated figure, facing Melonnie turns, giving Brahnt her back. He reaches for her hair.

With one Vigorous pull from top to bottom, Brahnt places his pistol silencer to her temple. He taunts at the pulling the trigger. "I hate being interrupted." A short flash and a muffled high pitch sound. Blood spills onto his hand. He wipes his mouth, filling it with a strange taste while he holds the nearly limp body up by a fist full of hair. Melonnie swings her saber and catches the rest of her throat. A flash of light leaves the wound. Brahnt drops her head and rushes over to Melonnie.

He feels revived. Somewhat stronger. Somewhat more alert. The crowd is nearly gone and the second group is now descended, now able to make visual contact.

The police, swarming the area and taking defensive posture, take aim. Brahnt and Melonnie camouflage themselves within the crowd. He cannot hear his heart beating, but he can hear the hearts of others running in the crowded mall. Up and to their left is a small sign dimly lit. Brahnt pushes his way toward it. Melonnie falls over some poor trampled woman's body. His grip strengthens and she pulls herself up. Reaching a few feet from the door, another coated figure reaches for them. Melonnie pushes Brahnt into the doors, forcing him to crash against it. His hips push on the rail and the doors open. A loud sound! The door slams open against the wall. He reaches out with his hands, preventing serious injury. His body meets with the ground in a loud exhale.

Coming to a stand and brushing himself off, he stumbles for the door with his vision is somewhat distorted. Reds appear where the void of darkness once set and blues where the light is too bright. He can hear pounding on the other side of the door. With a barely noticeable stagger, he reaches to the door. His head begins to feel a burning sensation. "uuuhhh" He rubs it. His ears, becoming sensitive catches the beating of his heart. 'Something strange is going on here.' He fears not death, but only for Melonnie's safety. "Melonnie, I hope you're all right." (a thunder) The door crashes open. His view looks into the door's passage. He catches a glimpse of Melonnie's arms retreating pulling back. Behind her the people race and yell, pointless in their direction. This was obviously a big hit. He notices the body propelled through the open passageway. Brahnt clamps down onto him with both of his hands, redirecting his travel.

A large sound! The body compresses against the stony wall. The structure of the hallway shakes with violence. "Fucking (spit rockets out of his mouth) Black Coats, who are you."

"My friend-" says the Black Coat a gasp.

"Fuck you!" Brahnt reaches inside the Black Coat's jacket, searching for a saber. He remembers seeing Melonnie through the door, that she has taken it. "Good, Good girl."

"Help me." The Black Coat pleads. Brahnt, while still pinning the Black Coat against the wall, searches frantically for a weapon. His fingers find an open wound, accidentally discovering that his heart has been removed.

"She stole your heart? She has a way of doing that." Brahnt's sarcasm holds no comfort for the Black Coat. The Coat, limp and dying, weakens further. His life though not expired, hangs by threads of time.

He pulls his hand out of the Black Coat's open chest wound. 'That smell?' He brings his hand out and up to his nose. "Hmmm." He licks the blood from his hand. His headache retreats and his senses become keen. Now, more determine than ever, he frantically searches the Black Coat for a weapon of any sort. He finds a dagger. Knife in hand, he throws the body to the floor. The Black Coat's back strikes the ground.

"I can help you."

"God damn right!"

"Vigore. (Brahnt stabs down at the stone floor near the Black Coat's neck) Vigore is here. He's the one you want." He says nearly breathless.

"Not quite the help that I had in mind." (a scraping sound) Brahnt slides the knife across the floor with both hands, pushed by his leaning body.

"Please let me-" His plead is broken off into silence as the knife is stabbed into the neck and cuts away at it. Blood pushes its way out of the creature. Brahnt wipes his nose. The vampire's eyes roll into his head until nothing more than empty cavities are visible. "Ahhh, you're gross!"

Tearing off a piece of his own clothing. Brahnt collects the creature's blood. Holding it to his mouth, he drinks. "Damn you taste horrible." He soaks more of his blood into it and again he drinks from it. A flicker of light, and life is no longer within the creature. Brahnt turns to the exit door, estimating the distance at forty feet away. Bringing himself up to one knee, he sprints towards it. The door is there before he can even blink or let out his first breath. Pushing his shoulder into it, the aluminum door bends and breaks open. "That didn't even hurt!"

Exiting the building, the streams of rainwater fall onto the parking lot. Examining the structure of the building, he seeks out any method of accessing the rooftop. Catching a hint of movement, he feels the sudden and overwhelming urge to leap to the top. However, the thought registers as absurd.

"How the hell can I reach the top? Regardless!" He leaps. The feeling, foreign to him, causes him to doubt his newly discovered ability, reducing his velocity. With the side of the building in sight, he reaches out hoping to take a hold of it. "Got it!" His hand slips, reaching out with his other hand. "Got it again!" (a sense of relief)

Placing his elbow on the edge of the roof, he pulls himself up. In the center of the roof looms a very large man. He too wears a thick leather Black Coat. The larger man points down into the broken glass. Silently, other Black Coats follow his orders. He must then be the leader.' Engrossed with the chaos below, the muscular man breaks away to study the eastern horizon.

Branht's elbow slips. His foothold gives way and he begins sliding down the coarse face of the granite wall. His fingers extend, trying to grasp a hold of the building's surface. Sparks ignite as he claws through the stone leaving permanent gouges in the formerly impenetrable surface. He falls twenty-four feet, then suddenly he comes to a halt. Amazed at what he has done, he inspects his hands finding that they are black. Enameled. Drawing from unfamiliar instincts, he jabs desperately at the building. Hand over hand, claw over claw, he climbs his way to the top of the building, as would any Vampire. Each lift increases his confidence ten fold, until he reaches the top. Once there, he steps onto the rooftop, proud and feeling invincible.

In the mall, the black and white uniforms give their last warning to the Black Coats. Their devilish eyes turn to the group of policemen. Their weapons fire, raining vertical bullets. Smoke from the hot barrels fills the air accenting it with the scent of burned gunpowder. Their bodies shake as the bullets penetrate. The policemen's eyes focus every shot fired, hoping for minimal casualties from innocent bystanders. Vigore, looking down and through the glass windows, is infuriated by the human's display of terrorism. Holding his fist in the air and waving it in a circular motion, the last group of Vampires begins their second wave.

The group takes to the glass plates. Their dark talons shine against the streaks of lightning. The rain comes down even harder now. They wedge small holes, small enough to insert one talon through. With their other hand, they cut out a circle around the smaller one. The circular cut is large enough for their bodies to slither through one by one. Below, the shower of bullets forces the vampires to fall onto the tile painted red. Their bodies shiver and shake as they lay in pools of their own blood.

There is obvious pain in their injuries. Twitching in their own blood, their lips tremble as they try to inhale. Overhead Vigore's last group of vampires enters the building, crawling quickly under the ceiling. Down like scorpions, their bodies move nearing the unsuspecting Police. Quickly and steadily they descend, coming only closer and closer to their prey. The last few vampires standing fall to their knees between the rain of bullets and the police reloading of their guns. The scent of gunpowder is sharp in the air. The crowd lay still on the floor, most of them covering their heads. For the few brave enough to watch they peep upwardly, a glance at a time. Among the laying crowd Melonnie lays still. Waiting to make her escape. She notices the black Coats moving under the ceiling, as painting the white ceiling black.

Seeing them tremor on the floor, the police cease-fire.

The captain wipes his head, confused and disgusted at the blood and carnage. He gives the signal for the others to close in. They approach carefully. Neither of the troopers can believe, what has just taking place. Blood has never been so plentiful.

"Why are they shaking?" asks one of the policemen.

"Quiet! Officer." says the captain from the corner of his mouth, afraid to move his eyes away from the Black Coats.

Vigore's men, now in position, leap from the walls snatching the officers one at a time.

Attacking from their blind side, in a swift medley of assorted acrobatic stunts, the police officers find themselves at the mercy of the reaper. Some of their bodies are pushed into walls, while others are sent several feet into the air exploding on the hard floors.

The swift creatures, run passed the officers grabbing shoulders, necks, ribs and whatever else the they can mangle in the first phase of their blitz kreig. Viciously and without compassion, they puncture holes into the officers as if they were rag dolls.

Unfortunately for the officers, the classical music played through the mall speakers brings the irony of terror to a more vivid realization. Like human voodoo dolls, their bodies are manipulated into a blood-bathing feast. The crowd becomes uneasy, as their safety is threatened again. Their screams begin once more in fear. Motion among them, Melonnie is the first. Using her speed to her advantage she runs to the nearest elevator away from the enemy. "I must climb." She says in a low voice. "I have to find Brahnt." The elevator door opens. The beautiful amber color lights illuminate the floor numbers. Her middle finger frantically jabs at the circular buttons. No response. She moves her finger to the next highest level, marking them with bloodstains.

Again she jabs at the button. Through the mostly glass elevator, she can see the crowd has become wiser and now they move, running, doing everything and going everywhere, as if they dance to the tune of chaos. The doors close behind her.

She witnesses as the Black Coats leap from wall to wall. Taking hold of the innocent humans, they drag them to the wounded Black Coats. The elevator rises, as the people become smaller. During her view of panic and .despair, flashes of the Angelica stories come to surface, from embedded memories within her mind, passed down through generations. Her eyes seem frantic, filled of hurt, and still within them display her determination. The doors behind her, open. As the doors slide open and her eyes move to their direction, she gasps for air, watching her enemy standing at the doorway.

The shape shifter, caught between man and creature, seems grotesque. Bearing his teeth, he lunges his deadly jaws at her. Its snout misses her face by mere inches, as she dodges her destruction. Taking advantage of her position, she knees him hard breaking his pelvis bone. She can feel as its bones break, splintering further into his body. The lower jaw of the creature drops down onto her shoulder. Shooting out with her talons, she digs into him. With her strong hold, she rolls the creature onto her back and through the glass window. The glass cracks, shatters, and then explodes. The creature falls through and to the hard surface below. She turns to leave.

'Darkness?' She focuses again. 'Shit! Another-' Her breath is cut short. A sharp pain! She feels the cold steel penetrating her chest. Lifting her eyes, she locks eyes with the Black Coat. She jabs a punch at him, while holding on to his saber by way of the blade. Blood quickly fills her blouse, still more. Thunderstruck by her punch, he loosens his grip. Regaining his balance, the Black Coat kicks out burying his heal into her abdomen. Falling backwards, her hands slide on the blade. Blood drools from the corner of her mouth, as she falls backwards and out of the elevator.

Plummeting onto the floor, she somersaults landing on her feet. Though feeling the bite from the stab wound and rapidly losing strength, she seeks out her next play. Taking a few steps backwards, she stumbles over a mangled body, falling onto her back. Forced to look up towards the ceiling, her eyes come to focus on a lone man watching down. 'Those eyes! It's Vigore!' Their eyes lock, each enraged with each other's presence. The look on his face turns maddening, realizing not what she is, but who she is.

[On the Roof Top]

Hidden from Vigore's immediate view, Brahnt has been watching. Vigore removes his dagger from his vest. Raising it into the air, Brahnt sights the hilt of the blade, as Vigore prepares to throw it down. With a single violent thrust, his hand swings downward, releasing it. Noticing that the large man is preoccupied, Brahnt rushes for his attack.

Below, Melonnie rolls onto her right hip. Assaulted by yet another Black Coat, she is lifted from the ground and forced to stand upright. The knife still falls.

Brahnt's clawed hand tears through Vigore's leather armor. Surprised of the attack Vigore swings his foot, taking a leap backwards and opening his hands as if expecting an army. But to his surprise there is only one. Vigore's, seemingly insulted, regards his enemy with even greater disgust. "You?" He says still filled with disbelief. "Is that all? Just one person?"

[Below]

Clutching Mel tightly within his sinister grip, the Black Coat opens his mouth preparing to bear down on her. Mel rolls her eyes towards him. It is evident that this is a very old Vampire. His teeth are tarnished and some of them slightly chipped. The knife, falling, comes to sudden stop, burying itself into the Black Coat's skull. The weight from the falling knife, forces him to one knee. Mel, gathers her strength, as best as she can. Holding the hilt of the knife in one hand, she allows the other to touch his chest. Feeling his broken ribs, she is prompted for a visual inspection. She confirms her suspicion true; his ribs are cracked and protruding. "Here (she grits her teeth) let me help (pulling the knife) with that!" With blade in hand she reaches across and around his neck. Placing the dagger to his throat and holding him by a fist full of hair, she stands. Strenuously, she pulls her shoulder to the rear, allowing the knife to ride across the Coat's neck.

Blood streams out like little dams, bursting. Coming to her knees she sniffs out the scent of the blood. "I see you've just eaten." - sarcastically. "Oh and fresh soul of human. (she reaches over to her ear) She was only thirteen! Bastard!" Regretfully Melonnie closes her eyes, plunging her fangs into the open wound. With blood painting her face, she slakes her thirst. Opening her eyes, she examines her surroundings, insuring her safety. The few human souls witness her action, causing her to feel shame.

Her mind flashes back to the Angelica. *Gabrielle the angel had come to speak with them after the war was nearly over its first deciding factor. He places a blessing on them, brought down by higher order. The gift of knowledge and understanding. This would help them adapt through all times, so long as they fought for the good of man. Man? What a joke! They were truly God's children. For they would never become of age.* - Her mind returns.

Her heart stops. With her next breath, it begins to beat in reverse. "I'm going to be sick." She says surviving the pains in her stomach. Feeling a slight disorientation, the shape and color of her eyes change. Shades of black move about in front of her, while her eyes come to an agreeable fix. Breathing deeply, she gains her composure and with that, her eyes adjust. For the time being, her eyes are split vertical and horizontal, imaging a cross. Changing her point of reference, she whips her head upward. Fully energized she comes to her feet, still looking into the sky peering through the broken glass. Twisting her ankles, she digs deep into the floor, mixed with blood and rain. With a firm foothold, she crouches. Coiled and compressed, she leaps towards the roof's opening.

She leaps spontaneously into the air. Black coats descending are torn and ripped apart, as her body spirals upward with her talons extended. Nearing the opening, the rainwater falls against her body and clothing, cleansing her from the blood of others. The winds press down against her, while she comes near to the openings. She places her hands over her head and closes her eyes. (the sound of splintering glass) It explodes. Once through the thick glass ceiling, she shakes her head and opens her hands, clearing away the small shards. With her legs apart, she places her feet carefully on the steel frame supporting her weight. Her frowning eyes, scan the rooftop hunting for her man's whereabouts. Leaping to her the side, she cartwheels onto the rooftop. Her feet land on the roof, soft like a feather and without a sound they make contact with the puddled rain and splintered glass.

Hearing the sounds of clashing swords, she brings her hands down beside her feet. Moving cat-like across the wet gritty floor, she crawls towards the sounds of a duel being played out. Reaching the edge of the roof, her eyes fill with horror and fear. At its edge, Vigore and Brahnt swing blades, attempting to defeat each other. Though proud, she fears that he is no match for Vigore. Vigore, with merely two flesh wounds swings his blade with great strength. (her eyes move to Brahnt) He fights courageously, but he bleeds.

Melonnie, leaping, falls between Vigore and Brahnt. Crescent kicking at Vigore's muscular arms, she disarms him. Spinning towards Brahnt, she pushes him off with one hand while taking his sword with the other. Turning toward Vigore, she raises the sword and continues the assault.

Leaning and placing one knee onto the rooftop, he wraps his leather fingers around the hilt of the fallen sword. Wrapping his leather glove around the hilt of his sword, he lifts his blade blocking the assault. His blade, though meeting with hers, falls down onto his shoulder. It is obvious that her fortitude is comparable to his. She spins her sword and cuts down at him, but again the expert swordsman stops her deadly blade.

"Come to my side! Join my army!" He invites her using his most sinister voice. (she looks at him with profound hatred)

He swings down at her collarbone. She blocks, catching and holding his blade. Breath to breath they look into each other's eyes.

"Never! Your life was doomed from the start." She throws her knee to the outside of his ribs. She makes contact, injuring a previous wound. "Picking people out like raspberries in a garden is not my idea of power." He bends. She draws her blade in and pushes down at an angle. He catches her sword. Arching her shoulder and tilting her blade forward, she uses the leverage to slide the sword across his face. He grits his teeth, bearing down the pain. Blood flows down his face and onto the sword, accompanied by the chilling sound of two sharp blades sliding against each other. Inhaling deeply, he thrusts forward pushing off her leaning body. Using great effort, his thrust projects her several feet away.

Crashing down on her back, she slides a few feet further. The sword lies beside her. Seemingly having the advantage, Vigore reaches for his dagger. Cocking it back and starting to throw the weapon. He takes a sudden, but dramatic, pause. His other hand drops the sword. His expression is frozen.

Melonnie takes the advantage, rolling onto her side and grabbing her blade. Coming to her feet she raises her sword. Vigore's hand reaches for his chest, uncertain of the origin of pain and unable to breathe. Reaching down into his belt, Vigore grasps his other dagger. He pulls, but the dagger cannot be lifted. His hands tremble.

From behind the bricklayers, Brahnt appears with his drawn semiautomatic. Small flashes, produce by gunpowder, fire out the barrel. The first bullet, aimed at Vigore's head, penetrates its target. Lowering his weapon, he fires once more breaking the Giants knee and forcing him to fall down upon it. Brahnt fires again, blasting his only remaining support. Again Vigore's knee gives way collapsing him onto both knees. Melonnie looks at Brahnt, as he fires repetitively with accurate and deadly aim. For the moment she is impressed, hearing the sound of empty shells falling down in the cold rain. Water pours down his face, washing out the wounds from his battle. He breathes heavy, and though seemingly on his last breath, he moves forward firing his weapon. It fires consecutively. The chamber is empty. He releases the clip from it's housing.

Reaching into his jacket and pulling out another clip, he reloads his weapon. He pulls the slide, takes aim, and fires at nearly point blank range. "Finish it!" His mouth moves between droplets of water, but his voice carries slowly into her ears.

Carrying her saber low and near to the ground, her feet come down against the rooftop separating the small puddles of water, as she focuses on her sword stroke. Her expression is contorted and her attention lifts towards Brahnt. Only a few feet away, the tip of the saber prepares for the fatal kill like streaks of highly polished lightning. Brahnt's firing arm bend at the elbow. The word "NO" begins to leave his lips. Brahnt's firing hand begins to point in Melonnie's direction. She stares at the barrel seemingly facing her and down the arm of the man holding it. A flash of light the weapon jolts backwards then falls forward again. Another bullet is fired. Behind her, the summoned Black Coats, gather. Brahnt turns his attention to the group gathering behind Melonnie. It seems unbelievable. Behind Melonnie two of Black Coats fall, struck to the head by Brahnt's deadly aim. The darkness fills even greater darkness, as the scorpion like objects come waking from their nests.

Nearing the shots fired, Melonnie shakes her head acknowledging the sound. Her sword, losing its focus, (she presses against Brahnt) grazes the side of Vigore's neck. Vigore moves only enough to prevent serious injury. Melonnie, holding Brahnt firmly against her body, pushes Brahnt off the edge of the building disappearing into the cover of night.

Pulling off his leather gloves, he drops them to his side. A deep breath. Reaching for his back, Vigore pulls at the knife thrown by the human. Each motion brings the knife further outward. The Black Coats stares at the leader, marveled at his stamina. His hands fall onto the rooftop. (a faint sound of metal on a stony floor). He coughs out blood, as his heart begins to pump once again. Servanté breaks through the crowd of Vampires. Trapped within his hand he has a fresh girl. Aside from the foreign bloodstains and the wet rain, she is pure and innocent. Fresh blood, for a wounded king. Servanté throws the meal down to Vigore. She stumbles then falls to the floor. Frightened, she looks into his face. He pants a bit. Looking down they compare hands.

Hers are soft and pink. Her fingernails painted red, contrasting the blood washing away from her hand. His are harder seemingly made from tough leather. Aside his fingers smaller sets of talons pierce the skin of each finger. At the end of his finger is one large claw like nail. A Talon. A Black Talon. He admires her soft eyes, as they become the eyes of despair. Hope has disappeared for this soul.

Vigore's mouth bursts open, replacing her despair with horror. Two sets of fangs, two upper and two lower, expose themselves. He motions forward tearing into her neck and collarbone. It snaps like brittle bone. Shaking his head left to right, he shakes the rag doll. Filling himself with her essence and having her still trapped within his mouth, he comes to a stand. The Black Coats, waving their hands and raising their voices, cheer him on, as Vigore's wounds dry and heal. The thunder carries on, not worse and not better, when it rains on heroes it rains not better or worse upon villains. Fully energized, the beastly creature rises to his feet. His large and steel like talons pierce through her as if she were no more than a rag doll amongst a pack of wolves.

Servanté approaches Vigore. "There are more of those Black and White Uniforms outside. There are also others with guns dressed in dark blues and masks. Every one has a uniform and a human weapon."

Vigore throws the doll like into the crowd. The Black Coats pull and tear at it, rejoicing. Soon the Limbs give way, tearing the rag doll. "How are we strong?"

"All well? Is he one of the two naturals?" Says Servanté

"He is not a natural."

"But his strength. He was so efficient."

"I know." Nods Vigore "Kill them all! No survivors will live to tell of us tonight. Take of their uniforms and close the streets, leading to this place. Work not in terror, but in shadow. With all of us well fed, this should take no more than a matter of hours. Burn the place down. No witnesses."

"The area is too big. There are too many witnesses."

"What is our alternative?"

"I don't rightfully have one."

"Then pick the bodies of our soldiers. Bring the gunmen to me and kill the rest. This has not gone according to plan."

"As you wish Vigore. Let the chase begin." His smile increases and taking a step backwards, he turns facing the crowd. He opens his hands. The crowd silences. Servanté begins explaining the military tactics. Vigore stares into the sky, carefully burning to memory each step Brahnt had made.

Chapter 10

Shadow Behind the Face

Falling Heavens

Rotating globe
In two directions
Motion of streets passing and coming
Tires turning and moving toward destinations
The driver whistles a tune, untoned
And he drives enjoyably on the road to hell.
Next stop,
Falling heavens

The Dawning of a New Day

Having carried him on her shoulder for miles of travel, Melonnie places her first foot on the ground. Aching and exhausted with defeat, she places Brahnt on a small cleared pasture. She must have flown with him on her shoulders for hours. Now resting her heavy and exhausted body on the natural floor of the Earth, she kneels with her hands outstretched absorbing nature's energy. Surges of the same energy, brush lightly on the surface of his skin.

"Where are we? Mel?"

"I'm not sure where we are, but I know that we are much closer now."

"Closer to what?" He asks out of breath.

"Closer to the gathering." Her voice is steady, as she continues to absorb nature's energy.

"How can you tell?" He raises an eye to her, studying her concentration.

"I can."

"So? Aren't you tired?"

"Non. Not really. You should eat better and stay away from those hamburgers. You would feel better too!" She says displaying a small smile at the corner of her mouth.

"You've got to be kidding me? What the hell do you put in that stomach, girl?"

"Blood. Life from other animals. You've seen me. (he holds out his hand)" Her tone is coy.

"I know. I know. You didn't have to answer. That was a rhetorical question." He holds his hand to his mouth. "You know? The kind of question that you don't answer." Bending forward, he places his hand on his knees. Inhaling deeply he satisfies his immediate need for oxygen. Making his best impression of a man trying to look his best, he exhales. "God I feel sick."

"Why, what did you eat?" Her voice is livelier and seemingly teasing.

"I drank some of that vampire blood. Gross, I don't know what came over me." He says leaning over onto the ground.

He spits out.

"The effects of the UnNaturals blood will probably wear off. You'll be ok." Her words, however, are not very comforting to him. Glancing over to his direction, she watches him cough and spit out the poison.

Curiously she crawls on her hands and knees to where he sits, suffering. Her eyes look down at the mixed serum. Placing her finger in it, she makes little swirls observing the color and the smell. "Good!" She comments with a little excitement.

"Gross! (he inhales) What's *good* about it?"

"It's not yours." Her tone is a bit coy. Finished with her professional examination, she wipes her finger.

"So how the hell do you stay so powerful? I mean why aren't you tired? You must have taken out thirty of those guys."

"And don't forget. I had to rescue you." She snickers at him.

"Hey I was doing OK for a simple-cell human."

"Yeah (she smiles at him and leans on the slanted tree next to him) you did OK." Kindness, filling her heart, compels her to touch his shoulders and bring him closer to her. From this view, she can see the heat ventilating from his body and transforming into steam. "Amazing!" He doesn't respond. He only looks at her in that unique way that only Brahnt can. "Are you cold?"

"Getting there." She rubs his shoulders.

"Come here you big scary human guy." She pulls him between her legs and plays with his hair. Her eyes become dreamy, perhaps even wondrous. "You must be something in *your* world. Hiding in the shadows. Killing all those *bad* men. You kill women too?"

"Oh yea. I'm an equal opportunity employer." He says with a humorous gesture. "But only the bad ones." He smirks.

Striking across the very top of his head, she smacks him. His head cants to a side, and he laughs even louder. "You think that everything is funny?"

"Only the funny things. Sad things are not so funny. Then there are those ludicrous things- You know?" He feels her pointy finger, jabbing him in the ribs.

"Boy! I really screwed with your life." She says with a taste of despair.

"No! Not at all my life has always been screwed with from the beginning. Really. Ever since I lost my soul."

"Darling. Your soul is the purist in the world. You see a cause and you fight for it. You don't even look back. You enjoy your life to the very end. And you don't give up, until you have tried everything. And you know when to quit. I wish that I could have been more like you. You are an incredible person."

"I'm not all that. Melonnie, I've had my share of bad hands."

"I know. But let me continue please. I've never really had the choice. I've never had that much free will. I didn't decide to fight this war. This war is as old as time itself. And until a few days ago, you people were just tools. You are the only means we have to fight our way back home. Without your souls being judged by the creator, we may never be able to enter through the gates of heaven. (her fingers run through his hair) And until recently, you humans were only a meal. You've taught me how to respect that."

"And you've taught me that there is more to life than I alone could have ever seen. You've shown me that there is an incredible world out there and great mysteries that slip past our noses. I owe you more thanks than I could ever repay. Figure this, I think I know who God is. I mean I have been giving it some thought and I believe. I'm not sure how it happened, but I believe. And I feel it here."

"I guess (she cuddles his head) we're just two different creatures finding out that we are not so different." she says to him

"Still there is a lot of anger in me. I wish that I could change the world. I haven't changed, but I know I'm not the same," he says. She is deep into her thought and experiencing the discerning feeling of love, but it is unknown to her. And within her, she struggles. "I'm an assassin too Mel. I know what you're thinking. I'll make it easy for you. If you can't love me, then let me fill your blood line." He ends sadly and leans his head to her knee.

"I've killed better men than you. (she pauses struggling with her conflict)" Tears form into droplets. "I hate the world today. I can't change. And though I've tried at the words, I can't find them. You look at me as if I am an angel undercover. How can I tell you I'm not? I live for the moment and not for the past. In many ways- yes! We are similar. D'Accord! And yet in many ways I'm not. You live within your social truths. I still am living for the survival of the fittest and though we both fight for the preservation of humankind. The difference lies in that you are the children of a race forgotten, left to fend for yourselves. We are the pursued- the hunted. We are hunted by your kind and another kind. Haven't you realized this yet?"

"That is the reason I am with you." He says to her.

"No offense. In your world you are feared and perhaps within that fear you are respected. In my world you are a bug waiting to be squashed."

"No offense taken." His sarcasm shows through.

"Please (she places her fingers to his lips)." He takes her hand, pressing it further into them. Inhaling, he closes his eyes. She, on the other hand, filled with tears, feels the strength of his passion towards him. Her heart beats making erratic sounds, skipping beats and moving out of time. Her chest falls and rises rapidly. He opens his eyes, looking into hers. She inhales, closing her eyes. Taking a hold of his hand, she brings it to her face. He exhales. His eyes gently open. She opens hers, meeting his.

"Just say it." He says in form of a question. "All my life (she feels the dark cloud of his mind), I've waited for something important. Something that would distinguish me from the other scum, from the other pollution that watches as people are killed and burned." His energy increases with each word, each motion. She weakens with each word listened to. "Just say it! (pressing her face in his hands) Say it!" Tears of desperation fill the cavity of her existence. The barrier fills. The muscles around her eyes twitch uncontrollably. He presses her face harder and falls his forehead to her chin. Her mouth shivers. Her fangs protrude, as she loses more and more of her control. Her hands take his face. Gently making passage to the back of his neck, by way of his hair. Her breathing is now erratic. Bringing his forehead to her chest, she feels his warm breath. There is a slight moisture to it. Tears from his eyes fall on them. "Say it. I know it's there." The words begin, but catch at the top of her throat. Her mouth, slightly deformed, mimic the word the best she can and without sound. He feels her struggle. "Do it! Finish it!" She takes a small glimpse of his exposed neck. Her mouth salivates. He can feel the salivation falling against his neck, forcing him to swallow hard. A sharp motion and he is within her clutches, vulnerable. Canting his head to a side, he tries to look at her. Anticipating death, he takes in a hard breath of air. Still he leaves his eyes open. The last thing I want to see is the beauty of her eyes, he thinks to himself.

Her hair dangles onto his neck and his shoulders. (the painful sting of piercing icicles) The muscles to the right corner of his mouth push down. Her bite becomes gentle. He can feel his blood leaving his body. "That doesn't hurt too badly. It feels calming, like water that flows from a gentle river." His breathing matches the sensation. The small cold droplets of her tears cool the warmth of his skin. Opening her mouth, she pulls away from her bite. Red and teary eyes reveal what he has already known to be the truth. Blood, his blood, trails down the sides of her mouth. Lips trembling, she blinks her eyes slowly.

"You're human." She says regrettably

"MNNNO!"

"Oui vous êtes!" (Yes you are!) Her head lowers.

"It doesn't matter."

"My kind will never accept you." She pleads for his forgiveness.

"I don't care." - he interjects

"I can't change."

"I don't care."

"You'll take me as I am?" She says between segmented tears. Reaching to her face he wipes away a few of the them.

"Say it! Please say it! Remove yourself from your social prison."

"I love you." The words are bearably recognizable at first, though every consonant and vowel is mimicked and not heard. (her nostrils flare, inhaling the fresh early morning air) "Je t'aime! I Love You- I Love you. (a gasp of air) I love" She finishes in sounds of whispers.

She places her face to his. Cheek to cheek, she rubs it back and forth against his. Pulling her face away from his, she touches her mouth with his. Their lips meet, mouths open, and they engage with a kiss.

"You bit me." He says pulling away from her full lips.

"Yes?" She says surprisingly.

"It hurt." Looking at his facial expression, one would think he is a big baby.

"And?" she says almost in the same tone.

"It hurts!" His eyebrows raise up to her, as she focuses on his neck. She is all but too familiar with the way vampire wounds sting and burn, if not properly sealed with their own saliva. This is such a puncture.

"Hold still." She bites down on her finger, lightly.

"This doesn't mean you're going to have to eat again? Does it?"

"No. But it will heal the wound." He watches a single drop of blood, bead and fall from her finger.

Careful not to foolishly spill it, she carries her finger to his wound, allowing it to fall on the small punctures. His blood crystallizes upon impact. "Hold your breath." He does. Massaging the wound, the blood flakes and falls away from the wound. Only there is no wound left there. All but a small pigmentation is left and in a few hours that effect will vanish as well.

"Well that feels strange," as his eyes suddenly shift their visual perception.

"That is not supposed to happen!" She says at the effects changing the appearance of his eyes.

"What is not supposed to happen?" He looks up at her confused. "Are you all right?" He says to her, as her appearance has somehow changed. He sees her hair dancing in slow motion. The rays of light, escaping through the trees, stop at the reflection of her beauty. Her face is simply perfect in every way imaginable. Imagination has surpassed all that is of fantasy.

"Honey? Your eyes are dark like mine?" She says to him delicately and with humor. "You poor thing."

"My God! You are beautiful! How can I remove my eyes from you?"

"Brahnt? (she approaches him carefully, yet amused) What ever you are feeling, my love. It will pass."

"No! Melonnie. (he looks down at his hands) You don't understand. This is beautiful. I- I believe that I can finally see through your eyes."

"Brahnt? What do you mean?"

"You're glowing! You have this fluent ambiance surrounding you." She blushes. The color of the ambiance changes. Realizing what he can see, she brakes into smiles; then laughter. "You know what this is." He states the question.

"Escussie? Is that a question?"

"Yes. Sorta'."

"Its nothing."

"Then why do you laugh? Why does it change like this?"

"It's nothing really."

"No! It's something all right. What is it? Mel? Mel?"

"Brahnt? Brahnt?" She returns mocking him. "It's a sensitive issue."

"Are you- No?"

"No! (she slaps down on his arm) How did I learn this- (she searches for the words) I have the hots for you."

"Wow! Do I have this glowing thing?"

"No." she is short.

"No?" Looking at his hands and legs.

"Well, look you have a faint line here. (touching the outline of his face) Oh! And look! There is another one here." She points out the rim of his lips. Reaching to their comfort once again. She engages him in a kiss.

The kiss turns to sudden passion, as her hands move about him, vigorously. With her eyes closed and lips still engaged, she brings his image to the eyes of imagination. He moves in time with her, touching her shifting shape. He allows himself to be captivated by her natural essence and though not knowing what to expect, he knows to trust and believe in her. Her fingernails extend like small claws. She passes them lightly across segments of his flesh. In her mind she can hear his heart beat ten times stronger. His motion moves in time with hers. The images of his blood rushing through his veins come clear into her imagination, painting a picture of perfection. The once gentle pulses of life are careful notes, tuned by a perfect musician.

He feels her heavy breathing; her rapid motion. She is like a lioness over her prey. He feels helpless and vulnerable. The feeling is foreign to him, but then again so has his life become. Nonetheless, the new feelings are welcomed. And for a man that has never fallen in love before, it is a feeling and an emotion well passed overdue. Her skin is cool, but pleasant to the touch. He, on the other hand, feels warm; something that she could only dream of.

They touch each other with great curiosity and equal passion. Each kiss is delivered with the precision of a sniper. Slipping his hands around her waist, he feels the newly found pleasure. Her hands finger through his hair with aggressive gentleness. He watches her smile from time to time, sometimes nervously, while other times displaying her happiness. However strong her emotions are for him, within her body and heart lays a seriousness. There will be consequences to this. She knows it. Equally he knows the truth. Still, tomorrow they may not live, and so today is all that matters. Her fingers claw slightly, as part of her normal mating ritual. His infected blood, brings forth changes unfamiliar to him and so, everything is at a balance.

Still lip-to-lip and upright on her knees, she unbuttons his shirt. His hands pass gently over her face, down her neck, and onto her shoulders, leaving behind small traces of warmth indicative of his passion.

Down between her straddle, there is another feeling. A feeling of longing. A feeling of wanting and being wanted. She reaches the last button. His hands pull at her blouse, exposing her strong shoulders. Reaching over to them, he places light kisses on them, each one an inch apart. The sensation stimulates her, sending more sensual pleasure to the pit of her stomach.

"Butterflies?" He asks her, noticing her goose bumps.

"Butterflies." She confirms, while smiling. She pushes his head backwards. His body follows. Now leaning over him, her semi long hair tickles his face. Moving from side to side and then up and down, the cool strands of hair, leave gentle pleasures. How can so many pleasures be derived from such subtlety? Placing her weight on one hand she uses the other to glide down his chest, admiring the hard work and effort that has brought his chest to this design.

Taking her finger, she follows the outline of each individual curve. She smiles. Her fangs show brightly and unashamed. Leaning his hand to her face, he follows the contour of her fangs, finding comfort where there was none. Returning her hand to brace herself, she reaches down to his chest. Lapping at his chest, much like a cat would out of a bowl of milk, she runs small circles on his masculine hair leaving tiny spirals. Pressing her face deeper into his chest, she bites lightly at small pockets of flesh.

The first nip is a little hard, and his body flinches. She smiles at his vulnerability. Taking another hold, a gentler hold, she nips at him again. The combination of pain and pleasure brings an erotic sensuality to surface.

"Butterflies?" She inquires. She hears nothing more than a concealed moan. Within the pleasures of his mind that he feels, she senses the dark cloud. "You needn't be afraid." 'This is love. True love', she thinks to herself. Equally as erotic to her are the methods and stories of his thoughts. She finds herself involved with his thoughts dating back into his childhood, his dreams, and his history. She absorbs his life and in doing so she finds herself falling deeper in love with the man and not the image. 'This is a good man. A very good man. And though we all do things against the way of mankind, this man fights for what he believes. This is why he is here with me.'

Tapping into momentary images produced from the dark cloud within his mind, she brings forth an image of a small hand. *A large bulky pencil, within his hand, and a crumpled piece of paper. The hand writes distorted words, but she can only make out the word soul.* The image is distorted by another image. The image of herself within his eyes. She feels the way he sees her and it feels good to her. Extending her tongue, like the erotic woman she suddenly has become, she paints a path to his neck. His blood pumps behind thin walls and she knows it. The sensation to bite down against his throat comes to the surface of her desires, but there is very little struggle here. She knows that there is true love traveling within those very veins and within his touches and love, displays itself as the most powerful of the emotions. She nips at his chin.

Unable to remain passive, he reaches around her back and takes a hold of her shirt by way of her collar. Pulling down into opposite directions, the shirt rips from top to bottom. With her back exposed and his hand actively caressing her, he absorbs the pleasure of feeling between each rib.

Reaching down between her legs, she takes a firm hold of his belt. With one hand and still pressed lip to lip, she unbuckles it. Her elbow bends and pulls away. Her arms swing out wildly, belt in hand.

She reaches down once again, this time, unbuttoning his pants. He pulls her blouse away, throwing half to each side.

Breasts exposed and heavy with excitement, he places his nose and mouth between them. Inhaling deeply, filling himself with her sent. The soothing musk scent makes his passion become greater. His hands explore the area of her thighs, delicately savoring the sensation as most would a meal. He is pleased that he has found his way.

Attentive to his needs, she strokes his masculine ego as she would one of her own kind widening her hips, allowing him better comfort. At their full natural extent, he stretches out his hand around the soft semi-muscular flesh. Further exploring each other, they continue to explore each other's uniqueness. Reaching over her hips and taking a hold of her waist, he sits her down on his lap. Comfortably they unite, becoming one inside her, he takes another moment to contemplate his position.

"Mel?" His whisper carries over to her ear.

"Yes Brahnt?" She smiles back with dreamy eyes filled of sensuous pleasure.

"The Preying Mantis kills its prey, after mating."

"Yes Brahnt?" She asks moving her hips into his.

"Well so does the queen bee." He asks a little detached to his masculine desires.

"Yes Brahnt?" She asks again with the same sarcasm and the same rhythm.

"Well and the black widow also- I was just thinking. I'd like to know if-" He watches as her smile becomes wider. Her fangs are young. There are no chips. No scratches. They are so white and perfect.

"I guess that is something you'll have to find out for yourself." She answers back. Somehow he expected that response. Her mystery and her elusiveness are things that make her so interesting.

Feeling her motion, "I've never in my life have experienced a woman quite like you."

"You'll get tired of me."

"No I won't!" He says to her, as she continues moving. The fallen leaves brush by them, raked by the gentle finger of the wind. His eyes welcome the strange and unique sensations produce by the glaring trees high above them. The aroma of flowers mesh with her scent, as the alchemist mixes the intricate aphrodisiac. Continuing to move in time, she looks down to him. His shirt, wide open, displays an array of interesting muscularity. She focuses on each follicle of hair and each indentation. But, never having been with a man, this proves too hard to absorb all and in complete.

He observes the way the light has fallen on her, creating vast shadows that are ever changing within her movement. Small beads of sweat form on her back, as he continues moving with her. Her hands, with buried finger, dig further into the ground at each side of his face. (sweat rolls down the center of her back) Her breathing becomes rapid and steadily increasing. He finds it enjoyable.

Managing to stretch his hands to her face, he caresses her soft skin with the backside of his hand. Her face moves against his touch, maximizing contact. Truthfully either one of them is no virgin, but the height of pleasure produced and brought forward feelings that would contradict their individual experiences. Placing his hands around her cheek, he forces his thumb to make contact with the side of her brow. She responds by opening her mouth. Her tongue sits down at the edge of her full lips, caressing them and anticipating affection.

One finger after the other, he wraps them around the base of her neck. Pulling down, he brings her closer, delicately collapsing her arms. The tips of her cool strands of hair touch the sides of his face and the nape of his neck producing sensual comfort. The soft feathery feeling tickles, bringing forth his smile. Not knowing whether he would live or die after this event, he pushes on with all of his heart and soul.

With his palm against the side of her hip, he presses down on the ground for support. She rolls over onto her back. The hem of her skirt slides up, exposing her thighs. Looking down to her he pushes up, standing himself on his knees. Pulling off his sweat filled shirt and rolling it, he makes a pillow of it. Reaching down to her, he lifts her head and places it down behind her neck. She smiles and is marveled by his shivery.

Resting his elbows to the side of her face, he places a kiss on each one of her beautiful and delicate eyes. Repositioning himself he delivers a kiss on the peek of her cheekbones. Moving down further, his lips press another kiss on each corner of her mouth. Her eyes roll up wards and then down to him again. He places a kiss delicately on each side of her collarbone.

Moving down further he places his mouth slightly underneath the round of her breast. Delicately cupping it with his mouth, he creates suction. She becomes even more aroused and takes a hold of him by his hair. Like a scavenger in dire need of substance, they search for something more than emotions to cling to. And unsatisfied she reaches down to the belt of his pants. She pulls him slightly aggressively into her hips, securing her pleasures.

They continue to make love, like lovers that had fallen to earth, explicitly for each other. Love like this could never exist apart from these two. Closing his eyes he allows further penetration. Without many words, they express to each other all they can in way of their love.

The wind carries both their scents into the air, for all to witness that love between two different people and two different beings can exist. And how beautiful, delicate and magical are the feelings that only love can produce. The Sun, who has forever seen, witnesses this ritual with pleasure. And for proof, the Sun will offer its warmth and splendid rays of hope. Hope that true love can prevail. Hope that this will serve as an indicator pointing toward the beauty of love.

The wind caresses their every move as if never tiring of displaying its affection. And they make love as beautifully, as roses blossom.

Chapter 11

Melonnie Attacks

A Song Without a Voice

Once I heard a song without a voice.
Its motions were the words,
Its beauty the music,
And my heart the ear
That allowed it to enter
And there it sings until I fall asleep.

Deep Discoveries

Windshield wipers move from right to left and then right again. The large raindrops explode on the windshield, like marbles falling on a hardwood floor. The wind chases away the rainwater from the windshield, placing Brahnt in a pensive state for the while. Random thoughts occupy his lack of expression within the moving vehicle.

Melonnie's attention persists on the road ahead, however his ideas bleed all into her conscious.

"I have something for you Melonnie."

"I know its is very hard for you to believe I have such strong feelings for you." She snaps.

"What?"

"Oh sorry, you think so loudly."

"I have never heard of quiet thinking." His statement masquerades the question. "Anyway, it's not what I meant."

"What's the matter?" She asks.

" I was just thinking. I'm going to this castle, to this place, cove, coven, whatever you can call it. To meet more of these people-, creatures-, beings that are like you-, not like me. And.... And... you eat people. And-, well-, I'm a people." He finally lets out not knowing exactly what he's just said.

"You are frightened? You went up against the man that we're after. I think that you did very well against him." Her nose wrinkles and eyes squint at him.

"Yes- No! I'm not. Wouldn't you be if you thought that a stake through the heart may be what you get?" He says trying to reason between her and his fear.

"We are not Hollywood monsters. Mon Dieu! Keep your thoughts pure. (a desperate pause) Think of making love to me, that will throw them off (he looks at her face)"

"Is that all you're going to suggest to me?" He looks down her chest and at her legs admiring and remembering.

"That's more like it." She says in a humorous tone

"Beside you gave those wampires a run for their money."

"Why do you do that?"

"Do what?"

"Say wampire all the time instead of vampire. It a 'v' not a 'w'." He says stalling her. Her dark eyes roll to his direction. "Hasn't anyone ever told you that you have fascinating dark eyes?" She smiles.

"Quit teasing my intelligence." She says slowly.

"OK. But the comment about your eyes still remains-"

"The question? Please."

"OK. Doesn't it get boring for you to be able to hear everything from everyone?"

"We actually cannot hear everything. It's not like I read your mind. Everyone knows that you mind stores everything chemically charged. (he looks at her surprised) There is a certain energy you produce at a moments thought. Just when you're thinking it, it appears as an energy source. It isn't like that. I can't read your actual thoughts. It's more of a sense. Sometimes I can hear when you speak inside yourself. And yes most people are boring, but I've never been inside the mind of a professional killer - and can I add successful killer assassin."

"Can you explain that with a little more detail."

"Simple. Sometimes you clearly express ideas with words inside your head. It is just as if you were speaking to someone. This is where I have the least bit of difficulty in finding your thoughts. Then there's that emotional language. This is where you think without words. You merely focus. The eating of your favorite food, for example."

"Get off the Hamburgers!" He warns her.

"You just merely feel good. And though you think 'mmm, this is good' you don't repeat the words in your mind. This is really hard to read for us. Then finally there's the instinct.

Where you practice what you need to do ahead of time, so when the time comes, you become spontaneous. But like anything else the older you are the better your reflex. With the elders, I would just think happy thoughts."

"Yea." He replies.

"What is the matter now?"

"You eat people." In a complaining tone of voice. (she grins) And I Thought you liked me?"

"I do." She answers

"Well, they eat people"

"And?"

"I'm a people!" He finally lets out bright eyed.

"You're my people and I'll protect you."

"You're a (he stutters) girl."

"Yeah (she mocks), but I pack a punch" She jabs him in the ribs.

"Hawaiian, maybe." He looks away into the side of darkness. "So you read energy sources? What is that electrically cable (he points off the road) saying right now?"

"It's not the same. Humanity has a unique way of thinking. The simple fact that you've existed so long, is scientifically amazing. But there are greater powers in the universe, than just you and I."

"Mel?"

"There is magic and good and evil."

"Mel! - Mel?"

"Oh sorry." She smiles at him.

"I'm glad I asked you. Really. How have you come to know so much?"

"Years and years of experience."

"Oh, yea! I forgot how old you really are." His attention steers to the moving terrain outside the window.

"And what is that supposed to mean?"

"Nothing."

"Brahnt? You know it's an awfully long way to have to walk."

"It only means, that I wish I would have been the one to fill those beautiful memories inside you. Who knows? Maybe things would have been different."

"Don't flatter yourself. Most of our memories are passed down through generations."

"We, on the other hand, sit and tell stories and then we tell our children those stories."

"Is that how you humans do it?"

"Do what?"

"Pass down stories?"

"Yeah what other way is there?"

"We are born with them." -Mel

"What?"

"We are born with the memory traces."

"Does that mean that you know everything?"

"Non. Just what we trace back on our own. It's Sort of the way you remember things yourself. Except that we don't have to live it to remember it."

"Wow! Lot of pain in there?"

"Sometimes. But mostly it is important for our survival. Like I said, it is a wonder that you humans have lived as long as you have."

"I don't know. It seems a bit romantic, having to sit there and listen to the stories during Christmas time and having someone correct them when you're wrong."

"Are you talking about you adoptive parents?"

"Yea." He says sadly.

"Listen. You know that it isn't your fault?"

"I think I know that now. Meeting you has definitely opened my mind. I just hope that this isn't the end of us. It's a wonderful feeling to have a wonderful friend."

"You often sleep with your friends?" She says to him, surprisingly.

"No, just my good ones."

"And how many of these good ones do you have?"

"Oh (he moves his eyes around in a circle) Just one."

"And it better stay that way! I know how you humans are."

"Oh! And how are we."

"Ticklish!" She reaches over and runs her fingers on the side of his ribs. He bends to one side and laughs. Releasing him of his laughter. She stops the car.

"Nous sommes là!" She says to him.

"We are here! Right?" He asks trying to remember the words.

"Hey that little yellow book of yours really works. It is just a small distance ahead. I'll go there and meet you here in the morning." She says to him.

"No! I'm coming with you." –Brahnt

"There is no telling what will happen there."

"You said you'll protect me." - Brahnt

"I will but you'll have to stay here."

"I'm not leaving you! I'm very serious about that. Besides I can kick some wampire butt." Bringing her hand up to her face, she laughs at him. "What?" he asks, "I've just said *wampire,* didn't I?" She nods her head, while holding her hands to her to her mouth.

"*You* can be dangerous?" - Mel

"Danger is my middle name." _ Brahnt

"You may not like what you see."

"I have a gut of steel." - Mel

"And if you see your relatives in a cage, about to be eaten, there will be nothing you can do."

"Gotcha!"

"On more thing love. *I* do all the talking!" She says seemingly in arrogance.

"Ok-" He feels her hand against his mouth. He winks at her.

Opening her car door, he fastens his weapons and grabs the bulky book wrapped several times in lambskin. He follows her lead closely and they start their way through the brush, quietly and a step at a time.

Pushing leaves and branches away from their path, they move in careful time of each other. Some branches crack, dried and badly weathered, while others whip back into place. For the most part they keep it very quiet. Each step leading them into the unknown, is one more step committed to Brahnt's memory.

"I can't see them, (whispering) but we're being watched." Brahnt says into her ear.

"I know." She answers back, continuing on and pretending not to be the wiser.

Breaking through the other side. Brahnt and Melonnie find themselves at the base of a large spur.

The ocean waves, crash its white crests against a narrow walk way. Strange, cold chills pass by the both of them. And like tether-like fingers, whispering warnings, they are touched. The ghost like feelings intensify, as they both walk out the narrow walk way.

Despite the eerie feelings, the view is beautiful. The dark choppy water is more than inviting. A few hundred yards into the ocean is another landmark. Like a spiraling tower of rock erecting for the water, the land mass seems to reach towards the moon. In all of his travels in the world Brahnt feels the power of this monument. Reaching out to him she takes his hand into his and they make their way to the end of the rocky walk. Nearing the end, Brahnt looks at her. Her hair dances upwards, as so does his.

"What now Beautiful?"

"We go that way." She rolls her eyes in the direction of the sky.

"How?" He returns the question, unable to see any passage up the steep cliff. Taking his hand into hers and coming face to face, his feet become lighter. "Well?" She looks down at his feet.

"Oh my-" His hands clench hers, as he watches the ground below as it becomes smaller by the second.

Releasing her right hand, he reaches for her neck. Bringing himself closer to her, fear touches him like a thousand little needles.

"Hey (she says softly)relax. I got you. You wouldn't want all the other wampires to make fun of you? Would you?" Her voice is soothing. So soothing that it relaxes him. "Look there." She says pointing.

Between the fingers of the large ocean rock, the moon shines through. The night is of a pale dark blue and her beauty bewitches Brahnt.

Coming over top, they land on the soil. Brahnt carefully looks down. Vertigo. 'That is a long way down.' " Is that the only way back?" She nods her head. In the distance there is another erection, but this one has been created out of purpose. "Wow! I've never seen a castle like this before. How long has it been here?"

"I don't know. A long time I suppose. This is where the highest and mightiest of creatures bring their problems to be solved. Many languages and many great minds. I hope that someday I will be the one called Headmaster."

"Onward then. Friend."

"Together then!" She smiles back at him and together they make their way to the castle.

[Entering the Castle]

The wet soil gives way to each step they take, as the doors near themselves closer with each independent motion. The gusty wind stumbles on the uneven terrain, picking up leaves and carrying them off in miniature whirlwinds. Melonnie approaches the door with extreme caution. She cants her head to one side, as if looking at the clouds east of her. Reaching out with her ear, she searches for any sound that may lead to understanding the extreme quiet amidst. Her feet reach up to the cold stone stairs and set themselves down upon it. The grit trapped beneath her feet only alarms her further. His feet too touch down, making the same gritty sounds, prompting them to look at each other.

Placing one foot over the other, they both reach the wooden doors. Iron wedges and large bolts hold up the door. The wood seems olds and weathered. Much of it is splintering and pitted. Melonnie's gentle and soft knuckles strike out against the hard wood, but little sound is made. Or at least so it is believed. Giving each other a stare and without much else said, (her lip curls) she takes the lead.

Taking the handle firmly into her hand, she grips the iron ring from the lion's mouth and twists the door open. Releasing a series of metallic explosions echoing down the halls of the castle's entrance, the rust breaks suddenly from the old hinges and gives way to her thrust. The sounds, hollow, pound waves of echoes down the hall giving definitions to its depth. The rust catches Brahnt's attention, as he is left wondering if there is anyone truly there. And for a moment he has doubts. Angered by the noise, which obviously would announce their entrance, Melonnie pushes the doors with greater strength. They respond and swing reluctantly hitting the inner walls. As they crash into the walls, the wood metal and stone come to an agreeable but eerie harmonizing note.

One footfall after the other, she steps beyond the six foot entrance way. Continuing forward, they enter the main room. As they walk deeper into the center of the room, Brahnt quickly makes mental notes of the burning candles. However, he takes heed to a more eminent danger.

Twitching her nose slightly, she sniffs at the freshly poured glass of Blood Wine resting on a well-set table. Her eyes scan, the room searching out for the mysterious reason behind the wine glass and the burning candlelight. Narrowing her eyes, her nose catches the scent of another danger. However, as she so searches out the reasons for the mystery, the eyes of reason fall upon them. Unknown to her the room has many eyes observing each of their moves.

Ghost like images wait patiently as the two bodies make their way into the center of the room, where fate would be their deaths. High above them, many cling to the ceiling. Against the walls, they defy gravity.

It is apparent that they have camouflaged themselves well, blending into their surroundings, by bending light and mocking the appearance of the objects surrounding them. As the strangers step deathly close by them, within a breath away, they are oblivious to the ambush. As he does, they sniff at him and her. She smells of familiarity. However, he does not. The male's shoulder brushes lightly against one of them, which stands near a tall candleholder. Behind the candle light the stranger looks directly through him and to the other side of the room. As it seems the strange man is not aware of their presence.

Walking closer towards the nearest dinner table the ghostly creatures watch as the male reaches out for a delicate glass of poured blood wine. He places his nose to the rim, inhaling. Judging by his immediate thoughts and his facial expression, the scent is almost recognizable and for the moment he cannot remember where he has smelled it before. The act of his memory will buy him time. 'Who is this man and this woman who have come through the halls of ancient warriors and masters of the underground world?' Most curious is the question, 'How have they come up from the ridge and ocean front, when the castle sits so high on a cliff? Has humanity invaded or discovered them and if so what is their purpose of their visit?' Still, like a fixed ornament, many wait confused and unaware of the results and waiting for directions from their leader. As the strange man passes by, eyes open revealing their black lacquered expression. A subtle sound of a sheath bringing birth to cold steel. He takes a sip of the wine. "Foul!" He spits it out, landing on the face of one of the ghost like creatures sitting before the wine. To his surprise, the wine camouflages on impact, also bending light.

Brahnt's looks turn onto Melonnie. He projects to her the thought of glass breaking. Melonnie takes the Que. Quickly changing her body, Melonnie camouflages herself. For a moment Brahnt notices her outline standing before him. But as she takes speed there is merely even the evidence of a cool breeze.

Brahnt throws his leg over the table, kicking off the candleholder, forcing it down into the chair. The image of a heavy man appears first outlined in flames and then outlined in their natural environment. The man stands to a scream. Brahnt swings his weapon across the way, taking aim across the table. (his tie falls on his shoulder) He removes his weapon, coming to rest on one knee. (impulses to his brow and finger) his trained eye calibrates with his weapon and he fires. Drawing back the dagger, the vampire motions for the throw. The bullet strikes at the hilt of the blade. Blood spurts out from the wound. The vampire brings his hand to his chest, succumbing to his wound and camouflaging himself once more, while two others rush towards Brahnt in their invisible state. Melonnie, also camouflaged, charges at them. In mid air, she collides with them one at a time.

Projecting them away from Brahnt and into the floor underneath. He watches with amazement, as their invisible bodies smash the table and chairs. Turning to the higher landing, Brahnt fires quickly at the posts of the thrown. The bullet splinters the lion heads.

A figure of an older man materializes, next to the target. As he stands, he holds his hand out and yells out. "Enough!" The room is stilled. Looking around carefully, searching for the strange woman, he addresses the strange man holding a weapon. "I take it you were trying to capture my attention?"

"Yes sir." Brahnt says to him with direct intentions.

"I can see that you are not a man that kills for the sport or fear. So tell me what brings you here?"

"I have something for you." He says careful not to tip his hand too soon.

"What could you possibly have for me, child?" He smiles with amusement. Brahnt reaches behind him, pulling up at his sack. Throwing it onto another table it lands, hitting hard and heavy. Not removing his aim or his eyes from the man standing before him, his finger reaches out taking a hold of the back end. Pulling it up and shaking it, the book slides out and hits the table as if it were a brick and unyielding. Members at the table come out of camouflage and move away from the table, some tripping, while others only stumble on each other. A deep look of regret forces its way to the man's expression, fastening itself to the image of his face. (dropping his head) "I am sorry." He picks his head up and redirects his attention towards Brahnt. "You are human?"

"Yes." He answers with a tone of caution. No sooner said, whispers surface filling the silence.

"Holster your weapon, Human. We will do you no harm." More whispers. This time only louder. "I have spoken!" He says pointing his finger at all parts of the room. The room silences.

"Brahnt." He says to the elder.

"Ah yes. Your name?" He asks outwardly for reassurance.

"Yes. My name."

"Tell me Brahnt, who was the Angelica?" He says disregarding the question for his own.

"Tell me first. Your name?"

"Quantis. And leader of the clan? Your accomplice? Is it... (he points the woman standing next to him) Melonnie?"

"You know her well?"

"No! I only her knew mother. We thought she had been killed a hundred years ago on the raid of Mount Bejaux. Come out girl! I will insist on your safety." There is no sound. Brahnt clears his thoughts. "Ah yes and the safety of Sir Brahnt."

Melonnie reappears and he is surprised to see that had he not been agreeable, his life would have ,been ended abruptly and without sound. Standing before him, she places her dagger back into its sheath while maintaining her cold, angry stare. "Welcome. Please dine with us. We did not expect for you to bring a human with you. Keeper! Kill a swine and roast it for our human guest. They have brought us what we need to defeat our enemies! Make it the best pig there is!" Melonnie drops her guard and brings the knife to its sheath. Quantis' look seems more relieved. Melonnie walks to where he stands and looks him dead in the eye. Her look is one that is filled with disgust.

"Don't you recognize your own kind?" Her words are threatening. "Besides fat-man. You skills are too rusty. Like the door that lead me to this place." Her mood is obviously dangerous.

"It wasn't you, child. It was he! (he looks over her left shoulder) He stinks. (she doesn't look amused) Maybe if you would have walked upwind- but." Still looking into his eyes, she sees that he is sincere. One of her eyes comes to relax. And she bursts out in laughter. The room, able to hear all by way of thought, laughs aloud. Brahnt is in the center, with obvious confusion. And all eyes come to greet him.

"What?" Brahnt asks aloud, shaking his head and throwing out his hands in defeat.

"Monsters? Who can understand them?" He reaches down to the table before him. The burned man sits still, with only light stains caused by the fire. Brahnt takes a hold of the wine bottle and pours himself a drink. Before anyone there can give any warning him, he swallows. The flavor is foul! His mouth, rejecting the horrible flavor, secreting even more saliva. His cheeks puff outwardly with the increased volume. Turning to where the burned man sits, he prepares to spit. Locking eyes with the burned man and realizing that this would be a repetition of the same event, he holds steadfast. The burned man squints one eye down against his eyelid. The look is overwhelmingly threatening.

Brahnt swallows and swallows hard. The room breaks out to laughter once more. The burnt man comes to a stand. Reaching over at the pail Brahnt, he pats Brahnt's back offering his chair. Looking to the kitchen, he says nothing and gestures very little. A small figure moves about quickly and through the doors leading into the cooking room. Brahnt can see little of what is beyond, though he is intrigued.

"We have no time for curtsy, your kingship. Vigore has trailed me since the beginning of my journey!" Melonnie calls out. Two guards take the unsuspecting Brahnt by the shoulders. Melonnie looks at Brahnt then at the Headmaster. "What are you doing?"

"He won't be harmed! He needs only to be inspected. Reluctantly, Brahnt's body is detained. The two guards sniff at Brahnt expecting to find or detect anything out of place.

"He doesn't smell like a witch." One of the guards exclaims.

"Now isn't *that* surprising!" Brahnt sarcasm goes by seemingly unnoticed. Melonnie smiles at his remark, but stares directly at the Headmaster. From under the floor rises an iron cage. "Look you old fool! (the cage is opened) Can't you find another way of finding out the truth?" A jolt and Brahnt is pushed inside. The door locks behind him.

"Your clothes Man!" The guard calls out.

"You got to be kidding?"

"The sooner we inspect them, the sooner you'll be released. It is not you we are worried about. It is what you may be carrying. Your clothes?"

With those words he begins undressing. The crowd observes with interest. The women are especially peaked. Bearing his chest the room fills with sounds of amazement. Melonnie laughs the while.

"All humor aside Headmaster, we may not have enough time. We may need to break the information within this book, at another adjournment. We have to appoint someone to guard over it. (a flash of Vigore) Have you men at each tower?"

"We have a location over top that looks out in all direction."

"Good." She nods her head taking a glance at Brahnt's naked body. There are stares of amazement and disbelief.

"Look at him! He's gorgeous." A woman cries out from the back room. Brahnt feels enlightened. Melonnie smiles at the comment.

"No he's not." Calls out another female from the opposite corner of the room. Brahnt's hearing searches out the hidden speakers. Looking from one corner of the ceiling to the other, he finds nothing more than stones and for the moment it would seem that the stones are speaking to him.

"This is not the time ladies!" Melonnie interrupts. "Besides, he's mine." The room mutters with astonishment.

"Melonnie!" The headmaster exclaims with disbelief.

"How many human women have you bedded? It's OK when its a man, but when it comes to a woman's life the rules change?" Her tone takes on a stronger and deeper anger.

In the background, Brahnt shakes his head and waves his arms. Melonnie's eyes fix themselves on his. Two guards, fearfully take his side. "When is it that a female can live her own life, without some fat male sitting on fat chair giving orders of something he knows nothing about? Well, (she draws her talons) unlike yourself, I have love of this man." The Headmaster swallows hard.

"Now Melonnie. I only meant that it was sudden and unexpected. But for love everything is possible." He holds out his hands, palms open.

The doors reopening suddenly interrupt all thoughts. The room shivers and quakes, as the steps of Erasmus' boots enter the room. Entering with a proud stride, he studies every face, recognizing some while memorizing others. All heads bow.

"I say," Erasmus speaks, "that if the world cannot get over this prejudice and these double standards, a woman should take her own equality into her own hands. Behead the bastard!" Erasmus continues his confident strolls towards Melonnie. Passing the cage he looks at Brahnt, "Hello mister. Nice to see that you stuck it out."

"Ah! Erasmus, nice of you to come through." Fearfully, the head master steps back as so does his guardsmen.

"Look you fat tub of lard! That's my friend in that cage. And if you don't free him, I'll have to take your eyes and wear them as a souvenir. That's of course provided that Melonnie doesn't need them first." Erasmus says drawing his sword.

"The human must be inspected. We are living in a high-tech world. (turning to the inspectors) Please check Mr. Brahnt's clothing. Enough with the fat jokes! Sit Erasmus. Drink." The Headmaster invites them.

Chapter 12

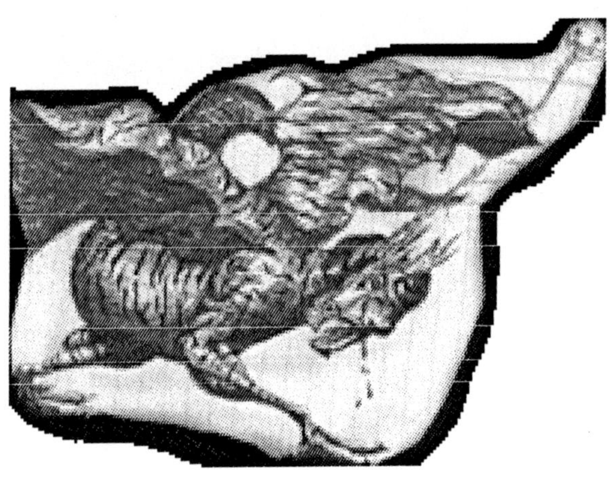

Shadow Creature

Nunca
(Spanish Version)

Tocarme es
Liberal tus deseos.
Ya no te de
Miedo del futuro.
Yo te deso
Besar tu boc.a
Dejame sentirte
Y
Nunca despertar.
Nunca le realidad nos alcansara

Twisting tides

[Guards on the tower]

Looking into the chilled and frigid night air, approaches a small cloud of darkness. Within them is the presence of evil. The purest form of evil known to earth. The guards at the tower study the approaching cloud. The blue psychic closes his eyes, allowing his mind to stretch out as far as the ocean can take him. Closer and closer to the cloud his mind reaches. His partner, standing beside him, watches the sweat make its way down his blue face. Reaching out further and further, his soulless body fills with fear. There is a sensation present, but one that is unknown. His face twitches. "What do you see? Sign to me, old friend." In the near distance and seemly coming closer, he sees the black cloud. As it obstructs the sight of the moon, there is more definition to it. In fact it doesn't seem to be a cloud at all. 'In fact-' (he thinks).

Blood runs down the face of the blue Natural. The guard, standing, observes the flowing blood. Unable to believe what is happening, he is temporarily paralyzed by shock. Still mind melting with the distant cloud, his closed eyes bleed. His muscles flex, tensing to the point of pain. The muscular spasms force his body to shake violently. Bringing his hand to his chest, he draws the letter "V" with his own blood. Unable to breathe, his lungs pull at the walls of his throat caving them in. His nostrils flare, pulling down towards his upper lip.

Concerned, he moves between the blue Natural and the cloud. However, his attempt to shield the bleeding Natural is meek compared to the dark forces at hand. Looking desperately for a sign, he stumbles across his unclenching fist.

Feeling out the stiffly jointed Natural, he can clearly define the letter "V" within his fingers. "Vigore?"

[Vigore]

Dark figures riding upon dark winged creatures near the castle. Each rider carries the face of death, as they ride manifested creatures summoned from darkness and created from their own energy. There is a deathly silence among them. The wind swirls strangely between each rider. Maintaining their focus toward the castle, the only sensation in common is the harsh breeze of the wind pulling at the strands of hair. Picking up strands at a time. Each flap of their wings, carries the Black Coats closer. Vigore feels the life force of the Blue Psychic escaping his body, and so continues reaching out to him. Mind melting with the Blue Psychic, he tries forcing his eyes open. However, the distance is too great, therefore unable to obtain complete domination.

Leaving his dying companion, the guard darts to the door, pressing his kinetic energy against the wooden mass. Stones crumble, making powder trails, as they swing against the walls.

[Inside]

"Brahnt? You may have your weapons and your clothes. Welcome to our castle. All hear this! That Brahnt has been cleared and he is not a spy. Please rele-" Quantis' voice is cut short, by the sounds of the doors blasting open and slamming their immense weight against the walls. The sound arrests all the silence, removing all sound within the room. Melonnie's compassionate eyes turn to the intruder. He too is out of breath, but for other reasons. Pushing himself through, he rushes down the stairs and into the crowd with the look of urgency. Struggling to understand, the crowd turns to him maintaining fearful silence and waiting for his next words with greater anticipation.

"Speak!" Quantis yells. Struggling to breathe, he falls to one knee, extending his fingers forming the letter "V".

"Vigore!" Melonnie says. "I hope that it's not to late."

"It is never too late to have some fun. Besides, I owe some of those boys a run for their money." Erasmus turns to Melonnie, grinning.

"Nice Expression!" Melonnie compliments.

"I saw it on TV! Thanks." Answers Erasmus.

Having been heard the guard's hands falls over the iron rail, trailing with blood. The others, stunned, stand amazed and with little motion. Realizing the gravity of the situation, Melonnie and Erasmus clear the table. Reaching into his wardrobe, Erasmus pulls out his dagger and commences carving a battle plan. Melonnie, points at strategic areas of the table, while Erasmus engraves the battle plan close to her vocal specification.

"Priests! (with authority) To each post! In two's! Take your holy symbols and cast your spells. Fire! Wind! Godspeed. Two guards per Priest! Point North, East, West, and South. Assemble a fourth to meet battle in the air. Assemble a fourth to meet battle at the foreground. A fourth to the see barrier and the rest to hold the integrity to the castle." She points her finger about and motions for the dispatch.

The room moves about swiftly and without question. From the walls they pull ropes, opening old hidden doors. With their cavities they find weapons. The lines are long, as they move as swiftly as they can, taking a hold of their familiar weapons. "Erasmus!"

"I know I'll take to the sky." He says. Meet me back here when this is over."

"Erasmus your weapon?" She calls out to him.

"I am all the weapon I need! If I need one, I'll just borrow it." Erasmus runs forward and dives into the air chanting phrases. With his hands open in legs straight back, he nears the glass window in form of a cross. Closing his eyes, beneath his projection manifests a Shadow Creature. He reaches out to it, straddling it as one would a horse. The glass breaks, as he passes through it. The stained fragments fall to the stone floor.

Brahnt calls out her name, but it is of no use. There is too much noise surrounding them. He watches as three other vampires suit her, for the armed combat. Beside her, Brahnt's clothes and briefcase are placed on a table. Brahnt looks at his weapons with desperation and hungry for a piece of the excitement.

"Let me out! Mel. Let me fight by your side!" Brahnt's hands reach for her between the iron bars, but no one takes notice of him. To them he is just a child, who would serve better to have him sit still and take his chances at not being noticed, than dying a tortured death at the hands of the world's worst villain. The Priests stumble through stonewalls, climbing stairs leading them to their rehearsed position. Brahnt, still in the cage, yells for his release. But Melonnie is much too far to be reached by his calls.

Dark clouds begin surrounding the sky, darkening it even further with an unnatural feeling of power. Melonnie turns to Brahnt's direction. Her hair whips around her, as she turns her face towards him. Her eyes meet with his. She takes a hold of her gear, handed to her, and places it into position. Looking at the headmaster, she points to Brahnt's cage. He moves about the cage, trying to understand what she is saying. But only bits and pieces can be understood. Melonnie turns to Brahnt once more and mimes the words "I love you". Brahnt eyes look to the distance with displeasure, sug gesting his disagreement. The elder's hands fumble through his clothing, searching for something. To his side, barely hidden by red cloth, is the Book of Vigore. Finding the key to the cage, the Elder releases a sigh of relief and begins making his way to Brahnt.

He tries to maintain his view of both of them. (another battle group leaves for combat) Brahnt can see their years of training reflected in their efficiency and calculated movements. It is almost as if not a single action is wasted. A group of fighters crowd, taking Melonnie away from his sight, while the Elder forces his way through the crowd of naturals.

[Brahnt]

Reaching Brahnt, the headmaster pushes the key into the whole and opens the door. Embarrassed but proud, the headmaster looks into Brahnt's eyes with compassion and concern. "Our love be with you."

"And with you. Where did Melonnie go?" Brahnt replies.

"She is in charge of the water troops. You shouldn't follow that path. I know of a hiding room for you. You can wait there until the fighting has passed. You may not survive, but it will prolong your life." The Headmaster tells him while pointing and leading the way, but Brahnt will not move.

"This is not the time to run and hide. (walking over to his weapons) Not when so much is at stake and definitely not when the Vampire I love is at battle. I will not live this between cowardly shadows. (arming himself) I've come to prove myself and if destiny has brought me here then here is where I shall fight!" He tightens his belt.

"Melonnie thought you were going to behave that way. Take this!" He reaches out to him, extending a metal goblet.

"What is it?" He says while looking at the Headmaster's hands. To the side of one he sees the Elder is bleeding.

"It is my blood! It will give you a chance to have our strength. It's temporary, but it is the only chance you have."

Briskly, he walks to him taking the goblet into his hands. Without so much as lifting his head, Brahnt places the goblet to his mouth and drinks. Making several faces as the warm liquid fills his stomach, he feels the burning sensation of the liquid brewing. Cramping, he falls to his hands and knees. "Don't fight it child. It'll only hurt worse!" Brahnt lifts his face, staring at the Elder through new eyes.

"But you taste to bad." The priest looks into his devilish eyes and realizes the power within the man. For the first time he can see what Melonnie loves so much of him. "Go forth and conquer or hell will have us all!"

[Brobova]

Already in place, the Priests focus on their individual tasks. Holding their magical staffs in one hand while the other hand stretches outward, their guards surround them, lifting their shields protecting them of any attack. Chanting in the ancient Angelic Languages, the skies take on different forms. Thunder rolls across the clouding sky, while lightning travels among the clouds, like a stalkers searching out for its prey. The array of colors make for beautiful sky flowers, however there is no beauty in its intention. For tonight the reapers will rise to take from the earth and fill the void of their dominion. Their chanting increases with power and so do the clouds that surround them. Brobova, chants among them.

In the distance, Vigore sits high on his Shadow Creature also chanting. Extending one of his hands towards the castle, he projects a ball of fire. The glow lightens the faces of many that ride near the lord of darkness. But unaffected they ride on with only one thought on their minds, death to all that oppose.

Cumulonimbus clouds, above the riders, obscure as Vigore's spell leaves his hand in a blinding light.

Brobova, opening his eyes, becomes aware of the oncoming fireball. Concentrated and determined to his fate, he moves not nor is he led astray. Bravely, he continues to chant increasing his power. One of the protectors moves in front of him. Looking at his comrade he reaches out for his hand.

Accepting his hand, he is given a shield. The glowing force surrounding Brobova, is near complete. Showing its true size, the flaming ball appears ominous. The dark moving flames weaves within itself, illuminating the stone balcony. The UnNatural lifts the heavy shield to his shoulder and braces himself, he prepares for the impact. Bringing the shield between him and the approaching ball of death he braces himself. Impact!

The UnNatural staggers backwards, trying to maintain his equilibrium. Rooting his feet into the ground, his muscular body prevents further movement. Deflected by the curved design, he drops the red-hot shield to the ground. With scorched hands he prides himself at having deflected the fireball. "It's empty! It was only fire." Curious, he turns to the wall where the fire still burns though scattered onto the stones. "Is that supposed to happen?" He says to the other, receiving only a shrug of the shoulders for a response.

Reaching down to the cooling shield, the UnNatural brings it to his shoulder. Upon the touch of his fingertips and like a trigger, the flames revive. Burning brighter, the UnNatural turns, looking over his shoulder. The flames have grown! They leap from the wall and onto the UnNatural. Like a hand gripping its victim, the flames bring him to his knees, consuming his flesh. Kicking and screaming, he rolls from one side of the balcony and onto the other. His comrade, steadfast, is unable to move for fear that Brobova's life may be at jeopardy. Though his orders are simple, they suddenly become unbearably painful to obey. But, he knows and understands that he must protect the Priest until he has established himself fully powerful.

Vigore, leading the army, reaches to his shoulder grabbing at his crossbow. Bringing it to his lap, he stocks it with an arrow. Simultaneously, as if rehearsed a million times, the Black Coat's and Red Wolves perform the exact same task. Vigore, sighting his target, takes aim. They aim, following his lead. All together they launch their arrows. Slicing through the night sky, they leave blue traces of light trailing behind them.

Brobova's protector reaches down for a second shield. The smell of his comrade's flesh burning, fouls the night air. Letting out a fierce scream, he takes the smoldering shield and places it in front of the Priest. The pain from his hand races through his body and into his heart. Bringing up his second hand he leans the heavy shield on the stonewall. Small loose stones fall to the hard floor beneath his feet. Shifting and twisting his foot he prepares for the worse.

Sounds of ricochet and sparks illuminate the night air, as most of the arrows are deflected. However, a few of them, catching at the exact angle penetrate the shield at its weakest point. One. Two. Three. The metal rings out, giving way to the steel tips. One of the bolts buries itself through his knuckle and into the base of his forearm. Each blow, forces him to take a step in retreat. The walls beside them both become embedded with other such destructive objects. Small pieces of the stone wall chip and strike Brobova's hand. Blood falls from the wound upon impact. Like a mystery in reverse the blood returns to its wound. Though not healed. The wound bleeds no more. The vampire turns to Brobova and holds out his hands. Brobova heals his wounds and charges his body with the power of his soul, mind and wholeness. The vampire turns to the night air.

Dark wings emerge from the back of his shoulders. With just one leap he takes to the air. Sword in hand he heads off to join his fellow warriors.

[Erasmus]

On a Shadow Creature high above, he waits for the enemy. Watching carefully, he allows the last of his enemies to pass him. Leaning down at the neck of his winged creature, he and his mount descend from their perch. Falling down to his enemy's plane, Erasmus closes in on his target. His Shadow Creature pushes onward and steady, reaching the first of his victims. He watches the wings of a Shadow Creature fold and unfold, carrying the red wolf in front of him. Reaching to his back, Erasmus draws his crossbow. Already loaded, he takes aim. At sights end he waits for the right moment. His finger presses on the trigger. He tugs and the steel bolt is released. The shiny, black object travels forward and true from its messenger. Breaking through his back and puncturing through the front of his chest, he feels the stiff and unyielding rod lodged inside of him. Reaching his hand to his heart, his fingers cut. His face, pale, is forced to look upward, as his muscles of his neck, reject the pain burning within his chest. As his life weakens, his Shadow Creature loses altitude and velocity. It's dark void lightens to transparency, as the victim holds on to his last moments. Breathing becomes heavy, as his life force weakens.

Erasmus' Shadow Creature nears his victim, closing in. Looking down into the dark, choppy waters below him, he sees a familiar shape traveling swiftly underneath the surface of the water. Bending his arm to his waist, he draws his sword. Squinting his eyes he refocuses all of his attention onto his first victim, waiting and estimating for the perfect timing. Leaning forward on the Shadow Creature, he increases velocity.

Below, the shadow breaks through the surface of the water, taking flight. Its cloak, however, looks dry and tattered. Its head reflects against the light of the pale moon. Directing its hollow eyes, seemingly onto Erasmus, it extends a long bone-like finger. As if pointing to Erasmus, the creature takes flight in his direction. Almost instantly the creature closes distance. Now located slightly above his shoulder, Erasmus tries to ignore the bulky creature. "Hmm? The Grim." He says with a slight disgust.

The Reaper, taking short glances at him, glides through air mimicking his every move with great ease. It looks at the dying vampire and then at Erasmus. Letting out a horrible sound, much like a dissonant chord composed of the millions of souls it has captured through its existence, Erasmus' strikes at the reapers face with the hilt of his sword. "Shut it. You're going to give me away!" (metal to bone) The Reaper is pushed aside and for the moment is cloaked. "I got work to do! Reaper!" (moving his sword upright)

Leaning back, the Shadow Creature sails downward and over the dying vampire's shoulder. Erasmus raises his arm, extending the sword eagerly waiting for the first blow to be delivered. Closer and closer to the dying creature he comes, until it's within striking range. Erasmus swings his sword diagonally. The center of the sword comes into contact with the flesh at the base of his victim's neck. As it penetrates deeper through, Erasmus feels the metal separating what seems to feel like the bones of the neck.

Feeling the vibration of his splitting bones vibrating up to the hilt of his sword, Erasmus grins devilishly. The sword rides through and out the other side, separating the victim into two oddly shaped falling pieces. Blood sprays into the open sky with no ground to rest upon. The victim's Shadow Creature disappears from underneath him, as his powers have been removed from within him. Looking over his right should, Erasmus briefly glimpses at the Grim, falling over the severed body. Outstretched, like a bird of prey, the Grim hides the two halves within his dark cloak and with them.

Down… Down into the depth of the dark and mysterious choppy waters they plummet.

"Now you can have him." He says.

Erasmus, observes the breaking of the wave below him, spying more Grim Reapers swimming under the natural camouflage of the choppy waters. He wonders if perhaps within this battle there will be such a reaper that holds his name. For surely heaven has closed the doors on him centuries ago. But as the Priest's words also ring in his ear, he still believes that there may be hope. 'Besides,' he thinks to himself, 'I haven't finished with all of the Hail Marries.' For now only time will tell. Lifting his view, he notices flares approaching him, while blue streaks of fire attack the castle. Leaning forward, he looks on at the unsuspecting enemy with eagerness to combat.

Using his blade as a lance he rides forward. The eyes of his Shadow Creature gleam, reflecting its power. Nearing another one of his enemies from behind, he pushes his saber through its back. The creature lets out a short sound, releasing the air from his lungs. But his expression is what coins the moment. The Vampire places his hands on the blade of Erasmus' sword. Holding the blade, with all of his might, he can only watch as the bold steel slides between his fingers, while Erasmus pulls it back. The Vampire, heavily bleeding, feels his life draining rapidly. All that comes to consciousness, is the sound of him breathing.

The dying Vampire's Shadow Creature releases a small whimper, distracting two more Red Wolves next in rank.

Surprised, by the image of Erasmus, they draw their crossbows. Leaning hard into the dying Shadow Creature, Erasmus grabs a fist of the Vampire's hair. (they fire their crossbows)

Pulling his dead weight off of his mount, Erasmus uses his limp body as a shield. The two bolts penetrate, completing his death. Pulling up on the reins, he climbs towards the lightning clouds. He glances down at the Red Wolves, reassembling for their next attack. Grabbing the head of the dead Vampire, he tugs and pulls until the head severs. Clinging to the reins, he spins in place. The circular motion forces the dead severed body to fall into the open sky, but not before he grabs the Vampire's crossbow. With the severed head in one hand and the crossbow in the other, he leans towards the back of the Shadow Creature and commences descending.

The body plunges down into the hands of the Reaper. Erasmus' eyes focus upon the two Vampires approaching steadfast. Coming out of the spinning circle, Erasmus throws his double-edged sword, while laying the crossbow on his lap. He Fires!

Tumbling through the air, the sword finds its way to one of the Red Wolfs approaching. The hilt of the weapon strikes his chest, bringing him to a sudden stop. The second Red Wolf leans over the neck of his Shadow Creature, placing Erasmus into his sight. He too fires his crossbow!

But Erasmus' projectile lands first. The Vampire's eyes glaze with death amidst. Charging at him, Erasmus leans away from his saddle, taking the dying Vampire's sword. With the bolt wedged into his heart, the Vampire leans over his Shadow Creature out of breath. Holding on to it, he realizes that his fear is well founded. Erasmus was the greatest to have ever fought for their cause. 'A shame', he thinks to himself trying to catch his breath, 'he should have remained on our side'. The wings of the creature come to a halt, as so does his life. But before his body descends it is snatched away by the powerful hands of the Reaper.

Swooping down, as would the eagle, he reaches the vampire to his right. With the sword buried to the hilt against his chest and gasping for air, Erasmus places one foot on his chest and one hand on the hilt. Kicking out with his foot and pulling at the sword, it is freed to terrorize.

Still alive, he grits his teeth. Erasmus, leaping onto his saddle, places the blade of his sword to his throat.

"How did you know where to find us?" He asks. The Vampire trapped and bleeding. Says nothing. Erasmus removes a dagger from his waist and places it between the blades of his enemy's shoulder. "Now you know that this will hurt." (reloading his crossbow he fires at the squadron) The bolt, flying deathly close to other Black Coats traveling in the swarm, turn to define its origin. Much to their surprise, they can see Erasmus' approach toward one of their squadron members.

"I don't care." He squeezes out of his drowning mouth.

"Not a good answer." Erasmus says to him, while pushing the dagger into his shoulder. (the point penetrates)

"Erasmus wait! Please wait! (he gulps, clearing the blood from his mouth) You use to be one of us." Gritting his teeth and opening his eyes wider, he feels the knife penetrating further.

"Ok! (exhaling)" He takes in a breath of air. He inhales. "And what of me when I tell you."

"I'll let you fall Michael. You might live to fight another day."

"Vigore is at the front of the line. He fears that with the book you may find a way of defeating him."

Erasmus pushes the knife deeper into his back. "Holy war brother! Have some patience! I'll tell. Vigore has acquired the allegiance of psychics."

"Good enough brother. Fall now and next we meet I shall kill you swiftly." He pushes him off the Shadow Creature. Erasmus, no longer preoccupied, faces the oncoming Vampires.

Arrows approaching! Erasmus leans down on his Creature, starting his evasive descent. The spray of arrows, skimming overtop, barely come to miss. Following his lead and determined to kill him, the large group of Red Wolves turns their Shadow Creatures and begin to follow. Skimming the water, his enemies pursue reloading their crossbows. Erasmus, approaching the choppy waters pulls on the reins. The dark waters underneath touch his boots, as so does the tips of the Shadow Creature's wings. Erasmus looks into the sky. (more sparkling objects) The Enemy having taken aim, have fired their weapons once again. Standing up on his saddle and leaning all of his weight forward, he forces the Shadow Creature's nose into the cold waters. A powerful sting! He Yells! A bolt stabs its way into Erasmus' shoulder, as he dives. But before, any more can stab him he is safely into the ocean. Bubbles! He watches the assortment of arrows fall into the water, losing their fury. Raising his eyes, and using his night vision he can only see the distortion of the shadows of the enemy passing over him.

A shower of bolts rains upon them, burying themselves with no prejudice. Moans become a real part of their surroundings. The squad leader looks behind, at his elite soldiers. He watches the bolts lodging themselves into their necks, chests, knees, and thighs. The blood spilling from their bodies, is caught be the choppy waters. Pain! A bolt lands against his arm. He looks up. Something else shines. Reaching up he grabs the falling object.

As sudden as it came, the death rain stops. All is quiet for the moment, as they assemble searching out for Erasmus. The leader signals to of his me to swim underneath the water in search for him. There is nervous laughter in the ranks. Though most of them had only heard of the Legendary Vampire Warrior, the stories all seem to leave their deep impression of doom to all that opposed him.

Bubbles! More Bubbles! Two bodies float to the surface of the water, each of them with severed heads. More fear strikes into the heart of the troupes. Their Shadow Creatures, once steady move about, colliding against each other. "Calm yourselves!" commands the leader. "Draw your swords! Regain your will. We'll take flight to the castle!" But, before he can give the final command, the thought of Erasmus comes back to haunt him. He looks below him, trying to see into the deep water. It becomes disturbed and violent.

"Sir?" calls out the squad leader. "Do you wish us to continue?" The squad leader studies the expressions posted on his troupes. They seem as nervous as he is, if not more.

Turning his head to the squad leader, the water suddenly sprouts out with a massive death attack! From within the depth of the mysterious waters, emerge Melonnie and her troupes. Springing from underneath, they take a hold of the Red Wolves striking out with their swords and tearing out their life force with razor like talons.

Melonnie rises from the choppy, bloody waters, holding a knife between her teeth. Jumping onto the leader's Shadow Creature, she lands behind him. Reaching out to, she takes a hold of his head with gouging claws and a knife pointing into his heart with her other hand. Making a move for his sword, she claws at his neck. Melonnie's talons tear at him.

His fingers slip, losing the grip on the sword's hilt and he is forced to lean back. Displaying her intentions, she pushes at the knife slightly. Blood spills onto the blade, snaking its way to the opposite end, where it drips into the water.

"You!" (with a raspy voice)

"That's right! Lets see if you can get it right this time." She twists the knife deeper into him.

"Tell your men to surrender." Melonnie says gritting her teeth and holding him tighter.

"Never!" He yells out.

"Cut his head off! I'm through being nice." Erasmus says to her, coming out of the water on his Shadow Creature.

Silently, A singular arrow moves between soldiers. Erasmus, circling his hands in front of his body, snatches the arrow from the air. With the same motion and energy he buries the arrow into the leaders leg. The leader screams out horribly. Removing a dagger from his leather harness, Erasmus flicks his wrist toward his aggressor.

The aggressor is silenced, falling into the water where his head is now severed. Erasmus looks into the crowd with great distaste. Terror and intimidation fill their hearts like never before. "I can take you all on! Last chance!" (Erasmus draws his sword)

"Halt! Bleib bitter still!" (Halt! Be still!)

'German?' Erasmus questions. 'Why?' The soldiers drop their weapons into the choppy water below.

"Smart move." Erasmus says to them. Like a fly caught in a spider's web, they await for the next instruction. The cold, bloody waves crash on their faces.

Now, seeing her enemies unarmed, Melonnie gives her last order. Erasmus, kicks his heels into his Shadow Creature. Extending his saber and rushing down the center of the squad, he decapitates several Red Wolves. The Naturals leap onto the unsuspecting squad slaughtering Black Coats with extreme prejudice.

Melonnie observes, as the enemy troupes are taken down into the water. "Nice?" She whispers into the leaders ear. "Isn't it? When the shoe is on the other foot. Tell me Tiak? What are you feeling now? Fear? This is no fear compared to what hell is going to have in store for you."

Biting down into his neck, as taught in combat training, she remembers the beautiful things that Brahnt has shown her. And comparing her world to his, she wishes she could wash her hands of the madness. 'Why can't we live as one? Why since the beginning of time?' (remembering the castle) She lifts her head. "To the castle! Find the Book of Vigore and Guard it with your lives. Vigore is here and so is his witchery! Beware!" She wipes her mouth of his blood and pulling out his heart, she drops the body into the water. Clenching her fist, she squeezes his heart, until it is no longer recognizable. The crazy sounds from Erasmus, brings humor back to her senses.

"What about Brahnt?" One of them calls out from the waters.

"Yeah the Human? What about the human?" Calls out another voice. A silence grows on the surface of the choppy waters. Melonnie takes a deep breath before answering.

"Find him, guard him! But guard the castle first. We must not loose tonight's battle for the short life of a human. If we fail tonight all of humanity will suffer and so will we." Melonnie answers confidently.

"If you find yourselves weak. Drink from Vampire blood. They have taken it from the humans giving them super strength."

One by one they all sink into the ocean's salty water. And for the moment it would seem that there had never been a battle.

[The castle]

The enemy nears. The priesthood has come to complete strength. Fire lights the sky in form of fireballs and lightning. Each, with their witchery, both Evil and Holy fight to dominate the sky. Casting a spell, Vigore creates darker clouds concealing themselves. Lightning from the castle penetrates the cloud. A vampire feels the power of the lightning, as he is struck down by one of the bolts. His hands burn and become dry down to the bone. He and his Shadow Creature, are carved into statues, crumbling into the wind as they fall. And, unaffected, the warriors move on.

Brobova looks deep into the approaching cloud. He knows that the spell will have to be soon lifted and he fears that his enemies are aware of it too. Still, as he waits for the second part of the plan to come into phase, he dispels any idea of weakness or defeat. Lightning flashes, come out from the forces surrounding him, as well as the other three priests. The blue-white lightning strikes at the approaching clouds, striking down more men. Brobova, opening his eyes, looks into the sky. "They are too close! Where are the sky troops?" Guiding his attention below, he sees more of the naturals surrounding the castle perimeter stabbing crosses into the ground and holding their crossbows. Their shiny long swords glisten, reflecting the lightning streaks and small fires.

Unable to ward off Vigore's magic any longer, the villainous cloud comes into contact with the building. A fascinating flash of brilliant light! Lightning strikes at random bodies unable to distinguish the good from the evil. The balance of power is now equal. Having lost valuable time and a great deal of his soldiers, Vigore understands his odds. Taking to the walls and the higher levels. Vigore's men fall off of their Shadow Creatures and into battle with their swords in hand.

Sword to sword, brother to brother the sounds of metal cling and clash. A thick mist surrounds them. Bringing his Shadow Creature lower to the ground, Vigore kicks his leg over the head of his Shadow Creature and allows his heavy body to fall onto the earth. His weighted feet bury themselves into the soil, before the great doors of the castle as his Shadow Creature blends into the mist.

From behind him come two of his greater warlocks. Observing his dead, he watches his men killing and destroying as well as being killed. Among the crowds battling, reapers take away the evil dead. The two warlocks spring from their creatures, landing near their master, side by side. Absorbing the impact of their fall, they land on one knee. Simultaneously and like rehearsed, their dead expressions come afoot. Opening their hands they chant out with deep-rooted evil. Dusty pieces of the cracking wall fall to the earth, leaving its hazy residue. The wind picks up. Small whirlwinds (dust devils) arise at will, lifting small fragments of residue and catapulting them. A small flash of light from nearby.

The warlock, standing right of Vigore, receives a sudden puncture to his chest. Falling to the ground with the eyes of death forming to his appearance, Vigore studies the blood exiting the puncture wound. He turns to the dead Warlock. Leaping onto the dead man's chest. The remaining Warlock, extending his hands, creates a magical shield protecting Vigore and himself, while Vigor digs his finger into the wound and removes a semi-dull object. "What? (examining the object) A Human!"

He releases the bullet, dropping it onto the dead man's body. Vigore's irritated voice distracts the Warlock failing his spell. Another flicker of light. A sudden sharp pain to the back of his knee and Vigore falls onto it. Turning his attention behind him, his eyes catch the glimpse of another flash, almost impossible to detect.

His hand reaches for the Warlock. But it is too late. A dead thud. He is struck a second time. This time blood flows from another wound. Before another word is mentioned, there is yet another flash. Vigore reaches out for the safety of the Warlock, but again he is too late. The Warlock's head rocks violently back, as he is force to stagger. A bead of blood forms on his head, leading a blood trail. As the blood escapes his head, the Warlock drops making no other sound but that of deadfall as his body strikes the earth.

Ignoring his injury, Vigore comes to a stand. Creating a fireball within his hands, he lunges forward throwing it. Walking to the dead Warlock, he presses his glove on the opening wound. The crimson lifeline glistens against the moonlight. Vigore turns, facing the fireball just thrown.

"Brahnt! Curse you!" He releases the head of the Warlock. It hits the ground.

The fireball strikes at the tree. The flames explode stretching outward. Like magical fingers reaching in all directions, the fire waits for its next command. Brahnt leaps off the tree limb, allowing him to free-fall. Holding his rifle up and over his head, it catches on one of the many branches. The fingers of the flame reach back and around tree above him.

Burning fragments tumble beside him. Able to place his foot on one of the lower limbs, he scurries to safety. Adrenaline filters through his veins, causing his body to react with the serum. His outer skin becomes plated with an exoskeleton. Not understanding how the effect was created and having no time to ponder, he straps his rifle to his back and climbs down the burning tree.

Vigore finds Brahnt ability to be most impressive. Holding out his arm, he flags down three other centurions. Leaping off of their Shadow Creatures they fall to the Earth, landing near to Vigore.

"There is a human among them. Entertain yourselves, but capture him alive."

"But sire?" Warns one them, "he is a human and on their side. Is he not a threat?"

Without hesitation, Vigore points his finger at him. A flash of light! A sharp burst of flames. The insolent creature is immediately engulfed by a rage of flames. There is a short scream. But as he opens his mouth, the flames make their way into his body burning him from the inside. Vanishing, the flames leave only an object of ashes, poorly resembling the creature's form. "I should be the one to fear. (the wind picks at the statue) Any more questions?"

Without so much as another word or an expression. The first centurion morphs into a wolf, a red wolf. The other extends its arms creating leather-like wings. The two shape shifters take to the pursuit.

Vigore scans the surrounding battlefield. He looks above, where the battle rages. Fallen are from both sides, his and theirs alike. Behind him more of the UnNaturals fall leaving their Shadow Creatures vanishing in mid flight. Taking a deep breath he absorbs the stench of battle. And though knowingly a stench, he breathes it as if it were the fragrance from roses budding. Taking a step forward, he receives a blow to his arm. At a quick glance, his blood seeps slowly from the wound. Lifting his view to the castle's defensive perimeter, he focuses on another arrow falling to his direction. Lightning hands take the arrow from its path and with a swing like motion he returns it to its messenger. The arrow cuts through the air at twice the speed as whence it came.

The archer receives a jolt of pain, as the arrow twists into his stomach. Placing his palms against the stone mid-wall, he coughs out his own blood.

Below, Vigore reaches for the arrowhead. Unable to attain it by way of hand, he pulls it out in reverse. Though the pain of the wound is evident, however he is too proud to display any signs of discomfort.

Once removed, he takes aim and throws it into the crowd of combatants. Sinking into the heart of a natural, he is content in knowing there is one less natural claiming right to breathe his air. Vigore's wounds heal almost as quickly as they form.

Focusing on the doors of the castle. Creating another fireball, he throws it. It strikes the door with generating ground tremors. Stones crack giving way to breaking stones. Though a powerful blow, his face is one that carries disappointment. Again, his hands come together, creating yet another ball of fire.

[Brahnt]

Falling down onto the mossy ground, he finds that his new flesh is unharmed. He touches his it. It feels soft but impenetrable. (a sound from overtop) Flamed particles fall to his right and left. He moves his eyes upward. (a gasp) A brilliance of yellow. Pressing his feet into the tree trunk, he squats and then pushes off with all of his might. The flaming treetop falls upright. (sounds of tree branches cracking and burning) Brahnt comes to a sudden stop, taking hold of another tree trunk. Rolling over onto his back and pushing franticly away with his feet, the soil gives in part way until his back is completely rested on the trunk of the tree.

He feels the unequal bark scratching at his back. But that is of no comfort. In between breaths, he hears dangerous sounds.

Sounds of something coming forth. (rustling in the leaves. Bushes moving) Motioning, as if to stand, he moves forward. A flash of darkness! Hair! Lots of it! He is unable to breathe. Feeling out with his hands, he feels out the beast that has attached itself to his throat. Trying to pry the creature's mouth open, he prevents further injury. But knowing that his strength will not last, Brahnt releases one hand. He feels the moisture of his own blood spilling down to the base of his neck.

Reaching down into his left boot and still pinned to the tree, he obtains his stiletto. Pressing his wrist aggressively against the base of the creature's neck, he finds the hollow. 'Sweet spot' he thinks to himself.

He stabs. The knife slides easy. The large dog-like creature releases its hold of Brahnt. Falling to the ground it kicks trying to regain composure. Resembling a half human and half beast, it maintains its life between the two dimensions.

A foreign shape. Brahnt notices a figure looming high above. Coming to his feet he hides behind the tree nearest him. Around the tree, scouting both the high grounds and the low grounds he moves. The creature descends to the ground nearest the fire. Brahnt watches the creature spread its wings. The shape shifter changes his appearance into human form. He reaches for his sidearm. Walking over to his partner, he leans to him. But there is nothing he can do. He cocks his weapon, pressing his body against the tree. The sting from his neck wound agitates him. 'All this for trying to impress a girl?' He asks himself. 'Yeah (he smiles) but what a girl!' Watching the once winged creature kneel down besides the half-wolf, Brahnt takes aim.

The creature reaches for the knife pushed into the base of his partner's skull, sliding it out. The Red Wolf lets out a howl, starting the regenerative process. The other comes to a stand, scouting out with his narrow eyes and bat like nose. Charging from behind the tree, Brahnt fires his two automatic pistols simultaneously. One bullet to the chest, one bullet to his shoulder, another bullet strikes the buckle fastening his sword to his back. The heavy sword falls. Barraged with projectiles, the creature leaps to flight. Brahnt drops and rolls. Taking a second to aim, he fires once more. The small rocket penetrates its chest, puncturing through the creature's heart. Taking a hold of his chest, it bends forward.

The bullet breaks through his back, followed by a small stream of blood. He watches the creature fall against the earth. It sounds odd, hard and heavy. Brahnt chases up to him. Taking the sword from the mossy floor, he takes a hold of the hilt. Squeezing the hilt, the moisture on it collects and rolls down the blade. Brahnt swings down against the creature. As its only defense, it places its arms out against the blade. But it is of no use. The creature is slain. (a sound from behind) He swings his sword around.

The sword catches, decapitating the enemy. However, for the moment, he pays little mind to the body falling to the ground. He is content hearing the two heavy sounds smacking down onto the soil. His attention turns to the powerful presence of Vigore's men scouring the fields and storming the castle. Looking down at his victim, he grins. "Damn! Is that all he sent for me?"

Grabbing at his shirt, Brahnt's fingers make their way to his buttons. Unable to unbutton them quickly enough, he rips it away, leaving his chest and back exposed. His muscular arms reach down for his belt. He unbuckles the metal latches and pulls his pants down. (he falls) Naked, his body glistening against the unsteady glow brought from the burning tree limb behind him. Kneeling, he grabs at the decapitated body. Opening the long jacket, he takes notice of the apparel. Looking waist level, he can see no waistband or buttons. He rolls the body over and pulls the jacket off. "Still no buttons?" He looks at the jacket and then at the body. "You've got to be kidding me. I can't go around fighting naked! There's got to be a zipper or something?"

He takes to his feet and throws on the jacket. It closes around him like a glove. He feels the clothing moving about. Its flaps open suddenly. Brahnt looks down at himself, he finds his body covered in the same way as his enemies. "Cool!" he says running his hands around his shoulders. The material is very soft, but very strong. Bending down on one knee, he takes a grasp of the sword sheath and fastens the buckle at chest level. Leaning over towards the sword, he takes the hilt and drags the blade closer to him. Hilt facing the torn skies and blazing rays produced from the fires, he pushes further upright. Blade in hand and empowered, he straps his pistols around his waist. Stepping over to the burning tree limb, he finds his rifle and munitions bag. Looking into the crowd far beyond his human reach, he makes his way out of the woods one foot in front of the other. Each step brings him closer to the crowd of killers.

[Vigore]

Vigore's men assemble on the fields surrounding the castle. The castle doors have been broken open, but their attempts to enter have failed. Opposed by the naturals, they have been unable to enter. From underneath the moss-covered battlefield, emerge the naturals. Vigore's men are taken by surprise. Swords clash back and forth like deadly chimes on a windy day.

Lightning from the Priest's scepters and fire from the hands of Vigore exchange illuminant attacks back and forth. Arrows skim the surface of the land catching hold of opposing forces. Men from the tower fall to the ground, where Vigore's men sever their heads finishing the job. Creatures as old as time fill the night air with cries of pain and just like the mist it fills terror in the hearts of men and women alike. Vigore's men land their Shadow Creatures and combine forces on land. Moving forward, with swords and daggers their deformed faces continue the bloody war. As they fight, they look to the sky, where their brothers fight the same war from a different perspective. Marching on, the sounds are distant but are warning beacons, to what awaits if they survive fields. The sound of their leather uniforms and swords sing in a chaotic harmony, while their bodies perform the deadly ballet.

Between the fields and the castles stands Vigore. Looking backwards into the them, Vigore's eyes fill with a sense of power. Drawing two swords from his harness and leaning forward, he lunges towards the castle. Moving his sword across his body in the shape of X's, he creates a chopping barrier. Arrows launched at him falling from the skyline and are immediately reduced to splinters. A step at a time he moves onward, each time increasing speed. Each time coming closer. Vigore reaches the doors. Passing through them he comes to a complete halt. The tips of his sabers simultaneously strike the stone floor. (sparks!) The two deadly blades gouge out symmetrically at the stone floor and come to a haunting stop. Vigore's cold breath creates a cold mist, and in silence he looks around. The room is well lit, but seemingly vacant. More of his men appear. As one by one they stop at the edge of the door, they crowd the entrance. Vigore moves forward with caution, using his sense of smell and other heightened senses, as he moves forward. His eyes search for any sign of what can be an ambush.

He gives the signal. His troops enter with the same degree of caution. Some of them wear the blood of others, while others wear their own. Most of them however pant, trying to catch their breaths. A step at a time they move forward, with their eyes fixed on anything and everything. The sand trapped between the soles of their boots and the hard surface of the floor, makes for an eerie sound. Vigore takes a healthy whiff of the air. There is a strange scent to it all, but it is muffled with the scent of candles burning.

His men move closer to the middle. Hunched and with bent knees. Their coat tails drag on the floor creating and eerie scraping sound, as their dirty jackets trap and drag the small sand crystals. Small noises from the walls and ceiling echo the silent chamber. In its center and to the right of Vigore's sword is an open cage. Looking to the door Vigore's keen senses notice the slight deformity by the doorframe. Rolling his eyes, he observes the ceiling. The meaning of the word "ambush", heeds warning in his mind.

"Beware the walls!" He calls out, drawing his sword and twisting them slicing at the air. He spins them for a brief moment longer, turning his body in circles. Then he pauses. He removes a dagger from within his holster and aims it at one of his men. Quickly and without anticipation he throws the dagger. The others watch as the dagger comes to full spin and towards the soldier. The dagger halts buried in mid air. The faint shadow of a natural holding a sword is evident. As his ability to bend light dissolves, Vigore's men witness the natural falling to the floor, dead.

A scream! And the silence is broken. The battle begins again. From the walls and the floor, from the ceilings and from behind dark corners, warriors become visible as the naturals come forth, attacking Vigore and his red wolves. Tables are broken in two and smashed to the ground, as enemies of the realm lift each other and throw each other down for the kill. Swords are barely the weapons of choice as they fight in close range. Taken by surprise Vigore finds himself fighting and killing from one person to the next, and this is the way he would have it.

[Melonnie]

At the shoreline the Naturals blend with the mud, the rocks, and the water. They wait for Vigore's survivors that have fallen and now swim to what they believe to be safety. The choppy water submerges Melonnie's face. Erasmus swims to her, bringing his mouth to her ear. "Melonnie? The sun has not risen." Melonnie's eyes look into the sky. He's right the stars are all out of alignment.

"It's a good thing for you." (splashes in the distance) Melonnie motions to two scouts to attack silently.

"I beleive Vigore is using psychics and Warlocks." He whispers to her ear.

"Where would they be hiding?" She questions. (two Red Wolf Soldiers suddenly sink to into the water) She smiles. "The peak!"

"Ah of course. But it's seemingly unguarded." Erasmus says back to her.

"Of course. Leaving it obvious so that we would overlook it. It would take us twenty minutes to swim there."

"I can make it in less than that." He whispers back.

"Erasmus. If you take them out, the sun will give rise and you my friend-"

"Melonnie we'll lose. You know that. Besides If I remember correctly it'll take more than just one of them to cast such a powerful spell."

"You got a point?" She snaps back.

"One dead for the many? The sun will rise slowly."

"And if you're wrong?" He reaches over to her and places a kiss against her forehead.

"We all die Melonnie. But not all of us truly live. If I sacrifice my life for all of you, you'll keep me alive forever."

"God be with you my friend." Erasmus rises from the water. Beneath him the Shadow Creature carries him toward a small towering rock that stands peacefully in the ocean like a giant iceberg. Someone else approaches Melonnie.

"Commander?" Whispers the young female.

"Yes. Come closer." She whispers back.

"Vigore has penetrated the castle. There are at least a hundred soldiers scattered on the field. And they're scaling the walls. They still battle in the skies." She says in manner of a report.

"And Brahnt?"

"They have seen him alive. Killing them in the battle fields."

"Take charge of the troops here. I'll tend to matters in the castle."

"Brahnt is in disguise-" She says to Melonnie, but she is gone.

[The Castle]

Vigore's hands fight through with great power. His saber glides through his enemies flesh as easily as one would cut through butter. Crossing his blades overhead, he blocks his opponent. Sliding his right hand down and swinging backwards he manages to cut through another who fights one of his men. He kicks forward, pushing his heal into his enemy's stomach. His enemy bends over, reacting to the painful blow. Leaning forward he drops the hilt of his weapon onto the bent man's back. A strange sound comes through, as the sharpened hilt penetrates breaking his spine. Drawing his hilt back, (smiling) he swings upward with his other sword. The swing, unobstructed cuts his head cleanly off of his shoulders. "This feels good." He thinks aloud. "Ah what foul stench!" He turns around with his two blades forward. Before him is a figure. His eyes focus. "You!" A shiny flicker. Pain draws his face. Another shiny flicker and more pain is introduced.

"Oui! Je suis là!"

He moves away from the figure that has just scarred him. "Ah! Melonnie? (he wipes his face with his glove) Why are you so angry?"

"You know why! Don't stand here and play God with me! You need to die by my hand!" She moves forward, carefully monitoring her surroundings for potential threats. Vigore lunges forward with the blade carried in his right hand. Pointing the tip of her sword down, she blocks. He swings his left blade. She raises her sword and blocks once again. As the tip of her blade points to his face, it grazes his neck. Feeling the edge of the blade scratching at his neck, he dodges her next strike. It is too close for comfort. They engage blades once again. Swinging in a circular momentum, he attacks at her with twin steel. Melonnie blocks left, right, high and low being unable to strike beyond his speed and precision. "The book girl. Where is the book?"

"Do you think I'm foolish because I'm a female or is it because I'm blond?"

"Melonnie, your gender means nothing to me. (he swings low to her feet)" She blocks low and swings high and across his body. "You naturals bleed all the same way." A Red Centurion swings at her from behind. Leaning slightly forward, she back-kicks. The centurion is caught off guard. His breath escapes him. Vigore moves in for the kill. Kneeling on one knee and spinning around she raises her sword, blocking Vigore's blade.

Bringing herself to a stand, she comes face to face with the centurion. She reaches him and hissing, he is distracted. She spins around him placing between herself and Vigore. Vigore's blade penetrates his back, stabbing through to the other side. Melonnie takes hold of the centurion's blade, while swinging across with hers. Her cut is true and it severs the centurion's head. The tip of her blade slices Vigore's neck, but the damage is minimal. As it bleeds it also repairs itself. She can hear

Vigore's scratchy voice, announcing his surprise. Now with two sabers at hand she stands even more confidently.

"Now old Vampire. Let's dance to the sound of the pail moon, by which we are brothers of the same fate." Twirling her swords they charge at one another. Sword over sword and hand over hand their blades meet leaving sparks and ominous threats, with every motion and every swing.

Using the back of his right hand, he blocks outside to inside, catching her sword. With his left hand he does the same, Leaving Melonnie's chest and stomach unguarded. Leaping slightly forward, he kicks at her. The impact is deep. She falls viciously backwards and against the wall. The back of her head strikes against it. (blurred vision. A long silver object) She staggers to the left. The sword misses wedging in between the stones. She swings her sword across her body, striking the wedged sword. The sword shatters. He swings diagonally across towards her. Pushing herself away from the wall, she rolls onto the ground, passing by him. His sword strikes the wall, once again missing its target. A single spark blazes into thousands of tiny sparks.

Coming out of her roll, she takes notice of a centurion approaching. Lunging her sword forward, she stabs his heart. The centurion drops his hands. His sword falls to the floor. Leaving no time to finish him, she turns to Vigore. Sliding her sword a few feet about the floor, she aims for him. He pushes off of the floor, missing the sword's deadly stroke. She lets out a grunt. "Impressive Melonnie. One might think you were my daughter."

"I would never be your daughter. Bastard!" She answers displaying her deepened hatred. Removing two small throwing spikes from his belt, he cocks his arm and throws them at her. Dropping her shoulder, she rolls away. The spikes stab into the floor. Gliding toward the stairway. He makes his way to the second level. Melonnie pulls at the spikes. Being only able to remove one of them, she quickly takes aim at Vigore, throwing the weapon and sinking it into his left thigh. He lets out a sound of agonizing pain. Using his hands he breaks his fall. He turns his head and focuses on Melonnie's figure.

Sprinting forward, she approaches with a deathly threat. Leaping, she lands her foot on a centurion's shoulder. Using him to propel forward, he falls as she rises. With her two blades crossing in the air, she summersaults on the stairs.

Vigore is no longer there. Fearing that he may know where the Book may be hidden, she stumbles up the stairs. "Vigore!" She yells out. A glowing light. A man screaming. At the top of the stairs falls a man, besieged with, flame consuming, pain. She takes a moment to roll him over and over again, trying to extinguish the hell fire. (pressure on her shoulder) Feeling a strong hand lifting her. Her body is forced against the uneven semi-jagged stones of the wall. Out of breath and in pain she faces her assailant. "Vigore! Merde!" (reaching for her weapon) She spits at him with a mixture of blood and saliva. Balling a fist with his spiked gloves, he punches at her stomach. She lets out an exhausted sound of pain and bends over. Her face falls against his shoulder. Her nose bends into his leather. Striking upwards, the back of his fist propels her head back into the stonewall. He removes a spike from his belt. Weakened by the might of his blows, she remains limp and struggling. Holding her hand across her body he drives the iron spike into her hand. She yells! But though it is a horrid sound, it is like music to his ears.

Looking over his shoulder she notices the change in the clouds. "I am going to save you. I will burn you like I burned your mother!"

"No you won't." Her whisper is faint, as she gains her strength.

"A last plea for survival?" He questions her in a mocking tone.

"No. Look." She raises her eyebrow to the breaking clouds. "You'll never make it out of here alive." She reaches with her free hand, wrapping two of her fingers around one of the remaining spikes. Vigore turns his view to the clouds. He sniffs the air. It smells of sun.

"But how?"

"Go ask Erasmus. He knows you best." She says in a stronger whisper. She raises her hand. He turns to face her. She strikes down. The spike catches in the nape of his neck. Unable to breathe and disoriented by the lodged spike, he staggers backwards. Sliding her hand down his side armor, her fingers fasten themselves to what seems to be a canteen strap. "Where are you going daddy? You're staying here with me!" Feeling the call of danger, Vigore pulls himself away. Spiked to the wall, she balls her fist, but is unable to hold on. The strap breaks, leaving Vigore to escape. He pulls the spike out with both hands. But the expression of defeat is permanently engraved in his mind.

"You will die Melonnie. Watch the skies with care." His raspy voice warns her. His chilling voice fills her with fear. Her lips quiver, trembling. Her eyes are widened. Vigore turns to the window and with open arms glides out into the night air disguised in a hell creature. Or is it a disguise?

She pulls at the spike, but is unable to remove it. Grabbing her wrist, she pulls her hand away from the wall. The spike tears her fleshy hand. More of her blood streams down her arm like external veins. Suddenly giving way, her hand becomes free. Falling to her knees exhausted and abused, she places the drinking pouch on her lap and pulls the nub. Bringing it to her nose she takes a sniff. Cautiously, or perhaps with exhaustion, she brings it to her lips.

Taking in as much as she can swallow, she feels the sensation of replenishment. Though the taste is somewhat stale, it is blood. Human blood. Looking down at her wounds she watches them heal. But her judgment is impaired. The body can heal, but her mind needs rest. Still there's no moments here for resting. There are no more sounds of heavy battle coming from underneath. And the sky is not completely covered with the rays of the sun. It is a time of transition. Coming to a stand and arming herself with two daggers and a sword, she makes her way from where she came. Next to the stairs, a fellow natural vampire is laid to rest, burned by Vigore's magical fires. Back pressed against the wall, she climbs down the stairs.

Her view fills with the sight of a badly beaten dining room. The serviette and dining dishes are spread out around the area carelessly. Her feet touch the ground floor, with the lost hope of defeating Vigore. Eyeing the cage, she races towards it. As if she were unable to stop herself from hitting it, her hard body slams against the cold metal bars of the cage. Her eyes close for a moment. And she thinks. Steering her eyes to the black iron cage door and seeing that Brahnt is missing, she hopes for the best. She can only hope that he has somehow managed to escape, for his sake. Her thoughts are those of him securely hidden, for he is outnumbered and out skilled. The room now echoes her breathing. Her head spins around. Her hair follows. Her eyes now affixed to where the Book of Vigore rested. The book is no longer there. Across the roof there are sounds of battle. (the sound of wood splintering) She looks upward. The ceiling above gives way and down fall two creatures grappling with each other. Each struggling for the superior position, they descend. The lower body crashes first while the other has his fall broken. The moment though, would show otherwise. Upon impact their bodies squeeze together and their heads hit against each other's.

"I thought that would break my fall." Says the winner of the plunge. He looks up at the woman standing there. "Is there something the matter little one?" He asks looking down and shaking his head.

"Brahnt! Erasmus? Where is he?" She says, holding her hands to her hips, while watching him dust himself off.

"That boy has no manners. He smells so foul that even the Black Coats will avoid him. Actually I take that back (he places a finger to his lips). Yes actually he is on the south wing. I believe that he has been fighting the Black Coats and the Red Wolves. He is doing rather well for a Human. (Melonnie looks worried) Mel?"

"Don't call me that! (a gentle thought crosses her mind) Only he calls me that."

"Don't call me that- " his mimicking stops once she stares him down. "He'll be fine."

"And I thought you were going to make the sun rise?" She says to him sarcastically.

"There were two of them. I killed thirteen guards and then I killed them. I did what I could."

"Comme tous les homes! (Like every man!) You complain because you had to kill only thirteen men." They look at each other and smile, realizing the incredible odds they have just beaten.

More sound comes from the rooftop. Standing back to back they look upwards. Both, with swords in their hands, they follow the sounds overhead. The ceiling splits sending down debris. Melonnie and Erasmus come back to back, holding the razor-sharp swords loosely in their hands. They know that their brothers are at war and though they fever for the battle, they also know they must fight with intelligence. (the roof splinters and gives way) From the rooftop fall two more Black Coats. Melonnie and Erasmus run across the floor avoiding the falling creatures. The two bodies crash to the floor. Dead on impact.

They walk over to the bodies, inspecting them. Dead already, both Melonnie and Erasmus wield their swords decapitating the motionless bodies. Blood pools and soaks onto the floor. Having severed the heads of their enemies, the two warriors look at each other. "Finish it!" Another sound! The doors swing open with strange force. Another Black Coat enters the room hurried and with his head facing the floor. Searching for the kill zone, she spots bloodstains no doubt from her own people. His sword drags low, but no matter. She reaches for one of Erasmus' daggers. Taking a hold of the hilt she cocks her hand, drawing the weapon away from its sheath. Erasmus sniffs at the air. It smells foul.

Without wasting so much as a breath, she throws the dagger allowing her message of death to be carried by way of air. The Black Coat's head rises. The hair from his face clears. Her eyes meet with his. Once locked into each other's view. He smiles at her. She on the other hand calls out to him in horror. But it is all moving much too slowly. And the voice of her mouth doesn't carry. (a small object approaches) He focuses on it. (a deep sound of penetration) Power Drain! It is suddenly hard for him to stand. The floor pushes against his back. There is no pain- no sound.

He brushes away the moisture from his brow. Noticing a red coloring on his hands. He moves his hands down to his chest. Oddly enough he feels a foreign object holding firmly and affixed to it. It's odd, heavy, and solid. "My God! She thought I was a Black Coat!" Blood escapes his mouth slowly but its deep rich color is not easily disregarded. The sound comes back again. He can hear in the distance the sound of feet, 'her feet.' 'It must be her feet. Wait! It is out of time. Erasmus must be coming too.' The thoughts seem out of sync with from reality. "No, this can't be."

"Brahnt! No! Don't die on me! I love you!" She calls out to him. Each step brings them closer. With little strength he holds out his hand signaling them to stay clear. Erasmus, running beside her, takes a hold of her and pulls her back. Bringing themselves to a stop, they watch his hands drop to the floor.

From beyond the doorway other figures approach. Flashes of darkness appear entering the room, creating a linear outline of the wall. Melonnie draws her sword! She watches quietly as Brahnt's eyes close and his breath becomes shallow.

The coated figures extend their hands. From them protrude shiny dark objects in the shape of crescent moons. Melonnie lifts her sword and crouches. Hurdling forward, she charges at them furiously. Her deep and embedded rage takes to her form. Swinging her sword accurately, she strikes one of the approaching knives. The contact of the two metals, spark and illuminate her deadly rage for a brief moment. Spinning away to her left and extending her hand, she takes a hold of the other knife.

Completing her revolution, she cants her arm and releases the blade with the same momentum of her spin. The knife takes flight, sinking into the chest of the furthest Black Coat. Stabbed and bleeding, he falls to one knee. Facing the floor, he pants to catch his breath. Melonnie extends her sword, hacking the other Black Coat's arm. The arm is severed and falls to the floor, further painting the floor red. She returns the swing. The blade strikes at the Black Coat's neck. His throat is sliced. Reaching up to it with both hands, he watches himself bleed. Completing its second rotation, the blade severs the head. She enjoys watching his body fall to the floor, while his only arm twitches.

Taking large steps towards Brahnt's direction, she reaches down to his limp, dying body, kneeling down to his side. Picking up his head in one hand, she caresses his hair with the other. He looks peaceful, she says to herself, trying to fight back the rage and hurt. And though peaceful, there seems to be a certain devious look to his face. Melonnie's hands touch his face, neck, and chest. Tears fall down her face without barriers. Her lips curl forming odd shapes of deep pain. Touching his chest, her hands come across something very hard and heavy secured within his jacket. She unbuttons it. Noting the streaks of gold and leather, she pushes the jacket further revealing the Book of Vigore. Her eyes are not large enough to bare the tears that fall from them. "And it wasn't even your fight." (the sounds of hooves striking the ground outside) She takes firm grip of the jacket and begins to pull him away from the door. Erasmus takes his sword and gives flight to himself, while Melonnie struggles with his body. Passing over her head, he holds his place above the large, wooden doors. The sound of hooves rearing becomes louder now.

Two Red Wolves push the door open. Their defined bodies filled with muscles, display their immediate threat. Erasmus' heart comes to a still. Melonnie, having moved Brahnt's body to safety, comes to a combative stance. She removes the Book of Vigor from her mind, preventing them from discovering it within her thoughts.

Replacing her thoughts with memories of loving Brahnt, she pulls her sword up. Holding it vertically to her side and shifting her weight, she prepares to engage her enemies. The two Red Wolves charge in her direction. Having traveled half the way to Melonnie, Erasmus drops down from behind them. As if rehearsed one of them turns to face Erasmus, while the other one continues forward. Erasmus lets out a calm laughter, as if to ridicule his enemies. The Red Wolf Centurions halt with death gripping at their souls.

"Erasmus!" The one facing him calls out.

"That is right! Erasmus!" He mocks.

"I do not wish to quarrel with you. I must have the Book of Vigore. Give me the Book and I shall pretend I have never seen you." Again the calm laughter. The two centurions stand back to back.

"Do you know who that is over there?"

"This female?" Asks the centurion with sarcasm in his voice.

"Female?" She yells out offended by his tone.

"Let me ask you an easier question. Do you know that dead man laying there?"

"That man laying there killed many of my men. He was a good warrior. One of the best I have ever seen. But as you can see death has embraced him. The Book Erasmus and we will quarrel no longer!"

"That (he points to her with his sword) is Melonnie." (smiling) They gasp, turning for a better look.

"And that (he points to Brahnt's body) is Brahnt." He finishes in a stronger tone.

"Melonnie's human companion?" Their eyes fill with hesitant fear.

"And *they* are my friends." He nods his head. Erasmus' words shoot through like daggers, penetrating the very heart of fear.

"Spare our lives Erasmus, but give us the book."

"Now how would that young lady feel if I did that? Especially after your stupid attacks have cost her the lives of all the ones she has loved?"

"Enough talk! To the death then!" Both Red Wolves press forward towards Erasmus. With their attention distracted,

Melonnie reaches down to the stone floor, picking up a dagger. The dragging sound of the blade carries to the centurion's ear. One hits the back of the other with his palm, alerting him of danger. Melonnie cocks and throws the dagger. The centurion turns extending out with his hand. The dagger penetrates his hand. Blood falls on either side of his palm and onto the stone floor filling its grooves. Grinning and bearing it, he reaches over with his other hand dropping his sword for the moment. Melonnie charges at him. He pulls out the dagger. In his peripheral vision, beyond the focus of his hand, her image changes holding her blade low to the ground. Melonnie swings from the floor to his head. With the dagger in his good hand, he blocks the rising sword. The force of her blow brings Melonnie's saber down towards his neck. The sword's edge cuts at the base. Leaning into it, Melonnie pushes the sword with both hands. (a gun shot!)

His knee gives way, collapsing his body to the ground. Melonnie achieves the leverage she needs. With a powerful swing, twisting at her hips, she generates the strength she needs to slice him through and out the other side. The centurion reaches up for his throat, collecting in his hands the very streams of blood that escape him. The pain burns like that of the sun against his very flesh. Looking up at Melonnie he watches the saber returning for another swing. His head detaches cleanly. "That feels good!" She says feeling the vibration of the blade produced by the separation of the vertebrae. The sound of his head striking the ground insures the cut has been successful. She looks at Brahnt. His eyes are barely opened. Reading his thoughts, she hears him warning her not to be distracted.

Erasmus' sword swings against the Red Wolves' acting out the dances of death, he has seen only much too often. He thrusts, as the centurion deflects. He carries the momentum of the deflection to a circular attack. His blade spins horizontally.

Taking to a knee Erasmus' blade extends its reach to his enemy's legs.

A snap and a chime. The chopping wet sound of cutting meat sounds good to Erasmus' ear. His lower limb snaps away from his body, leaving a trail of his blood. The centurion falls to the ground. The stub of his foot rests on the stone floor, still pooling his blood. He yells out, making his pain known. Melonnie brings her sword high over her head. With great effort she bends her body forward, bringing down the power of the sword. It carries through to the centurion, penetrating his chest at an angle. Blood immediately stream lines from his mouth. The sun breaks from the clouds, shining its rays through the doorway.

Erasmus is pushed away by the power of the rays. Falling, still in the hands of the rays, his flesh burns. Smoke fills the deathly still air. She leaps, grasping his body and pushes him beside the door, shading him from the harmful rays of the sun.

Shaking, Erasmus' hands shake uncontrollably. Behind her the Red Wolves catch fire, along with the blood he spilled. Melonnie takes a glance at the burning body behind him. Redirecting her attention to Erasmus, she looks at his burned face. He is singed and curled with dead flesh. His lips shake uncontrollably. Melonnie carefully places her hands to his cheek. She feels his flesh trembling. His odd face smiles back at her.

"Thanks," he says to her, "I was not in the mood for a barbecue." He comes to a stand and walks over to the odd wooden doors, She closes the doors locking out the rays of the sun. Erasmus kicks his feet out, pushing his back further in to the wall. The room, partly lit from the burning bodies, feels cold and empty. There is a silence that death only can recognize. Her blood stained dress and body moves to Brahnt. There where he lies, he pants desperately for air. (Erasmus comes to a stand and staggers over to them both). Gulping air down to his lungs, his eyes can barely focus. Saddened with grief, she kneels down to him and gently touches him on his shoulder. She pushes him over to his back. He rolls and looks to her. Shaking her head side to side, her lips tremble out the words "I'm sorry."

"It's OK. Mel." (blood trails down the side of his mouth) Struggling. She moves her hand down to the Book and removes it from his hold. Erasmus' feet stop scraping, coming to halt beside them. Erasmus kneels to him. Melonnie opens his jacket further. She places her hand delicately around the knife buried beyond his bloody shirt. She touches the blood on his shirt and brings it to her lips. Tasting it, small memories of their romance enter her mind. More tears fall from her eyes. She turns his attention to him, once more. Erasmus comes to his knees.

"Let me take you to my world, Brahnt."

"No (he struggles) Let me die here loving her as I can. (he coughs and blood drools down the side of his mouth) All men die. But so few truly live. To live having loved you, is immortal." He reaches down for the knife. Melonnie can read his thoughts. Tears blur her vision (droplets of his blood tap at the floor). She reaches for the knife.

"No!" Erasmus yells out. "Let me help you. Please! Allow me this chance to give meaning to my life! Please!" Erasmus' hands tremble violently holding Melonnie. "Please man! Brahnt don't leave us this way." He looks to the doors, sensing that someone else is approaching.

"You have brought meaning to my life! You have taught me to live for more than just my revenge or my (he coughs) hatred. You have given this soulless body a soul." He says then smiles.

"How ironic my friend. That what you have learned from me, I have learned from you." He pulls his hand away from

Melonnie's and lowers his head. Tears of sadness fill her eyes. Melonnie pushes her hair around the back of her ears.

"Wait! Wait! Wait just a moment." She comes to a stand and rushes over to the table they once cheerfully sat underneath. Kicking away broken and splintered chairs, she searches. The feelings of desperation overwhelm her. She pushes away the tears from her eyes, smearing blood on her face, while trying to clear her vision. Underneath a broken cushion she finds a folded piece of paper. "Wait! Here it is. I have it. I have it!" She turns to him and runs over stumbling and nearly tripping over broken obstacles. Reaching his body. She smiles of a sad-joy. "Look (her voice breaks)! I have this for you. I found it! I swear to God! I found him and I got this for you. You see! Right there!" She looks at the writing on the piece of paper. Brahnt's tiring eyes focus on the note he had written during his innocence. "It says it here! 'I owe you one soul' It your handwriting! We have it now. The bet is forfeit! Join our side, sweetheart. Join our side!" He smiles at her. His eyes blink.

"Kiss me, Melonnie. Let my lips feel your lips once more." He says to her. She reaches down to him and places her mouth to his. He struggles to fit his fingers into her hand, still tightly wrapped in the dark coat that betrayed him. His warm lips turn cold. (a slow but hard knocking at the door) And she feels as his soul escapes his body. There, lip-to-lip, her tears fall to his eyes and her uncontrollable breath enters his mouth. (sounds of deep lament) Her body trembles severely, as she slowly and gracefully pulls away from him. Trapped within her fingers, she still grasps the sheet of paper. "Hold this!" She yells at Erasmus, holding out her hand. Erasmus faithfully obeys and takes a hold of the paper. She returns her attention to Brahnt, who now lies still.

Taking a hold of the knife buried deep within his chest, she pulls it out. His blood no longer flows, but now oozes slowly, lifeless. Putting her hand down on the stone floor, she stabs it with the tip of the blade. Her blood pools within her palm. (slow hard knocking at the door) Making a fist with her hand and extending her index finger, she allows her blood to travel down to her nail. Carefully she writes the words, "I love your soul. Till we meet in heaven..."

Splintering wood. The door locks break, as the door bursts open. A dark creature stands tall, filling the frame of the door. Melonnie wipes her last tear. Smears of his and her blood paint her face. Taking her sword into her hands, she raises it for combat. The creature lets out a horrible shrieking sound. The sound is like that of a millions souls crying out in pain. The large heavy body turns to look at Erasmus. He draws his sword. "Sorry! I may be slightly burned, but I'm not going anywhere with you!"

"Erasmus?" Melonnie calls out concerned. "What is that?"

"It's the Reapers, love. They collect the bodies and take them to Hell. But this one seems to be lost." It turns to Erasmus and lets out another yell. Swinging its arm, it strikes Erasmus, causing him to tumble on the floor much like a rag doll.

Slamming his body hard against the stone floor, he takes a glimpse of Brahnt's dead Body. "No!" He yells out. Melonnie alarms even more. Erasmus comes to his knees and brings his hands under his chin. He reaches into his pocket, pulling out his Rosary Beads. In quiet breaths he begins to pray.

"Who are you? Don't take him from me." The creature continues his march. His heavy body moves forth, fearless. Dust clouds form and swirl like little tornadoes near to his feet as he strides towards the woman and her weapon. Melonnie lifts her sword, charging at the large creature. As she approaches it, she can see that this creature has no face, but only bares a skull. Melonnie spins around with her sword outstretched, rushing the creature before her. She screams with a bloodcurdling piercing yell and lunges at her opponent. The blade chimes, striking the creature's face. (bone fragments splinter off) Having struck the creature against his jaw, its head jolts backwards with only a small nick to its massively powerful face.

Turning back to face her, the creature realizes that her saber swings across for yet another strike. The creature raises his arm in defense. His long ragged sleeved arm becomes bare. From within its mystery is yet another mystery. His arms too had no flesh. She continues her swing, as if unaffected by what she is seeing. The blade chimes again. The walls whisper echoes of the blade striking the mysterious creature. And again only fragments of the arm appear to be effected. She swings overhead and to the creature's neck. Reaching across itself, with his hand, the creature extends his bone-like fingers and grabs the sword by the blade. (it shrieks at her) It twists at the wrist. The sword bends slightly. Melonnie reaches for her dagger. Removed from her waist, she lunges forward with the dagger in her hand. The sword shatters. Steel dust and splinters suddenly shine and dance in the morning sunbeams.

The dagger penetrates the creature's heart. Only, once through the tough material, there is a sense of hollow. Swinging its other arm, he sends her soaring through the air. Her body strikes a candle staff. Tumbling onto a chair and crashing through a table, it splinters and breaks like brittle twigs. Falling on top of another table, it too collapses under her weight, breaking in half. Her body falls heavily to the floor where her breath is completely squeezed from within her, leaving her lungs but collapsed.

Forcing her lungs with air, once again, she coughs and gasps loudly, regaining her strength and posture, prepared for another assault. The creature moves on, nearing Brahnt's body a step at a time. She looks at Erasmus. He still prays. Coming to her feet, she takes a healthy look at the creature then at Erasmus. "The Reaper!" She whispers its name. "The Grim tales of the Reaper! May God himself strike me down if you take him from me! Stop! Reaper! Arrêt!"

Feeling the pressure of time. She breathes more deeply. She crosses her arms, absorbing the pain. "Arrêt! You can't take him!" The creature stops and turns to face Melonnie. "I have it here on this paper, that he has no soul. For the moment the Reaper stands puzzled. She points at the small piece of paper resting as quietly as is Brahnt. The creature, confused, takes another look at her. Noticing the tears in her eyes, it realizes that it is of no consequence to him. Its march continues. Falling to her knees, "Mon Dieu, help me."

At the sound of her words, the creature stops but a few feet from Brahnt. For the moment there is no sound. 'Has he taken him? Did he leave?' She is afraid to open her eyes. For the moment she much rather close them and never open them again. She is even too sad to cry.

"Melonnie?" A soft voice filters through the excitement. A familiar voice. "Melonnie? Open your eyes."

"Brahnt?" She shakes her head, with closed eyes.

"Please I only have a few moments."

"But you're dead. (shaking her head) And if I open my eyes I'll know this."

"Humans all die. It's the breath of life that allows them to live on." The voice is gentle and soothing to her pain.

"Gabriel!" She opens them filling with hope. Before Brahnt he stands. His body is slim. Except for a flat black garb and a sword suspended by a red sash, he looks plain. He looks different than in the dreams that her ancestors had genetically passed down. "Are you still an Angel? Right?" He says nothing, "Tell me that I can save him. Tell me how. I'll do it! I'll do anything."

He stands with no words. “There is a place where we all go once we die. I’m afraid that he shall not be in heaven with your kind.”

“I can’t let this happen!” she moves forward. “He was a good man. He taught me to love. He taught me to respect humanity; He even showed me how to smile. Doesn’t God think that is worth something?” The Angel says nothing.

“I can not tell you what needs to be done here?” The Angel says. “I can tell you that the universe revolves around love. It was created from love. Love has been the source of power here on Earth for a long time.” Walking closer to his body, the Angel kneels down next to Brahnt. “Tell me, Melonnie? Is this one man more precious than all who have died here tonight?”

“Though there may be beautiful roses throughout the gardens crossing land. My Rose will always be the most beautiful. For within its thorns it guards my love.” Bending down near to him she caresses his face.

“Then you know what to do.” The Angel disappears.

Standing where he once stood, is his sword. Melonnie’s eyes reach first, then her hands. The creature, seemingly unaware of what has happened, continues to move forward. She dives to the sword. Taking a hold of it by its hilt and rolling over top of it, she comes to a stand bringing it to shoulder level.

Letting out a heroic scream, she charges at the creature. The creature extends its claw like arms. Melonnie swings across with greater strength and speed, as if her actions are more guided by the blade than by her skill, both of which have been sharpened by experience. The creature blocks with its forearm. (sparks) Bone fragments appear to break away from its hardened body. She swings down forty-five degrees, using the strength from her shoulder to bring down the blade. The creature stretches its arm in a rising block. The sound of bone shattering vibrates through the sword. "That feels good," she says to her self.

The mighty blow forces the creature to back away. Along the windows more of the dark creatures appear silently still bearing witness. From the corners of the room even more, like shadows coming to life, appear. The creature lets out a roar and lunges forward. Melonnie turns about him. He misses his mark. Now behind him she swings horizontally to his head. The creature holds out his hand, wrapping its fingers around the blade.

Melonnie's powerful stroke splits his hand apart. (the creature screams louder) "You're not taking him! You're not taking him!" Blood spews from her mouth along with her fury and determination to succeed. The creature's jaws snap at her. The sound of his jaws crashes together echoes in the silence of the room. The other reapers too click their jaws, but that is all they do for the moment. With just one arm the Reaper pushes forward towards Melonnie.

Swinging his arm across, he clutches at her neck. Turning against the strike and with her sword laid horizontally, she swings once more meeting his blow with the sword's blade. Melonnie's blade makes contact. Sparks combined with chipped bone fragments disperse upon impact. His blade falls helplessly to the floor (in the same motion). Melonnie spins her body around, extending her blade. It catches at the base of its throat. A large hollow snap! The Reaper's head falls to the floor. The bony sound of his head breaking against the stone floor sends chills to all reapers to witness. Silently, mystically, they back away. As they disappear into dark corners, they know they have born witness to the power of love.

Melonnie looks to Erasmus. He rests against the stonewall, sheltered by the shadows of darkness and witness to the dark side of truth. Waving his hand, Melonnie understands that he is all right. She places her attention to Brahnt's body.

Coming over him and lying on top of his body, she places her hand against his chest. His blood is still moist. "If I could trade my life for yours… If I could leave my ways for yours… I would have. I'm so sorry. I didn't know it was you. I should have recognized your hair, your scent. The way you walked. Something! But know this my love. I shall see you in heaven. For as God as my witness my once soulless body now carries your soul and your love." She rubs her head against his chest, and within her fantasy, she is with him. Today and forever more.

Tracing the fatal wound with her finger, a blue flick of light escapes it. Pausing for a brief moment, it is suspended between her body and his. She feels its warmth. It enters her body. Passing through her chest, it leaves a small burn. She drops her head and begins to cry. The words "Pourquoi mon Dieu? Pourquoi." She repeats the words over and over as the sounds within the room fall deaf to her ears…

Chapter 13

MoonShade

Surrendering into the arms of sorrow and with tears breaking through her once ignorant eyes, she leans her head onto his chest. Realizing that a simple mortal and his simple napkin poetry had turned her harsh view of humankind to one of human compassion, she recites a small note of discourse she had hoped to share with the man of her dreams, while leaning on a hillside speaking of things passed and yet to come.

MoonShade

The moonshades underneath the water's skin
Refract and flow in the current,
Hiding
The shadow remains below
The rocks.
The soaked dust
Is dancing with the moon
Dancing with the remains
Of what used to be
My reflection.

Special Features

FolkLore

'Every story has a lore untold'

Before man imprinted his foot on the earth, there were majestic creatures that decorated and adorned it. Among the Unicorn, the Cyclops, the mermaid and the winged horse, were the most astonishing creatures of all -The Angelica.

The Angelica was a combined creation of man and angel in a pure form. Their twelve-foot wingspan covered the sky like miracles born from a romantic fantasy. Hundreds of them adorned the sky, defying gravity, searching for fruit to harvest from the pastures that never went a season without bearing. They were designed to be a reminder of celestial angelic representation.

Then man was created and given a soul, breaking the boundaries between all creatures in the heavens. During this time Lucifer was planning a revolt against God. Unlike other creatures from God's creation, man had a soul and he was given the right of free will. And man looked upon all creatures and gave them a name, thus bringing meaning to their existence. Among these creatures was the Angelica, properly named for their representation of the Celestial Angels.

Then woman was born as an equal to man and the two singular halves opened the gates of knowledge. Upon which, the order was given to remove all celestial creatures from the face of the earth as Lucifer raged his war.

Between the conflict of the Luciferian Angels and the Celestial Angels, the order was written that the sword from heaven should strike down all creatures sculpted by the hand of the creator resembling the heavens. But the gates of knowledge were opened and the Angelica, who shared a part of man's existence, was also filled with ideas brought forth from the tree of knowledge. The Angelica followed their natural instincts and fought back in the attempt to preserve their lives.

Troupes from both sides, Luciferian Celestial and Angelica, lost their lives on the initial battlefield of Earth. When the fighting stopped and each group given their rights to exist, man was sent out of the Garden of Eden.

Man was blind to the consequence of his deeds. However, the Angelica would remember this day for eternity.

The message was sent down to the Celestial Angels, the Angelica had earned their right to live. Their once beautiful wings were torn from their backs, leaving blood filled scars that would someday be representative of their race. The beautiful long white teeth would no longer sip from the nectar of sweet fruit, but would now be regarded as fangs that would hunt down their prey and drink their blood.

As if this was not punishment enough, they were ordered to live far away from man, their half brother, and sentence to exile for several hundreds of years.

Luciferian Angels approached the Angelica proposing the un-life. Many confused and despaired Angelica went the Luciferian route and became known among themselves as UnNaturals.

As for the other Angelica (the Naturals) their eyes were turned to dark voids and left to survive on their own.

Gabrielle, having pity on his half-kind, brought to them an immortal secret. They would have to drink from the rain on the seventh day.

Several hundreds of years later, Natural scholars found the loophole that man overlooked. In order for them to be recognized, man would have to be judged for their individual sins.

This created the rift between the Naturals and the Un-naturals, as Lucifer would fight to gain and corrupt the souls of every human, preventing humanity from having good judgment passed on them.

Many have hidden a darker secret that protects the realms of evil and goodness. Now a handful of the Angelica descendants fight to keep the fate of man in order, hoping to restore their rightful place in the heavens.

"All creatures no matter big or small will make their way home."

The Book of Vigore:

What is the history of the Book of Vigore?

This book was created during Vigore's, early years as a sorcerer.

Under the misconception that the Priest had killed his father, Vigore murders him and creates the Book of Vigore using the Priest's flesh and blood.

However, not satisfied, he entraps the spirit of a young demon into the pages.

Unaware of the consequences of his actions, the book becomes a living, breathing entity that is at opposites with itself.

The Book of Vigore:

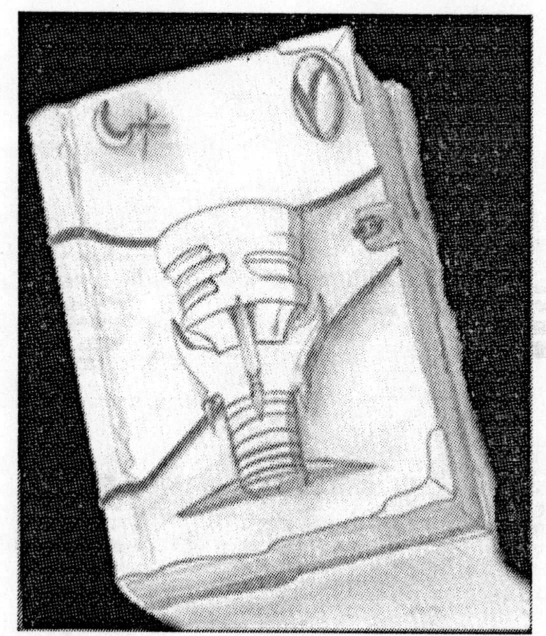

By

D'Avion

Reading Tips D'Avion Novels

The clever details of How to Read the books.

It is not hard to get into the flow of way the books read. However, for those of you sticklers for English Grammatical structure.

Please understand that certain rules have been replaced, so that the energy and emotion of the book is kept in flow. It is almost like listening to a drama or comedy from the old theatre. If you don't understand the rules of the language being used you may miss certain meaning. Fortunately being able to read the book over you can catch all the subtleties.

There was an example that I read in a book. It was about a prince that had taken care of a peasant woman. As it turns out the peasant woman was pregnant at a time where an unmarried woman was frowned upon. The Prince took care of her, but she insisted on comprehending how she had gotten pregnant. The author of the book cleverly placed a dash during the time he found her unconscious and the time she came to.

That singular "dash" denoted the time period where he made love to her.

Without further explanations here are a few simple rules.

Example 1.

"Ouch! (touching his eye) That *hurts*!" He says demonstrating great pain.

This example has many different items

1. (touching his eye) = lower case/ this is action happening at the same time he says "Ouch!"

2. *hurts*! = Italicized words are for tone inflection and stressing the meaning of the word
3. He says = as opposed to "he says." This is also for affect further separating the vocal meaning from the narrative meaning.

Example 2.

"Je suis ici! Ici !!" (I am here! Here !!)

1. "Ici!!" = The double exclamation is to double the emotional interpretation of the word.
2. (I am here! Here !!) = Done to mimic the sentence, this is the closest meaning to the translation of the language being used.

The Credits:

I have always believed in a team effort, weather it's someone closely cooperating with you on a project, or it's someone holding a screwdriver. It is important to understand that all small efforts are an intricate part of the whole. It is more than obvious that the materials here and on the web (www.deavion.com) are of the best quality.

I would therefore like to give credit where credit is due.

"Good friends are hard to find. A compliment insures they know that they are well appreciated."
- D'Avion

Kim Yung Im

Special thank to Yung Im. Her supervision and comprehensive analysis of the story helped insure good character integrity. Cooperative efforts with music, and art helped design the realism of the characters. Lastly, her help in the musical score, specially created for Melonnie: The Dark Side of Truth is noted, is well appreciated.

If you would like to see what this powerhouse is made of, visit the World Wide Web.

Mark Donnaruma

Heartfelt thanks to Mark, who's business savvy manner has made it possible for readers to discover the world of horror that I've created. I am especially grateful for his direct contribution of Melonnie: The Dark Side of Truth, helping maintain the focus of the character's "Relevant Point of View".

Leslie Krüger

Very special thanks to the sexy, Leslie who offered her time and creativity in bringing the characters to life on the World Wide Web.

"I love that girl!"

Christian Martin

I would like to extend a unique thanks to Christian Martin, who currently suffers from Cerebral Palsy and doesn't know it.

Owner of Christian's Café, located in Rochester NY, he has proven to be an inspiration to all who visit. His attention to story content and genius contributions, have furthered the assurance of the novel's of popularity.

Ryan Cupp

Thank you Ryan for your poetic contribution. For those that haven't figured it out yet, Chapter 13 was his idea. I met Ryan at Christian's Café. This young poet aspires to complete his book of poetry early next year.

Mathew Bernius

Inspiration is his middle name. Matt's inquisitive line of thinking, alluding to the higher complexities of style and design, have made a tremendous impact on presentation and delivery. His ingenuity design and research have helped immensely.

Thanks

Mark Cardona

Ok so you've enjoyed the technical fighting scene. Well where do you think most of it came from? You got it! Thanks to Sifu Cardona's clever knowledge of the Chinese Martial Arts fighting system, I have been able to detail comprehensive fighting scenes that feel and seem more realistic.

Cover
Melonnie: The Dark Side of Truth
Cover Art: - by - D'Avion
Composer/Photographer – by D'Avion

Chapter 1
Poetry Credit - **Shadow Show** - by Ryan Cupp
Wolf's Eyes: **Model:** - by Kim Yung Im
Composer/Photographer – by D'Avion

Chapter 2
Melonnie Rises – by – D'Avion
Poetry Credit – **When the Wind Whispers** – by Ryan Cupp

Chapter 3
Melonnie Rumani – by – D'Avion
Poetry Credit – **When the Wind Whispers** – by Ryan Cupp

Chapter 4
Brahnt Vaughin – by - D'Avion
Poetry Credit – **Unspeakable** – by Ryan Cupp

Chapter 5
Finding the Book of Vigore – by – D'Avion
Poetry Credit - **Shadow from within without** – by – *D'Avion*

Chapter 6
Thulis Ruchanka – by – D'Avion
Poetry Credit – **Fatal Blow** – by D'Avion

<u>Chapter 7</u>
Cloak and Dagger – Artwork – by – D'Avion
Composer/Photographer – by - D'Avion
Poetry Credit – **Thief of Moments** – by - Ryan Cupp

<u>Chapter 8</u>
Watching over Brahnt - by – Kim Yung Im
Poetry Credit – **I Can** – by D'Avion

<u>Chapter 9</u>
Melonnie's Rage – by – D'Avion
Poetry Credit – **Soon to Victory** – by – D'Avion

<u>Chapter 10</u>
Shadow Behind the Face – Model: Kim Yung Im
Composer /Photographer – D'Avion
Poetry Credit - **Falling Heavens** – by - D'Avion

<u>Chapter 11</u>
Melonnie Attacks – by – D'Avion
Poetic Credit - **A Song Without a Voice** – by – D'Avion

<u>Chapter 12</u>
Shadow Creature – by – D'Avion
Poetry Credit - Nunca – by – D'Avion

<u>Chapter 13</u>
Poetic Credit – **MoonShade** – Ryan Cupp

The following is a sneak preview of D'Avion's next exciting novel, Nichole: A Kiss for the Dying

Nichole: A Kiss for the Dying

[G-MAN dialogue begins]

The sun dwindles on the horizon, like a playful child waiting to see what lies within the secret shadows of the night. I can hear the sun whispering secrets to the twilight. With very deep and profound attention, the twilight listens and carries on as it has done for so many millions of years. Still like a foolish child, the sun asks about the night as if asking for the first time ever. When dawn appears the moon will ask the same of the day. The dawn will listen as her brother does and the cycle will continue as it has for so many millions of years. I believe that once a very, very long time ago both the sun and moon where lovers inter-twined by some mystical force. Perhaps it was love or perhaps harmony. What love so pure could hold these two forces together? I don't know.

I know though, that when the moon appears there will be other things to come. I know that now. But believe me I didn't once upon a time. It is true that between the shadows creep things humans cannot come to comprehend. And for those who believe in these things, I fear the worst. For they are the unfortunate casualties of a silent war. I refer, of course, to the war between the good and the evil.

I don't know how or where this all began. I guess I should say that I don't know exactly. I only know a few of the names and a few of the places. However, I know someone that may have the answers. It is to my fortune that she favors me. I would fear the wrath of her kind, if I were at opposites.

To whom am I referring? Her name is Nichole Rumani. Though I know her best as Nichole. My name is Marcus G. The network calls me the G-man. I was the best at my field. That is until I met Nichole. Frankly she fascinates me. But I won't tell you that. I rather you find out for yourself whenever you have the misfortune of meeting her. She chases criminals, gangsters, power mongers, and political figures. She is the best of her profession, but with a greater advantage. Her skills are totally unmatchable and her methods are unpredictable.

Let's see. Where do I begin?

How about filling you in on some of the details. Why don't I start with the date? It is August 10th 2090. Technology has been downplayed severely today. But that wasn't the case in 2072. The streets were hot with techno-drug. That is the slang term for technological over-load. The world had become a terrible danger to itself. Technology was an inconceivable cyber-organism. But you can't say that all these things have materialized over-night.

The late 20th century lead the world into an angry state. Road killings were taking the lives of the weak. Pop music had turned youthful resources into a brain washed frenzy. Individuality was replaced by a stereotypical null-like state. It was as though humanity was dead. The world gave way to selfish pride and inferiority complexes clashed against the empowered. It was like someone flipped the switch and all the nerds came to power, becoming suddenly popular. You may think that this is humorous, perhaps even ridiculous to mention. Perhaps I would agree, if the world hadn't changed so radically. Technology advanced at a quickened rate. It was so competitive that one week's newest discovery was the next week's obsolescence. It led the country into technical saturation. With only a hand-full of individuals to protest, the technically inclined destroyed humanity. It is true that humans exist but humanity is gone. The boundaries that were once so important for the balance of the universe were now fading into the blue seas of terror. When a handful of people formed an alliance against the world, it seemed an effortless task. They bonded with other individuals with the same realization as they had. Blinded by power and money the small handful of humans grew into a most powerful organization.

When the world calendars introduced the year 2006, a man named Anderson Wilkons formed a unified super-power called Group 52. Wilkons, a priest empowered by the Priesthood of the Third Division, persuaded other divisions and commoners of the Reality Churches to join forces throughout the world. Their mission was simple. Empowerment. Some rumors have it that he is dead. Still, other rumors have it that he has become a product of his own creation. Encased in a formidable armored shell, it is said that he can live forever.

Near to more recent time, life has evolved once again. The poto-mems that once occupied the world are becoming more educated, but they have a long way to go. Ask yourselves, "what would an 18th century man do with the technology of nuclear missiles? And what would he do if he could reproduce that technology? Worse yet, ask yourselves if his enemies would stand a chance?"

Group 52 has grown to be one of the most powerful components of the world to date. Very few agents have been able to escape the organization once they were committed to their ring of espionage. Most of them are either dead or deep underground assassins. Others have gone to other countries, forming devastation groups with the idea that they can bring balance to the world.

China and Japan, though united with the U. S., have experienced problems of their own. Large sectors of the Asian population have protested the union of the greater powers. Rumor has it that an underground rebellion has created a new secret weapon! It seems that late in the 19th century, the Department of Defense, in combined efforts with the Supreme Court, were forced to pass the Technology Evolution's Act (TEA). Pushed by the Cyber-Trash, the empowered nerds open the world to their current threat. Today every organization is secretly collecting any type of information about the silent killer that affects only humans.

Placing aside their differences China, Japan and the US have built an underwater city. With a great concern of Biological Warfare weapons, they resulted to the depth of the sea. A wise choice since XV-35 could not be used on underwater targets.

XV-35 is what they are currently speaking through the secretive vines of the underground. The weapon is said to send out an alternating low frequency that disrupts the cells of the human brain. The victim suffers a small headache seconds before his brain collapses in on itself. No one knows what the weapons look like. They only know the names of its victims the weapon has claimed during its testing period.

XV-35 was the hottest weapon on the market. Every nation wanted their blooded hands on it. Prototypes were found in the form of police P-876 riot control rifles. Later it was found in simple objects such as pens and wristwatches. The poor souls that have been unlucky to have survived have been left with less than a breathing carcass kept alive only for experimental purposes. Retirement of these so called experimental is only after their brain has collapse. Word on the street is that the weapon cannot be perfectible with the current solid state nor cube technology. But, that has never stopped the Chinese before. It is common knowledge that underground movements such as these, have unpredictable patterns of behavior. The word on the street is that they are close to perfecting the technology.

In an open response to the sudden fear, kept quiet within walls of government houses, the World Unity Alliance has created a tactical unit called the Black Shield. BS is a world wide and highly secured organization operating on their own council. Licensed to kill and armed only with cutting edge technology, the secret and unseen Black Shields are the only adversaries that Group 52 fears.

For fear of revealing their strength and weaknesses, assassins are often sought to clean up the mess opening one of the oldest professions known to our beloved world.

Between the cracks of this confused world lurks another enemy. Though a new enemy, it is also ironic that this enemy is the only chance humanity has.

Rumors have said that they are as unseen as the shadows that lurk between night and day. They are as old as time and as powerful as all of man's technology combined. It has been told that they are the only creatures on earth that have the ability to defy humanity and their weapons of mass destruction. At first I wouldn't have believed it either. But after meeting Nichole, I am apt to think anything is possible.

This new world technological advancement is the most impressive witnessed, since the U.S. put a man on the moon. I read one of those old dusty books a quote that ironically set the tone for our era of new discovery. "If we can put a man on the moon, we can do anything."

My God! If those poor people of long ago only knew where that would lead, they would have been more careful. Perhaps they would have kept music and art ahead of technology. But you and I both know that the world is about money and wherever that green is, is where you'll find most people of wealth running.

I used to be that way myself, until Nichole happened. Until I got a bullet lodged in my stomach. I remember that night well. I was told a story that would forever change my life and make me a prisoner of her cause.

[G-MAN dialogue ends]

About the Author

Quite simply stated "America was not ready for this!"

D'Avion's writing career began in Europe, where he has written and traveled extensively. His recent popularity has encouraged him to make his Horror/Fantasy Novels available to the general American Public. However, if you think that this is his first Novel you are in for a big surprise. D'Avion has been writing since grade school, where his first short story was about a werewolf set loose in a little town near his home. At the age of 8 he received an A++ for his effort in creativity and attention to detail. He has also published other Novellas in other countries. So why here why now?

According to D'Avion, the American Entertainment Industry was not ready for a face-lift. D'Avion's method of writing deals more with the Psychological profile and the alteration of reality as it pertains to the individual characters. He also makes clever use of allowing the reader to focus on more than just one character. So it is not surprising to have mixed emotions about the characters in his book.

In the words of the Author:

> "I think that the general Book Industry has created a formula that people are accustomed to read. The Entertainment industry won't change unless people force it to change. The stories that I write get fantastic reviews by readers from all walks of life. I have received letters and calls from agents expressing their approval for my writing, but they are afraid to take the plunge. It's nothing new, really. That's the way big business is. However, it's the little people that drive that

business. I write for the people. I write so that they are not only entertained, but are also challenged." –D'Avion

Raised and instructed under the European influence, horror fiction writing takes on a new face.

"Today's social and professional functions strip us of our personal daily resources. Most people do not have the time to read some of the longer more formal novels. Trying to compete with the fast action of films is really very difficult as well. I have studied the psychology of television and have found the hybrid that allows readers to enjoy the same adrenaline rush as when they see a movie, only better. I write for people that have a good head on their shoulders and are usually on the go. I personally enjoy reading some of the books that are detailed and very in depth. But I find that books written with extensive descriptive prose often constrict the imagination of the reader. I like to return the reader their sense of participation in creative process of imagination. My job is to rejuvenate creative and imaginative souls. I prefer to lay the cards out on the table and let the readers decide for themselves if the character is a good guy or bad guy."

–D'Avion

"If I had to make a singular statement about what our society needs in books today it would be –
Hot, swinging and sexy- Baby!"

Challenge your imagination visit www.deavion.com

9 781588 208576